T0147099

THE VIRGIN AND LORD GRAY

"I need you, Sophia. Come here."

She hesitated for a moment, as if trying to decide whether it would be more fun to obey or defy him, then she flung herself into his arms.

"That's it, pixie," Tristan whispered. He tumbled her onto her back in the bed, the long, hot length of his body pressing against every inch of hers, from her shoulders down to her toes. He dropped a sweet kiss on her lips, and cupped her face in his palms, his gray eyes serious. "Tomorrow, when I wake, I want to find you right here, in my arms. Don't leave me again, Sophia."

Sophia's heart rushed into her throat. "I didn't want to leave you yesterday morning, Tristan. You were asleep, your limbs flung wide and your hair falling over your face. You looked so warm, so peaceful, I wanted to curl up next to you and fall asleep with my head on your chest."

He touched his forehead to hers. "Then why didn't you?"

Sophia heard the hurt in his voice, and a soft sob rose in her throat. "Because it's hopeless, Tristan. Surely you see that? You're the Earl of Gray, and I'm no—"

"Brave and passionate. Clever, kind, and beautiful." He tipped her chin up. "You're everything. I don't want only a single stolen night with you, Sophia. I want all of you, always."

She sucked in a shocked breath, but his lips took hers in a devastating kiss, and her thoughts scattered...

Books by Anna Bradley

LADY ELEANOR'S SEVENTH SUITOR
LADY CHARLOTTE'S FIRST LOVE
TWELFTH NIGHT WITH THE EARL
MORE OR LESS A MARCHIONESS
MORE OR LESS A COUNTESS
MORE OR LESS A TEMPTRESS
THE WAYWARD BRIDE
TO WED A WILD SCOT
FOR THE SAKE OF A SCOTTISH RAKE
THE VIRGIN WHO RUINED LORD GRAY

Published by Kensington Publishing Corporation

The Virgin Who Ruined Lord Gray

Anna Bradley

LYRICAL PRESS
Kensington Publishing Corp.
www.kensingtonbooks.com

LYRICAL PRESS BOOKS are published by
Kensington Publishing Corp.
119 West 40th Street
New York, NY 10018

First Electronic Edition: October 2020
ISBN-13: 978-1-5161-1037-7 (ebook)
ISBN-10: 1-5161-1037-4 (ebook)

First Print Edition: October 2020
ISBN-13: 978-1-5161-1041-4
ISBN-10: 1-5161-1041-2

Printed in the United States of America

"Justice will not be served until those who are unaffected are as outraged as those who are."
—Benjamin Franklin

Prologue

Sophia Monmouth was the first.

She'd been six or seven years old at the time, a tiny, grubby little thing, indistinguishable from every other ragged street urchin in London. Lady Amanda Clifford might not have noticed the girl at all, if it hadn't been for the blood.

It had dried by then, Sophia's mother having met her fate some days earlier, but such a quantity of blood—great, dark red gouts of it streaked across the child's pinafore—wasn't the sort of thing one overlooked.

Then there'd been the child's eyes. Green, rather pretty, but mere prettiness would not have swayed Lady Amanda in Sophia's favor. No, it was the shrewdness in those green depths that decided her, the cunning.

It was far better for a woman to be clever than beautiful.

Lady Amanda chose the child's surname to please herself. Arrogant of her, perhaps, but it was best when Lady Amanda was pleased. As for everyone else...

In the Year of Our Lord 1778, Seven Dials was a sweltering, fetid warren of narrow streets, each one piled on top of the next like rotting corpses in a plague pit. One could only assume the doomed souls residing in Monmouth Street weren't pleased either by the name or by their fate.

But it couldn't be helped. It was pure arrogance to think one could leave their past behind them, the past being, alas, a devious, sneaking thing, apt to spring up at the most inconvenient of moments, in the unlikeliest of places. One could never entirely escape their origins, and Sophia Monmouth—tiny, grubby little thing that she was—was no exception.

And so, her surname was Monmouth, despite it being a name that pleased no one, aside presumably from the succession of dukes who'd borne the title, excepting perhaps the first of them, who'd been beheaded several hundred years earlier.

Treason.

Grisly business, but then it so often was, with dukes.

If Lady Amanda had suffered any misgivings about upending the child's fate, she didn't recall them now. And truly, who was to say what fate had decreed on Sophia Monmouth's behalf?

Not Lady Amanda Clifford.

After all, if the son of a king could lose his head on the edge of an executioner's blade, there was no reason to suppose a Seven Dials orphan—tiny, grubby little thing that she was—couldn't someday turn the tide of history.

Chapter One

Great Marlborough Street, London
Late July, 1793

There was a boy, lying on the roof of Lord Everly's pediment.

Tristan Stratford, Lord Gray, frowned down at the glass of port in his hand. No, it was still half full. He wasn't foxed. Delusional, perhaps? It didn't seem so far-fetched a possibility as it once might have done. Even the sanest of gentlemen could be harassed to the point of hallucinations.

But a boy, on his neighbor's roof? It seemed a curious choice, as far as delusions went.

Tristan abandoned his port on the corner of his desk and crept closer to the window. He closed his eyes, drew in a deep breath, then snapped them open again.

Blinked.

There was a boy, lying on the roof of Lord Everly's pediment.

He was a puny specimen, all in black, more shadow than substance, more figment than flesh. Tristan was a trifle disturbed to find he'd conjured such a singular delusion, but questions of sanity aside, a boy on a roof must spark a tiny flicker of interest, even in a chest that had remained resolutely dark and shuttered for weeks.

The boy wasn't doing anything wrong. Just lying there on his back, quite motionless, staring up at the sky. Still, a boy, on a roof? No good would come of that.

Perhaps he should alert someone. It was what a proper neighbor would do. No doubt Everly hadn't the faintest idea there was a boy on his roof.

Even the most perceptive of men might overlook such a thing, and Everly wasn't the most perceptive of men. Tristan had never cared much for his lordship, Everly being a shifty, squinty-eyed creature, but neither would he stand about gaping while a child thief stripped the man of all his worldly possessions.

Whether the boy was real or a product of Tristan's fevered imagination remained in question, but if he wasn't a phantom, he was certainly a thief. There could be no innocent explanation for his presence on Lord Everly's roof.

After all, Tristan knew a thief when he saw one. He'd been a Bow Street Runner, once upon a time. He couldn't say what he was now. An earl who lazed about and sipped port while his neighbor was robbed, apparently.

Another useless earl. Just what London needed.

Still, since fate had doomed him to a lifetime of aristocratic idleness, he was obligated to do the thing properly. So, after weeks spent haunting his townhouse, Tristan had reluctantly agreed to accompany his friend Lord Lyndon to White's tonight. He'd had vague notions of engaging in activities earls were meant to find amusing—drinking, wagering, that sort of thing—but Tristan hadn't been amused.

He'd found it all utterly pointless. He'd left early, and was nearly home before it occurred to him White's was *meant* to be pointless.

Pointlessness was, in fact, rather the point.

Given that the evening had been a spectacular failure, Tristan didn't hold out much hope for any of the other gentlemanly pursuits London had to offer. Indeed, after tonight, he couldn't think of a single reason to remain in the city at all.

Aside, perhaps, from the boy on Lord Everly's roof.

Tristan retrieved his port, sank down into his chair, and tipped his glass against his lips. A proper earl didn't waste perfectly good port. The boy was bound to do something interesting sooner or later. Tristan was content to sip his port, and wait until he did.

And wait, and wait, and wait…

Time didn't hesitate to take liberties with Tristan—the past few weeks had dragged on for *years*—but never had the minutes crawled by as reluctantly as they did now. The shadows lengthened, the fire burned to embers, the long-case clock on the first-floor landing chimed the hours, and somewhere, an entire civilization rose and fell again.

And still, Tristan waited.

Surely it was unnatural for any boy to remain motionless for so long? But even when it started raining, the lad never twitched. He simply lay there, still as a corpse—

Tristan jerked to his feet, his empty glass tumbling to the floor. He peered down at the still figure, but it was too dark for him to tell if the boy's chest was moving.

Was it possible he *was* a corpse? How the devil would a corpse end up on Lord Everly's roof? Then again, if a phantom thief could appear on a roof, mightn't a phantom corpse do so, as well?

No, no. That wouldn't do. There were limits to what Tristan would tolerate in his delusions. A phantom thief was one thing, but a corpse quite another. That was one hallucination too far. And so, Tristan was left with a single, unavoidable conclusion.

There was a dead boy, lying on the roof of Lord Everly's pediment.

A dead boy on one's neighbor's roof wasn't the sort of thing a gentleman could overlook, and that, Tristan would later reflect, was the cause of all the chaos that followed.

If the situation had been even a trifle less alarming than a dead boy on a roof, he might not have ventured out at all. He might have remained in his library, helped himself to another glass of port, and gotten sotted, like a proper earl was meant to do.

As it was, chaos found him, and once she had him, she showed him no mercy. She seized him by the neck, sank her talons into his flesh, and hurled him headlong into a tumult without even the courtesy of a second glance.

* * * *

If Sophia Monmouth had realized how easy it would be to scale the front of a London townhouse, she'd have left her footprints across every rooftop in Mayfair by now.

A single leap, and she was balanced on the top edge of the wrought iron railing flanking the stone steps. A bit of a scramble and a discreet shimmy or two, and she was clinging to one of the columns on either side of the front door, her arms and legs wrapped around it, albeit in a most unladylike fashion. From there it had been easy enough to haul herself up and clamber over the edge of the pediment.

Unnecessary risk, Sophia.

Lady Clifford's voice often found its way into Sophia's head at times like these. If ignoring it caused her the *tiniest* pang of guilt, Sophia had nonetheless become accustomed to shrugging it off.

It wasn't that Lady Clifford was *wrong*, exactly. Strictly speaking, Sophia hadn't *had* to scale the front of Lord Everly's townhouse. She could have hidden around a corner or behind a tree like an ordinary intruder, but she'd been curious to see if she could manage the thing. After all, a lady never knew when she'd be obliged to make use of some lord or other's rooftop. It was a simple matter of knowing one's capabilities.

Besides, where was the fun in being ordinary? She was here now, snug as you please, lying on her back on Lord Everly's roof. Goodness, he had a great many windows, didn't he? Six of them on the first floor alone, marching in a tidy row across the front of the townhouse. The symmetry was pleasing, but then aristocrats did like for things to be in their proper places.

All things, not just their windows.

Curious, she nudged the toe of her boot into a tiny gap at the bottom edge of the window above her and pushed. It slid open, and an amused snort fell from her lips. Heavens, the nobility were foolish. It would be the easiest thing in the world for her to slip inside the house and pinch the family silver.

Truly, it was a pity she wasn't a thief, because she would have been a tremendously good one. Most of the townhouses on Great Marlborough Street boasted wrought iron railings and columns on either side of the doors with lovely, wide pediments on top. No doubt the aristocratic owners were proud of their pediments, and considered all the cornices, columns, and canopies to be the height of elegance.

Ah, well. Pride was a wicked, detestable sin.

Really, what was a wrought iron railing but a footstool, a column, a makeshift ladder, and cornices and decorative arches footholds and finger grips? Rooftops all across Mayfair were now crooking their fingers at Sophia, daring her to attempt them. That was the glorious thing about London, wasn't it? Just when one thought they knew her, she offered an entirely new landscape, ripe for exploration.

As for Lord Everly, his silver was safe enough from her. Fortunately for him, Sophia wasn't here to steal. She wasn't here for Lord Everly at all.

No, she'd come for someone else, and now there was nothing to do but wait for her quarry to venture out the door. He might not do so tonight, but she'd happily come back for him tomorrow, and every night afterwards until he did.

Sophia hummed to herself, gazing up at the dark sky as she waited. After a short time, it began to drizzle. The fat raindrops struck the slate roof in varying notes, transforming what might otherwise have been a dreary evening into a symphony.

She lay still, listening to the rhythmic patter. She'd never minded the rain, but neither had she ever noticed how pleasant the sound of it was. Then again, she'd never been as close to it as she was now. It didn't have the same pleasing resonance when it hit the pavement, but from up here it was like music, or clocks chiming.

The sky above Sophia deepened to an opaque midnight blue as the moments slipped past. The clouds that had been hanging over the city all day skidded this way and that, playing a game of hide and seek with the moon. Yes, she'd be spending more time on London's rooftops, once this business was done.

Her heartbeat took up the soothing tempo of the rain, and it might have lulled her into a doze if the creak of a door opening below hadn't roused her. Sophia kept her head down, but rolled over and slid on her belly to the edge of the pediment and peered over the side, taking care to keep out of sight. The street was thick with shadows, but the faint light from the entryway briefly illuminated the figure of a man before he slammed the door behind him.

Sophia's lips curled into a smile.

He was a small, rat-like thing, stoop-shouldered and twitchy, easily distinguishable. A flaw, in Sophia's opinion. Far better to blend, if one was a criminal.

He had a pipe between his fingers, and he paused to suck on it before he ambled down the steps and turned left onto Great Marlborough Street, toward Regent Street. A thin stream of smoke trailed after him like a second shadow as he disappeared around the corner.

Sophia let him go. There was no need to rush after him. She'd never once lost her quarry, and she wouldn't lose him now. She waited, still humming, until the sound of footsteps faded and a glance revealed nothing but the empty street below.

She threw her leg over the side of pediment and dangled there for a moment before her foot found the narrow edge at the top of the column. She steadied herself, then shimmied down in the same shocking manner as she'd gone up. She didn't bother with the railing this time, but dropped lightly down onto the top step, and tugged her dark cap down over her face.

She'd been following this man for several weeks now, and knew far more about him than she ever cared to know about any man—which public houses he frequented, which Covent Garden prostitutes he preferred—all to no purpose.

But Sophia had been patient, knowing he'd return to the scene of his crime eventually.

They always did.

* * * *

The corpse had moved.

That is, the boy—he was very much alive, as it happened—was of an acrobatic turn. He'd rolled across the roof with the ease of a billiards ball across the baize, and now he hung over the edge of the pediment, his legs braced on the roof while his torso hung suspended in midair.

He might yet end up a corpse. An unexpected twitch of a muscle or a sudden breeze and he'd topple over the side like overripe fruit from a tree. Tristan might have put a stop to the business right then—thief or not, he didn't care to see the boy plunge to his death—but before he could stir, Lord Everly's door opened and a man emerged.

He closed the door behind him, snuffing out the faint light coming from the townhouse, but Tristan got enough of a glimpse of him to determine it wasn't Everly. He was much smaller than his lordship, who was thick and squat, more spherical than otherwise. Tristan couldn't see the man's face, and given the number of people who went in and out of Everly's townhouse on a given day, he didn't bother to hazard a guess as to his identity.

The man paused to raise the pipe between his fingers to his lips, and then he was off down the street, his gait cocky. Too cocky, the fool. He hadn't the least idea he was being watched.

Tristan didn't bother to note his direction. His gaze darted back to the boy, who'd turned his head to follow the man's progress. He hadn't moved, but Tristan sensed a sudden tension in that slight frame, the taut stillness of a predator in the seconds before it burst into movement.

What were thieves, if not predators?

The familiar, restless energy Tristan had given up as lost was now rioting in his veins. A few minutes passed, then a few more, and then... quickly, but as cool as you please, the boy was on his feet and over the side of the pediment.

Tristan's muscles tensed instinctively, as if preparing to catch the boy midfall, but he needn't have worried. The lad made quick work of the column, scampering down like a monkey. In the next breath he'd dropped onto the street and was gliding after his prey, dark and silent as a shadow.

Not a phantom, then, and not a figment. Not a corpse, and not a thief. Oddly, it was this last that surprised Tristan the most, but it didn't appear as if the boy had been there to steal.

At least, not from Everly. He might intend to pick the pocket of the man he'd followed, but there were plenty of pockets in London ripe for the picking, none of which required a rooftop adventure.

Why would this boy risk his neck for the privilege of picking the pocket of a man who, though small, was several heads taller than he was, and outweighed him by at least two stone? Tristan hadn't the vaguest idea what the boy thought he'd do when he caught up to his victim, but he'd find out soon enough.

He was still wearing his boots, and didn't bother with his greatcoat.

Ten seconds later he was on the street in front of his townhouse. By then there was no sign of the boy, but he couldn't have gotten that far ahead. Damned if the little imp hadn't perfected the art of disappearing, though, just like a proper phantom.

But phantom or not, in the end it wouldn't matter.

Tristan could cross from one end of the city to the other as easily as strolling from his library to his study. He knew every road, every hidden alcove, and every filthy back alley in London.

The boy was clever and quick, but Tristan would catch him.

* * * *

He was going to make a fatal mistake tonight. Tonight, after tedious weeks of chasing this villain all over London, Sophia was going to catch him out at last.

She could smell it, feel it, as if it were a scent in the air, or the glide of a fingertip across her skin. She no longer found it odd she should be able to sense such things. She must have been born with the mind of a criminal, if not the heart of one, because she knew instinctually how they would behave.

She headed west down Great Marlborough Street, clinging to the shadows, pure intuition guiding her steps. Once or twice she thought she heard footsteps behind her, but when she paused there was nothing aside from the light patter of rain falling on the ground.

Even if there *was* someone following her, they wouldn't catch her.

No one ever did.

She kept to the shadows as she prowled along behind her prey, who plodded toward Tottenham Court Road, utterly oblivious to the fact he was being followed. It seemed not to occur to him he might be held accountable for any of his crimes.

His nonchalance wasn't a result of innocence, but of arrogance and stupidity.

It wasn't until he turned onto Aldwych Street and she could see the dome of St. Paul's Cathedral and the spire of St. Clement Dane's Church looming in the distance that Sophia's heart began to pound. Of all the places a man might haunt on a dark night in London, this man had chosen to come *here*.

Strange, considering what had happened to him the last time he'd lingered in this neighborhood.

That is, what he *claimed* had happened.

How strange he should wish to return by himself, at night, to a place where he'd been the victim of a crime.

But it was no accident he'd come here, and no coincidence.

Sophia glanced about, paying particular attention to the shadowy corners before prowling after him, knots of excitement tying and untying themselves in her chest as she paused at one side of St. Clement Dane's Church, waiting to see what he'd do.

He didn't appear to be concerned someone might see him, but approached the entrance to the church, checked his pocket watch, then fell into a casual slouch in the arched doorway and turned his attention back to his pipe.

Another person might have been fooled by this show of unconcern, but not Sophia. His actions were too self-conscious, too practiced. To her well-trained eye it looked as if he were waiting there for someone, but wished to appear as if he'd just happened upon the church by chance, and by chance had been overcome with an irresistible urge to smoke his pipe while he was there.

She smothered a derisive snort. He wasn't very good at this.

She ducked behind the column of a building across the street from the church. She had a clear view of her man from here, but she was already scanning the churchyard, searching for a better hiding place. She'd need to be closer to him if she wanted to hear anything.

Her gaze landed on the small, round portico to the west side of the church. It was nothing more than a half-circle of slender columns with a roof, but it would do, and she was already fairly close to it—just on the other side of the street. If she could reach it, she could creep around the side, closer to the entrance of the church. From there she'd be able to see and hear whatever passed.

The dash across the road might prove a bit tricky, though. If the man happened to look in her direction while she was crossing, he'd certainly see her. But then he hadn't proved particularly observant so far, had he?

Sophia assessed the narrow street in front of her, calculating the distance, then glanced back toward the entrance to the church, where her quarry was still slouched against the archway, looking about as alert as a sleepy child at a church sermon.

Yes, she could make it. Once that thick bank of clouds crossed the moon, she'd go. She waited, her muscles tensed to run, but just as the clouds began to edge out the moonlight, she heard a thin, high-pitched sound coming from behind her.

It sounded like…yes, it was. A man was coming down the Strand towards St. Clement Dane's Church, and he was whistling.

Sophia froze for an instant, her heart pounding, then as quickly and quietly as she could she melted back into the shadows. Another glance toward the church revealed her quarry had jerked to sudden attention. For one breathless moment Sophia thought he'd seen her, but he wasn't looking in her direction.

He was waiting for the man who was making his way down the Strand. The man himself seemed not to realize he was the object of so much intense interest. He ambled along, whistling tunelessly, utterly at his ease.

Whatever criminal enterprise was about to unfold, the whistler wasn't a part of it.

No, he was its victim.

She held her breath as the whistler drew closer to the archway where Lord Everly's man was waiting. Even from this distance she could see the villain was already creeping forward, ready to pounce on his victim like a rat on a crumb of bread.

Then, just behind him, Sophia saw a flicker of movement in the shadows. Her eyes widened, then narrowed as she strained to make it out. For a moment it had looked as if there was someone else there, lurking behind the church door, but she couldn't be certain.

Her head snapped back toward the man coming down the Strand. He was moving steadily toward the front of the church, still whistling cheerfully, unaware of the mischief that awaited him.

It was pure foolishness for her to try and stop it now. She'd only expose herself, and put her mission at needless risk. Even so, Sophia's mouth was opening, a cry of warning rising in her throat.

She never got the chance to voice it.

Just as it was about to burst from her lips, a gloved hand came down hard over her mouth. Sophia gasped in shock, but even when a long, muscular arm snaked around her waist, she kept her wits about her. This wasn't the first time she'd been grabbed, and she wasn't the sort of lady who succumbed to hysterics.

No, she was more the sort of lady who bit anyone foolish enough to put their hand over her mouth, and that was what she did now. Without any hesitation, she sank her teeth into the closest finger. She got a mouthful of an exceptionally fine kid glove for her trouble, but she clamped down onto the knuckle like a hunting dog with a bird locked between its jaws.

Her attacker didn't think his glove fine enough to be worth saving, because he tore it off and let it drop into the dirt between them.

When the bite failed to secure her release, Sophia landed a practiced kick to his shin, her lips curling in a savage grin when her heel hit bone with a satisfying crunch. The arm around her waist went slack for an instant, but he seemed to have a good deal of experience attacking people, because he didn't release her. Anyone else would have, but he held her fast, a muttered curse escaping his lips.

So she kicked him again.

He let out a pained grunt. "You'll regret that soon enough."

Before she could land a third kick, he jerked her off her feet and dragged her backwards into the shadowy graveyard behind St. Clement Dane's.

Someone *had* been following her, and now he'd caught her.

Chapter Two

The kick found its mark as surely as if Tristan had a bullseye painted on his shin. It was a swift, vicious blow, and unexpected enough it might have secured the boy's release if Tristan had been anyone other than who he was.

As it happened, the lad was out of luck. Tristan had been kicked by every blackguard in London, most of whom were stronger and burlier than this meager slip of a boy. Still, for all his flimsiness, he was fierce enough to have spoiled a rather nice glove with those sharp teeth of his.

Tristan left the glove in the dirt where it had dropped and grabbed the scuff of the boy's neck with his bare hand. "Struggle all you like. I have you now." He pinned the boy's arms to his sides, wrenched him off his feet, and dragged him into the gloom behind St. Clement Dane's churchyard. "Ah, here we are, lad. We'll transact our business in the dark, shall we? We won't be disturbed here, and I can question you for as long as I choose."

A sound burst from the boy's lips. Given his current predicament a cry of fear was to be expected, but this wasn't fear. It was a cry of wrath. In an instant he was struggling again, his slight body thrashing and twisting like an enraged fish on the end of a hook.

An exceptionally sneaky fish.

If he managed to squirm free, Tristan had no doubt he'd scramble up the nearest column and vanish in an instant. "Enough!" He tightened his arms around the boy. Not so tight he'd hurt him, but tight enough to hold him still. "You're wasting your strength, lad, and trying my patience. You're not going anywhere until I've questioned you, but I won't hurt you. Now cease writhing, if you please, and I'll put you down."

Tristan expected his advice to go unheeded, but to his surprise the boy ceased struggling and went as limp as a sack of flour.

"There's a good lad." Tristan set him on his feet, but he was careful to back him up against the wrought iron fence surrounding the graveyard. "Now, if you agree to keep quiet, I'll remove my hand from your mouth. Not a single sound until I give you leave, understand?"

Tristan waited, one hand on the boy's shoulder to prevent him from bolting until at last the boy gave the briefest of nods. "Well then, lad." He eased his hand away from the boy's mouth. "What have you to say for yourself?"

Not a damn thing, it seemed.

Tristan studied the narrow shoulders and bent head, and a reluctant chuckle escaped his lips. "You're a proper little thief, aren't you? Quick-witted, agile, and you know when to keep your mouth shut. I've seen grown men with less self-possession."

The boy was, in fact, just the sort of clever, tight-lipped little miscreant who'd prove invaluable to older, more sophisticated criminals—criminals like those responsible for a recent rash of robberies plaguing London. The thieves had evaded the law for months, but five weeks ago a botched attempt at a theft had led to a grisly murder, and one of the gang of culprits had been taken up for the crime.

Strangely enough, he'd been taken up right *here*, in St. Clement Dane's churchyard. A curious coincidence, really—or it would have been if Tristan believed in coincidences.

He didn't, nor did he believe in innocent explanations. Those who engaged in suspicious activity invariably proved to be guilty, and this boy, in his dark clothes with his cap pulled low over his eyes, was the very picture of a pocket-sized villain. "Come now, sir. Surely you have something to offer in your own defense."

No reaction from the boy. He kept his head down, his face carefully concealed behind the brim of his cap.

"I'm happy to keep you here all night." Tristan's tone was pleasant, but he tightened his grip on the boy's shoulder.

That earned him a shrug. Delicate bones shifted under Tristan's fingers, but not a single word crossed the boy's stubborn lips. Irritated, Tristan reached out and snatched the cap from his head. "You'll look me in the eye when I speak to you, lad—"

He broke off, and the cap slipped through his fingers and dropped to the ground. A few hairpins went with it, and the long, silky hair that had been stuffed underneath fell down in a dark cascade of waves.

Tristan stared at her, flabbergasted. "Hell and—"

"Damnation," the girl finished, with a toss of her gleaming head.

Some flowery scent wafted over Tristan, something rather like... honeysuckle? What sort of girl smelled like honeysuckle after a rooftop escapade and a mad dash through London's filthy streets? No sort of girl Tristan had ever seen.

He turned his attention to the face that had been hiding under the cap, but it was as distracting as her scent. She had smooth, olive-tinted skin, heavily lashed light green eyes, and a stubborn, dimpled chin. That face was enough to scatter any man's wits, and that was *before* he noticed the plump lips that somehow contrived to look fetching, despite the fierce frown she wore.

"What, you've nothing to say now?" She waved a hand at him. "You were about to deliver a proper lecture, I believe. I beg you won't let the fact I'm not a boy dissuade you from your scold."

Tristan was rarely struck speechless, but it wasn't every day one found the boy he'd been chasing—the boy who'd climbed to the roof of his neighbor's townhouse and then back down again, as cool as you please—wasn't a boy at all.

He...that is, *she*...was a woman.

A woman, not a girl, for all that she was a small, dainty thing, no higher than Tristan's shoulder, and didn't look to be above nineteen or twenty years old. Indeed, she was so resoundingly feminine, so delicate, his instinct to protect those weaker than himself might have rushed to the fore if he hadn't caught the spark of a formidable temper in her green eyes.

The lady was far from weak, and even further from innocent.

It was the reminder he needed before he made an utter fool of himself by offering to escort her home, or some other gallant nonsense. She might be female, but it didn't make a damn bit of difference to him whether she was a villain, or a villainess.

She'd been hiding on Everly's roof, disguised as a boy, waiting for her victim to emerge so she could follow him here—a feat she'd accomplished with the practiced ease of a born thief.

The lady was up to no good. The only question was, what sort of no good?

She regarded him with one slim eyebrow arched, waiting to see what he'd do next. Tristan liked to think he was a gentleman of some presence of mind, but it took every bit of sangfroid he could muster to say calmly, "You didn't answer my question, miss. Why are you sneaking about London in the dark, and what are you doing at St. Clement Dane's Church?"

"Why, saying my confession, sir." Her full lips curved in a mocking smile. "What else does one do at church?"

Much to Tristan's disgust, he found he had to make an effort to tear his gaze away from her mouth. "Perhaps I could accept that explanation, if it weren't midnight."

She leaned closer and whispered confidingly, "I thought it best not to wait until morning. I'm quite *wicked*, you see."

Her whisper hit Tristan right in his lower belly, but his only outward reaction was a quirked eyebrow. "I've no doubt of that, but there's the trifling matter of your never having entered the church. I found you skulking in the churchyard, if you recall."

"Skulking? Goodness, that *does* sound wicked. But you see, then, why I'd be so anxious to confess my sins."

So many lies, falling from such sweet lips was…disconcerting. Tristan had never seen a lady lie with such cool impunity before. He traded only in truth, yet there was something striking about her audaciousness. "Perhaps you'd like to confess your sins to me?" He'd have the truth out of her one way or another.

The green eyes went wide. "Oh, no. I couldn't possibly do that, sir. Whatever will you think of me?"

"What, indeed? But that puts us at odds. I can't release you until you've explained yourself."

"No, I'm afraid not, sir. Unless, of course, you're a vicar?" She swept an assessing gaze over him. "You don't look like one. You're far too…clean."

"*Clean?*" That startled a laugh out of Tristan. "Are vicars commonly dirty? I would have thought it was just the opposite."

"Not *dirty*, but neither are they so…polished and shiny as you are." She cocked her head, studying him, then gave a careless shrug. "You look like an aristocrat. Rather high, I think, given your accent and the quality of your gloves. A viscount, perhaps, or an earl."

It was on the tip of Tristan's tongue to say he wasn't anything of the sort, but that was no longer true. He *was*, in fact, an earl. Not just Tristan Stratford anymore, and not a Bow Street Runner, but Lord Gray. His lordship, despite having never aspired to the title, and being uniquely unsuited to it.

But this wasn't a ballroom, and he wasn't writing his name on her dance card. This was a deserted graveyard in the middle of the night, and she was…well, he didn't have any bloody idea *what* she was, but certainly not a lady, and very likely a criminal.

Tristan didn't explain himself to criminals. They explained themselves to *him*, and it was time she was made to understand that. "Perhaps you'd rather give your confession to the magistrate?"

"The magistrate!" Her eyes narrowed to slits. "On what charge, sir? There's no crime in visiting St. Clement Dane's Church, is there?"

"No, but I think the magistrate might be interested in knowing you're desecrating rooftops on Great Marlborough Street. Scaling a townhouse is a rather singular skill, and not one common in innocent young ladies."

That got her attention. Her gaze caught his before skittering away.

"Look at me if you please, miss. What you were doing on Lord Everly's roof? No sense in denying it. I saw you from my window, and followed you here. I took you for a thief, and I imagine the magistrate will, as well."

At mention of Lord Everly's roof her face paled, but if Tristan expected a confession to cleanse the lies from those plump lips, he was disappointed. "That would be a damning charge indeed, sir, but there's the small matter of my *not having stolen anything.* Insignificant, but there you are."

He gave her a cool smile. "Not this time, no, but given the rash of recent thefts in London, I feel certain the magistrate would choose to question you. But perhaps you've changed your mind, and would rather speak to me than him?"

She didn't seem to find that option appealing. She remained stubbornly silent, but by now, Tristan had run out of patience with her. "Let's try this one more time, shall we? Who did you follow here, and what do you want with Lord Everly?"

"Lord Everly? Why, not a thing."

She might deny it all she liked, but Tristan could see he'd struck a nerve. "This is your last chance to tell me before I take you before the magistrate."

"A kind offer, I'm sure, but I believe I'll save my confession for my vicar."

Tristan studied her, but not a crack appeared in that smooth façade. Whatever her reasons for tonight's adventure, she was determined to keep them to herself.

Unfortunately for her, he was as determined to find them out as she was to hide them. "Very well." He took her by the arm and half-turned, easing her away from the fence. "Perhaps you'll be more forthcoming with the magistrate."

He was hard-pressed to account for what happened next. He didn't feel her twist out of his grip, but one moment he had a hand around her arm, and the next he was grasping at air. He whirled back toward her, but somehow in those few seconds of freedom, she'd slipped through the wrought iron bars of the fence, and was standing on the other side of it.

Tristan gaped at her, open-mouthed. "How the *devil* did you manage that?"

The bars were generously spaced as far as fences went, but not so far apart it ever would have occurred to him she could slip between them.

It would take some clever twisting and maneuvering to do it. Even now, with her on one side of the fence and him on the other, he couldn't see how she'd managed it.

Scaling townhouses, climbing columns, scampering about on rooftops, and now slipping between the bars of a fence? Good Lord, who *was* this woman?

"As I said, I believe I'll save my confessions for my vicar." She dropped a curtsy so mocking it might as well have been a rude hand gesture, and backed away from the fence, out of his reach. "I wish you a pleasant evening, sir. Oh, I beg your pardon. I mean, *my lord.*"

Without another word she melted into the shadows, her delighted laugh echoing in the darkness. Oh, she was pleased with herself, wasn't she? But the lady was premature in celebrating her escape, because Tristan would be damned if he let her get away from him.

He was much too big to pass between the rails as she had, but the fence wasn't more than eight feet high. Tristan gave the wrought iron a shake, frowning when the rails gave a protesting squeak. A bit flimsy, but it would have to do, because there was only one way to go from here.

Up, and over.

* * * *

His exalted lordship—the Earl of Great Marlborough Street, or whoever he was—was utterly furious. Pity, but that was what he got for creeping about and making things difficult for her instead of squandering his fortune at the clubs or trifling with his mistresses, as an earl was meant to do.

Sophia tried to smother her laugh, but the look on his face when he realized she'd slipped through the bars of her makeshift prison was the most delicious thing she'd ever seen. She would have liked to draw that lowered brow, the glittering fury in those cool gray eyes.

He did look rather like a painting—one of those terribly elegant ones, where the gentleman posed rakishly at the bottom of a grand staircase, with a half-dozen hunting dogs sprawled at his feet. Yes, she could easily imagine him on a handsome stallion, clad in a pair of buckskin breeches and a dashing hunting jacket, on a quest to ruin some poor fox's day.

He certainly didn't belong *here*, though to his credit he knew his way about well enough to track his quarry from Great Marlborough Street to Westminster. His quarry being *her*, of all the devilish bad luck. But then he hadn't succeeded in catching her, had he?

Not for long, at any rate.

Like most hunters, he wasn't reconciled to losing his game, but short of climbing the fence there was little he could do about it. He couldn't come after her. The fence was quite high, and the wrought iron had been fashioned into spikes along the top edge. She hadn't come across many aristocrats who could match her for agility, and this one wasn't likely to be an exception, so—

Blast him, what was he doing?

Sophia stared, the hair on her arms rising in alarm as he grasped the iron rails and gave the fence a determined shake. If she didn't know it to be impossible, she'd almost think he was testing it for stability before he—

Climbed the fence.

She watched in horror as he swung himself up and reached out to wrap two impossibly large hands around the spiked tops. "What do you think you're doing?"

Perhaps the better question was, what was *she* doing? It was pure foolishness to stand about gaping and asking questions when it was plain to see he was about to clamber over the fence.

"If you intend to flee, I suggest you do so now." His gray eyes met hers through the iron bars. "After such an impressive escape, I'd be disappointed indeed if you didn't lead me on a chase."

No, surely not! She couldn't be so unlucky as to cross paths with the one aristocrat in London who could actually scale such a monstrous fence. Why, it was absurd, impossible, and yet even as she watched, open-mouthed, it was happening, his long legs making quick work of it, hauling himself closer and closer to the top…

Sophia retreated into the thick shadows of the graveyard behind her. Her muscles were tensed to run, and her mind was busily picking out the best route towards freedom, yet she stood as motionless as the gravestones in the graveyard at her back, unable to tear her gaze away from him.

His big, capable hands dwarfed the spikes at the top of the fence. The knuckles of his ungloved hand were covered with scars, and there were nicks and scratches on the back of it that were utterly at odds with his elevated rank in life. Why would a gentleman with such fine gloves have such coarse hands?

Sophia wasted so much precious time staring at his hands, by the time she gathered her wits enough to move, he'd made it to the top of the fence and was seconds away from dropping down to the other side. They stared at each other as he balanced on the top edge, a predatory gleam in his eyes. "Do you suppose you can outrun me?"

Those gray eyes. Dear God, he looked like a wolf about to devour an entire herd of sheep, and he was coming after *her*.

If he'd been another sort of man, Sophia would have said he'd never catch her, but this man was quick, long-limbed, strong. He'd gotten over that fence as easily as if he'd been mounting a horse, and there was no reason to suppose he was any less accomplished a runner than he was a climber.

Worst of all, he was cunning. So cunning he'd followed her from Great Marlborough Street to St. Clement Dane's without her knowing he was there. How had he managed it? She'd never blundered so badly before—

A thump echoed throughout the silent graveyard, the sound of boots hitting the ground, followed by a low chuckle. "I hope you're as quick as you are clever."

To Sophia's everlasting shame, her knees trembled at the sight of him. Why, he was positively enormous! If he'd been wearing a billowing black cape and had a bloody dagger to hand, he'd be every inch the sinister Gothic villain.

"Because if I catch you…"

The *anticipation* in his voice, his unmistakable *pleasure* in that prospect… A chill rushed over Sophia's skin. There was only one sensible thing to do.

"You won't escape me a second time."

Flee.

She didn't pause to respond to his threats, but whirled around and fled into the graveyard, praying the darkness would swallow her. If it came down to who was the faster of the two of them, she was doomed. He had the longest legs she'd ever seen. She hadn't a chance of outrunning him. Her only hope was to get far enough ahead of him that she'd lose him in the shadows.

Fortunately, there was no shortage of shadows in the graveyard. Crooked headstones jutted from the earth like so many broken fingers, beckoning her forward. The clouds had thickened again, and the night air had turned heavy with the threat of rain, but a few pale rays of moonlight struggled free of the gloom, and Sophia could pick out a path before her—a way around the headstones that would keep her hidden until she reached the other side of the graveyard.

Crouching low, she weaved her way silently through the haphazard rows. Some of the mausoleums were still intact, their crosses straight, the statues of the Virgin still safe in their recessed nooks, holding court over the dead. But as she passed into the older part of the graveyard the carefully tended plots gave way to weeds strewn with bits of crumbled stone, the once-smooth marble now marred by damp, mossy cracks.

She paused when she reached a derelict white marble crypt, its iron door hanging partway across the arched entryway, teetering on its broken hinges. For an instant she was tempted to squeeze past the ruined gate and duck inside to hide from her pursuer, but if he happened to see her and follow her inside, she'd be trapped, and at his mercy.

So, she crept on. The scent of soil and decay rose into the air in the wake of her footsteps, but Sophia didn't pause to remark it, nor did she look behind her, even when the heavy thud of his footsteps brought him so close, she imagined she could feel his hot breath on her neck.

Panic hovered on the edges of her consciousness, but she resisted the urge to bolt. She kept her gaze fixed on the street beyond the graveyard until she made it there by sheer force of will. She didn't allow herself to think about how far she'd come, or how far she still had to go, but simply kept moving, ducking down narrow alleyways and pulling out every trick she'd ever learned to evade a pursuer.

This man, though, was no ordinary pursuer. He seemed to know every hidden alcove and crevice in London as well as she did, and his determination to catch her never flagged, his long legs easily closing whatever distance she managed to put between them.

But this wasn't a game of distances. It was a game of cunning and stealth, and Sophia excelled at both. He was faster than she was, but she was wilier in the way of the pursued, who generally had a great deal more to lose than their pursuer.

Slowly, steadily she made her way to Beak Street, and from there to Kingly, then north as far as Tenison Court until Regent Street appeared before her, wide and open. Just to the west was Maddox Street, temptingly close, where Lady Clifford would be waiting for her, and Sophia might squeeze into Cecilia's bed with Georgiana and Emma.

She paused in the shadows of a building at the corner of Beak and Regent Streets, listening, but it had been some time since she'd heard the echo of his footsteps behind her. Was it possible she'd lost him earlier, closer to Golden Square, or was he still there, lurking in the darkness, waiting for her to come out of hiding?

She was close, so very close. Her throat ached with a desperate yearning to be safely at home, but she'd made it this far by suppressing her reckless instincts and letting caution and good sense guide her steps.

No unnecessary risks, Sophia.

She crept from her hiding place and dashed across Regent Street, her heart pounding and her harsh breaths echoing in her ears. As soon as she reached the other side, she ducked into the shadows again and crouched down, shivers darting down her exposed back as she waited for a heavy hand to land on her shoulder, a palm to cover her mouth, a deep, masculine voice to curse in her ear.

But when she dared to look behind her, there was nothing. No pursuer in a billowing black cloak. No ghosts, no bloody daggers, no Gothic villain. No aristocrat with one glove, scarred hands, and glittering gray eyes.

Regent Street was deserted.

Sophia didn't move, but remained crouched in the gloom, gulping at the air, one breath after another until her heart ceased its panicked thrashing. Then she rose on shaking legs and dashed down New Burlington Road to Savile Row, then to Mill Street, and from there—finally, *finally*—to Maddox Street.

It wasn't until she was mere steps from the entrance of the Clifford School that she realized she'd made a mistake.

A dreadful, dreadful mistake.

She saw his shadow first, ghostly and terrifying and growing more enormous against the white brick wall with every step he took toward her.

Sophia stared at him, dumb with shock.

No, it was impossible he could have known she was coming here, except somehow, he *had* known. She hadn't lost him near Golden Square. He'd gotten by her without her noticing, and he'd been here all along, waiting for her.

For long, frozen moments, neither of them said a word. She backed away from him, knowing even as she did so it was hopeless. He was too close, too big, and he was standing between her and her only escape. Even so, she turned to run, but she hadn't gone a step before that big, scarred hand closed around her elbow, stilling her. The sudden tug upset her balance, and she would have fallen if he hadn't snaked an arm around her waist and hauled her back against a chest so unyielding, she might have been slammed against a wall.

"You *are* wicked, aren't you?" His voice, so low and soft she might have thought she'd imagined it if his lips hadn't brushed her ear. "You told me as much. I should have listened to you."

So close, so close...

The words were a howl in her throat, but she had no breath for a howl, and they left her lips as a whisper.

"Indeed. But not close enough." His arm tightened around her waist—not so tight it squeezed the breath from her, but tight enough to be menacing. "I should have realized sooner you were one of Lady Clifford's…creatures."

Creatures? Dear God, that didn't sound promising. Sophia said nothing, but a drop of sweat trickled from her temple into the corner of her eye.

"You told the truth about one thing though, didn't you? You aren't after Lord Everly. You're after Peter Sharpe."

Sophia squeezed her eyes closed.

He *knew*. Lady Clifford, Peter Sharpe, Jeremy Ives…

Whoever this man was, he *knew*. Somehow, he'd put all the pieces together—

"Now, why would Lady Clifford have such a keen interest in Mr. Sharpe she'd direct one of her disciples to follow him? I can't help but wonder, you see, if it has something to do with Jeremy Ives—"

"Take your hands off the lady. *Now*."

Sophia's eyes snapped open at the sound of the deep, familiar voice, and relief flooded through her, so intense she sagged against her captor. "Daniel."

Her pursuer's body had gone rigid, but when he spoke his voice was calm. "Brixton. I should have known you were lurking about."

"Aye. You should have. Let go of the lady, my lord."

The arm at her waist dropped, and the chest at her back disappeared with such suddenness Sophia stumbled.

"Come here, Miss Sophia." Daniel Brixton held out a hand to her, but he never took his eyes off the man still looming behind her.

She took a hesitant step toward Daniel, but her legs were so wobbly she stumbled again, and he was obliged to catch her. "Daniel, thank God. I—"

"It's all right, lass." Daniel righted her with a nudge of his massive arm.

"I wouldn't have hurt her, Brixton."

Daniel's lips stretched in a grim smile. "Of course not, my lord."

Sophia turned to find her gray-eyed pursuer standing a few paces behind her, his hands tucked casually into his coat pockets, no longer the stuff of nightmares, but just a man now, albeit a big one.

Not, however, as big as Daniel Brixton, Lady Clifford's most trusted servant.

No one was as big as Daniel.

"Go on inside now, Miss Sophia." Daniel gave her a gentle push toward the entrance.

Sophia didn't argue, but stumbled up the steps on trembling legs and hurled herself through the front door. She slammed it closed with a deafening thud, then fell against it, tears in her eyes, and her lungs burning.

Chapter Three

"Sophia?" A voice drifted down into the entryway from above. "Is that you?"

Sophia glanced up and saw Cecilia hanging over the third-floor railing. She was clad in her night rail and she held a book in her hand, her finger marking the page.

"Where have you been? What's kept you so long? We thought you…" Cecilia trailed off when she caught a good look at Sophia's face. "Sophia? My goodness, what's the matter?"

Sophia turned, her lungs still clamoring for air, and peered through the arched window above the door. Nothing but darkness met her gaze. Daniel and Lord…Lord…well, she hadn't any idea what or who he was lord of, but he was gone.

Vanished.

No, no. Not vanished. Of course, he hadn't vanished. Daniel had sent him away, that's all. Aristocrats didn't simply disappear into the mist like specters—

"Sophia?" Cecilia was watching her with wide eyes. "Are you all right? You look as if you've seen a ghost."

"I think I…I think I *have*." Sophia slumped against the door, patting her chest to calm her racing heart.

"It's all right, Cecilia. Go back to your bedchamber, love. Sophia will be up soon." A cool voice broke the silence, and Sophia turned to find Lady Clifford standing in the doorway to the drawing room, a faint smile on her lips. "Well, Sophia. Here you are at last, dearest. I don't suppose I need to ask how your evening went. You look as if the devil himself has been chasing you."

The devil, a specter, or a very determined, *vigorous* lord. Sophia wasn't sure which, only that she'd never seen anyone run like that in her life. "Not a devil, my lady. An aristocrat."

But no ordinary aristocrat. Aristocrats were idle, sluggish things, with bloated bellies from too much beef and port, not—

"An aristocrat?" Lady Clifford raised an eyebrow. "My, how intriguing."

"That's not quite how I'd describe it, my lady." Terrifying, yes, and eerily reminiscent of a Gothic horror novel, what with the moon shrouded by clouds, the deserted graveyard, and the wicked, aristocratic villain.

Even now Sophia's body was convinced it was still tearing through the streets of London, fleeing her pursuer. Her poor lungs felt like cracked bellows, and she was bathed in sweat from her temples to her toes. Her black tunic was pasted to her back, and her breeches...well, the less said about them the better, and no doubt her cap was still lying in the dirt in St. Clement Dane's churchyard.

Her best cap, too, blast him, but then she'd gnawed on his glove, so perhaps they were even. "An aristocrat with the longest legs in London. He caught me just outside the door. Daniel came along and chased him off, but I doubt we've seen the last of him." Sophia thought of those wolfish gray eyes, and her head fell against the door behind her with a defeated thump.

Lady Clifford's gaze sharpened. "Who was he?"

Whoever—or *whatever*—he was, he had remarkably keen predatory instincts. Sophia didn't often find herself outwitted, being as wily as a thieving street urchin with a fistful of gold coins, but this man had managed to catch her out neatly enough. "Lord something or other. Daniel knows who he is."

"This is all very curious. Come along then, and tell me the rest." Lady Clifford turned back into the drawing room. "Will you have some sherry?"

"Yes, please." Sophia's throat was as dry as dust, and the inside of her mouth tasted like ashes.

Lady Clifford perched on the edge of a green silk settee, reached for a silver tray in front of her, and poured a modest measure of sherry into a crystal tumbler. "Here you are, my love. This will settle your nerves."

"My nerves might require the rest of the bottle." But Sophia didn't take up her glass, nor did she join Lady Clifford on the settee. Instead she paced back and forth in front of the fireplace, mumbling to herself as she tried to make sense of what she'd seen tonight before that tangle with the Earl of Great Marlborough Street.

After a bit more pacing, Sophia turned to face Lady Clifford and announced, "You were right all along. This whole business is suspicious from start to end."

Lady Clifford sighed. "Our business so often is, isn't it?"

"Someone's been telling lies, my lady." The sort of lies that led to an innocent man's neck in a noose.

Not just anyone's neck, either, but Jeremy's.

Jeremy Ives had appeared on the doorstep of No. 26 Maddox Street years ago, begging for work, a ragged little street boy with big, guileless blue eyes. He'd won Lady Clifford over with those eyes, though to this day she insisted he simply happened to come along when she needed a new kitchen boy.

Sophia's throat tightened. Her own heart wasn't the soft, pliable sort, but from the first moment she looked into Jeremy's sweet face, that frozen organ had melted like an icicle in the sun.

Jeremy wasn't just her friend. He was the closest thing she had to a brother.

He wasn't a pupil—the Clifford School didn't accept boys—but Sophia had taken it upon herself to teach Jeremy his numbers and letters. It had been a painstaking process, but now at age eighteen he could work simple sums and read from children's books.

Lady Clifford patted the seat beside her. "Come, Sophia. Sit here with me and drink your sherry. You look as if you're about to succumb to a fit of the vapors."

Sophia snorted, but she crossed the room and sank down on the settee. She took up her sherry, then set it down again without tasting it. "We all knew it to be a lie from the start, of course. Jeremy Ives is no more a murderer than I'm a debutante."

Jeremy had been locked behind the great stone walls of Newgate Prison six weeks ago, and they hadn't heard a word about him since. Even Lady Clifford, with all her connections, had been denied access to him.

Panic threatened, and Sophia curled her hands into fists to stop their trembling.

For all they knew, Jeremy could be—

"No, of course he's not a murderer." Lady Clifford squeezed Sophia's hands until her fingers loosened. "Tell me what you saw tonight. Did you go to Great Marlborough Street again?"

Sophia drew in a calming breath. "I did, yes. I waited on the roof of Lord Everly's pediment for Sharpe to come out, and then I followed him."

"The roof? My goodness, child. How did you manage that?" Lady Clifford handed Sophia her sherry, nodding with approval when she took a sip.

"It was easier than you'd think, what with all the fences and railings and columns everywhere." Sophia's lips curved in a sly smile. "All it took was a bit of climbing, and I had an excellent hiding place."

"You know what else is an excellent hiding place? The shadow of a tree, or around a corner, or across the street." Lady Clifford tutted. "Unnecessary risk, Sophia. Though I admit it was clever of you, especially since you don't appear to have tumbled over the edge. So, there you were on Lord Everly's roof. What then?"

Sophia sighed, but she didn't bother defending her rooftop exploit. She wouldn't be going back to Lord Everly's roof, not with his lordship's meddlesome neighbor lurking at his windows. "I waited until I heard the door open, and when I peeked out, there he was."

"Just like that? How kind of Peter Sharpe to be so accommodating," Lady Clifford murmured, a smug smile tugging at her lips.

"Oh, he was—even more accommodating than you think. I followed him, and where do you suppose he went, my lady?"

Lady Clifford's smile faded. "St. Clement Dane's Church."

"Yes. Astonishing coincidence, isn't it?"

"Quite." Lady Clifford set her glass on the table with a sharp click. "Not suspicious in itself, perhaps, but it is a bit strange Mr. Sharpe would return to St. Clement Dane's at night after he witnessed such a ghastly crime take place there."

Six weeks ago, a Bow Street Runner named Henry Gerrard had been stabbed to death in front of St. Clement Dane's Church. Peter Sharpe was the only witness to the crime, and he'd identified Jeremy—*their* Jeremy—as Gerrard's killer.

Dear, sweet, blue-eyed Jeremy was now an accused murderer.

A murderer, and a thief. The Bow Street magistrate had come to the wise conclusion that Jeremy— a young man incapable of doing all but the simplest of tasks—was part of a vicious gang of thieves terrorizing London. Jeremy, in league with criminals so clever they'd been thumbing their noses at the law since the thefts began earlier this year.

Henry Gerrard was meant to have unraveled the mystery of Jeremy's identity, and Jeremy to have slit Gerrard's throat for his trouble. Sharpe, who'd been loitering in the doorway of St. Clement Dane's Church at the time, claimed to have witnessed the gory scene unfold right before his eyes.

Now here was Sharpe, at St. Clement Dane's again tonight.

"You'd think he'd stay away, wouldn't you? But Mr. Sharpe didn't appear to be at all concerned for his safety. He didn't skulk about, or make any attempt to hide himself. He marched right to the front of the church, as bold as you please, and hung about there as if it were the most natural thing in the world."

"Hmmm." Lady Clifford tapped her lip, thinking. "How long did he stay?"

"Long enough for me to suspect he was waiting for someone. He had that look about him, too. He checked his pocket watch three times, as if impatient for someone to appear."

"*Did* anyone appear? Did you see anyone else?"

"Well, yes." Sophia huffed out a breath, furious all over again at the way the evening had unfolded. Peter Sharpe had gone to St. Clement Dane's Church for some nefarious purpose. She was certain of it. She'd been close to finding out what when the cursed Lord of Great Marlborough Street, who should have been off being an earl instead of sneaking about after her, had snatched her away. "But he wasn't there for Peter Sharpe."

"Who, then?" Lady Clifford asked, her brow furrowing.

"He, ah...I'm afraid he was there for *me*. Lord Everly has dreadfully nosy neighbors, you see. It seems this gentleman spied me from a window that looks out onto Lord Everly's pediment, and took it into his head to follow me when I went after Mr. Sharpe." Sophia snatched up her sherry and downed the contents in one swallow. "He plucked me up, dragged me into the graveyard, and threatened me with the magistrate."

Lady Clifford was giving her a strange look. "Lord Everly's neighbor, you say? A tall gentleman, rather forbidding, with dark hair?"

"He's taller than any aristocrat I've ever seen, and certainly much larger than any aristocrat needs to be. He did have dark hair, yes, and absurdly long legs. Rather alarming, taken all together." Even now Sophia hadn't fully recovered from the horrid sight of him coming over the fence.

"Well, that *is* a surprise. I heard he'd retired to his estate in Oxfordshire after his brother's death. I wonder what he's doing back in London?"

Sophia's mouth fell open. "What, you mean to say you know who he is?"

"My dear child, everyone knows who he is. He's Tristan Stratford, otherwise known as the—"

"The Ghost of Bow Street." Sophia's empty glass slid from her numb fingers and dropped onto the silver tray. She patted at her chest to calm a heart now pounding with delayed panic, and spluttered, "Dear God, the Ghost of Bow Street chased me across Westminster tonight."

But of course, it was him. Who else could have tracked her all the way from Great Marlborough Street to St. Clement Dane's without her noticing him? How many aristocrats in London could scale an eight-foot fence in under a minute? Who but the Cursed Ghost of Cursed Bow Street could have chased her such a distance, and through every back alley in London?

Naturally, Lord Everly's neighbor must turn out to be the Ghost of Bow Street.

The shock on his face when she'd slipped through the fence, the fury when she'd taunted him from the other side...

Sophia shuddered. The more arrogant the gentleman, the more fragile his ego. The Ghost of Bow Street was likely more arrogant than most, and not accustomed to being challenged. If he happened upon her again, he'd certainly come after her, and he wouldn't let her escape him a second time.

"I can't fathom why Tristan Stratford is in London at all. His elder brother died recently, leaving Stratford the Earl of Gray. He's resigned his place in the Bow Street Runners, and if the gossips have it right, he's not pleased about any of it. Apparently, he's never wanted the title." Lady Clifford shrugged. "It's his now, however, whether he wants it or not."

"He's Lord Gray." He really *was* an earl, then. An earl, and a ghost, and a Bow Street Runner, all at once. God in heaven, what a disaster. Of all the men whose notice she might have caught, why did it have to be *his*?

He knew her first name, where she lived, and he'd already figured out she'd been following Peter Sharpe tonight. He was so stealthy he was more apparition than aristocrat, and she'd done a remarkably thorough job of making herself memorable.

Just like that, any hope she'd had of avoiding him crumbled like so much dust in her hand.

Oh, *why* had she climbed onto Lord Everly's roof tonight? She'd known she could be seen from the upper floors of the townhouse next door, but it had been so silent, and without a glimmer of light to be seen. What business did Lord Gray have, wandering about in the dark and peering out his windows?

Sophia groaned and covered her face with her hands. Dear God, what a mess.

"Now, there's to be none of that." Lady Clifford tapped her on the head. "Go on up to your bedchamber, dearest, and put this out of your mind for the rest of the evening."

"Put it out of my mind?" How could she do that, knowing the Ghost of Bow Street was after her? "It's too late for that, my lady."

Lady Clifford gave her a distracted smile. "My dear child, it's never too late for anything. Now, off you go. Your friends are waiting for you."

Sophia stumbled to her feet. There wasn't a blessed thing she could do about Lord Gray right now. She'd think it through tonight, and come up with *something*. "Goodnight, my lady."

Lady Clifford patted her cheek. "Goodnight, my love."

Sophia dragged herself up the stairs, every muscle protesting. She wanted her bed, but when she reached the hallway outside the bedchamber she shared with Cecilia, Georgiana, and Emma, she paused.

"'Farewell all,' sighed she, 'this last look and we shall be separated forever!' Tears followed her words, and sinking back, she resigned herself to the stillness of sorrow." Cecilia, who was reading aloud, gave a dramatic sigh.

"She can't resign herself yet," Georgiana objected. "It's only the first page!"

There was the soft crinkle of paper, then Cecilia's voice again. *"'He now seized the trembling hand of the girl, who shrunk aghast with terror—"*

"Why are they always shrinking?" Georgiana demanded. "I've never shrunk aghast in terror in my life."

"Hush, will you? *'Shrunk aghast in terror,'"* Cecilia repeated in a louder voice. *"'She sunk at his feet, and with supplicating eyes that streamed with tears, implored him to have pity on her.'* My goodness. That does sound promising, doesn't it?"

"I do like it when their eyes stream with tears," Emma allowed.

Sophia heard more pages turning, then Cecilia said, "Oh, listen to this! There's a ruffian, a pistol pointed at someone's breast, and a scuffle with some banditti coming up. Also, it looks as if Adeline is going to fall dreadfully ill with fever, so that's something to look forward to."

"What do you suppose banditti is, precisely?" Emma asked. "Have either of you ever seen banditti?"

"In London?" Georgiana scoffed. "Certainly not. There are no banditti in London, only in Italy."

Sophia leaned closer to the door. They were reading Mrs. Radcliffe's *The Romance of the Forest*, despite the late hour, and in flagrant disobedience of the Society's rules. She burst through the door with the sternest frown she could muster. "You were meant to wait for me before starting the book! Those are the rules."

Three pairs of guilty eyes—blue, hazel, and brown—shot toward her.

"All members must agree on a book, all chosen titles are to be read aloud, and no reading shall take place unless all four members of the Society are present." Sophia ticked the points off on her fingers. "Shame on all of you."

"We've only just dipped into the first chapter a little bit." Cecilia was sitting on the bed, the book balanced on her knees. Georgiana was by her side, and Emma at her feet.

Sophia raised a brow. "You're only into the first chapter, and the heroine is already bathed in tears, and resigned to the stillness of sorrow?"

"Yes! Isn't that wonderful?" Cecilia rubbed her hands together. "I think it's going to be a very good one."

"Have any of the virgins swooned yet?" Sophia asked. "Unless the virgins swoon in the first chapter, it won't be as good as the last book."

"Well, no, but I believe there's a ruined abbey." Emma sounded doubtful.

"Surely a ruined abbey is a good sign? There's usually a ghost or two or a headless corpse when there's a ruined abbey."

Sophia shrugged. "Swooning virgins are better. There were loads of swooning virgins in *A Sicilian Romance.*"

Georgiana gave a derisive snort. "Swooning virgins. What nonsense."

Sophia and Emma nodded in agreement. All four of them were mad for Gothic romances, but with the exception of Cecilia, who had a heart wider than the Thames, they adored and disdained the heroines in equal measure. Adeline St. Pierre-de Montalt, heroine of *The Romance of the Forest,* wasn't likely to be an exception, no matter how engrossing her story. Soon enough they'd find themselves reacting to her with a mixture of breathless anticipation, amusement, and mockery.

Swooning virgins were all very well in romantic novels, but a lady fragile enough to fall into a swoon in London would soon find her pocket picked, her person assaulted, and her limbs crushed under carriage wheels and horses' hooves. Sophia in particular found it difficult to sympathize with a heroine who was continually either fainting, or bursting into floods of tears.

As for cruel villains and bloody daggers...

Sophia thought of Henry Gerrard, dying in the dirt in St. Clement Dane's churchyard, and a wave of sorrow washed over her. Blood and murder were only diverting until they became real.

"We did try and wait for you to come, Sophia, but you know Cecilia can't resist a romance." Emma cast a reproachful look at Cecilia.

Cecilia bit her lip and turned her big brown eyes on Sophia. "We should have waited. I'm sorry, Sophia."

No one—not man, woman, god, or mortal—could resist the plea in those soft eyes. "It's all right. Never mind, dearest."

"We'll start again, shall we?" Georgiana bounded off the bed and rushed across the room to seize Sophia in a hug.

Sophia let Georgiana tug her toward the bed and flopped down, joining her three friends in an untidy pile of limbs. Emma twisted a lock of Sophia's dark hair around a long, elegant finger. "Oh, your hair is wet. Is it raining?"

Sophia rested her head on Emma's calf with a contented sigh. "Not anymore. It was earlier."

"What in the world is that smell?" Georgiana pressed the back of her hand to her nose. "It smells like Gussie when his fur is wet."

Gussie was Lady Clifford's pinch-faced pug. He was dreadfully ugly, and had an unfortunate chronic nasal condition that made him snort. To add insult to these injuries, he'd been saddled with the name Gussie in his puppyhood, before anyone realized he was, in fact a boy dog. By then, the name had already stuck. Despite these drawbacks, he was much beloved at the Clifford School, especially by Emma, who was fonder of animals than she was of people.

"It's not so bad as all that." Sophia lifted her tunic to her nose for an experimental sniff, then winced. "Bad enough, though."

"You look as if you've been hiding in a gutter." Cecilia rose from the bed and crossed to the basin, then paused and turned back to Sophia with a doubtful look. "You *haven't* been, have you?"

It was a fair question, given Sophia had hidden in gutters before. "No, not tonight, but I did spend some time on Lord Everly's roof."

The room went quiet for a moment as Cecilia, Emma, and Georgiana exchanged looks.

"Is there any word of Jeremy?" Cecilia asked, an anxious frown on her brow.

Sophia bit her lip. Lady Clifford discouraged them from sharing information about their assignments with each other. The less her friends knew about Jeremy's predicament, the safer it was for all of them, yet Sophia knew they were as concerned about Jeremy as she was.

"No change there, I'm afraid."

Sophia didn't offer anything more than that, and her friends fell silent again until Georgiana approached Sophia with a damp towel in her hand. "Here. Take this, and give me your tunic."

"What's Lord Everly's roof like?" Emma asked. "Nice and quiet, I imagine."

"Not as quiet as you'd think. Not as private, either." Sophia peeled her black tunic over her head. "As it happens, Lord Everly's neighbor saw me up there and chased me from one end of London to the other."

The other girls looked at each other, then back at Sophia. "*Chased* you?" Emma asked. "No one ever chases you. Not for long, anyway. Is Lord Everly's neighbor a racehorse?"

"No, he's a Bow Street Runner." Sophia hesitated. "He's, er...he's Tristan Stratford."

Two mouths dropped open at once.

"The Ghost of Bow Street?" Emma breathed. "Lord Everly's neighbor is the Ghost of Bow Street?"

Sophia sighed. "Unfortunately, yes. If I'd known, I never would have climbed onto Everly's roof in the first place."

"Who in the world is the Ghost of Bow Street?" Cecilia looked from Emma to Sophia with a puzzled frown. "I've never heard of him."

"Only you would ask that question, Cecilia." Georgiana leaned over and grabbed a gossip sheet from the table beside the bed and handed it to Cecilia.

"I don't care a whit for the gossip. It's a waste of..." Cecilia's voice fell away, the rest of her lecture left unsaid as she stared at the drawing in front of her. "*That's* the Ghost of Bow Street? My goodness."

Emma took the paper from Cecilia and stuck it under Sophia's nose. "That's him? That's the man who chased you?"

Sophia glanced down at the page. Yes, it was him, all right. The drawing hadn't properly captured the slash of his cheekbones, the sternness of his lips, the severe, aristocratic elegance of his face, but there was no mistaking *him*.

For better or worse, he wasn't the sort of man one forgot. "Yes, that's him."

Emma gave her the slightly crooked smile that made every man she came across her devoted slave. "I would have let him catch me."

Sophia thought of his cool gray eyes and the pressure of his hand against her mouth, and a shiver tickled down her spine. "No, I don't think you would have. Not if you'd seen him for yourself. But never mind Lord Gray. Come, Cecilia. I want to hear about the banditti."

Cecilia opened the book and read to the end of the first chapter, then she turned down the lamp and they tucked themselves into their beds. Her friends were soon asleep, but Sophia lay awake for a long time, listening to the soft sounds of peaceful slumber around her.

Ghosts and headless corpses, swooning virgins and bloody daggers...

A man lying in the dirt in St. Clement Dane's churchyard, his life's blood gushing from his slit throat, and Jeremy, an innocent man—no, a boy, really—taken up for the crime, and facing a ghastly death at the end of a noose.

Do you suppose you can outrun me?

Sophia tugged the coverlet tighter around her shoulders, but she couldn't suppress a shudder at the memory of those huge hands gripping the wrought iron spikes, the pale scars on his knuckles, the icy challenge in his gray eyes.

I'd be disappointed indeed if you didn't lead me on a chase.

She rolled over onto her side and squeezed her eyes closed, but sleep eluded her until at last she threw the coverlet back and crept to the window.

The rain had returned. The street below was damp, but aside from the muted patter of the drops on the pavement, all was silent and still. Sophia stood there for a long time, staring into the darkness before drawing the drapes across the window with a determined tug. She returned to her bed, and this time when she closed her eyes, they remained closed.

She was no swooning virgin, and she wasn't afraid of ghosts.

Chapter Four

That night, Tristan dreamed of graveyards.

It began quietly, as dreams often do—quietly enough the dreamer is deceived into thinking he's found a warm, safe cocoon, just before he's hurled into a nightmare.

In the dream, he was alone in a graveyard, wandering among the headstones under the watchful gaze of a pair of sightless stone angels. Their wings were spread wide, the feathery tips joined over the arched doorway to a white marble crypt gleaming dully in the moonlight.

He'd come to the graveyard to fetch someone, to save her from some terrible but unknown fate, but each time he drew close enough to catch a strand of her long dark hair, she melted into the fog hanging low over the headstones. He might have wandered from one headstone to the next for an eternity, chasing that cool, transparent mist if he hadn't stumbled and fallen to his knees.

He'd tripped over something—

Someone.

Henry Gerrard, his eyes open, blank, staring at nothing, warm blood still oozing from the gash in his throat. In the next breath Tristan was running toward the church, his hands dripping with Henry's blood, a plea for forgiveness on his lips, but when he staggered into the confessional his voice was gone, and he was left alone with his sins and no hope of a blessing—

He woke with a jerk, his heart pounding and his nightshirt clinging to his damp skin. He sat up and dragged a hand through his hair, also drenched with sweat.

It wasn't his first nightmare, nor would it be his last.

At first, there'd been no pattern to them, no logic or reason. When Tristan crawled into his bed and closed his eyes, he never knew which of his demons would choose to haunt him, but over the past few weeks the nightmares all ended the same way.

When he opened his mouth to beg for forgiveness, he'd be struck dumb.

Sometimes he was begging Henry's wife, Abigail, to forgive him, but more often it was Henry himself. Sometimes Henry would be just as Tristan remembered him, with his trusting brown eyes and laughing mouth, but in Tristan's worst nightmares he'd be as he was tonight, soaked in blood, with vacant, staring eyes and a jagged slash across his throat.

Then Tristan would wake, shaking and panting, and trade his sleeping nightmare for his waking one—one where Henry was still dead, murdered in St. Clement Dane's churchyard, and Tristan was still the man who'd failed to save his best friend.

Before tonight, he'd never dreamed of priests and confessionals, or dark-haired ghosts and white marble crypts, but he could hardly fail to trace those particular demons back to their source.

I'm anxious to confess my sins. I'm quite wicked, you see.

Tristan *did* see. He saw a great deal more than she could ever imagine.

He didn't know how or when he'd realized she was running to No. 26 Maddox Street tonight. They'd still been a dozen streets away from the Clifford School when he'd changed course to get ahead of her. At that point, she could have been going anywhere.

But she hadn't been. And somehow, he'd known it.

Perhaps it was nothing more than the way she ran from him. He knew the city as well as he knew the pattern of scars on the backs of his hands, yet he'd lost sight of her more than once.

Tristan didn't lose people. *Ever.*

She was too clever not to have realized she couldn't outrun him, so what might have been a quick enough chase led to a race through every back alley in Westminster. She'd led him down one darkened street after another as if he were a clumsy, dull-witted cat and she—small and quick and like a shadow herself in her black clothing—a particularly wily mouse.

If there was a corner to duck into, she found it. Once she'd made it through the churchyard and onto the Strand, she stayed close to the sides of the buildings where the darkness gathered, clinging to the walls as she passed, slipping silently around London's edges.

All the way to No. 26 Maddox Street.

There was nothing unusual about the sprawling brick building there. Nothing to distinguish it from any other Mayfair residence, but then nothing about the Clifford School was what it appeared to be, least of all its inhabitants.

There was a brass plaque fixed to one side of the front door. It was small, unobtrusive—not meant to draw the eye.

The Clifford Charity School for Wayward Girls. Lady Amanda Clifford, Proprietress. Pupils accepted by private recommendation only.

Tristan hadn't approached the door tonight. He hadn't ventured from the shadows to read the plaque. He already knew what it said. He'd memorized it weeks ago, after Jeremy Ives, one of Lady Clifford's servants, was taken up for the murder of Henry Gerrard.

Ives was currently being held at Newgate. In another week he'd stand trial for his crimes, when he'd certainly be found guilty. Tristan was looking forward to his hanging with grim anticipation.

He threw the coverlet aside, rose from his bed, and made his way to the window. He shoved the drapes back to find only darkness waiting for him on the other side of the glass.

Not that the hour made much difference. He'd have no more sleep tonight.

He didn't keep track of time anymore, but he must have stood at the window for hours, staring blindly into the darkness, because when he came back to himself the sky had lightened, and the sun was edging over the horizon.

You look like an aristocrat, rather high, I think.

An accurate guess, on her part. He hadn't been quite so accurate, on his.

She wasn't a thief. Or perhaps it was more appropriate to say she wasn't *just* a thief.

He might have learned more if Daniel Brixton hadn't emerged from the shadows like some kind of disembodied spirit. If he'd been in his rational mind, Tristan would have been expecting Brixton to materialize. The man had preternatural instincts, and he was a proper watchdog.

Massive, but cautious. Quiet, and clever. Above all, deadly.

Lady Clifford chose her people well.

Even without Brixton's sudden appearance, Tristan might not have gotten anything more out of the girl. She'd been afraid, yes. He'd felt her slender body trembling against his. Fear did tend to loosen most people's tongues, but then *she*, like all of Lady Clifford's disciples, wasn't like most people.

Not that it mattered much by then. By then, Tristan knew enough.

He'd lingered in the darkness outside the school for some time after Brixton was gone, staring up at the dark windows, fury gathering like a storm in his chest. She'd told him she'd gone to St. Clement Dane's Church tonight to say her confession.

Perhaps she should have done so, while she still had the chance.

* * * *

"You look like death, Gray." Caleb Reeve, Lord Lyndon, threw himself into the chair across from Tristan's at the dining table and signaled the footman for coffee. "No use burying yourself behind that newspaper. I can see you're a bloody wreck."

Tristan peered over the edge of the *Times*. "What the devil are you doing here, Lyndon? It's not calling hours."

Lyndon snorted. "Calling hours are for debutantes and their marriage-minded mamas. I'm not here to court you, for God's sake."

Tristan set his paper aside with a sigh. "Why *are* you here, then?"

"I came for Mrs. Tribble's apricot pastries, of course." Lyndon rubbed his hands together as the footman set a plate of steaming tartlets in front of him. "I could forgive your ghastly appearance this morning if I thought you'd gotten up to a proper debauch last night, but you left White's before ten o'clock. No doubt you were in your bed by half ten. Now then, Gray. Why so feeble this morning?"

Lyndon spoke with studied nonchalance, but Tristan heard the note of concern in his friend's voice. He and Lyndon had been at Oxford together, and knew each other far too well to have secrets between them.

Henry's murder, the circumstances surrounding his death, Tristan's nightmares—Lyndon knew all of it, and though he'd scoff at any suggestion he was worried for Tristan, he'd appeared in Great Marlborough Street far more often these past weeks than he'd been in the habit of doing.

"You'll be pleased to know I wasn't in bed by half ten. I went out again after I left White's."

"Well, that sounds promising. Where did you go?" Lyndon took an enormous bite of his tartlet, groaning with appreciation.

"Well, since you ask, Lyndon, I spied a young boy on the roof of Lord Everly's pediment, chased him from Great Marlborough Street to St. Clement Dane's Church, discovered he wasn't in fact a boy at all, but a young woman, then I chased *her* through a graveyard and every back alleyway in Westminster until I caught her on Maddox Street."

Lyndon had been making happy noises as he devoured his tartlet, but by the time Tristan finished, he was choking on it. "Urg...Ack..."

Tristan waved over the footman. "James, if you'd be so kind as to thump Lord Lyndon before he expires in my breakfast room."

"Yes, my lord." James darted forward and whacked Lyndon on the back until soggy bits of apricot tartlet spewed from his mouth. "Beg your pardon, sir."

"Not at all, James," Lyndon gasped. "Good man."

"Well done, James. Thank you." Tristan took a calm sip of his coffee, and waited.

Lyndon coughed and spluttered a bit more, but finally he wiped his streaming eyes and turned an indignant look on Tristan. "Jesus, Gray. You might have warned me."

"I might have, yes." Tristan gave him a small smile. "I beg your pardon. I thought you'd appreciate a more dramatic telling."

"Well, of course I do." Lyndon, undaunted, took up the untouched tartlet on his plate and began to devour it. "Good Lord, Gray. That sounds far more entertaining than White's. What did you do with this young woman once you caught her?"

"I let her go again." Not by choice, but one didn't tangle with Brixton unless one was prepared for a brawl.

Lyndon paused with the tartlet halfway to his mouth. "What, just like that? After all that trouble?"

"She had more...resources than I anticipated. A protector, that is." The smile faded from Tristan's lips as he met his friend's gaze. "Daniel Brixton."

Lyndon's eyes went wide. "Brixton? You mean that large, terribly frightening fellow who works for Lady..." Lyndon trailed off, his eyes going even wider.

"Lady Clifford, yes. The young woman on the roof was one of Lady Clifford's, er..." What did one call them? Demons? Felons, perhaps? "One of her pupils."

Lyndon dropped the tartlet back onto his plate. "You mean to tell me you saw one of Lady Clifford's fiendish sprites on Lord Everly's rooftop and followed her to St. Clement Dane's Church?"

"She was following Peter Sharpe." Tristan hadn't realized it was Sharpe at the time, but when he'd caught the girl—Sophia—at the door of the Clifford School, the puzzle pieces had fallen into place quickly enough.

Of course, it was Sharpe. It was the only thing that made sense.

"Sharpe?" Lyndon gave a low whistle. "That's some trouble waiting to happen, that is."

"You may be certain it's already happening. The only question is, how far has it gone? Lady Clifford is no fool, and it's no accident the girl was following Sharpe. They mean to see what they can do to save Jeremy Ives."

"Not a bloody thing, from what I've heard. Everyone in London knows Ives is guilty."

Everyone but Lady Clifford. But then perhaps she did know it, and simply didn't care. "He *is* guilty, and I mean to see him brought to justice for his crimes, no matter what mischief Lady Clifford and her, er..." Hellions? Vixens, perhaps? "...students are doing to help him escape it."

"I see. You intend to remain in London, then?"

Tristan was only meant to be in London until the end of the week. He'd promised his mother he'd return to Oxfordshire then, and get on with the business of being Lord Gray.

But he'd made other promises, too. Promises to Henry, and on Henry's behalf to Abigail, and their infant son, Samuel. "For a brief time, yes. Another month, perhaps."

Lyndon had been tearing what was left of his tartlet into pieces, but now he pushed the plate aside and dusted the crumbs off his fingers. "Your mother won't like it."

"No." Tristan's mother had made it clear she expected him to fulfill the duties of a title his elder brother, Thomas, had been shirking for years, starting with resigning his place with the Bow Street Runners and ending with marriage to a lady from a neighboring estate Tristan had only the vaguest recollection of ever meeting.

"The countess's grief over Thomas's death is...extreme," Lyndon said carefully, but Tristan knew well enough what his friend meant.

The Countess of Gray had never been much interested in Tristan. He was more like his father—that is, dull and serious and far too concerned with tedious things like propriety and honor. Tristan's elder brother, Thomas, had always been her favorite child, and she'd petted and spoiled him since he was in short pants.

Thomas's death was a great loss, but not, unfortunately, an unexpected one. After he inherited the title and fortune a decade ago, he'd embraced dissipation with the sort of single-minded dedication that put a premature end to the lives of firstborn sons all across England. Tristan had loved his brother dearly—Thomas had been handsome, charming, and affectionate— but he hadn't been surprised when years of debauchery had sent Thomas to an early grave.

Now the countess's overindulgence of her elder son had led to predictably tragic results, she'd succumbed to a grief so violent it bordered on parody.

She'd declared herself mere steps from her own grave, and demanded Tristan return to Oxfordshire as soon as possible.

"She expects you to marry still?" Lyndon asked, his tone grim.

Tristan gave a short laugh. "Let's just say the countess has taken a much greater interest in me since I became the earl."

Lyndon shook his head. "You were better off before."

Tristan didn't argue that point. Lyndon knew him well enough to know Tristan didn't relish the future now laid before him, but he'd do his duty by his mother and his title.

First, however, he'd do his duty by Henry Gerrard, a friend who'd been dearer to him than his own brother. "My mother will have to reconcile herself to my absence a little longer. I have the rest of my life to be the Earl of Gray."

He hadn't meant to sound so bitter, but when Lyndon's gaze jerked to his face, Tristan knew he'd revealed himself.

"Yes, you do." Lyndon's face darkened with something that was part anger, part sadness. "And I'm sorry for it, Tristan."

Tristan was sorry for it, too, but he didn't voice his regret.

Lyndon took his leave soon after that, there being little, after all, left to say.

* * * *

An hour after Lyndon left Great Marlborough Street, Tristan arrived at No. 4 Bow Street, where he surprised the Bow Street magistrate at his breakfast. "Stratford—that is, Lord Gray." Sampson Willis set his teacup hastily aside and rose from his chair. "I didn't realize you'd returned to London. Last I heard you were in Oxfordshire."

"I have some final business to resolve here." Tristan waved Willis back to his seat and took the chair on the other side of the desk.

Willis cleared his throat awkwardly. "I was sorry to hear of your brother's passing. It's a terrible loss for your family."

"Thank you."

"How does your mother do?" Willis shook his head. "Poor lady. I imagine her grief must be extreme."

"Yes, I'm afraid it is."

When Tristan didn't elaborate, Willis cleared his throat again. "Well, then. What brings you to Bow Street?"

"I regret having to bring ill tidings, Willis, but there's trouble over at the Clifford School." Tristan saw no reason to mince words. "One of Lady Clifford's students was up to some mischief last night."

Willis had returned to his tea, but he set the cup aside again. "Oh? How did you discover this?"

"Quite by accident. I happened to catch the young woman in question prowling about in the dark after Peter Sharpe."

Willis frowned. "What, you mean Everly's man? Are you certain she was following him? Perhaps their being in the same place was merely a coincidence."

"A rather startling coincidence, wouldn't you say, for one of Lady Clifford's girls to be creeping through the streets of London in the same vicinity as the only witness to a murder her ladyship's servant is accused of committing?"

Willis blinked. "Well, when you put it like that—"

"It was no coincidence, Willis. The girl was waiting for Sharpe on the roof of Lord Everly's pediment. My library looks out onto the front of Everly's townhouse, so I got a good, long look at her. As soon as Sharpe came out, she was over the side of the pediment and down one of the columns as quickly as any cat."

Willis's eyebrows shot up. "The devil you say!"

"I saw her myself. It was rather impressive, really."

Willis leaned back in his chair, considering this. "No doubt it was. If it was anyone but Lady Clifford, I wouldn't trouble myself much about it, but her ladyship knows what she's about, and she's trained those girls to be as clever as she is."

"Clever under the best of circumstances. Ruthless, even dangerous, in the worst of them, especially when you throw Daniel Brixton into the mix."

"What, was Brixton on the roof, too?"

"No. He wasn't at Everly's or St. Clement Dane's, but he did make an appearance."

"Yes, he generally does whenever the Clifford School is involved."

"I can't imagine Lady Clifford was pleased when Jeremy Ives was taken up for Henry's...for murder. I heard Ives has been with her since he was a lad, and is one of her favorites."

"No, I don't believe she *was* pleased," Willis muttered, fiddling with a quill on his desk.

"No, and likely not reconciled to his arrest, either. There's every reason to suspect she's up to something, and with Kit Benjamin's assistance, she's a formidable enemy."

Willis's gaze shifted from the quill to Tristan's face. "You believe the rumors about Lady Clifford and Benjamin, then?"

"It's difficult to say, but if they're not lovers, they're certainly friends. There's no other explanation for Lady Clifford's amazingly…shall we say, comprehensive knowledge of London's nefarious element. If the good alderman isn't providing her with information, who is?"

Kit Benjamin was well-respected in legal circles and purportedly an honest, upright gentleman, but he was also clever and ambitious. If there was a man in London who had his fingers into every secret, dirty corner of the city's inner workings, it was Benjamin. Such a man as that could prove invaluable to a woman like Lady Clifford, who knew how to use whatever information she had to great advantage.

"There isn't any doubt whatsoever Ives is guilty. I saw him myself, Gray, sprawled next to the body, fairly dripping in Gerrard's blood. Lady Clifford isn't one to trifle with, but I don't see how even she can do anything to help Ives now."

Tristan didn't appreciate Willis's unnecessarily lurid description of Henry's murder scene, but he swallowed his ire. "Perhaps not, but that won't stop her from trying. Why else would she send one of her girls after Sharpe?"

"Hmmm." Willis sat quietly for some moments with his hands folded over his belly, frowning. "Where did Sharpe lead the girl?"

"St. Clement Dane's Church."

Up until this point Willis had taken Tristan's news in a surprisingly desultory fashion, but at the mention of St. Clement Dane's he straightened in his chair. "Ah, now that is interesting. Do you have any idea what Sharpe was doing there?"

"None at all, only that he didn't appear to be doing anything illegal."

"Hmmm. Was he alone?"

Tristan shrugged. "As far as I know."

"I see, I see. Tell me, Gray, did you happen to get the young woman's name?"

"Just her first name. Sophia. As you can imagine, she wasn't particularly forthcoming."

"No, I imagine she wasn't. You'd recognize her if you saw her again, though? You remember her face?"

Green eyes flashed in Tristan's mind. The better question was, would he be able to forget her? It was damn unlucky he'd thought her a boy at first. If he'd known she was a woman right away, it would have saved him that dramatic moment when her hair fell over her shoulders and he got his first glimpse of a face that now haunted his dreams. The suddenness of her appearance before him was, in a word, inconvenient.

But then a pretty face might hide a multitude of sins, and despite those wide green eyes, she was far from innocent. Innocent ladies didn't scale townhouse facades. They didn't slip through the bars of a wrought iron fence as if they were made of mist, and they didn't navigate the streets and alleyways of London with the ease of a master moving pieces across a chessboard.

Tristan met Willis's gaze. "Certainly. I'll have her full name soon enough, as well."

Willis eyed him. "Are you needed in Oxfordshire at once? Or is it possible for you to remain in London a while longer? It might be wise for us to keep a close eye on this young woman. Nip any mischief she might cause in the bud before Lady Clifford manages to set it all atilt, you understand."

"I do. That's why I'm here." His mother would put up a fuss, but there was no way Tristan was going to scamper off to Oxfordshire and let Lady Clifford interfere with Jeremy Ives's appointment with the scaffold.

He owed Henry that much. At least that much.

"You're no longer a Bow Street Runner, but I daresay you haven't forgotten how to chase a criminal down in the few weeks since you were. Keep an eye on the girl, that's all, and report what you find back to me. Can you do that, Gray?"

Tristan nodded, and rose to his feet. "Of course I can."

"Good. Go on, then, and make sure you report anything of interest to me at once. Oh, and send Poole in on your way out. He's been lurking outside my door all morning." Willis waved a hand in dismissal.

Richard Poole, another of Willis's Bow Street Runners was slouched on a bench outside Willis's office, tapping the tip of his walking stick impatiently against the heel of his boot and grumbling irritably to himself. Tristan paused beside him and nodded toward Willis's door. "He's waiting for you, Poole."

"Right." Poole shuffled to his feet and made his way toward Willis's office, but before he went inside, he turned back to Tristan. "Shame what happened to Henry Gerrard, my lord. He was a good man."

Tristan glanced at him in surprise. Poole hadn't been a Bow Street Runner for long, and Tristan didn't know him well, but Poole had known Henry, and they'd been friends, of a sort. Sometimes Tristan became so lost in his own grief, he forgot others were grieving, too. "I…that's kind of you, Poole. Thank you."

Poole nodded once, then went into Willis's office and closed the door behind him.

Tristan left No. 4 and headed north toward Brownlow Street. He'd go see Abigail and the baby, see they didn't want for anything, and then he'd find out everything there was to know about Sophia, the dark-haired, green-eyed ghost from his nightmare.

She wouldn't haunt him for much longer.

For a few weeks more, he'd be a Bow Street Runner, and once that was done...

He'd retire to Oxfordshire, marry a lady whose face he couldn't recall, and spend the rest of his life being Lord Gray.

Chapter Five

One week later
Old Bailey Courthouse, London

Sophia peeked out from under the brim of the monstrously ugly hat she wore and shuddered at the hideousness surrounding her. Everywhere she turned she saw clenched fists, bared teeth, and dozens of gaping mouths filthy with curses. The stench of unwashed bodies crowded into too small a space was so overwhelming she feared she'd swoon like one of Mrs. Radcliffe's fragile heroines.

Lady Clifford had warned her not to come to Jeremy's trial today.

Perhaps I should have listened.

Bloodthirsty spectators swarmed the Old Bailey's gallery this morning. The good citizens of London enjoyed a gruesome hanging every now and again, and there wasn't a single person here today who didn't want to see Jeremy sentenced to swing. The crowd shoving at each other in the yard was no better. It looked as if half the city was out there, all of them panting to see the notorious murderer condemned to the noose.

No one seemed to care much what Jeremy might have to say in his own defense. He'd already been tried and sentenced.

Sophia dove back under her hat, her throat tightening with dread. Lady Clifford had tried to warn her it would be like this, but Sophia hadn't been able to bear the thought of Jeremy facing such brutal hostility alone. He wouldn't be able to see her, tucked into the back of the gallery as she was, but maybe he'd sense her presence, and would know he had at least one friend among the crowd.

One, and only one.

Lady Clifford had made it clear she preferred they all stay away from the Old Bailey today, it not being wise to emphasize the Clifford School's connection to Jeremy just now. It wouldn't do for people to become suspicious, or to attract undue attention. There was, after all, a *possibility*—not a *certainty*, because no one could ever be certain of anything—but a possibility Jeremy Ives's fate wouldn't be *quite* what London expected, regardless of what happened in the courtroom today.

Sophia rose to her tiptoes and tried to peer around the shoulders of the rows of men in front of her. Jeremy hadn't been brought in yet, so there wasn't much to see, but it had been weeks since she'd laid eyes on him. She was desperate to catch a glimpse of him today, even as another wave of dread rolled over her at the thought of what she might find.

Newgate was infamous for the miserable conditions, the gleeful brutality of the gaolers, and the unimaginable suffering inflicted on the prisoners. A simple, sweet-tempered boy like Jeremy wouldn't have the first idea how to survive in such a place.

An expectant hush fell over the courtroom, and a few moments later the harsh reality of Jeremy's predicament was borne home to Sophia with pitiless clarity. She slapped a hand over her mouth to smother her horrified gasp as Jeremy—lovely, kind, gentle Jeremy—was dragged into the courtroom.

He looked...dear God, he looked as if he'd been starved and beaten half to death. If she hadn't known this poor, ragged creature to be Jeremy, Sophia wouldn't have recognized him. He'd always been a big, strong lad, but his body had been reduced to a pathetic wreck, his shoulders hunched, his chest sunken. He was dragging one foot behind him as if it had been injured, and his face was covered in bruises.

Nausea clawed at Sophia's throat, and she was obliged to reach out a shaking hand and brace it on the column beside her to keep from staggering. She hadn't expected he'd look well, but this...she felt as if she'd been plunged into one of her most frightening nightmares.

They had to *do* something, help him somehow. In another week there'd be nothing left of her precious boy to save. He'd be lost to them forever.

The trial began. Sophia tried to listen, to concentrate on the evidence, but everything spun in a confusing blur around her until Peter Sharpe rose and stepped into the witness box. The hiss of the spectators in the gallery and the drone of voices in the courtroom below all ground to a halt when he gave his testimony.

Gave his testimony, and *lied*. Glibly, and without a shred of remorse.

With every word out of the man's mouth Sophia's anguish and fury grew, until her hands were fisted at her sides and it was all she could do not to leap from the gallery into the witness box below.

"Never saw the like of it in my life, my lord. That poor man, the Bow Street Runner what was, lying on the ground with 'is blood all over, like, and that one there," Sharpe pointed an accusing finger at Jeremy. "Like to 'ave cut 'is head off!"

Sharpe preened as a shocked gasp rose from the gallery.

"Please be so good as to refrain from embellishment, Mr. Sharpe." Mr. Beddows, the thin, soft-spoken gentleman Lady Clifford had hired as Jeremy's lawyer interrupted him. "Simply tell the court what occurred on the night in question."

Sharpe blinked. "Aw right, then. It's like this. I were at St. Clement Dane's Church, not bothering no one, when all of a sudden this one," jerking his chin at Jeremy, "comes out of nowhere down the Strand, and attacks me!"

Another gasp arose, and Sharpe nodded importantly.

"You mean to say he came out of nowhere, and attacked you for no reason?" Mr. Beddows prompted.

"He had a reason, right enough. He were after my purse! Thieves are the scourge of London, sir, and make no mistake. But 'e didn't get it, ye see, because along comes the other gentleman—the Bow Street bloke, as he were. What were his name again?"

"Mr. Henry Gerrard."

"Right. Him. Along comes Mr. Gerrard, and 'e's going on about gangs of thieves or some such, and he must 'ave frightened that one." Sharpe jerked his chin toward Jeremy again. "'Cause next thing I know poor Mr. Gerrard's on the ground, sliced to ribbons like a Christmas goose!"

"Your testimony, Mr. Sharpe, is that Mr. Ives stabbed Mr. Gerrard in the course of a robbery. Is that correct?"

"That's what I said, innit?"

Mr. Beddows gave Sharpe a thin smile. "Yes, very good, Mr. Sharpe. What happened then?"

"Well, I…I couldna just let that big bloke—Ives—get away with murder, could I? So ye see I-I…well, I bashed 'im over the head with my cane, once or maybe twice, until 'is brains were like to be splattered all over the churchyard."

"And then?"

"Well, I weren't sure what to do, but then I think to myself, Bow Street ain't but a few streets over, so I run there and tell them there's a thief and a murderer in the churchyard, and one man dead, and t'other leaking brains, and Mr. Willis comes running, as ye do when there's a murderer about, and 'e took 'im up—Ives, I mean, sir—and tossed 'im into Newgate where 'e belongs."

"I see. Is that your complete testimony, Mr. Sharpe, or do you have anything to add?"

Peter Sharpe, who didn't appear to be in any hurry to leave the witness box, drew himself up with a sniff. "I've got plenty to say about murderers wandering the streets of London with us virtuous folks—"

Mr. Beddows cleared his throat. "Anything factual relating to the crime, I mean?"

Sharpe deflated. "Nay."

Mr. Beddows did what he could to call Sharpe's testimony into question, but Sophia could see it was hopeless. Peter Sharpe was the trustworthy servant of a well-respected peer. As far as anyone knew, he didn't stand to gain a thing from accusing Jeremy of murder, and Sampson Willis, the Bow Street magistrate, corroborated every word of Sharpe's testimony.

There was little Sophia could now do but wait, her heart in her throat, for Jeremy to be pronounced guilty. As for what she might do later, once she left the courtroom, well…that was a different matter entirely.

She waited at the back of the gallery, as unmoving as the column beside her. No one paid her any attention. If they had—if they'd happened to catch a glimpse under the wide brim of her hat—the cold malevolence with which she gazed at Peter Sharpe would have turned their blood to ice.

* * * *

The back row of the gallery smelled like flowers.

It was faint, just a hint of the sweet, honeyed scent wafting in the stale air. At any other time, Tristan wouldn't have noticed it, but given the circumstances in which he'd first inhaled that scent, it was imprinted on his senses.

She was here.

Sophia Monmouth, the dark-haired, green-eyed ghost who'd led him on a merry chase through every alleyway in Westminster, was in the gallery. He'd found out her name easily enough, but surprisingly, he hadn't been able to discover much else about her.

Lady Clifford's students enjoyed a certain notoriety among a select group of people in London, but none of them seemed to know anything about Sophia Monmouth's past, other than she'd become the Clifford School's first pupil a few months after Lady Clifford had secured the building at No. 26 Maddox Street. Miss Monmouth had been a child then, not more than six or seven years old, and she'd been with Lady Clifford ever since.

It wasn't much to go on, but Tristan had only just begun to dig into the mystery that was Sophia Monmouth, who'd sacrificed any claim she had to privacy when she climbed onto Lord Everly's pediment.

She hadn't been back to Great Marlborough Street since, nor had he caught her out in any other suspicious behavior in the week he'd been following her. No, since then Miss Monmouth had been a model of good citizenry, a veritable paragon of exemplary behavior. He might have grown bored of following her if he hadn't known it was only a matter of time before she slipped. No woman who'd gone to the trouble of scaling the front of a townhouse would give up so easily, especially not one of Lady Clifford's students.

Tenacity was their distinguishing characteristic.

Still, he hadn't expected he'd find her *here*. Criminals tended to avoid courthouses in general, but then Lady Clifford had likely directed Miss Monmouth to discover what fate awaited Jeremy Ives. Not that the outcome of the trial was much of a mystery. Ives was going to be found guilty, and he'd be sentenced to swing.

Simple enough.

Tristan cast a subtle glance over the spectators in the gallery. There weren't many ladies here, and none with the dainty features Tristan remembered so well, but then she was skilled at disguising herself—

Ah. There.

A few paces to his left was a lady with a bowed head. Her face was hidden under the wide brim of the ugliest hat he'd ever seen, but he could just make out a curl of dark hair at her nape, the tip of a pointed chin. She was partially concealed behind one of the gallery's columns—Miss Monmouth seemed to be fond of columns—but as luck would have it, he wasn't more than five or six paces away from her.

Slippery as she was, there was no way she could sneak from the courtroom without him seeing her, but Tristan suspected Sophia Monmouth would remain right where she was until Ives's trial concluded.

As it happened, Jeremy Ives was the first to come before the bench.

Tristan kept an eye on Sophia Monmouth as Ives was brought into the courtroom. She didn't move or make a sound, but her entire body went rigid as Ives was dragged, blinking, to stand at the bar before the court.

Ives was a big man with broad shoulders, and hands so massive he could snap a man's neck as easily as snapping a twig, but aside from his intimidating size, there wasn't much about him that spoke of violence. Tristan couldn't see him well, but from here Ives didn't look to be more than nineteen or twenty years old, and there was a soft, slack quality to his face that made him look even younger, almost childlike.

He was filthy, his ragged clothing hanging on his emaciated frame. Prisoners condemned to await trial at Newgate did tend to lose weight, even as much as a stone or two, but Ives's extraordinary height exaggerated the effect. He was gaunt, reduced to nothing more than a pale, wasted pile of flesh and bone, like a cock plucked of its feathers.

Ives had been accused of an unusually brutal crime, but he wasn't at all the hardened criminal Tristan had expected. He gaped at the assembly before him, bafflement mixed with abject terror on his face. He didn't seem to understand how he came to be there, or for what reason.

The courtroom stilled as Peter Sharpe, the only witness to the crime, stepped into the witness box to give his testimony. His mouth was pulled into a stern line, as befitted the solemnity of the occasion. He was seated in full view of the accused in the dock, but if Jeremy Ives remembered Sharpe, he gave no indication of it. He stared dumbly at him, mouth agape, as if he didn't recognize Sharpe at all.

As for Sharpe, he seemed to relish having the attention of everyone in the courthouse fixed on him, and delivered his testimony in a tone of self-righteous defiance.

It was one of the quickest trials Tristan had ever seen. Sharpe gave his account of the crime committed against him, then Willis briefly took the stand and testified that yes, Sharpe had come to No. 4 Bow Street that night in a panic, shrieking about leaking brains and murder. All the Runners being out at the time, Willis himself had followed Sharpe to St. Clement Dane's Church, where he'd found Jeremy Ives lying unconscious next to Henry Gerrard's body, his hands dripping with Henry's blood.

And finally, they heard from the accused, who professed himself innocent with tears running down his cheeks. When the judge demanded he explain the evidence against him, he could offer nothing but a fumbling account of having come across Sharpe in front of St. Clement Dane's Church, along with a somewhat incoherent insistence that he "'adn't hurt or stolen nothing from no one, if it please yer lordships."

The verdict was swift, and the sentence harsh.

Jeremy Ives was found guilty of the crimes of theft with violence and murder, and sentenced to hang. A hush fell over the courtroom as the punishment was handed down, but if the crowd wanted tears and wailing and pleas for mercy, they were disappointed. Ives didn't appear to understand any of what had transpired. He stared blankly at the judge as the sentence was read, and then he was dragged from the courtroom, his head bowed.

Tristan watched him go with an uneasy sensation in his stomach. He'd seen too many innocent people hurt by criminals in London to feel any sympathy for those who were convicted, but there'd been something off about the proceeding he'd just seen. He couldn't explain it, but he felt none of the fierce satisfaction he'd anticipated at seeing Henry's murderer brought to justice.

Sophia Monmouth didn't appear any more satisfied with the verdict than Tristan was. She followed the prisoner's progress from the courtroom, her gaze lingering on the doorway through which he'd been taken long after he disappeared. Tristan caught a glimpse of her face when her head was turned, and his chest tightened at her expression.

She couldn't have expected Ives's fate to be anything other than what it was, yet for all the grim resignation on that exquisite face, she looked...devastated.

Tristan moved away from the edge of the balcony and further into the shadows, poised to follow her from the courtroom now Ives's trial was over, but to his surprise, she didn't move. She remained where she was throughout the next trial, then the next. The day wore on into the late afternoon, and still she stayed in her place at the edge of the column, her slender form unnaturally still, as if she'd been frozen there.

She didn't move until the last trial concluded, then she left in such haste Tristan found himself having to chase her once again as she exited the courtroom and made her way into the yard. Most of the crowd had dispersed after Ives's trial, but there were still a few stragglers hanging about. She stationed herself to one side of the door where a small knot of people had gathered and lingered there, as if she were waiting for someone to emerge.

A few moments later, someone *did* emerge.

Peter Sharpe.

Tristan saw him before she did, and so he was able to witness Miss Monmouth's reaction when Sharpe paused on the courthouse steps, a satisfied smirk on his lips. As soon as she saw him, she tensed. Her expression darkened, and her green eyes narrowed to slits, but she didn't move toward him, or call attention to herself in any way. She simply stood there, her gaze never wavering, and waited.

She didn't have to wait long. Sharpe trotted down the courthouse steps and ambled off down the street as if he hadn't a care in the world. Miss Monmouth stayed where she was until he was a good block or two down Newgate Street before she darted after him.

Tristan went after her, a grudging sort of admiration in his chest. Sharpe hadn't any more idea he was being followed now than he had the other night. She didn't rush after him, or follow too closely. She was careful, but quick. Miss Monmouth knew how to keep her head, but as skilled as she was, she wasn't flawless.

After all, she didn't know *she* was being followed, either.

Just as he had the other night, Tristan found himself wondering what she intended to do once she caught up to Sharpe. Any sort of physical confrontation was out of the question. Sharpe was a pitiful enough specimen of masculinity, but he was bigger and heavier than Miss Monmouth was. At this point, Tristan couldn't have said which of the two of them was the more ruthless.

He soon found out.

Her hat was the first thing to go. She swept it from her head, and with a quick, furtive flick of her wrist tossed it down a narrow alleyway without a second glance. Then she went to work on the white fichu tucked into the neckline of her gray dress. It was the sort of plain, bland dress a shop girl might wear, but with one sharp tug of her fichu the prim little garment went from dully respectable to downright scandalous, the low-cut bodice revealing a generous expanse of smooth, olive skin even the most principled of gentlemen couldn't fail to notice.

She pulled some pins from her hair, letting a few long, dark locks fall loose, and just like that, she'd gone from a governess to a tempting siren.

Tristan came to a halt in the middle of the road, suddenly breathless. That was…well, that was one way to manage Sharpe. A rather ingenious way, really, with her curls brushing against the soft skin of her neck, and her…that is, the curves of her—

Damn it. She was a menace, a danger to society.

Tristan was torn between outrage and a very unwelcome surge of arousal, but this was no time to dawdle in the street with his mouth hanging open.

He went after her, biding his time as she drew closer and closer to Sharpe. She didn't approach him until he'd turned right onto Hatton Street, toward Ely Court, where a small crowd of degenerates was gathered outside of Ye Olde Mitre Inn.

That was when she struck. Tristan had been expecting it, but it happened so quickly he nearly missed it.

Just before Sharpe melted into the crowd, she reached under the gaping neckline of her gray gown and drew out something shiny. She darted forward with it clutched between her fingers, and with a subtle pass of her hand…

What the devil?

Tristan was behind her, so he couldn't see precisely what she'd done, but it looked as if she'd—

"Thief! Thief!" A high-pitched feminine shriek rent the air. Tristan froze, still a few paces behind her, unable to believe what was unfolding in front of his eyes. She hadn't…she couldn't have—

"Thief!" Miss Monmouth was pointing one trembling finger at Sharpe, her cheeks scarlet with outrage. "Why, that villain there took my dear, sainted grandmother's silver locket right off my neck, 'e did! He's a thief!"

She *had*.

Sharpe was gaping at her with bulging eyes. "Wot? Ye're mad, ye are! I never did no such thing! I never even touched 'er, much less took anything off 'er!"

Miss Monmouth stared at him, her lower lip wobbling, then without warning she burst into a deafening flood of tears. "What sort 'o scoundrel snatches a lady's dead grandmother's locket right off 'er neck, I ask you? Oh, my poor, sainted grandmother is like to be turning over in 'er grave, she is! Why, ye're a blackguard sir, and make no mistake."

Tristan tensed as Sharpe took a threatening step toward her, but he needn't have worried. Miss Monmouth was more than capable of taking care of herself. "Search 'is pockets if ye don't believe me!" she shrieked, turning her big, tear-stained green eyes on the crowd of men gathered around the entrance to the pub.

"Oi, Harry! Git on over 'ere and check 'is pockets, will ye?" Two of the men, both of them mean with drink, broke from the crowd and descended on Sharpe, grabbing his arms. "Give 'im a good shake, like," one said, with a menacing look at Sharpe. "We don't take kindly round 'ere to thieves."

"'Specially those what steal from a 'elpless lady." The other man wiped an arm across his mouth, leering at Miss Monmouth. "Not the pretty ones, leastways. Don't care much 'bout the harpies, eh?"

Helpless? Tristan nearly laughed aloud at this description of his wily little rooftop thief, who was about as far from helpless as a rabid dog. He hadn't the faintest doubt the men even now turning out Sharpe's pockets would find the locket. She'd been so stealthy about it even Tristan hadn't seen her do it, but there was no question she'd contrived to drop her locket somewhere on Sharpe's person.

Good Lord, she was clever. With one twist of her wrist and flutter of her eyelashes she had Sharpe at her mercy. Tristan couldn't prevent another reluctant twinge of admiration. He couldn't let her get away with it, of course, but it was a neat trick, and an effective one. The two men who had hold of Sharpe were moments away from throwing him onto the ground and stomping him under their boot heels.

Tristan had spent enough time on the London streets to know when a drunken rabble was about to take justice into their own hands. Once they found the locket—and they *would*—they'd pound the life out of Sharpe. Tristan didn't care for the man, but he also knew him to be innocent of the theft. He couldn't stand by and watch while an innocent man was beaten.

"Wait! Take your hands off him." He strode forward and wrapped his fingers around the slender arm of the real guilty party. "Pardon me, madam, but I saw you slip your locket into this man's coat pocket."

Miss Monmouth turned on him with a squeak of outrage. "Ye dare accuse me of—" she began, but as soon as she saw his face the words died on her lips, and her mouth dropped open in shock. "*You!*"

"Me, indeed. I'd be obliged if you two gentlemen would be so kind as to unhand that man. He's no thief." He may well have been worse than a thief, but Tristan didn't have any proof of that, and one didn't accuse a man on supposition alone.

Sharpe and his two drunken counterparts turned to gape at him. One of them let go of Sharpe at once, but the other had found the locket, and now he thrust it in Tristan's face. "I don't 'spose this belongs to 'im. If 'e's not a thief, then why does he 'ave the lady's locket on 'im?"

"Because she planted it there. I was walking right behind her, and I saw her slip it into his pocket." Tristan held out his hand for the locket, then added with a wink, "I believe we've stumbled upon a bit of a lover's quarrel, gentlemen."

"Lover's quarrel!" Miss Monmouth swept an appalled gaze over Sharpe, her mouth twisting with disgust. "You're either jesting, or you're mad."

"He's not mad. That's Lord Gray, that is, Stratford as was, afore his brother keeled over." Sharpe regarded Tristan for a moment in awe, then pointed a finger at his accuser. "If the Ghost of Bow Street says she planted it, then ye can be sure she bloody well planted it!"

As soon as they heard 'Ghost of Bow Street,' the two men on either side of Sharpe stepped back, their hands held out in front of them. "Beg pardon, Ghost—that is, beg pardon, sir. That is, yer lordship, sir. Didn't mean no 'arm. Just trying to help out this lady 'ere."

"Very chivalrous of you, and no harm's been done." Tristan took the locket the second man offered him and tucked it safely into his breast pocket. "You needn't worry about the lady. I'll take very good care of her. Go on back to your pints."

The two men were happy to abandon their heroics for their drink, and ambled off toward the pub. Sharpe, however, wasn't as agreeable. He stared at Miss Monmouth for a long, silent moment, as if memorizing her features, then turned to Tristan with a sullen look on his face. "I might 'a gotten my head kicked in just now. I want 'er taken up for lying, or making a false charge, or whatever it is ye call it."

"Yes, I think I must." Tristan turned to find Miss Monmouth assessing him with narrowed eyes, as if she were searching for all the soft places on his body where she might land a kick. "We can't have dangerous criminals roaming the streets, assaulting innocent gentlemen, can we? Come along, madam. You can explain yourself to the magistrate."

Chapter Six

"The magistrate, *again*?" Sophia tugged at her arm to free it from Lord Gray's grip. "My goodness, my lord. You have a troubling fondness for turning innocent citizens over to the law."

He gave a derisive snort at the word *innocent*.

Oh, very well, then. Perhaps in this case she wasn't *quite* innocent, but then questions of guilt and innocence were tricky, plaguing things, weren't they? She was far less guilty than Peter Sharpe. If the scales of justice were properly balanced, *he'd* be the one being marched down Hatton Street by a tight-lipped Lord Gray.

Sophia gave another fruitless tug on her arm. "I don't see what all the fuss is about. You said yourself no harm was done."

He didn't deign to reply. He didn't release her, either, but neither did he take her to the magistrate. Sophia was relieved by this at first, since she didn't care to explain her interest in Peter Sharpe to anyone, but when Lord Gray hustled her back to Newgate Street and stuffed her into a carriage waiting there for him, her relief faded.

Lord Gray had been intimidating enough when he was chasing her through a dark graveyard, but he was even more so when one was a smallish lady crowded into a carriage with him, especially with that ominous look on his face. "If I didn't know better, my lord, I'd say you were cross with me."

A slight pinching of his lips was her only answer.

He has rather nice lips.

Sophia hadn't gotten a proper look at him the night he'd accosted her at St. Clement Dane's. It had been too dark and she'd been too flustered to pay much attention to his features, but now she took a moment to study his face.

Emma thought him very handsome, and Sophia couldn't deny there was something pleasing about him—that is, pleasing in a severe, rigid, humorless, unforgiving sort of way. His features were almost *too* aristocratic, too harshly elegant, but the forbidding symmetry was offset by surprisingly wide, darkly lashed gray eyes, and a slightly crooked mouth with a small white scar carved into the left corner of his upper lip.

Sophia was perversely fond of scars, but of course there were scars, and then there were *scars*. Lord Gray's was of the latter variety. One couldn't help but wonder how it might bend and twist when he smiled.

If he ever did. Sophia hadn't seen any evidence he knew how. He'd likely be vastly improved if he did, but there was little enough chance she'd ever find out.

Certainly, there was no fetching smile hovering on those stern lips *now*. He was scrutinizing her with the sort of narrow-eyed suspicion usually reserved for ferocious dogs and poisonous vipers. Which was fair enough, really, since she *had* bitten him the last time they met.

At last he raised an imperious eyebrow, and crossed one long leg over the other. "If you've quite finished assessing me, Miss Monmouth, perhaps you'd be kind enough to answer a few questions."

Ah, so he'd discovered who she was, had he? Not surprising, and again, only fair, since she'd made it her business to learn as much as she could about him. "What if I'm *not* finished assessing you, my lord?"

In truth, she'd hardly begun. He had the sort of arresting face that deserved prolonged attention, and she hadn't had even a moment to consider the rest of him.

The eyebrow twitched up a notch. "Carry on, then."

His voice was pleasant, deep and smooth, if a touch frigid, and Sophia was aware of a low thrum of pleasure in her belly when he spoke.

"I've got all evening to devote myself to you," he added, removing his hat and tossing it onto the seat beside him as if he were settling in for a long, tedious ordeal.

"I'm flattered, my lord. What shall we do first? *Macbeth* is on at Drury Lane. Do you enjoy plays with villainesses, Lord Gray?" Sophia asked, stifling a laugh at his expression. No doubt the Ghost of Bow Street wasn't accustomed to such pert replies, particularly from a lady who was undeniably in his custody, and less than half his size.

"I'd rather see them on the stage than the streets. Does that answer your question, Miss Monmouth?"

Her own expression must have been priceless just then, because his stern lips gave a subtle twitch. It was a pitiful attempt at a smile, but even that little twitch transformed his face.

Sophia blinked at him, her gaze lingering on that little quirk at one corner of his mouth. On second thought, it might be best if Lord Gray kept his charming little quirks and twitches to himself. He wasn't her friend, and it would be a great inconvenience if she became intrigued by him.

Sophia settled back against her seat as if making herself comfortable, even as she assessed her situation out of the corner of her eye. The carriage door on the right wouldn't do for an escape. He was too close to it, his muscular body between it and her, but the other—

"I beg your pardon, but if you don't mind, Miss Monmouth." Lord Gray jerked his chin at her, a tinge of red creeping into his cheekbones.

Sophia stared at him, puzzled. Was he *blushing*? Why would he—

"Here." He fished around in his pocket and, to Sophia's shock, pulled out her fichu and handed it to her with a bow of his head that could only be described as courtly.

Oh. Her bodice. She'd forgotten all about it. The entire time she'd been tweaking him and congratulating herself on her cleverness, her breasts had been no more than two stitches away from bursting from her seams. "I...thank you. I beg your pardon."

Sophia wrapped the fichu around her neck and stuffed it into the neckline of her dress while Lord Gray looked out the window, at his hat, down at his hands—anywhere but at her exposed bosom.

She took her time patting the linen into place even as her gaze wandered back to the carriage doors. No, the one on the right was out of the question, but she might be able to manage the other. If she was quick enough, and could take him by surprise—

"I wouldn't attempt it if I were you, Miss Monmouth. You won't make it three steps down Newgate Street before I'll catch you." He didn't move, but he'd tensed like a coiled spring ready to explode into action. "You might also wish to consider I've just witnessed you commit a crime, and we're less than a block from Newgate Prison."

Sophia stiffened at the veiled threat. If she found herself locked into a cell at Newgate, she'd likely never come back out again. People like her never did, whether they were guilty or not. One needn't look any further than Jeremy's predicament for proof of that.

There was also the minor inconvenience that she was, in fact, guilty.

Sophia eyed Lord Gray, her brain spinning with a confusing mix of half-truths and outright lies. She wasn't good at talking her way out of messes. That was why she took such care never to get caught. Her talents lay more in the physical realm: scampering, scurrying, climbing—that sort of thing. But now here she was, at the mercy of Lord Gray, the cursed Ghost of Bow Street. He wasn't going to let her go until he got what he wanted from her.

Perhaps not even then.

She huffed, and forced herself to settle into her seat.

Lord Gray knew a surrender when he saw one. "Wise of you. Let's begin with something simple, shall we? You're a...student at the Clifford School?"

"Yes." He already knew this, so it cost Sophia nothing to tell him the truth.

"Ah. Very good, Miss Monmouth. Progress already." His lips quirked in that ghost of a smile again. "Now, this is the second time I've witnessed you harassing Mr. Sharpe. What is it you want with him?"

A fair question—a predictable one, even—yet not one Sophia was keen to answer. Again, it was more than likely he already knew what she was about, but any acknowledgment of it could be brought up in court as evidence against her.

But how to avoid it? She bit her lip as she tried to think of what Georgiana might do in a similar situation. Georgiana was an expert at argument, unmatched at wriggling her way free of a verbal attack, like that time she'd left the Society's copy of Mrs. Radcliffe's *The Castles of Athlin and Dunbayne* outdoors, and it had been destroyed by the rain. Every time Sophia had demanded an explanation as to its whereabouts, Georgiana had outmaneuvered her by...

By answering every question with another question.

Yes, of course! Why, it was just the thing.

"Miss Monmouth? You haven't answered my question." Lord Gray's hard gaze flicked to her mouth, and all at once Sophia realized her lips had curved in a delighted smile.

Well, that wouldn't do. Smirking would only make her look guilty.

She did her best to rearrange her lips into a frown. "What makes you think it isn't a lover's spat, just as you said? That would explain everything, wouldn't it?" It would, and rather neatly, too. She might have thought of it herself, but for the fact Peter Sharpe made her flesh crawl.

The judgmental eyebrow shot up again. Lord Gray almost looked as if he were disappointed in her. "Come now, Miss Monmouth. Is that truly the best you can do? A besotted lady doesn't attempt to frame the gentleman she loves for a crime."

"Certainly, she does. Have you forgotten your William Congreve, my lord? 'Hell hath no fury,' and all that. I'm a woman scorned who's seeking revenge, nothing more, and a lover's spat isn't really a matter for the law, is it? Well, now that's settled, I'll just be on my way—"

"I don't think so, Miss Monmouth." Sophia had reached for the door, but Lord Gray wrapped his fingers around her wrist, stopping her. "Mr. Sharpe gaped at you today as if he'd never set eyes on you before."

He had gaped, hadn't he? Yes, he'd gotten a good, long look at her. Another blunder, and she had no one but herself to blame for it. "Yes, well, gentlemen have short memories when it comes to their lovers, my lord."

To Sophia's surprise he laughed at that, the deep, rich timbre of it filling the carriage. "Some gentlemen perhaps, but I'm afraid your demeanor toward him isn't very lover-like. You looked at him as if you'd happily see him swinging at the end of a noose."

"Well, of course, I would. Really, Lord Gray. You don't seem to know much about love affairs, or about revenge. Do you expect anything else from a lady whose lover has forsaken her?" Sophia sniffed. "I may be disappointed in love, but I do have my pride."

"I don't doubt it. That may be the only true statement you've uttered since you got into my carriage, Miss Monmouth." He studied her, as if not quite sure what to do with her next, then he reached into the breast pocket of his coat and pulled out her locket. "Tell me about this. Rather a nice piece. How do you happen to have it?"

"Did I steal it, you mean?" Of course, he would think so. How else would *she*—a woman of no family, no name, and no means—have such a fine piece of jewelry if she hadn't lifted it off some unsuspecting aristocrat?

"I'll have an answer from you, Miss Monmouth."

Sophia huffed. "Fine. It belonged to my mother."

Lord Gray turned the locket over. "It's inscribed. 'To my beloved Arabella. Forever yours, Lawrence, 1774.'"

"Lovely sentiment, isn't it?" Sophia's laugh was bitter. "Forever, alas, turned out to be a great deal shorter than my mother expected."

Lord Gray had been studying the locket, but now his gaze shifted to her face. "What does that mean?"

"What it always means." Within three years of giving her mother the locket, Viscount Clifton, her mother's protector at the time, had pledged his undying devotion to another mistress. Arabella Clifton, as she styled herself, had drifted from one lover to the next after that, with lessening degrees of success, until eventually she'd been driven into the streets to earn her living.

Less than a year later, she was dead.

It wasn't a pleasant story, but neither was it an unusual one. Sophia didn't intend to confide any of this to Lord Gray, however. "I told you already. Gentlemen have short memories when it comes to their lovers."

"So you did." Lord Gray held up the locket, letting it dangle between his fingers. "You must bear Peter Sharpe quite a grudge, Miss Monmouth, to risk such a treasure. What did you hope to gain with such a trick? To see Sharpe taken up for theft?"

Sophia's gaze followed the locket as it swung gently back and forth in Lord Gray's long, scarred fingers. She clenched her hands in her lap to keep from snatching it away from him.

Her memories of her mother were worn and faded now, like a letter she'd read too often, but the locket was different. It was something Sophia could hold in her hand, tangible proof of a mother she'd loved, and failed, and now could no longer remember.

It was the only possession she had that was truly *hers*, that meant something to her. Losing it would be as painful as severing a limb, but planting it on Sharpe was the only way she could think of to gain the upper hand on him. She'd been willing to risk sacrificing it for Jeremy's sake, yes, but she'd had every intention of getting it back.

Lord Gray was wrong about one thing, though. She hadn't intended for Sharpe to be taken up for theft. Sophia didn't have any faith in the justice system, but she did respect the justice of the streets. She'd been well aware once she cried theft the men at the pub wouldn't bother to verify the crime before they threatened to beat Sharpe bloody.

Sharpe was a coward, like most men of his ilk, the sort who collapsed at the first threat of violence. Sophia had planned to let him panic for a while, then withdraw her accusation just in time to save him—provided, of course, he chose to be forthcoming about his reasons for accusing Jeremy of theft.

It wasn't, admittedly, one of her cleverest plans, but after listening to Sharpe's testimony this morning she'd been desperate to *do* something, to somehow hold him to account for his lies.

Lady Clifford was going to be appalled when she found out what Sophia had done. Above all else, she'd taught them to be cautious. Cautiousness, alas, had never been Sophia's strength. She tended to leap first, then figure out the rest while she was flying through the air.

Unnecessary risk, Sophia.

Except to Sophia's thinking, it *was* necessary. Jeremy hadn't committed any crime. Sharpe hadn't accused Jeremy because he was guilty, so he must have done it for some other reason. Sophia wanted to know what it was, and she'd been close to finding it out before Lord Gray had rendered all her efforts on Jeremy's behalf useless.

Again.

"Miss Monmouth? Would you care to explain to me why you attempted to frame Mr. Sharpe for a crime of which he's innocent?"

Another laugh rose to Sophia's lips, the taste of it bitter on her tongue. Peter Sharpe might not have taken her locket, but he was far from innocent. It mattered little to her which crime he was punished for, as long as he was punished.

But Lord Gray wouldn't see it that way, would he? No, the way he saw it, people like *him* decided questions of guilt or innocence. People like her and Jeremy explained themselves, then begged for forgiveness. Ironic, really, since pleas for mercy never seemed to mean much to men like Lord Gray.

She'd get nowhere with him, even if she told him the truth. Perhaps *especially* then.

The truth certainly hadn't done Jeremy any good, had it? Anyone who'd seen him today should have recognized he wasn't capable of deception, yet it had taken less than half an hour for him to be tried, found guilty, and sentenced to death.

Sophia tore her gaze from the locket and met Lord Gray's forbidding wolf's eyes. "Tell me, my lord. What was your impression of the court proceedings today?"

"Are you questioning *me* now, Miss Monmouth?"

She shrugged. "I simply wondered if you found anything distasteful about it."

His face hardened. "I saw a guilty man sentenced to death as punishment for a despicable crime. There's nothing distasteful in that."

"Yes, I suppose that's what you *would* see. I thought you more perceptive than that, but it's easier to see precisely what you expected, isn't it?"

With a quick snap of his fingers, her locket disappeared into his fist. "It sounds as if you're accusing me of something. May I ask what it is you think I've done?"

So polite, so correct and courteous, yet Sophia could see the arrogance there, his certainty that he must be in the right. "I accuse you of willful blindness, my lord. It's not an uncommon failing, but still a grievous one."

Oh, he didn't care for that. *That* accusation had gotten under his skin.

"Explain yourself please, Miss Monmouth."

"With pleasure." Sophia leaned forward, her gaze holding his. "Mr. Ives, my lord. Did his demeanor strike you as being at all strange?"

Lord Gray had remained expressionless throughout his questioning, his face a blank canvas, but now Sophia noticed a flicker of something in his eyes. Uneasiness, or consciousness. It was there and gone in an instant, but by then it was too late. Sophia saw it, and pounced. "You *did* find something strange about it." Perhaps there was hope for Lord Gray, after all.

He eyed her warily. "Strange in what manner?"

"Mr. Ives didn't offer much in his own defense, did he? He appeared dazed, baffled by the proceedings. I would have said he didn't understand the accusations against him, or indeed, why he was in the courtroom at all. Did you happen to notice that?"

Sophia expected a swift and firm denial, but it didn't come. Lord Gray considered it, his arms crossed over his chest. "I did notice it, yes."

Sophia's mouth dropped open. "You did?"

He let out an irritable sigh. "You sound surprised, Miss Monmouth. You're aware I *have* been in a courtroom before? Mr. Ives isn't the first defendant I've ever seen."

"I hadn't given any thought at all as to how you spend your time, my lord, but since you're so familiar with courtroom proceedings, I can only assume you remarked Mr. Ives's unusual behavior."

"I just said I did."

"You did say so, yes, but you don't seem to have drawn the obvious conclusion from it."

He shifted impatiently against the seat. "It must not be as obvious as you think it is, Miss Monmouth."

"It is when one is paying attention. Jeremy Ives is simple, Lord Gray. He appeared confused today because he *is* confused."

Lord Gray went still. "Simple?"

"Yes. Intellectually, I'd put him at roughly seven or eight years old. He doesn't fully understand what he's been accused of, and he certainly doesn't have any notion how to defend himself."

Lord Gray said nothing, but Sophia could see he was mulling over what she'd said, and she pushed her advantage. "How many seven-year-old children are such clever thieves they've escaped justice for months on end? Do you know of any eight-year-old children, my lord, who are capable of committing a murder?"

He regarded her with cool gray eyes. "Simple or not, Miss Monmouth, the court has deemed him capable to stand trial."

"My, such unerring faith in justice! I'm afraid I don't have your confidence. I find, my lord, justice often has more to do with who the accuser and the accused are than it does with matters of guilt or innocence. Do you agree?"

Lord Gray's jaw hardened. "No, I don't."

"No, I suppose you wouldn't, having never sat in the accused's place. But there's another thing I found strange about today's proceedings."

"Please do enlighten me, Miss Monmouth."

Lord Gray didn't look particularly eager to be enlightened, but it seemed today wasn't his lucky day, any more than it was hers. "Does Peter Sharpe strike you as the sort of man who'd carry a cane?"

He opened his mouth, then closed it.

"No, I didn't think so, and what's more, today was the first I've heard about a cane. No one other than Peter Sharpe has said a word about it. Surely if he'd had one on the night of Mr. Gerrard's murder, it would have been found at St. Clement Dane's?"

"You can't be sure it wasn't. The knife used to murder Mr. Gerrard is of far greater importance than the cane, and it was found next to Mr. Gerrard's body, covered with his blood. Are you denying Ives regularly carried a knife?"

"Oh no, my lord. He *did* carry one—a folding penny knife, gifted to him by Mr. Brixton, with a walnut handle and a three-inch blade. Three inches, Lord Gray. Quite a feat, to kill a man with a three-inch blade."

He gave her a grim smile. "Not if you slit his throat, Miss Monmouth."

"Sharpe wasn't carrying a cane today, either," Sophia muttered, her brow furrowed. "Indeed, I've never seen him with one, and I've been following him for weeks. It's difficult to see how he could have subdued a man of Jeremy's size and strength without it."

"Oh, I don't know, Miss Monmouth. *You* managed to get the upper hand with Mr. Sharpe easily enough. Twice, in fact. Once the other night when you followed him to St. Clement Dane's, and again today." His gaze strayed to her bodice, then skittered away again.

Sophia's fichu was firmly in place, but all the same she felt warmth creeping into her cheeks. She wasn't a blushing virgin any more than she was a swooning one, but for a brief moment she thought she saw a flare of heat in those gray eyes.

She cleared her throat. "Let's put the cane aside for the moment, shall we? What would you say, my lord, if I told you Peter Sharpe is a despicable liar?"

"I'd say I think it's much more comfortable for you to believe Sharpe is lying than it is for you to believe your friend Ives is a murderer. Unfortunately, the truth doesn't support that conclusion."

"Indeed? Which truth are you referring to, my lord? Yours, or mine?"

"There is only one truth, Miss Monmouth." The heat in his eyes cooled until they looked like sheets of gray ice. "The truth is Mr. Ives was found crouched over the lifeless body of Henry Gerrard, soaked in his blood. I regret that truth should be so disagreeable to you, but the facts are what they are."

Sophia studied him, considering his words. One truth? How naïve he was, to think a truth so absolute one couldn't find a dozen different ways to turn it sideways, to twist it until it became a lie. What must it be like, to have such faith?

Sophia supposed she'd never know. "Since you rely so heavily on facts, Lord Gray, I must assume you wish to have all of them before you draw any conclusion about a thing so crucial as a man's guilt or innocence?"

His shoulders stiffened. "Despite what you may think of me, I have no wish to send an innocent man to the noose."

"Of course not. May I conclude, then, you believe yourself to be in full possession of all the facts related to Peter Sharpe's accusation against Mr. Ives?"

"I do, yes."

"That's a great relief to me, Lord Gray. Tell me, then, what do you make of this business with Patrick Dunn?"

Sophia could see at once he hadn't the faintest idea who Patrick Dunn was. To his credit, he didn't try and pretend he did. "I'm not familiar with that name. Who is he?"

"A weaver, formerly of Clare Court. Until recently he lived there with his wife and their two young children. Now he lives on the Thames, aboard the prison hulk *Warrior*, awaiting transportation to a penal colony in Australia."

"His crime?"

Sophia leaned toward him. "Why, theft, my lord. Three months ago, Patrick Dunn was convicted of stealing a watch from Peter Sharpe."

Chapter Seven

If he'd seen nothing but triumph in her eyes, Tristan would have found it easier to look away from her, but the more time he spent with Sophia Monmouth, the less able he was to make sense of her. There seemed to be a dozen different versions of her lurking under that enigmatic exterior, each one an echo of another, like layers of warped reflections in a cracked looking glass.

Tristan muttered a curse. No, there was nothing simple about her. She wore boy's clothing, but she wasn't a boy. She climbed, ran, and hid as if she were fleeing a crime, but she wasn't a thief. She was one of Lady Clifford's creatures, but she wasn't a liar.

At least, not in this instance.

Even knowing what he did about her association with the Clifford School, Tristan was having a difficult time casting Miss Monmouth as a deceitful villainess. Her eyes, in particular, didn't mark her as dishonest, and he'd looked enough villains in the eye to know one could see their darkness at a glance.

As much as he wished otherwise, he couldn't question her sincerity on this. One look into those fierce green eyes and he knew she wasn't lying about Peter Sharpe. Whether what she'd told him was true or not, he could see *she* believed every word she'd said.

Not a boy, not a thief, and not a liar. So much for the facts being what they were.

"Peter Sharpe has been the victim of theft before, Lord Gray." She was assessing every shift in his expression. "Don't you find that curious?"

"This is London, Miss Monmouth. Crime isn't a notable occurrence here. Hence I leave my answer to your deductive powers."

"Very well. What would you say, then, if I told you the crime Mr. Dunn is meant to have committed against Mr. Sharpe is remarkably similar to the crime Jeremy is accused of committing?"

Tristan *did* find that curious. "How similar?"

"Peter Sharpe is both the victim and the only witness to both crimes, and they both occurred at St. Clement Dane's Church. Quite a coincidence, isn't it?"

Tristan didn't believe in coincidences, but he kept that to himself. "Unusual, perhaps, but not utterly implausible. People all over London are victims of theft every day."

She swept this argument aside with an impatient gesture. "Next you'll tell me Mr. Sharpe is simply unlucky. I wonder, though, why he spends so much time wandering about London at night if he's so often the target of thieves and murderers. St. Clement Dane's Church appears to be a particularly unlucky location for him, yet I followed him there again just the other night. Strange, isn't it?"

Tristan stroked his fingers over his jaw, considering it. "I'll allow it's a bit strange, yes, but it's not proof of any wrongdoing. Tell me, Miss Monmouth. How did you find out about Patrick Dunn?"

She shrugged. "The same way everyone in London finds out about crimes. I read it in the Proceedings."

"You went searching for Mr. Sharpe's name in the Proceedings?" That had been clever of her. Tristan also made it a point to read the Proceedings, and might have come across Patrick Dunn's name and made the connection himself, but he hadn't seen any reason to doubt Jeremy Ives's guilt—not with the evidence against him. In any case, he hadn't been in London when Dunn was taken up. He'd been in Oxfordshire by then, grieving for his brother and attempting to soothe his mother's hysterics.

"I did. I knew Sharpe to be a liar the moment he made the accusation against Jeremy. I knew he must have told similar lies before."

Tristan raised an eyebrow. "I fail to see how you could know such a thing."

"How many liars do you know, Lord Gray, who lie only once? In any case, I was right, wasn't I?"

"You're sure of yourself, Miss Monmouth. Forgive me, but it's possible he didn't lie either time. Mr. Sharpe could have been the victim of two similar crimes. As I said, crime isn't uncommon in London."

Tristan had the distinct impression she just managed to resist rolling her eyes.

"Mr. Dunn has never been accused of a crime before, my lord. He claims Sharpe accosted *him* while he was passing through St. Clement

Dane's churchyard on his way home from the Turk's Head Coffeehouse in the Strand."

Tristan blinked. How had she discovered *that*? "That information wouldn't have been in the Proceedings."

"No. I paid his wife a visit in Clare Court. She was more than happy to tell me about her husband's unhappy fate."

Tristan still wasn't convinced. "It sounds as if it may have been a crime of opportunity. They're much more common than you may think, Miss Monmouth."

"So are false accusations, Lord Gray. It makes no sense a respectable, law-abiding man like Patrick Dunn would suddenly commit a violent crime simply because the opportunity presented itself." Her face turned bleak. "Mrs. Dunn insists her husband is innocent—that he had no need to steal anything."

"She's his wife, Miss Monmouth. Naturally, she believes him innocent. This is why you've been following Mr. Sharpe, then? You think if you can catch him out in another lie it proves he's also lying about Mr. Ives?"

"My dear Lord Gray, I don't *think* it. I *know* he's lying, and I *will* catch him out at it. Indeed, I might have caught him the other night if you hadn't gotten in my way."

Tristan's jaw hardened at mention of the other night. "It's a damn good thing I did get in your way. If Peter Sharpe is the blackguard you say he is, you might have gotten your own throat slit." He'd never known anyone so careless of her own safety as she was.

Incredibly, she laughed at that. "I'm touched by your concern for me, my lord, but I'm perfectly capable of taking care of myself."

"You mistake the matter, Miss Monmouth, if you think my concern is for *you*." Tristan's voice was cold, but in truth, he *was* concerned for her—that is, merely in the sense that any decent man would be concerned for any young woman recklessly risking her neck. Nothing more.

He leaned back against the squabs, studying her. She wasn't going to care for what he had to say next, but it must be said, nevertheless. "I'm going to have to insist you stop chasing after Peter Sharpe from now on, Miss Monmouth."

Her eyes narrowed to slits. "You *insist* on it? *You* insist on it? I beg your pardon, Lord Gray. You may be an earl and the Ghost of Bow Street, but as terribly important as you are, *I* don't answer to you."

Tristan's fingers tightened around the locket still clutched in his fist. "You answer to the law, just as every other citizen in London does. As for Peter Sharpe, he hasn't been accused of any crime, despite your account of his perfidy. You, on the other hand, were caught in the act of accusing a man of a crime you knew full well he didn't commit."

He blinked at her as a smile curled her lips. "At least you didn't refer to him as an *innocent* man this time. I do believe we're making progress, my lord."

Tristan's gaze caught on her lips—surprisingly sweet, pink, bow-shaped lips, utterly incongruous with such a pert mouth. For one wild moment, he imagined leaning forward and brushing his thumb over her plump lower lip.

His thumb, or his mouth. Would she taste sweet, or—

Damn it. She was a miscreant, a threat to the public.

He tore his gaze away from her mouth and cleared his throat. "I won't catch you harassing Peter Sharpe again, Miss Monmouth."

It wasn't a question. She heard the hint of command in his voice, and her smile widened. "You won't *catch* me, no."

Pert mouth, indeed. "Let me make myself clear. If I catch you going after him again—and make no mistake, Miss Monmouth, I *will* catch you—I'll have you brought up on charges."

The pert mouth remained stubbornly closed.

"Well? Come now, Miss Monmouth. Convince me you'll stay away from Peter Sharpe, or I'll take you to the magistrate this instant, and save myself a great deal of trouble."

She shot him a resentful look, her pretty pink lips turned down at the corners.

"Nothing to say?" Tristan waited, his face impassive.

At last, she gave in to the inevitable with an irritated sigh. "Very well, Lord Gray. I give you my word I'll stay away from Peter Sharpe."

"Your *word*? Is that all you have to offer? Why, Miss Monmouth, should I accept your word when I have every reason to believe you'll fail to keep it?"

She huffed out a breath. "Well, what would you have in its place? A blood oath? A virgin sacrifice? Shall we summon a priest? Would you be satisfied if I swore on the Bible, or should I place my hand over my heart and vow on my eternal soul I—"

To Tristan's horror a laugh threatened, and he cut her off with a wave of his hand. "That's enough, Miss Monmouth."

"I don't go back on my word, Lord Gray. If I give it, I'll keep it."

He studied her for signs of deception, but she held his gaze, her green eyes clear and unflinching. Despite all evidence to the contrary, he sensed there was honor in her. He felt it in the same way he felt the utter lack of it in others he'd come across in his years as a Bow Street Runner. Oh, it was a twisted, jaded, backward sort of honor, to be sure, but she answered to some sort of internal code, flawed though it may be.

"I suppose your word will have to do." He wasn't entirely satisfied, but it was either her word, or a visit to the magistrate. A wiser man would choose the latter. As recently as a week ago, *he'd* been a wiser man.

Not anymore, it seemed.

He'd continue to follow her, of course. Not only because he'd told Sampson Willis he would, but because somebody had to keep an eye on her. It didn't sit well with him Peter Sharpe had gotten such a good look at her face today, and God knew she didn't bother to protect herself.

"Here. This belongs to you." Tristan held out the silver locket.

Her eyes widened. "Thank you, my lord." She reached out and took it from him, then sagged back against the seat.

Were her hands shaking?

Until he saw that tremor, Tristan hadn't realized she'd thought he wasn't going to give the locket back to her. His gaze darted to her face, but she wasn't looking at him. She was staring down at her hands.

She'd closed the locket in her fist, and she was stroking it in the same manner one would a beloved child, or a favored pet. Her thumb moved back and forth across the smooth silver face, but she didn't seem to be aware she was doing it. Her eyes were closed, and the pink flush that temper had brought to her cheeks had faded, leaving her pale.

All at once she looked painfully weary, and painfully young. She couldn't be more than twenty years old. Tristan's chest gave a strange little lurch at the thought, but he pushed it aside. Miss Monmouth wouldn't be his responsibility for much longer, and he preferred it that way.

He knocked his fist on the roof of the carriage to summon his coachman.

She looked up. "Where are we going?"

"My lord?" The coachman appeared at the window.

"The Clifford School, Platt. No. 26 Maddox Street." Tristan issued the order without taking his eyes off her. If he wasn't mistaken, Miss Monmouth preferred to keep him far away from Lady Clifford.

"Yes, my lord." The coachman disappeared, and a moment later the carriage jerked into motion.

She shoved the locket into a hidden pocket in her dress, and with it any vulnerability he might have glimpsed in her face. "It's terribly chivalrous of you to see me home, Lord Gray," she drawled, "But unnecessary, for all that."

He gave her a thin smile. "It's not chivalry, Miss Monmouth, but forethought. Peter Sharpe is mere blocks away from here. I wouldn't want you to be tempted to follow him again."

"For pity's sake. I just gave you my word I wouldn't, yet here you are, still not satisfied."

No, he wasn't satisfied—far from it—but he couldn't quite figure out why. He and Miss Monmouth had reached a truce of sorts, which was more than he'd expected to get from her. "I thought I'd pay a call on Lady Clifford."

She shot upright in her seat. "Lady Clifford! Why, whatever for?"

Ah. He wasn't mistaken, then. She didn't want him anywhere near Lady Clifford.

Tristan arched an eyebrow at her raised voice. "Such an outburst. I wonder, Miss Monmouth, why my calling on Lady Clifford should distress you so."

She shrugged, but her dark scowl remained. "I just don't see what you'd want with Lady Clifford, that's all."

"You'll find out soon enough."

She frowned. "I hope you don't expect a warm reception from her. She won't be pleased to see you."

Tristan's lips gave a traitorous twitch at her sulky expression. "I'll endeavor to hide my disappointment."

* * * *

There wasn't a single person at No. 26 Maddox Street who was pleased to see Tristan, but Daniel Brixton was the least pleased of all of them.

"I told you to stay away from Miss Sophia, Lord Gray. I thought I'd made myself clear."

Clear enough, yes. Keep away from the Clifford School, or else. Unfortunately for Daniel Brixton, Tristan didn't take orders from him. Still, now wasn't the time to get into a tussle with Lady Clifford's guard dog. "Easy, Brixton. I just came to deliver Miss Monmouth to Lady Clifford."

"It's all right, Daniel. I'd like to hear what Lord Gray has to say. Do wait here in the entryway, though, won't you?" Lady Clifford nodded to Brixton, then turned her attention back to Tristan. "Will you come into the drawing room, my lord? You too, Sophia."

Tristan followed Lady Clifford and Miss Monmouth down a hallway to a drawing room where three young ladies and a very ugly pug dog were seated on a green silk settee, obviously waiting for someone.

"Sophia!" One of the young ladies rose unsteadily to her feet. "Jeremy?"

Miss Monmouth met her friend's gaze. She didn't speak, only shook her head.

"No. Oh, *no*. Jeremy." The other girl went as pale as death, and dropped onto the settee as if her legs had given way beneath her.

"Emma, Georgiana, take Cecilia upstairs, please." Lady Clifford spoke with the air of one who needn't raise her voice to be obeyed.

The dark-haired girl—Cecilia, presumably—let out a choked sob, but allowed herself to be led from the drawing room.

Lady Clifford waited for the door to close behind them, then waved Tristan toward the settee the three young ladies had just vacated. "Please do sit down, Lord Gray. Sophia, you look rather limp. Come sit next to me, dearest." She patted the seat next to her.

Tristan hadn't been prepared to be received with such graciousness, but he took a seat. "Thank you, my lady."

"Now then, Lord Gray." Lady Clifford folded her hands in her lap and turned a politely enquiring look on him. "I confess myself surprised to see you here. How did you happen to come across Sophia today?"

"We met at the Old Bailey, my lady."

Tristan had assumed Miss Monmouth had come to the trial at her ladyship's direction, but Lady Clifford seemed surprised by this information. "Did you, indeed?" Her tone was mild, but there was a subtle shift of tension in the room. "I didn't realize you meant to attend Jeremy's trial today, dearest. It seems as though Cecilia did, however."

Sophia Monmouth said nothing, just twisted her fingers nervously in her skirts.

"Miss Monmouth didn't simply attend the trial, Lady Clifford. I'm afraid she took such great exception to Mr. Peter Sharpe's testimony she followed him from the Old Bailey to Newgate Street, slipped a silver locket into his pocket when his back was turned, then accused him of stealing it."

Silence. Aside from a slight twitch of her lips, Lady Clifford's expression didn't change, but Tristan had the distinct impression she wasn't pleased. Miss Monmouth, who was now squirming uncomfortably, seemed to have drawn the same conclusion.

"The, ah, gentlemen loitering outside Ye Old Mitre Pub were on the verge of beating Peter Sharpe bloody when I came upon them." Tristan glanced at Miss Monmouth. "Street justice is an ugly thing, Lady Clifford."

"Indeed, it is. What a fortunate coincidence you happened to be there to intervene, Lord Gray." Lady Clifford reached out to stroke a hand over the pug's head.

Tristan let out a short laugh. "There are no coincidences, Lady Clifford. I saw Miss Monmouth follow Mr. Sharpe out of the courtroom, knew at once she was up to something, and went after her."

"Is that so? I wasn't aware, Lord Gray, you were still a Bow Street Runner." Lady Clifford's tone was as polite as ever, but Tristan didn't miss the shard of ice in her voice.

"My interest is personal, Lady Clifford, not professional. Henry Gerrard was a dear friend of mine. I'm sure you can understand I'm eager to see his murderer brought to justice."

"Jeremy didn't murder Henry Gerrard!" Miss Monmouth shot to her feet, her face white with anger. "If you're so anxious to see Mr. Gerrard's murderer brought to justice, then you'll do everything in your power to see the wrong man isn't hung for the crime!"

"Sophia, my love. Please." Lady Clifford took Miss Monmouth's hand and urged her back down onto the settee, but her gaze remained fixed on Tristan. "I beg your pardon, Lord Gray. Jeremy Ives is rather a favorite of ours. Naturally my girls are upset at the dreadful fate that's befallen him. I wasn't aware you were acquainted with Henry Gerrard. I'm very sorry for your loss."

Tristan stiffened. "I don't want your sympathy, Lady Clifford. I want you and your…young ladies to stop interfering in this business."

"Miss Monmouth is right, you know," Lady Clifford said, as if Tristan hadn't spoken. "Jeremy is innocent. He isn't capable of committing a crime, much less one so heinous as murder."

"The court doesn't agree with you, my lady. Jeremy Ives was found guilty of murder today, and there's an end to it."

Miss Monmouth jumped to her feet again. "It's not an end to anything! For a Bow Street Runner, you're very disinterested in justice, Lord Gray."

"On the contrary, Miss Monmouth. I'm quite interested in seeing murderers hang."

"In seeing *someone* hang, at any rate. You're far less troubled about whether the man swinging at the end of the rope is guilty or innocent." Miss Monmouth took a step toward him. Her hands were clenched into fists, and her cheeks flushed with righteous fury.

Tristan gazed up at her, a disturbing range of emotions twisting in his chest. Her accusation struck a nerve, and he didn't care for it, but at the same time he couldn't help but admire her passion, misguided as it was. His eyes met hers, and for a long moment they stared at each other, both of them a bit short of breath, then Tristan rose to his feet so he was towering over her. "I'll take my leave now."

He'd said all he wished to say, but before he reached the drawing room door, he turned a sharp glance on Sophia Monmouth. "Remember your promise, Miss Monmouth. You gave your word. Good day, Lady Clifford."

"Lord Gray." Lady Clifford inclined her head.

For some time after Lord Gray left, neither Sophia nor Lady Clifford said a word. The only sound in the room was Gussie, snuffling and snorting contentedly as Lady Clifford stroked his head. Finally, when Sophia couldn't stand the quiet a moment longer, Lady Clifford murmured, "Unnecessary risk, Sophia."

"I-I'm sorry, my lady. I know you told me not to go to the trial, but I simply couldn't…couldn't bear for Jeremy to be left alone." Sophia swiped angrily at the tears on her cheeks.

"I understand that, my love, and I can't blame you for it, but this business with Peter Sharpe and your locket." Lady Clifford shook her head. "That wasn't well done of you. It could have gone dreadfully awry."

Sophia sank back onto the settee, her knees shaking. "I just…I'm afraid I let my temper get the best of me. Peter Sharpe *lied* today, without a single qualm, or even a trace of regret. I never made any conscious decision to go after him. I saw him leave the courthouse, and the next thing I knew I was following him."

"But to what end, Sophia? What did you hope to gain from such a risky scheme?"

Sophia grimaced. "I suppose I was thinking I could threaten him into a confession of some sort. I thought if I could prove he was a thief himself the court might dismiss his testimony against Jeremy. It was foolish, I know."

Lady Clifford sighed. "I'm afraid it was. Your recklessness will get you nowhere, Sophia. I only hope you'll learn your lesson before you get hurt. Now, Lord Gray said something about a promise. What did he mean?"

Gussie abandoned Lady Clifford in favor of Sophia's lap. He rolled over onto his back, and she rested a hand on his fat belly. "Nothing nearly as significant as he seems to think. I gave him my word I'd stay away from Peter Sharpe."

Lady Clifford raised a brow. "And will you? I know you don't give your word lightly."

"He wrung the promise from me by threatening to take me to the magistrate at once if I didn't agree to his terms, but I do intend to keep it, yes, mainly because it costs me nothing to do so. Sharpe got a close look at me today, close enough he'd recognize me in an instant if he saw me again. It's best if I keep out of his way."

"Hmmm. You'll have to find another way to go about this business, then."

"Yes, but I can't think how right now. My thoughts are all muddled. We're running out of time, my lady." Jeremy had been so terrified in the courtroom today, so wasted and defeated. Thinking of him made more tears spring to Sophia's eyes. "Jeremy's situation is desperate. If we don't act soon, it will be too late for him."

Lady Clifford rested her hand on Gussie's head. "My dear child, it's never too late for anything. But I have a suggestion for you, if you're willing to hear it."

"Of course, I am."

Lady Clifford chuckled. "Don't be so certain, because you may not like it. It occurs to me Lord Gray could prove quite useful to us."

Sophia's spine went rigid. "*Useful*? How? He's meddlesome and high-handed, not to mention rigid and condescending. Worst of all, he lacks imagination."

"That remains to be seen, but what matters here is he's an earl, not to mention the Ghost of Bow Street. If anyone can get into Newgate to see Jeremy, it's Lord Gray."

"I hadn't thought of that." At one point or other they'd each tried to gain access to Jeremy, but no amount of begging, pleading, threats, or bribes had done any good. Even Lady Clifford had been turned away.

But the Ghost of Bow Street? No one would dare turn *him* away. He likely had a dozen different ways to get inside the prison. If she could see Jeremy, even for a short time, he could tell her in his own words what had happened that night at St. Clement Dane's. He'd give her something she could turn to account—she knew he would.

"But how can it be done, my lady?" Lord Gray believed Jeremy was guilty, and he despised the very sight of *her*. "Why should Lord Gray choose to help us?"

"Well, my dear, I can't say for sure he will. He may refuse, but I think it might be worth asking him, just the same." Lady Clifford chucked Gussie under the chin, then turned to Sophia, an odd little smile on her lips. "After all, there's no crime in asking, is there?"

Chapter Eight

"Manipulative, at best. At worst, she's devious." Tristan slid one of his pawns across the chessboard without giving much thought to where it would land. "She gave me her word she'd stay away from Sharpe, but I'd be a fool to rely on her keeping it."

God knew he'd been fool enough already. He should have taken her straight to Sampson Willis while he had her in his carriage yesterday. Perhaps then he wouldn't have dreamt of a dark-haired phantom with a scandalously bare bosom.

"Yes, I believe you've said so once already." Lyndon was toying with his knight and didn't look up. "Check."

"She's shrewd, too. Lady Clifford has chosen her pupils well. Miss Monmouth is a perfect, pocket-sized pixie in boy's breeches." Except she hadn't been wearing breeches yesterday, had she? It was no wonder he'd acted such a fool. That gray gown with its plunging bodice had addled his wits.

Tristan plucked his defeated king from the board. He set it aside and rose to his feet, abandoning any further attempts at concentration. "I tell you, Lyndon. She's the most exasperating woman I've ever encountered."

"Vexing. That was the word you used. Vexing, and tenacious." Lyndon gave a delicate shudder. "Dreadful combination, especially in an attractive woman."

Tristan abruptly ceased his pacing in front of the fireplace and turned to give his friend a wary look. "I never said she was attractive."

Not aloud, that is.

Lyndon abandoned his study of the game and blinked up at Tristan. "Didn't you? I thought I just heard you say she's perfect."

"I said she was a perfect *pixie*, Lyndon. It's not a compliment."

"No?" Lyndon frowned. "Well, what the devil is a pixie?"

"They're...aren't they demons, or elves, or some other sort of devious, manipulative mythical creature?"

"Are they, indeed? I thought they were meant to be like fairies. I've always thought fairies sounded rather nice." Lyndon thought about it, then turned his attention back to the chessboard with a shrug. "You didn't need to say she was attractive, in any case. I already know she is."

"You don't know any such thing." Lyndon's only answer was a knowing smirk, and Tristan muttered a curse. "*How* do you know?"

The smirk widened, and Lyndon waved a hand at the chessboard. "I know because I'm beating you at chess. I *never* beat you at chess unless you're agitated, and you're never agitated over a woman unless you find her attractive." He swept a critical gaze over Tristan's mussed hair and crooked cravat. "I've never seen you quite *this* agitated, though. Miss Monmouth must be lovely, indeed."

Tristan turned his back on Lyndon and stalked over to the window.

Lovely? Certainly, if one found Machiavellian tendencies lovely. That is, she was clever—he couldn't deny that—but she had a barbed tongue.

A barbed tongue and soft, full pink lips.

Damn it. Her lips were of no consequence. She was an outrage, chaos in boy's breeches and a black cap, roaming London's rooftops and stalking innocent citizens in the streets.

Silky dark hair, bewitching green eyes...

An irritated growl rose in Tristan's throat. Very well, Miss Monmouth was lovely, but she was also sly, and with the way she scaled townhouses and wriggled through fences, distressingly agile.

Delicate but strong, lissome, with perfectly proportioned curves—

"Well? Is she, then?"

Lyndon's amused voice broke into his musings, and Tristan turned from the window. "Is she what?"

Lyndon raised an eyebrow at him. "Lovely?"

A denial rose to Tristan's lips, but all that emerged was a resigned sigh. "She is, damn her. Exceedingly."

"Ah. I thought so." Lyndon shot him a satisfied grin, then slid his queen across the chessboard. "Checkmate."

Tristan turned back to the window, and his gaze fell on the roof of Lord Everly's pediment. Cursed Everly and his cursed pediment. This was all *his* fault.

"Come away from that window, will you? She's not there *now,* for God's sake, and your incessant hovering is irritating me." Lyndon was tidying the chess set away in its wooden box, his lips tight with annoyance. "Why are you in such fits over this woman, Gray? So, she's attractive. London is teeming with attractive ladies, and you've never gotten into a dither over any of *them.*"

"They aren't liars or felons." It wasn't a convincing reply, but what could he say? That he found Sophia Monmouth, with her pert mouth and barbed tongue far more tempting than any of the noted beauties in London?

Lyndon's face darkened. "I beg to differ. Lady Clarissa Warrington is a thief. By the time I broke with her she'd squeezed a fortune in jewels out of me."

"That's not the same thing, Lyndon." Tristan crossed the room and threw himself into one of the chairs in front of the fireplace. "I wouldn't hold Lady Clarissa up as a model of virtue, but I never saw her commit an actual crime. I *saw* Miss Monmouth slide her locket into Sharpe's coat, as stealthy as any thief."

Lyndon sank into the chair opposite Tristan. "Perhaps he deserved it. He may be every bit the liar Miss Monmouth claims he is, and as guilty as any other criminal locked up in Newgate."

"He may be, but he hasn't been convicted of any crime, and it's just as likely Miss Monmouth is the liar. She doesn't have any evidence against Sharpe. She accuses him, but of the two of them, she's the only one I've caught in a crime."

He'd been a fool to let those pink lips and green eyes seduce him into taking her at her word, especially given her association with Lady Clifford, who balanced on a fine line between guilt and innocence herself.

"It's a bit of a mess," Lyndon agreed. "But I'm not sure it matters as far as you're concerned, Gray. You're not a Bow Street Runner anymore. Fulfill your promise to Sampson Willis, then put Miss Monmouth out of your mind."

Tristan sat quietly, studying the flames dancing in the grate, then muttered, "It's too late for that, Lyndon."

Part of the trouble was, Tristan couldn't quite convince himself Miss Monmouth wasn't right about Sharpe. He didn't have any real reason to suspect the man, but his instincts warned him there was something off about Sharpe, and he'd spent enough time scraping London's criminal underbelly to know people were rarely as they seemed.

She'd taken an enormous risk, forcing herself on Peter Sharpe's notice as she had. Sharpe was a dull-witted sort, but even he must have realized

Miss Monmouth intended to do him mischief yesterday. If he really was the villain she claimed, she'd just made herself his next target.

"Miss Monmouth isn't your responsibility, Gray—not beyond what Sampson Willis has asked of you," Lyndon reminded him.

"I've already gone beyond that. Willis asked me to follow her, nothing more. It was my choice to interfere in her dealings with Sharpe. I'm involved now, whether it's convenient or not."

He should have known the dark, mysterious figure on Everly's roof would lead him into trouble. A wise man would have tossed back the rest of his port and gone straight to his bed without a second glance.

A wise man, yes, but not a Bow Street Runner.

Lyndon gave a heavy sigh. "Scruples are inconvenient things. You do realize yours will be the end of you, don't you?"

"No, my mother will be the end of me when she finds out I'm not returning to Oxfordshire straightaway. Go and see her, won't you, Lyndon? There's a good fellow."

"*Me?*" Lyndon gulped. "I thought we were friends, Gray. What have I ever done to deserve such a dreadful fate as—"

"Careful, Lyndon," Tristan warned with a grin.

"I only mean to point out the countess is…well, you must admit she's a—"

A subdued knock on the library door saved Lyndon from having to articulate *what*, precisely, the Countess of Gray was.

"Yes?" Tristan called. "Come in."

Tribble, Tristan's butler entered. "There's a young lady here to see you, Lord Gray. A Miss Monmouth."

Tristan's startled gaze met Lyndon's, and they both shot to their feet at once.

"Miss Monmouth! Attractive lady, Tribble? Looks rather like a pixie?" Lyndon's voice had risen an octave.

Tribble blinked. "I, er…as to that, I couldn't say, my lord."

"Never mind, Tribble." Tristan shot Lyndon a warning look. "Did she say what she wanted?"

"No, my lord, only that she must see you at once. I tried to send her away, you not being home to callers, but the lady is rather…*insistent*."

"Insistent?" It seemed an awfully tame word to describe Sophia Monmouth, but perhaps she was on her best behavior. "Yes, she is that, among other things. By all means, send her in, Tribble."

Tribble bowed his way out, leaving Tristan and Lyndon standing there silently, staring at the door like a pair of fools. It wasn't long before Tribble's heavy footsteps sounded in the hallway, followed by a lighter tread.

A few moments later, Miss Monmouth appeared on the threshold. "Good morning, Lord Gray." She strode into Tristan's library, as if she had a perfect right to be there.

Lyndon stared at her, his eyes about to fall out of his skull, then he turned to Tristan with a half-dazed, and half-pitying look. "It all makes perfect sense now, Gray."

She was wearing a day gown the color of the sun just before it burst over the horizon. It was simple, plain even—nothing at all remarkable about it—yet somehow, she made it look as if she'd wrapped herself in sunbeams. It wasn't a shade of yellow many ladies could wear, but with her dark hair and skin and those bright green eyes, she looked like a spring day.

Tristan, amazed and appalled at himself at once, shook the fanciful notion from his head. "Miss Monmouth." He bowed. "What an unexpected surprise to see you here."

"Yes, I imagine it is. But my appearance isn't as surprising as it might have been, my lord. I was planning to come through your window if your manservant turned me away." She gave him a—*damn it, there was no other word for it*—a *sunny* smile. "I daresay I'd have managed it easily enough. Your pediment is very much like Lord Everly's."

There was a moment of stunned silence, then Lyndon gave a shout of laughter. "It's a great pity you didn't. I would have liked to see that."

Miss Monmouth dipped into a polite curtsy. "I may yet be able to accommodate you, ah…ah…"

She turned to Tristan, who only stared at her like a fool until Lyndon cleared his throat. "Lyndon. I mean, the Earl of Lyndon. That is…Miss Monmouth, may I present Lord Lyndon?"

By the time Tristan finished this fumbling introduction his face was hot with embarrassment, and Lyndon was shaking with silent laughter. Miss Monmouth, however, only swept a cool gaze over Lyndon, then drawled, "How do you do, Lord Lyndon. I never realized Great Marlborough Street had such an overabundance of earls."

Lyndon bowed. "Wherever you find columns and pediments, Miss Monmouth, you'll find earls and marquesses and the like. Perhaps even a stray duke or two."

Miss Monmouth laughed. "Which of the lovely townhouses on this street belongs to you, my lord?"

"None of them, I'm afraid. I live in Berkeley Square. No one ever climbs onto our roofs *there*, a circumstance I never regretted until now."

Tristan's gaze bounced back and forth between them with a frown. Lyndon was *flirting* with Miss Monmouth. Rather pathetically, yes, but flirting nonetheless, and Miss Monmouth seemed to be enjoying it immensely, her green eyes twinkling.

Tristan glared at Lyndon, more irritated with his friend than he had any reason to be. "What can I do for you, Miss Monmouth? I confess I can't think of a single reason for your presence here."

She waved a hand, dismissing this. "Yes, yes, this is all very irregular, but we haven't time to ponder it now, Lord Gray."

"I beg your pardon?" Tristan's gaze narrowed on her, and for the first time he noticed the hectic flush on her cheeks, and the nervous way she fiddled with the fingers of her gloves.

Miss Monmouth wanted something from him.

Well, whatever it was, he'd already made up his mind to refuse her. "Are we going somewhere?"

She glanced at him, biting her lip, then drew in a breath and ceased fidgeting, dropping her hands to her sides. "Yes. We're going to Newgate Prison."

The silence that fell after this announcement was once again broken by Lyndon, who took up the coat he'd tossed aside with a low whistle. "On that note, I'll just take my leave, shall I? Miss Monmouth, it was a great pleasure meeting you." He gave her an elegant bow, then turned to Tristan, his lips twitching. "I wish you luck, Gray."

"What a pleasant gentleman," Miss Monmouth remarked, once the library door had closed behind Lyndon.

Tristan ignored this. "Whatever mischief you're up to this time, Miss Monmouth, I don't want any part of it."

"How do you know? I haven't told you what it is yet." She glanced up at Tristan from under her lashes. "It may be a perfectly charming mischief. Aren't you the least bit curious?"

Tristan swallowed. Damn it, anything could happen if she kept looking at him with that hint of bright green iris peeking through the thick, dark fringe of her eyelashes. "All right, Miss Monmouth. Let's have it out, shall we? What's your business at Newgate?"

She met his gaze. "I must speak to Jeremy."

Tristan stilled. Of course, he'd known what she wanted as soon as she mentioned Newgate, yet even so it was, quite literally, the last request he ever would have imagined she'd make of *him*. "Your business with Ives has nothing to do with me."

"Neither did my business with Peter Sharpe, but you didn't let that stop you."

He raised an eyebrow at her waspish tone. "Is this how you persuade me to grant you a favor, Miss Monmouth?"

She took a breath, and when she spoke again, her voice was softer. "We've all been forbidden to see him, likely to prevent him from having a chance to give us his side of the story. If he dies in Newgate, which he most certainly will, we'll never know the truth about that night."

"I already know the truth. Jeremy Ives slit Henry Gerrard's throat, and he's been sentenced to hang for his crime." Tristan heard the words leave his mouth, and wondered if they were true. There was a part of him that wanted to believe it could be that simple, that justice could be that accurate, that absolute. That part of him wanted to take Miss Monmouth by the arm and see her out of his library, his house, and his life.

But the other part of him stood there and gave Sophia Monmouth a chance to persuade him to act against his better judgment. Not because of her soft lips, or her green eyes, but because he couldn't forget the lost look on Ives's face as he was led from the courtroom yesterday, a death sentence hanging over his head.

"Please, Lord Gray." She wrung her hands, all pretense of nonchalance gone. "You saw Jeremy at his trial yesterday. He's in desperate need of help."

Tristan hesitated. He wasn't sure he liked Sophia Monmouth. He certainly didn't trust her, yet at the same time he found it difficult to refuse her. "If what you say is true, and someone has taken the trouble to keep him quiet, what makes you think I'll be permitted to see him?"

She took a step toward him. "You will be. You're the Ghost of Bow Street."

"Not anymore."

"You must know someone who can get us inside. A guard, perhaps?" She laid a hand on his arm. "Yesterday you claimed to care about justice. If that's so, how can you condemn a man to the noose without hearing his account? If you have even a shred of doubt about Peter Sharpe's testimony, I don't see how you can refuse me."

Neither did Tristan. That was the trouble.

He gazed down into Sophia Monmouth's pleading eyes, and with a muttered curse, Tristan reconciled himself to a visit at Newgate.

* * * *

"To tell you the truth, Lord Gray, I didn't think you'd agree to this scheme."

For all Sophia's careless confidence when she'd breezed into his library this morning, she hadn't truly believed Lord Gray would take her to Newgate Prison.

He gave a short laugh. "I've no idea why I did."

"Well, I-I'm grateful to you, my lord. I realize you would much rather have refused me."

It cost Sophia a few pangs of wounded pride to say it, but he merely nodded as if he didn't notice her discomfort, then cleared his throat with the sort of awful dignity only an earl could command. "Let me be plain, Miss Monmouth. I don't trust you. I'm not convinced you're not a thief, or worse."

Sophia blinked. Well, that was plain enough.

"Be warned," Lord Gray went on. "I don't expect to hear anything this afternoon that will change my mind about Jeremy Ives. Peter Sharpe may be every bit the blackguard you claim he is, but that doesn't make Ives any less of a murderer."

"I understand, my lord." Sophia's voice was meeker than usual, but in truth she hadn't expected Lord Gray would miraculously start believing in Jeremy's innocence. Her best hope for today was to see Jeremy, listen to his account of that night at St. Clement Dane's, and ease him in any way she could.

Sophia peeked at Lord Gray from the corner of her eye. He had a strong profile, with a proud, aristocratic nose, sharp cheekbones, and a jaw that looked as if it had been coaxed from a block of marble by a sculptor's hands. It was the sternest face she'd ever seen.

Lady Clifford was right. If anyone could get access to Jeremy, it was this man.

She suppressed a sigh. Emma was right, too. With his broad shoulders and piercing gray eyes, Lord Gray was undeniably handsome. Certainly, he was the most aristocratic, the most ruthlessly elegant gentleman she'd ever seen. Every inch of him shrieked nobility. Looking at him now, it was difficult to recall he'd ever been a Bow Street Runner, but for…

"Where did you get that scar?"

He raised a self-conscious hand to his top lip. "It's a dull story."

It wasn't a large scar, but one noticed it because it was in a curious place, just above the corner of his mouth, a narrow line of white bisecting the red of his lip.

All at once, she had an overwhelming urge to touch it. It was the sort of scar that told a story, and rendered a face more interesting. The sort of scar that begged to be touched. What would it feel like under the pad of her finger? Sophia traced a finger over her own top lip, trying to imagine it.

The next thought came out of nowhere, like a lightning strike from a cloudless sky.

What would it be like to kiss him?

The tip of her tongue darted out to touch her upper lip. She didn't realize she'd done it until a flicker in the gray eyes drew her gaze back to his. He'd followed the movement, and was now staring at her mouth.

Well, that was…strangely titillating. She didn't realize she'd instinctively parted her lips until his eyes darkened, and suddenly flustered, Sophia rushed awkwardly into speech. "Were you injured while chasing down a criminal? Is it a knife wound, or—"

"No, no, it's…nothing like that."

She cocked her head to the side to study it. "Were you struck? A fist, one with a jeweled ring on the finger might have left such a scar as that."

"I assure you, Miss Monmouth, the story will disappoint you."

She rested her hand on the seat between them, leaning closer to get a better look at his lips. "Was it a thief with long, sharp fingernails, or—"

"No!" He jerked his head back. "As I said, it's a dull story."

Was he *blushing*? Goodness, the origin of that scar grew more fascinating by the moment. "I think it must be something terribly exciting, for you to be so secretive about it." Sophia tapped her lip as she considered the scar. "Was it a quarrel with one of your mistresses? Or a duel over one of your mistresses? Or perhaps one of your mistresses found out about another and she—"

"For God's sake, Miss Monmouth!" The hint of color on his cheekbones had deepened to crimson. "Your fevered imagination does you no credit at all, and in any case, we've arrived."

Sophia glanced out the window. They had indeed arrived, and Lord Gray was mightily relieved at it. She frowned. There must be quite a story behind that scar if he preferred a wander through Newgate Prison to divulging it.

She hopped out of the carriage without waiting for the coachman's assistance, but Lord Gray stopped her with a hand on her arm when she stepped toward the main entrance of the prison. "Not that way. Follow me, Miss Monmouth."

He led her to a smaller doorway on the left with an arch above it, and two narrow windows set high into the brick on either side. He reached up to rap the end of his walking stick against one of these windows, and a few seconds later a face appeared behind the glass. Lord Gray jerked his head toward the left, and the face disappeared.

A few moments later, the door opened and a grimy man with a long, narrow chin peered out. He didn't look pleased to see Lord Gray, but he managed a sullen bow. "Afternoon, yer lordship."

"Hogg. Just the man I'd hoped to find." Lord Gray twirled his walking stick between his spotlessly clean white gloves. "I need your assistance."

Hogg glanced from Lord Gray to Sophia and back again. "An' what kind of 'elp would ye be needing?"

"Nothing too taxing. This lady and I need a word with one of your prisoners."

Hogg ran dirty fingers over his stubbled jaw. "Aw right. What prisoner ye want, milord?"

Lord Gray studied the silver tip of his walking stick for a moment, then lowered it to the ground and met Hogg's gaze. "Jeremy Ives."

Hogg's face went white. "Nay, milord. Can't help ye there. No one sees Ives, on orders from the guv'nor."

"But you'll make an exception for me, won't you, Hogg? It's the least you can do, given our long and mutually beneficial…friendship." Lord Gray reached into a pocket of his coat and drew out a small pouch. Coins clinked together as he tossed it into the air and caught it again. "I'll make it worth your while, of course."

Hogg's gaze locked on the pouch with a look so greedy, Sophia half-expected to see drool run down his chin. He glanced around, then peered behind him into the dim hallway. "I'll lose me place if anyone sees—"

"The longer you keep us standing here, the greater the chance someone will. Best make up your mind quickly, Hogg."

"Aw right then, but ye'll have to be quick, like. No mor'n a few minutes, milord," Hogg hissed, backing away from the door.

Lord Gray pushed it open with the tip of his walking stick. "After you, Miss Monmouth."

Sophia ascended the step, but hesitated before passing through. She wasn't a timid sort of lady, but that darkened doorway looked like the very portal into hell.

To her surprise, a large, warm hand settled on her back. "I'm right behind you," Lord Gray murmured into her ear, his deep, rough velvet voice sending shivers down her spine.

If he noticed her reaction, he didn't comment. He urged her over the threshold, tossing the pouch to Hogg as they passed. Hogg snatched it out of midair and slid it into his pocket with an ease that hinted at a past life as a street thief, then led them through what looked like an anteroom of some sort.

"The turnkey's lodge," Lord Gray muttered.

Sophia paused to glance into the two cramped rooms on either side of the center chamber. Each contained a stool, a table, a cot, and nothing else.

"I said move quick-like, miss," Hogg snapped. He reached out to tug Sophia forward, but before he could lay a finger on her Lord Gray's walking stick sliced through the air and landed near Hogg's arm. He didn't strike him, but he'd made his point, nonetheless.

"Don't touch the lady." Lord Gray didn't raise his voice, but his low growl was far more menacing than a shout would have been.

Hogg blanched, and didn't reach for her again. He took them through the turnkey's lodge to a passage on the left, then down narrow, shallow stone steps into the dungeons below. From there they passed into a serpentine maze of narrow stone passages with what seemed an endless series of heavy iron gates between them.

Sophia had been to Newgate once before, to see a friend of Lady Clifford's who'd been imprisoned for debt, but the female debtor's ward was a palace in comparison to the filth and misery of the dungeons. She resisted the shudders wracking her and plodded along silently behind Mr. Hogg until they emerged from the maze of passageways into what could only be described as a tomb.

One lone prisoner was slumped against the damp stone wall. What little she could see of him in the darkness made Sophia's stomach clench. Hogg lit a candle, and the gloom receded. She drew closer, and the shape of the man on the floor emerged from the shadows.

That was when Sophia's calm deserted her.

Chapter Nine

Jeremy's condition was so terrible as to defy description.

His wrists and ankles were cuffed with wide iron bands, their heavy chains attached to an iron ring in the floor. Filthy, naked skin gaped through the scraps of clothing covering him. His emaciated body was crawling with lice and other vermin and riddled with seeping sores. He seemed to have been singled out for the harshest sort of treatment at the hands of his guards, as well. Sophia could see at a glance his cheeks and jaw were bruised, and his legs were a mess of festering wounds.

Sophia rushed forward with a soft cry and fell to her knees beside him.

"Oh, Jeremy. Oh, sweetheart." He'd looked so feeble in the courthouse, and Sophia had prepared herself for the worst, but this...

She'd seen appalling suffering in her life—drunkenness, starvation, disease, women and children beaten bloody by the very hands of the people who professed to love them—but never in her life had she seen anything more shameful than this. Dear God, it was a miracle Jeremy was still alive.

But someone was doing their best to see he didn't remain that way.

"Jesus." Lord Gray's voice was hoarse. He followed her to the corner of the cell and crouched down on Jeremy's other side. "Ives?"

Jeremy's chin was slumped on his chest, but at the sound of the deep voice, his head came up.

"Jeremy." Sophia touched his cheek. "Can you hear me?"

He blinked, as if he thought she must be an apparition kneeling beside him, but then he burst into a flood of tears. "I didna think ye'd come," he choked out.

"Remove his irons," Lord Gray ordered.

Sophia looked up. The lantern light slanted across Lord Gray's face as he turned toward Hogg, and she caught her breath. His skin was stretched tight across the sharp bones of his face, and he'd gone dead white. His eyes had all but disappeared under a lowered brow, and his full mouth was a thin, grim slash in his face.

She'd never seen a man more enraged in her life. His features looked as if they'd been carved from ice.

Hogg shook his head. "Nay. He's a dangerous one, milord—"

"Do it now. Then get out." Lord Gray rose to his feet, and the candlelight threw his enormous shadow onto the stone wall behind him. He looked like a demon sent straight from the netherworlds.

Hogg gulped, then hurried forward, fumbling with the heavy set of keys dangling from his waist. "No mor'n a few minutes, milord. Ye promised." Once he freed Jeremy from his irons he leapt backwards, out of Lord Gray's reach.

The moment Jeremy was free, he threw himself on Sophia's neck. "I didna think ye'd come, Miss Sophia."

"Hush now, sweetheart. Of course, I came." Sophia brushed his limp hair away from his forehead and did her best to give him a reassuring smile. "Have I ever abandoned you, Jeremy?"

"Nay." Jeremy sniffled, and dragged his arm across his eyes. "But the man yesterday said as I'd done a bad thing, an' I thought ye wouldn't like to see me again, now I'm a bad man."

Hogg snorted, and Lord Gray turned a frigid look on him. "I told you to *get out*." He didn't spare Hogg another glance, but the man took to his heels readily enough, the clang from the iron door ringing like a death knell long after he'd slammed it behind him.

Sophia tried not to flinch at the sound, and turned her attention back to Jeremy. "You're *not* a bad man. Did you hurt anyone?"

Jeremy hung his head. "Nay, Miss Sophia."

"Look at me, Jeremy." Sophia raised his face to hers with a nudge to his chin. "Did you steal anything from Mr. Sharpe?"

Jeremy sucked in a shaky breath. "Nay, miss."

"Then you're not a bad man, Jeremy, no matter what the man said. You haven't done anything wrong. This is all a dreadful mistake. We've come to help you." She took his hand in hers and began to gently chafe his wrists to force the blood to flow.

Jeremy made a hoarse, rusty noise that sounded, incredibly, like a laugh. "Ye shouldna have come 'ere, Miss Sophia. This isn't a good place for ye, and there ain't no help for me now, no ways."

"Don't say that, sweetheart. Lady Clifford would tell you it's never too late for anything, wouldn't she?" More words rushed to Sophia's lips—arguments, denials, reassurances—but she couldn't force them past her lips, because they felt like lies. No matter what Lady Clifford said, the odds were against Jeremy surviving even another few nights in Newgate.

Tears started to her eyes, and it was all she could do to hold them back. Dear God, how could they have done this to Jeremy? How could they do this to anyone? Guilty or innocent, no man deserved to die in this place, like this.

"I didna do it, Miss Sophia. I didna hurt that man." Jeremy caught her hand in his, grasping it weakly. "Ye'll tell Lady Clifford an' Mr. Daniel I didna do it? An' Miss Cecilia and Miss Emma, and Miss Georgiana? Ye'll tell 'em I didna do it, and I'm sorry—"

"Hush, now. They know you didn't do it, sweetheart. No one is angry at you. Now, let's clean you up a bit, because I've brought someone to see you today." Sophia took a clean square of white linen from her pocket, wiped Jeremy's eyes, then gave the cloth to him. "This gentleman here is Lord Gray."

Jeremy turned wide, guileless blue eyes on Lord Gray, then ducked his head to whisper to Sophia, "Ye brought me a lord?"

Sophia smiled. "I did, yes. Lord Gray is an earl."

Instead of cleaning his face, Jeremy used the handkerchief to scrub at a place next to him on the stone floor. When he was finished, he turned bravely back to Lord Gray. "How do ye do, my lord? Will ye sit down?"

Sophia held her breath, dreading the moment when Lord Gray would coldly refuse Jeremy's invitation, but to her surprise he crossed the cell and crouched down next to Jeremy. "Thank you, Jeremy."

"Jeremy," Sophia began, brushing a filthy, ragged clump of hair away from his face. "Lord Gray and I need you tell us as much as you can remember about what happened that night in St. Clement Dane's churchyard."

Jeremy gave her an apprehensive look. "I don't know how to talk to a lord, Miss Sophia."

"You needn't worry, sweetheart. Lord Gray will be good to you. How did you happen to be in St. Clement Dane's churchyard so late that night?" The judge had asked Jeremy the same question at the trial yesterday, but he'd been too frightened to give more than a stammering, incoherent answer.

Jeremy gave her an uncertain look. "I weren't doing nothing wrong. I were just passing through the churchyard."

"All right," Sophia agreed with a reassuring smile. "And where were you before that? What had you been doing?"

Jeremy's brow pinched, as if he were trying hard to remember. "I were at the Turk's Head."

Sophia's stomach dropped. Patrick Dunn had been coming from the Turk's Head the night Peter Sharpe accused him of theft. It *could* be a coincidence—the Turk's Head was a quick walk from St. Clement Dane's Church—but the coincidences were piling up in a way that wasn't coincidental at all. "You mean the coffeehouse on the Strand, Jeremy?"

"Aye, miss."

Sophia exchanged a look with Lord Gray. "Do you go there often, Jeremy?" Jeremy shook his head. "Nay. I were only there that once."

"All right. How did you happen to go there that night?" The Turk's Head was a lively place, popular with London's political set, and always crowded with young radicals and reformers. It was likely Jeremy had just been attracted by the noise, but if someone had lured him there…

Jeremy's lower lip began to wobble. "I-I'm a bad man, Miss Sophia."

"No, Jeremy." Sophia pressed his hand. "I already told you you're not, and I've never lied to you, have I?"

"Nay, Miss Sophia." Tears streaked down Jeremy's cheeks, but he bravely met Sophia's eyes. "There were a lady in there, with yellow hair, an' I thought—she were pretty, Miss Sophia, so I went in, but I didna do anything wrong. I didna touch her. I just wanted to see her closer, like."

"It's all right, Jeremy. Did this lady talk to you? Did she ask you to go into the coffeehouse with her? Invite you to follow her?" Jeremy's mind was as innocent as a child's, but he had a man's body, with all the attendant physical urges. If someone was trying to lure him into the Turk's Head, a pretty lady would be an effective way to do it.

But Jeremy shook his head. "Nay. She didna notice me. There were a lot of people about."

Sophia blew out a breath. It sounded straightforward enough. "That's fine, sweetheart."

"What else happened that night, Jeremy?" Lord Gray peeled his coat off his shoulders and handed it to Sophia. "For the boy," he said gruffly, before he turned back to Jeremy. "You claim you didn't kill Henry Gerrard. If you didn't commit the murder, who did?"

Jeremy's face paled at the word *murder*. "I c-could never…I w-wouldna hurt no one, milord. It were s-someone else who d-d-done it."

"Was it the man in the courtroom yesterday?" Sophia asked, draping the coat over Jeremy's shoulders. She had as low an opinion as one could of Peter Sharpe, but he was a petty, trifling sort of villain. She couldn't quite convince herself he had the savagery to take a man's life.

"Nay, not him. It were…it w-were the other one." Jeremy squeezed his eyes closed, shuddering.

Beside her, Lord Gray stilled. "The other one?"

Sophia's heart began to pound. According to Sharpe's testimony, only himself, Jeremy, and Henry Gerrard had been at St. Clement Dane's at the time of the murder. He hadn't mentioned a word about a fourth man. "How many men were there that night, Jeremy? This is important, love, so think carefully."

Jeremy stared at her with wide, frightened eyes. "Four, miss, if ye count the one as got hurt."

Four? Sophia turned to Lord Gray, speechless with shock.

"Can you tell us who each of the four men were, Jeremy?" Lord Gray asked in a calm, measured tone.

Jeremy thought about it, his face screwed up with concentration. "There were me, and poor Mr. Gerrard as was, and t'other one—the one who said as I'd taken his watch and fob, but I didna, Miss Sophia! I never took nuffin. I didna even get close enough to him to take nuffin, but he set up screaming, an' calling me a thief—"

"The fourth man, Jeremy," Lord Gray said, gently guiding him back to the question at hand. "Did you recognize him?"

Jeremy's shoulders sagged. "Nay, milord. I never saw him a'fore."

"All right. That's all right, Jeremy." Lord Gray was making an obvious effort to curb his urgency. "Can you tell us what he looked like?"

Jeremy leaned forward, eager to tell the story he'd been unable to communicate in the terror of the courtroom. "He were biggish, milord. Not big like me, he being thinner, but tall, like, with black hair."

"Very good. Anything else?"

"I-I'm not sure. Something hit my head, and I can't remember very well—"

Jeremy didn't get any further before succumbing to a hacking cough. Sophia patted and soothed him, but her gaze met Lord Gray's over Jeremy's head, and she saw at once they were thinking the same thing.

Peter Sharpe was a liar, and the fourth man…

The fourth man was a murderer. Whoever he was, he'd killed Henry Gerrard.

Eventually Jeremy's cough faded to a wheeze, and his head fell against the stone wall behind him, his face pale with exhaustion. Sophia waited as long as she dared for him to catch his breath, but she heard a step in the corridor beyond, and knew they were running out of time. "You did very well, sweetheart. Now, tell us one more time everything you remember from that night, but you'll have to do it quickly, all right?"

Jeremy nodded. "I come down the Strand from the Turk's Head. Mr. Sharpe were at the front of the church, sort of wandering about, ye see. I were about to pass through, but Mr. Sharpe started carrying on, calling me a thief, and I were arguing with him when Mr. Gerrard came up, sudden, like. Mr. Sharpe were still shrieking, an' I thought Mr. Gerrard were going to take me up for theft, him being a Runner."

Sophia cast a fearful look over her shoulder toward the corridor. "He didn't, though?"

"Nay. It were strange, Miss Sophia. He didna pay me much mind at all. He turned on Mr. Sharpe and started going on, saying he knew what he were about, knew everything, like, an' then Mr. Gerrard tried to take up Mr. Sharpe, an' that was when t'other man came out of the shadows, like he were there the whole time, and he...he..."

"What did he do, Jeremy?" Sophia whispered, squeezing his hand.

"Quick like that, he s-stabbed poor Mr. Gerrard in the chest. Mr. Gerrard fell down, an' the man, he...he grabbed his head and run the sword across his throat—"

"Sword?" Sophia interrupted. "Mr. Gerrard was killed with a sword, Jeremy?"

"Aye, Miss Sophia."

Not with Jeremy's knife, then, but something much larger. There'd been a fourth man there that night, and he'd vanished into the shadows with the murder weapon.

"An' then there was all blood everywhere," Jeremy said, his voice thick. "An' Mr. Gerrard, he fell onto his back in the dirt, and I...it were so q-quick. I couldna think what do to, but I tried to help him. I got down on my knees next to him and I tried to stop him bleeding, but it were too late. He was blood all over, and there weren't nothing I could do. He made a noise—an awful noise, a kind of gasp, like, and then he weren't breathing no more, and I knew he was dead."

"This all happened in front of St. Clement Dane's Church?" Lord Gray asked, his voice not quite steady.

Jeremy nodded. "Aye. An' then the man, the one what hurt Mr. Gerrard got angry, an' he started carrying on at Mr. Sharpe, an' I don't know, something about me, and Mr. Sharpe getting the wrong man, an' then I felt a terrible pain in my head, an' the next thing I know I wakes up here, an' I've never spoke to a single soul since that night until you come."

Sophia leaned back on her heels, stunned. It was a strange story, but she knew Jeremy was telling them the truth. It was too complicated a tale for him to have concocted on his own, and he was trembling with horror at the memory of it. No one could feign such anguish.

Lord Gray had gone still when Jeremy described what happened to Henry Gerrard, but now he asked, very quietly. "Henry Gerrard, Jeremy. Was he…did he say anything before he died?"

Just talking about that night had sent Jeremy into a panic. His breath was sawing in and out of his chest, but he calmed at the sound of Lord Gray's soft voice. "Nay. He couldna talk, my lord, but he…he…"

"Yes? I'd be grateful, Jeremy, if you could tell me anything more."

"He were looking at the spire of St. Clement Dane's Church when 'e passed, my lord. Just staring up at it, like, and he…he were calm there at the end, just staring up at that spire, an' I thought 'e must a' been a good man, 'cause he died peaceful."

"He *was* a good man." Lord Gray pulled himself to his feet like a man who'd aged a lifetime in the past half hour. "He was the best of men."

Sophia's throat closed at the pain in Lord Gray's voice, and tears stung her eyes. She'd been so caught up with saving Jeremy she hadn't given as much thought as she should have to Henry Gerrard. But now, witnessing Lord Gray's stark grief, she wanted to shrink away from a pain so dark and heavy, so suffocating.

All at once, she understood his desperate need to see someone pay for the crime. Such grief as his couldn't go unanswered. Sophia understood that sort of grief. She'd suffered it herself when her mother died. As young as she'd been at the time, she'd never forgotten the pain of that loss, the burning need for justice, the paralyzing helplessness of not having been able to stop it.

The shame of surviving.

"Jeremy wasn't Sharpe's target," Lord Gray muttered to Sophia. "He mistook Jeremy for someone else."

"Yes, but who?" They had more questions than they did answers.

Jeremy had simply happened to wander through St. Clement Dane's at the wrong time. Sharpe had been lying in wait for someone else to pass through the churchyard, with the intention of leaping out at them and accusing them of theft. He'd seen Jeremy coming from the direction of the Turk's Head, and he'd thought Jeremy was his man.

But why would Sharpe want to frame an innocent man for a crime, and at whose bidding had he done it? Sharpe wasn't clever enough to come up with such a scheme himself. No, he was a mere pawn in something far, far bigger than a random theft.

And how was the Turk's Head involved in this mess? Who was the fourth man? Of all the information they'd learned from Jeremy, the presence of a fourth man at the scene of the crime was the most shocking.

Whoever he was, he was a murderer, and Jeremy was going to hang for his crime.

* * * *

Neither Sophia Monmouth nor Jeremy Ives seemed to remember Tristan was there.

He watched, his chest tight, as she held Jeremy's head to her shoulder, stroking his hair. Tristan could hardly believe this lady with her low, sweet voice and soft eyes was the same sharp-tongued hellion who'd defied him in St. Clement Dane's churchyard—the same calculating thief who'd slipped her locket into Peter Sharpe's pocket as coolly as if she sent innocent men to prison every day.

Except that wasn't what she'd been doing. Peter Sharpe *wasn't* innocent, but Jeremy Ives was. Miss Monmouth hadn't been trying to send an innocent man away. She'd been trying to set an innocent man *free*.

Tristan hadn't gotten a good look at Ives's face at the trial. When they'd entered his cell today, he'd been stunned to find Ives was hardly more than a boy, seventeen at most. He looked to have been a hearty enough lad at one point, but now his flesh hung loose on his wasted frame, and Tristan could see by his stooped shoulders and the tinge of gray in his skin the weeks he'd spent in Newgate had taken a dreadful toll on him.

Before he came here today, Tristan had thought nothing could change his mind about Jeremy Ives's guilt, but he'd been mistaken. There was simply no way Ives could have committed the theft Peter Sharpe had accused him of, much less a murder. Not just because he was simple, although that alone was reason enough to question his guilt. He'd looked at Tristan with that same slack-jawed misery and confusion Tristan had noticed in the courtroom the other day. It wasn't the look of a murderer.

One only had to look at the boy to see he didn't have the viciousness to commit a crime. Ives didn't even know why he was here, or understand in any meaningful way what he'd been accused of. He couldn't make sense of the concept of guilt or innocence. The judge had told him he was a bad man, and so he believed it to be true, even if it contradicted what he also knew to be true—that he wasn't a thief, or a murderer.

Or a liar. The account he'd given of the night at St. Clement Dane's, the tussle with Peter Sharpe, the existence of the fourth man…there wasn't a chance Jeremy Ives could have invented such an extravagant lie.

Tristan dragged a hand down his face. Jeremy's agitation had calmed when he described the last moments of Henry's life, when Henry had been gazing up at the spire. It had comforted Jeremy to know for those few fleeting moments before he died, Henry had been at peace. That said more about the boy's heart than words ever could.

Jeremy Ives didn't know it, but he'd given Tristan a gift today—a single tiny, precious drop of peace in an ocean of rage and despair.

Tristan was grateful to him, so unbearably grateful—

"Time's up, milord." There was a harsh jangling of keys, then Hogg slammed the cell door open with a crash.

Miss Monmouth stiffened at the sound of Hogg's voice. She'd been whispering to Jeremy, but now she rose to her feet. "Jeremy, I'll be right back, sweetheart. I need to have a quick word with Mr. Hogg here. Perhaps Lord Gray would be kind enough to wait with you?"

Tristan's gaze followed her as she and Hogg moved into the corridor, then he turned back to Jeremy, who was watching him with wide eyes. It was clear the boy couldn't think of a single thing to say to an earl, and Tristan was equally at a loss.

"I've never talked to a lord much before," Jeremy said at last, ducking his head shyly.

Tristan's chest tightened. Someone had taught the boy his manners, but they were little enough use to him here. He opened his mouth to say something comforting—what, he hadn't the faintest idea—but before he could get a word out, he heard raised voices coming from just outside the door of Jeremy's cell.

Hogg was standing there with his arms crossed over his chest, and Miss Monmouth was saying something to him, her words quick and urgent. Her shoulders sagged when Hogg's face remained hard, but then she reached into the pocket of her skirt, pulled something out, and held it out to him.

Her silver locket. She stared down at it for a long moment, then offered it to Hogg.

Tristan watched, anger searing his veins as Hogg snatched it up, and turned it over in his hands to test its weight. Finally, he nodded.

A bribe for…something. Something she wanted badly enough she was willing to part with the locket once again. He'd seen the way she looked at it when he held it out to her yesterday, had heard the slight break in her voice when she'd told him it had belonged to her mother. He hardly knew her, and even he could tell how dear it was to her.

She turned her face away as Hogg stuffed it carelessly into his pocket. Tristan got a glimpse of her bleak expression before she schooled her features into the same calm cheerfulness with which she'd greeted Jeremy when they arrived.

That one glimpse was enough.

When she joined Tristan and Jeremy again, she wore a bright, false smile on her lips. "I have good news for you, sweetheart. Mr. Hogg says you don't need to wear the irons anymore, and you're to have some broth, and a blanket."

Tristan stood silently next to her as she related this welcome news, the knot in his chest choking off his breath. She'd traded her locket for better accommodations for Jeremy. She'd given up something dear to her, and gained very little by it. Between the violent treatment from the guards and the disease that infected every corner of this cell, Jeremy Ives was going to die in Newgate. A blanket and some broth wouldn't change that.

Tristan cornered Hogg while Miss Monmouth was bidding goodbye to Jeremy, who, despite the improvement in his circumstances, was weeping piteously. "That locket the lady gave you. I want it back."

Hogg eyed him sullenly. "She change 'er mind?"

"No. *I* did." Tristan moved a step closer, so Hogg could feel the difference in their height, and held out his hand. "Give me the lady's locket."

"Nay. It's too late fer that, milord. She gave it up fair like, and I'm keeping it."

"No, I don't think you are." Tristan voice was soft, but menacing. The wardens at Newgate were some of the most loathsome, corrupt men in London, and Hogg was no exception. There wasn't a drop of honor or compassion in him, but what he lacked in sensibility, he more than made up for in greed.

Tristan drew a handful of guineas from his pocket. "You can take these, hand over the locket, and consider yourself fortunate, or I can take the locket off you myself, and keep the guineas."

Hogg sized him up, then he snatched up the coins, dug around in his pocket, and handed the locket over to Tristan.

"Wise choice." Tristan slid the locket into his waistcoat pocket. "It would be a great pity if I were to discover young Mr. Ives didn't receive his broth and blanket, or has been mistreated in any way. You don't want me as your enemy, Hogg. Be sure you keep your end of the bargain, or I'll haunt your every bloody step."

Hogg's face drained of color. Satisfied, Tristan strode back across the cell, where Miss Monmouth had managed to calm Jeremy to some degree. The lad's pale blue eyes were still swimming with tears, but he offered Tristan a wobbly smile. "Goodbye, my lord. I thank ye for coming to see me today."

Tristan managed a smile and a goodbye for Jeremy, but the boy's words echoed in his head as he and Miss Monmouth followed Hogg back through the dank stone passageways and into the turnkey's lodge.

Thank ye for coming to see me today.

For all the good it had done, Tristan thought as they emerged into the fresh air, leaving the hell that was Newgate behind them.

For all the good any of it had done.

Chapter Ten

It was some time after they returned to the carriage before either Sophia or Lord Gray said a word. The minutes ticked by, but Lord Gray didn't instruct his coachman to drive, and Sophia, who was staring blindly out the window, didn't ask him to.

It had taken every bit of her strength to leave Jeremy's cell just now—every bit of her forbearance not to collapse with fury and grief when she saw what they'd done to him. She'd been on the verge of sinking to her knees with each step through that endless, winding maze of stone and iron. She gripped the folds of her cloak in cold, numb fingers, her eyes dry despite the misery lodged in her throat. The brutality of Jeremy's fate, the injustice of it was too profound for tears.

"I believe you, Miss Monmouth."

Lord Gray's voice was so quiet Sophia might not have heard him but for the stillness inside the carriage. She turned away from the window and found him staring straight ahead, his face strangely blank.

"About Jeremy Ives," he clarified, when she didn't reply. "He's no murderer. He didn't kill Henry. I...don't know who did."

He turned to face her then, and Sophia's breath hitched in her throat at his lost expression, the bleak hopelessness in his eyes. She hadn't known Henry Gerrard. She'd grieved for him still, even shed tears over his fate, but she hadn't truly understood the depth of the loss of him until she saw it in Lord Gray's eyes.

Henry Gerrard had a life, and friends and family. How could she have forgotten, even for a single moment, Jeremy wasn't the only victim of this crime? She knew better than anyone a tragic loss, especially a violent one, couldn't be kept inside a clenched fist. It couldn't be contained. It was like a contagion, infecting everyone it touched.

"My mother was murdered," Sophia whispered, then froze, shocked she'd said the words aloud. She never spoke of her mother, not to anyone, and she was choosing to start with Lord Gray?

It seemed so.

"I saw it happen. I was hiding in a cupboard, and saw it through the keyhole." It hadn't been the first time she'd been in that cupboard, or even the first time a man had knocked her mother down.

But this had been different. This time, her mother hadn't gotten up again.

"There was...a great deal of blood." Sophia didn't look at Lord Gray as she spoke, but she was aware he'd gone still beside her. "I was very young at the time, but I remember trying to staunch the blood." Even at seven years old, Sophia knew what to do when there was blood.

Bits of wadded linen for blood, and kisses for bruising...

It hadn't worked, of course, but she'd stayed there for hours, crooning to her mother and stroking the matted dark hair until the light in the window faded, then lightened—once, then again, and again a third time. Three days. By the time Lady Clifford and Daniel came, her mother's body had begun to decay.

Sophia had fled back into the cupboard when she heard their steps on the splintered boards in the hallway. Years later, Lady Clifford told her they'd known she was there because she'd left a trail of bloody footprints from her mother's body to the cupboard door.

Sophia risked a glance at Lord Gray. His stern face had softened, and his gray eyes had gone dark with shared grief. "Will you...will you tell me a little about Mr. Gerrard?"

His throat worked, and without thinking, Sophia reached across the seat and took his hand. He jerked in surprise at the touch of her fingers, but he didn't pull away. "He was...*alive*. I know that sounds foolish, but no other word fits quite as well as that one. He loved to laugh." He made a helpless gesture with his hand. "It's been weeks, and even now, I still can't believe he's gone. It seems incredible a life like his could end so quickly, with so little fanfare, like...snuffing out a candle."

Sophia gave the long fingers in her hand a hesitant squeeze. "How did you know him?"

"The three of us—myself, Lord Lyndon, and Henry—were at Eton together, and later Oxford." A sad smile lifted one corner of his lips. "His high spirits got us into no end of trouble, but he always managed to talk his way out of being sent down. He had a good heart. No one could stay angry at him for long."

Sophia nodded, waited.

"His son, Samuel, is just two years old. His widow, Abigail...all she and Henry wanted was to be together, to watch their son grow into a man." Lord Gray trailed off with a shake of his head that said more than words could have. "They should have had that chance. None of them deserved this."

"No, they didn't." How wrong it was, that a man like Henry Gerrard should suffer such a tragic fate, while men like Peter Sharpe went about their lives unscathed.

Lord Gray met her gaze. "Jeremy Ives doesn't deserve it, either."

Sophia's heart twisted at his words. Until he said them aloud, she didn't realize she'd ached to hear them. Not from Lord Gray, exactly, but ever since this nightmare began, she'd been waiting for someone, anyone from outside the Clifford School to listen to her, and believe her.

Believe Jeremy.

The tears she'd been holding back stung her eyes. They didn't fall, but Lord Gray saw them. He brushed his fingers under her eyes and caught the moisture on his fingertip. It was the last thing Sophia expected him to do, and from the stunned look on his face, the last thing he expected of himself.

They stared at each other, tension crackling between them, until Lord Gray broke their gaze. He cleared his throat. "I intend to speak to Sampson Willis about Jeremy. He may be able to do something to help him."

Sophia nodded, but she already knew it wouldn't do any good. The courts had pronounced Jeremy guilty. Sampson Willis wouldn't challenge the verdict, and even if he did, it would come too late to save Jeremy.

But she didn't say so. There was no point.

Yesterday she'd accused Lord Gray of not caring if an innocent man were sent to the gibbet, but she'd been wrong. He *did* care. Perhaps he even cared as much as she did, but he was still the Ghost of Bow Street. He still had faith in men like Sampson Willis. He still believed in justice, in courts and witnesses, in magistrates and scaffolds.

Perhaps she'd believed in those things once, too, but if she ever had, it was so long ago it was a mere echo in her memory. But perhaps once, before her mother's death, there'd been a time when she believed in justice. She'd been too young to call it that then, of course, but when her mother had promised her good little girls were rewarded for their behavior, Sophia had believed her.

She'd been a good little girl, once upon a time, but it hadn't made any difference. She'd still been that little girl who'd torn strips of linen from the hem of her mother's petticoat to try and bandage her head. She'd still ended up in a dismal, empty room, her pinafore soaked with her dead mother's blood.

Somehow, it was this image of her childhood self, still young and naïve enough to believe a bandage could heal every wound, that haunted Sophia. A child, crooning broken fragments of lullabies to her murdered mother, waiting for her to wake up.

Good little girls didn't get rewards. Justice didn't have anything to do with goodness, any more than it did with evil. So, there was really no point in being good at all, was there?

That was the lesson Sophia took with her on the day of her mother's death, when she left the only life she'd ever known behind. A small, hard kernel of knowledge, buried deep inside the layers of her heart.

It was a lesson she never forgot.

But she wouldn't try and explain this to Lord Gray. He'd never learned that lesson, because he'd never had to. For him, one made a wrong right again by taking the matter to a magistrate.

There was nothing Sampson Willis could do for Jeremy. Sophia looked down at the hand still cradled in hers and thought about the scars on Lord Gray's knuckles. She'd been surprised to find he hid old wounds under his fine kid gloves. Perhaps she shouldn't have been. Perhaps she should have realized no one, not even an earl, escaped without scars.

Lord Gray was a better man than she'd accused him of being, but he wasn't the man to save Jeremy. No, she'd have to do that herself.

"I'll take you home." Lord Gray withdrew his hand from hers and rapped on the roof of the carriage. "No. 26 Maddox Street, Platt," he murmured when his coachman appeared.

Platt bowed, and a moment later the carriage started with a lurch and they were off, the dome of St. Paul's Cathedral looming over them, and Newgate Prison at their backs.

* * * *

"Sophia, are you listening?" Cecilia paused in the middle of her dramatic reading and laid the book across her lap. "The Marquis de Montalt is scheming to make Adeline his wife."

"Not his wife, his *mistress*. He's already married, if you recall. He hasn't any business marrying Adeline, but even so, he isn't the sort to take rejection well. Next thing you know he'll be vowing to murder her, and she'll be forced to flee the abbey." Emma, who was lounging on Sophia's bed, shifted to rest her head in Sophia's lap. "Are you not diverted, Sophia?"

Sophia sighed. "Adeline won't become the Marquis's mistress." Mrs. Radcliffe's heroines never became mistresses, nor were they ever murdered, for all that they spent most of their time running through dark forests, fleeing from dagger-wielding dukes and sleeping in haunted abbeys. "She's in love with Theodore."

"He's in love with her, too. Listen to this. *'She is yet, I fear, in the power of the Marquis,' said Theodore, sighing deeply. 'O God!—these chains!'—and he threw an agonizing glance upon them.'* Theodore's falling into paroxysms of grief and despair. Those bits are always good. Don't you think so, Sophia?" Cecilia peered hopefully over the top of the book.

"Clara's about to weep on Adeline's bosom, and a few passages later, Adeline is going to start weeping as well, so you see, everyone is shrieking and weeping. Love and honor will prevail, of course, but there will be some delicious torture and suffering before then." Georgiana shot Sophia an anxious glance. "Doesn't that sound delightful?"

Love and honor always triumphed in Mrs. Radcliffe's novels, and villains always confessed their wrongdoings. It was one of the things Sophia loved best about her books. There was something reassuring in everything wrapping up so tidily.

But with Jeremy facing the noose and the true villain content to see him swing, Sophia couldn't lose herself in the story. "Of course, it does. I suppose I'm just a bit weary tonight."

Cecilia flipped ahead a few pages, skimmed to the end of the chapter, then set the book aside with a sigh. "Adeline's going to retire to her bedchamber and fall so ill she won't be able to quit it again. Nothing unusual in that, really. Why don't we stop for tonight, and pick the book back up again tomorrow?"

Nods and murmurs of assent followed. Quiet fell over the room as they each became lost in their own thoughts, until Cecilia roused herself and crossed the room to join Emma and Sophia on Sophia's bed. Georgiana piled on next, and they all lay there together on the crumpled coverlet.

"What does Lady Clifford say?" Georgiana asked at last.

Her friends hadn't asked Sophia about Jeremy. She could see they wanted very much to know how he did, but they knew her well enough to see her emotions were too raw to speak of it with any composure yet, and they'd resisted quizzing her.

Sophia had been feigning interest in Cecilia's reading, but now she let herself collapse against her pillow. "Nothing at all yet. She said we'd talk later, and sent me upstairs."

When she'd returned from Newgate, Sophia had found Lady Clifford waiting for her in the parlor. She'd braced herself for a painful discussion of Jeremy's pitiful condition, but instead, Lady Clifford had studied her for a moment, then murmured, "Go on up and see your friends, dearest. We'll talk later." She patted Sophia's cheek and sent her up to her bedchamber, where Cecilia, Emma, and Georgiana had welcomed her with soft exclamations and a tangle of enfolding arms.

"She has a plan, that much you can be sure of." Georgiana plucked up a lock of Sophia's hair and began plaiting it. "She always does."

A small spark of hope flared in Sophia's breast. Surely, Georgiana was right. Lady Clifford would never stand by and allow Jeremy to hang. Surely, she had a plan to save him, only...

The feeble hope sputtered and died. Nothing less than a prison escape would do Jeremy any good, and no one escaped Newgate.

"Jack Sheppard escaped Newgate," Emma said, as if she'd read Sophia's mind.

He had, yes, but he'd been sparse and lithe, with enough strength to climb up a chimney and through a ceiling into the chamber above. Jeremy couldn't even rise to his feet on his own, much less scale a chimney—

A soft knock on the door interrupted these musings, and Lady Clifford poked her head into the room. "Good evening, my loves. Ah, I see you've all taken good care of Sophia, just as I knew you would. Sophia, dearest, are you fit to come downstairs with me? Daniel and I would like to have a word with you."

Sophia rose from the bed. "Yes, my lady. Quite fit."

Emma, Cecilia, and Georgiana also rose as if to follow them, but Lady Clifford held up her hand. "Just Sophia this time, dears. I know you want to help, but this is a rather delicate matter, and it's best if we keep as few of us involved in it as possible."

The four girls traded hopeful glances. This was it, then. Lady Clifford *did* have a plan to rescue Jeremy, and from the sounds of it, it was a promising one. If her ladyship didn't think it stood a chance of succeeding, she wouldn't feel the need to keep it private.

"Come along, then." She held out a hand to Sophia, but paused at the door to throw an amused glance over her shoulder. "Remember, my dears, there's to be no reading any Radcliffe until Sophia returns. Those are the Society's rules, after all, and Clifford students always respect the rules, don't we?"

Emma muffled a snort. "Of *course,* we do, my lady."

"Very good, dears." Lady Clifford closed the bedchamber door and took Sophia's arm. They made their way downstairs, where Daniel was waiting for them in Lady Clifford's private sitting room. His hard, dark gaze roamed over Sophia's face. "Gray minded his manners today?"

Sophia managed a smile for Daniel, despite the nerves churning in her belly. "He did, yes. He agreed to take me to Newgate with very little fuss, and now he's spoken to Jeremy himself, he believes he's innocent. He was kind to Jeremy. He even gave him his coat."

Daniel raised one thick eyebrow, and Sophia's cheeks heated.

Was she...defending Lord Gray?

"Aye? Is he going to do anything about it?"

"He's bringing the matter to the Bow Street magistrate," Sophia muttered, knowing as she did how scornful Daniel would be at that answer.

"Sampson Willis?" Daniel let out a harsh laugh. "May as well do nothing."

"Lord Gray is a decent man, particularly as far as Bow Street Runners go, but I think we can all agree we can't leave this matter in his hands. He's well-intentioned, but he's a bit too, ah...shall we say *ethically rigid,* to be of much help to us." Lady Clifford waved Sophia to a chair, then took a seat across from her. Daniel remained standing, with one arm braced against the mantel.

"Now then, Sophia. How did you find our Jeremy?"

"Worse than you can possibly imagine. Another day or two at most, and he'll succumb to the appalling conditions at Newgate." Sophia winced at her own bluntness, but this was no time to mince words. "Whatever is to be done, it must be done at once."

"It will be. Tonight, in fact. We've come up with a way to get him out, but we'll need as much information as you can give us, starting with where he is. Once we're inside, we'll need to remove him quickly."

"He's in the dungeons under the turnkeys' lodge." Sophia had paid close attention when Hogg had taken them out, and she now gave a precise description of the route they'd taken from the entrance through the maze of passageways. "Even with my directions, finding him may be tricky," she warned. "It would be much easier with a guide."

"Is he locked in irons?" Daniel asked.

"He was, but Lord Gray insisted the guard remove them." She didn't mention she'd traded her locket to ensure the irons didn't reappear. "His keeper, a Mr. Hogg, is quite susceptible to the flash of a coin."

"Is he, indeed? That *is* good news." Lady Clifford glanced at Daniel, who gave her a quick nod. "Very good, dearest. What else can you tell us?"

"Jeremy's not in any condition to walk, or even to stand on his own." Sophia shuddered at the thought of the wreck her healthy, strapping boy had been reduced to. "He'll need to be carried."

Daniel grunted. "I expected as much. How's the lad's mind? Is he confused? Likely to resist me?"

Sophia thought of the heartbreaking gratitude on Jeremy's face when he'd seen her today, the way he'd hung on her when she had to leave him. "He's confused, yes, and scared witless, but there's no question he'll do as you say. He'll be tremendously glad to see you, Daniel."

The first time Sophia had laid eyes on Daniel Brixton, her entire body had gone numb with terror. She'd been a child, yes, but he was still the most forbidding man she'd ever seen, with his black hair, huge hands, and tight, unsmiling mouth. But Jeremy was a decided favorite with Daniel, and even his harsh face softened slightly at Sophia's words. "And me him, lass."

There wasn't much more Sophia could tell them. Lady Clifford asked another question or two about Mr. Hogg, but she looked anxious as she studied Sophia's face, and it wasn't long before she sent her back to her bedchamber with strict orders to go directly to bed.

Sophia wasn't in the habit of challenging Lady Clifford's commands, but in this instance, she didn't go to her bed, or even to her bedchamber. Instead she wandered into the dark library tucked into the back corner of the house. She remained there for a long time, staring out at the tiny terrace and handkerchief-sized garden.

She was still standing there much later when she heard the front door close behind Daniel. She closed her eyes and leaned her forehead against the glass doors, her lips moving in a silent prayer that tonight would be the end of Jeremy's nightmare.

Of all their nightmares.

Somehow, though, without Sophia being aware of it, her thoughts turned from Jeremy to Lord Gray. She couldn't forget the anguish in his voice, his grief when he'd spoken of Henry Gerrard.

Jeremy might yet survive his ordeal, but there would be no rescue for Henry Gerrard. No triumph of good over evil for his son, Samuel, or his wife, Abigail.

Sophia didn't doubt Lord Gray truly believed Jeremy was innocent. She'd seen the shock on his face when Jeremy had told them his story today. He'd been kind to Jeremy, compassionate toward him. She thought of Lord Gray's coat resting on Jeremy's shoulders, and her breath tangled in her throat.

Lord Gray didn't wish to see Jeremy hang for another man's crime any more than Sophia did, but there was little chance he'd approve of the way they'd chosen to right this wrong. Tomorrow, when he woke up and discovered Jeremy had been taken from Newgate, he'd be furious. Disappointed, even. So much so, he'd likely never wish to see her again.

Sophia rested her hands on the glass, pressing her fingertips against the cool, hard surface. Jeremy was the only important thing here—the only one who mattered. In the end, it should make no difference to her what Lord Gray thought.

It shouldn't, but it did.

Chapter Eleven

There'd been no ghosts last night. No blood, no daggers, and no murder. Neither gravestones nor confessionals nor white marble crypts had haunted Tristan's dreams. Even Henry, who died anew every time Tristan closed his eyes, hadn't appeared in his nightmares last night.

No, last night he'd been haunted by shifting images of an emaciated boy with dull, frightened blue eyes. His thin wrists were locked in irons, but instead of Newgate he was imprisoned in a while marble crypt, and with him a lady wearing a silver locket, tears glittering on her lashes.

It wasn't the grisliest of the nightmares he'd had, but it disturbed Tristan like no other nightmare before it. He was still in bed, propped up on a stack of pillows, and he might have remained there for most of the morning if Tribble hadn't appeared with a note from Lord Lyndon.

Gray,

Jeremy Ives is dead. He died in Newgate Prison last night, or so we're meant to believe. There's some mischief afoot, Gray, and your pixie is involved in it.

Lyndon

Tristan stared down at the note, his lassitude giving way to shock and then anger as his gaze darted over the paper. Miss Monmouth, involved in some sort of mischief regarding Jeremy Ives? Of course, she was bloody involved in it.

He'd seen the despair on her face when she'd knelt beside Jeremy yesterday, chained to the floor of his cell as if he was some kind of wild animal. He'd seen the glitter of fury in her eyes, the thrust of her chin, her cold determination. How had he not anticipated something of this sort would happen?

Ives, dead? No. Tristan would wager every guinea he had Ives was still alive when he was taken from his cell. But how could they have managed it? He'd been as deep in the bowels of Newgate as one could get, locked behind thick iron doors hidden at the end of an endless stone passageway. One didn't simply wander into Newgate, then wander out again with the prisoner of their choosing.

Jeremy Ives had been hanging on to life by a fraying thread. It would surprise no one to find out he'd succumbed to the brutality of Newgate, just as so many others had before him. It would vex the citizens of London he'd escaped the noose—they did like to see their murderers hang—but no one would question Ives's death.

No one, that is, who didn't know Lady Clifford. If anyone could steal a condemned murderer right from under the noses of Newgate's guards, it was *her*. No doubt Daniel Brixton was also involved.

Brixton, and Sophia Monmouth.

She'd used *him* to do it. The tempting curve of her lips when she'd smiled at him yesterday, all that nonsense about his scar, the sweet way she'd taken his hand in his carriage and asked him to tell her about Henry—had it all been just a ploy to distract him so she could gain access to Newgate and plot Ives's escape? His instincts had screamed at him not to trust her, but he'd done so anyway, and for no better reason than a pair of pretty green eyes.

She'd fooled him. *Him*, the Ghost of Bow Street.

Tristan crushed Lyndon's note in his fist and tossed it aside. He snatched up the *Times* Tribble had left on the table beside his bed, and there it was, right on the first page. It wasn't much—just a short notice that the notorious murderer Jeremy Ives had died in Newgate Prison the previous night.

Whatever Lady Clifford had done, it was plausible enough to convince the papers Ives was really dead. The rest of London would follow suit, particularly those who'd attended his trial and seen for themselves how feeble he was. There would be no public outcry, no demand for his return. Miss Monmouth and her conspirators had done the impossible.

They'd committed the perfect crime.

Tristan threw the coverlet aside, dragged on a pair of breeches, and tugged a shirt over his head. He had to see Lyndon at once, and after that he had a call to pay at the Clifford School. If he had his way, he'd wring a confession from Sophia Monmouth, and then—

He paused, his foot hovering over his boot.

Then what? An arrest? Could he truly bring himself to arrest her? He could still see the despair in her eyes, still hear her soft voice, her tenderness as she'd soothed Jeremy. And Jeremy himself, an innocent man—a boy—starved, beaten, and chained up like a dog…

Tristan's boot slipped from his hand and dropped to the floor.

Had she truly had any other choice? If it had been Henry in that cell, or Lyndon, wouldn't Tristan have done the same in her place? Did saving her innocent friend make her a criminal?

Tristan dragged a hand through his hair, his jaw ticking.

Damn her. Damn her to hell.

This wasn't complicated, no matter how much she tried to make it so. She'd helped a condemned murderer escape from Newgate Prison, and she'd implicated Tristan in the crime. Perhaps he could understand her reasons, but she'd still broken the law. At the very least, he'd have the truth from her.

He snatched up his boot, shoved his foot into it, and stalked towards the door of his bedchamber, shouting for Tribble to see his carriage readied.

He'd do what he must, green eyes be damned—

"Lord Lyndon is here, Lord Gr—"

"For God's sake, Tribble. Do you suppose he can't see me for himself? Step aside, man, and let me through."

Tribble stood in the doorway with Lyndon right on his heels, huffing impatiently. "It's all right, Tribble." Tristan waved Lyndon in, then motioned to Tribble to leave and close the door behind him.

Lyndon frowned after him. "That manservant of yours has gotten awfully high and mighty of late—"

"How do you know there's mischief afoot?" Tristan wasn't in any sort of mood to quibble over servants. "It's not difficult to imagine Ives is really dead, given his condition."

"No, but he's not dead, for all that. I've got a man or two at Newgate, just as you have. Damn clever bit of work, how she got Ives out, but then Lady Clifford and her collection of sorceresses know how to execute a crime."

Tristan didn't argue that point. Sophia Monmouth had all the behaviors of an accomplished criminal. He'd known that since he'd spied her on Everly's roof. He should have listened to his instincts from the first.

"Seems Ives was taken out in a coffin well before sunrise this morning, but curiously enough, not a single soul saw his corpse aside from one guard, and what do you suppose has happened to him?"

"Disappeared," Tristan muttered through clenched teeth. "Who was it?"

"Hogg."

Tristan had been pacing in front of the fireplace, but now he stilled. Of course, it was Hogg. Who else would it be? He may as well have handed Hogg to Miss Monmouth on a silver platter.

"Hogg's fond of a gold coin, from what I understand," Lyndon said. "Newgate Prison's secure enough, until you bribe a guard."

Tristan muttered a curse. He'd shown Miss Monmouth precisely which guard to approach with that bribe. "Jeremy Ives is proclaimed dead. Someone shows up at Newgate with a coffin and takes his corpse away, but no one aside from Hogg sees either the dead body or who took it, and now Hogg is gone. Do I have that right?"

"Yes. I'd hazard a guess Hogg isn't returning anytime soon, either. Lady Clifford has the means to make it worth his while to stay far away from London."

Tristan had heard enough. He snatched up his coat and threw it on over his shirt, not pausing to bother with a cravat or waistcoat. This wasn't a social call.

"Off to the Clifford School?" Lyndon asked, following Tristan from his bedchamber. "I'll go with you, if you like."

Tristan shook his head. "No, thank you, Lyndon."

He had quite a lot to say to Miss Monmouth, and all of it for her ears alone.

* * * *

Tristan's lips twisted as he gazed up at No. 26 Maddox Street. The utterly unremarkable stone steps led to the utterly unremarkable front door of an utterly unremarkable house.

But inside? A half-dozen or more criminals, hiding in plain sight.

He marched up the steps, pausing on the landing. It wasn't calling hours, but his fist met the door with the sort of vehemence that made it clear he wouldn't be denied entrance, no matter what time it was.

After a short wait, a lady with tight gray curls opened the door. Tristan stared down at her, some of his righteous anger fading. A part of him wanted to rage at anyone associated with the Clifford School, but it was difficult to shout at a lady so tiny he could see the top of her head.

"Good morning, Lord Gray." She stepped back from the door and ushered him into the hallway. "Please do come inside."

Tristan raised an eyebrow. He'd never laid eyes on her before, but she knew who he was, and she didn't look at all surprised to see him on the doorstep, despite the early hour.

There was no sign of Lady Clifford, or, thankfully, Daniel Brixton.

He stepped into the entryway. "I've come to see Miss Monmouth. Indeed, I insist upon it." Saying her name made anger surge through him again, but he could hardly give vent to it while he was looming over this small lady like the hulking monster from every child's nightmare.

Why were all the ladies at the Clifford School so tiny?

She answered him with a serene smile. "Of course, my lord. Miss Monmouth has been expecting you."

Yes. No doubt she has.

"This way, if you would, my lord. Ladies," she added. "If you'd be so good as to return to your work, I'd be grateful, indeed."

Tristan heard a shuffle of feet above his head, and looked up to find three pairs of eyes gazing down at him from the third-floor landing. The three young ladies he recalled from his previous visit were measuring his progress down the hallway as if calculating how quickly they could drop down onto his back from their places on the landing if he dared to threaten their friend.

Miss Monmouth wasn't the only one who was expecting him.

He followed the little gray-haired lady down the hallway and into the elegant drawing room he'd been shown into at his last visit. A tray of refreshments waited on a table, a cheerful fire was roaring in the grate, and Lady Clifford's stout little pug was snoring contentedly on a rug beside it. It was all very comfortable and proper, a glossy veneer of respectability concealing a multitude of sins.

"I'm Mrs. Browning, Lord Gray. I'm Lady Clifford's housekeeper. If you require anything, please don't hesitate to ring the bell." Mrs. Browning punctuated this polite speech with a nod and left the drawing room, closing the door behind her.

Tristan didn't spare her another glance. His gaze was fixed on Sophia Monmouth, who was waiting for him in front of the fireplace, as still as a marble statue, with her hands clasped neatly in front of her. "Good morning, Lord Gray."

She was wearing a dark green gown today. The muted color shouldn't have suited her, but every color seemed to flatter Miss Monmouth, even the dull, somber ones. This gown emphasized the unusual color of her eyes, turning them a soft, mossy green.

Tristan didn't bother with pleasantries. "How did you do it?"

Her expression didn't change, but her shoulders stiffened. "Do what, my lord?"

"Don't," Tristan grated. He stalked across the room to stand before her, so close a deep breath bathed him in the seductive scent of honeysuckle. "Don't pretend you don't know what I'm referring to. It demeans both of us."

She lifted one slender shoulder in a shrug. "I beg your pardon, my lord. I'm afraid I don't understand you."

"I think you do, Miss Monmouth. I think you understand me perfectly." Tristan edged even closer to her, studying her face for the faintest hint of guilt, the merest twitch of consciousness, but there was nothing. "Very well, if that's how you wish to proceed. I'm speaking of Jeremy Ives's miraculous escape from Newgate."

"Escape?" Her smooth brow furrowed. "Jeremy Ives is dead, Lord Gray. His death was announced in the *Times* this morning. Surely you saw it?"

"I saw it, yes," Tristan bit out. "Saw it, and knew it at once for the lie it is."

Her chest rose and fell as her breathing quickened, but otherwise she showed no signs of agitation. "Lie? I don't know what you mean."

Tristan's lips twisted, but it was a cold mockery of a smile. "Come now, Miss Monmouth. Of course, you do. Tell me, was the coffin your idea? I don't deny it was an ingenious one. Jeremy Ives was in no condition to rise to his feet on his own. You sidestepped that problem neatly enough."

She said nothing, just stared over his shoulder, her green eyes blank.

All at once, Tristan couldn't bear her silence, her icy composure a moment longer. "If you're going to lie to me, you'll do me the courtesy of looking me in the eye, Miss Monmouth." He caught her chin in his hand and turned her face toward his. He wasn't rough, but he wouldn't let her look away from him, either. "You owe me your gratitude. Aren't you going to thank me for my part in Jeremy's escape?"

"Your part? I don't under—"

"You don't understand? Curious, that a clever, clever young lady like yourself should be at such a loss this morning. I gave you Hogg, Miss Monmouth. If it weren't for me, you never would have known which guard to bribe."

"Mr. Hogg? You mean the guard from yesterday? Has someone bribed him?" She took care to keep her voice flat, but her green eyes darted away from his.

"No. Don't look away from me." He tightened his fingers on her chin, forcing her to meet his gaze. "You've implicated me in this debacle. Have you forgotten I brought you to Newgate, and called Hogg to your notice? Should news of our visit to Ives reach the magistrate, they may choose to conduct an investigation. Don't suppose they won't discover we were there, and spoke to Ives."

Her chin rose. "There will be no investigation, my lord, and even if there was, you didn't commit any crime. According to your own words, you have nothing to fear from the law if you're innocent."

"What would you know about innocence?" He swept a hard gaze over her, lingering on the pulse fluttering under the smooth skin of her throat. "You seem nervous, Miss Monmouth. Committing a crime does tend to agitate people, but then this isn't your first crime, is it?"

"It's curious, Lord Gray. I recall you telling me just the other day Peter Sharpe hadn't been convicted of a crime, and therefore was an innocent man." She spread her hands wide. "I haven't been convicted of any crime. Am I not to be allowed the same courtesy as Mr. Sharpe?"

Tristan tipped her chin higher, and brushed his thumb over her cheek. "You look innocent, with that delicate face and those wide green eyes, but you're not, are you?"

The eyes in question flashed with temper. "Do you truly believe *you* know anything about guilt and innocence, Lord Gray? You *know* Jeremy isn't guilty of any crime, yet even knowing that, you still believe the courtroom the best arbiter of justice."

"You're right, Miss Monmouth. I *do* believe it. How else do you propose to judge guilt and innocence? With your intuition?" He released her chin, but he didn't step back, and she refused to back away, either. Her body was nearly flush against his, so close he could sense her trembling, feel the warmth of her through his clothing.

"It truly is that simple for you, isn't it, Lord Gray? I envy you. How comfortable it must be, to live in a world of absolutes."

"Is that how you see it? How strange." He dragged his finger over the hollow of her throat, fighting the urge to close his eyes at the sensation of her warm, soft skin under his rough fingertip. "I would have thought it was far more comfortable to determine guilt and innocence according to whim, as you do."

Her lips parted at his touch, and God, he was so furious with her, yet at the same time he was desperate to kiss her, to sink his hands into her thick dark hair and still her for his mouth. A low moan of lust and despair threatened to burst from his lips. He shouldn't want her like this, but he could no longer deny he *did* want her. That pert, pink mouth drove him to such madness he didn't know whether to arrest her, or devour her.

Whatever this strange pull was between them, she felt it, too. He knew it by the way the color flooded her cheeks, the flash in her eyes, the wild throb of her pulse under his finger.

She raised balled fists to his chest, but she didn't push him away. "Did it ever occur to you, *my lord*, that the laws work best for those who wrote them and enforce them? Do you suppose they work for the men and women in Seven Dials? For the ragged street urchins? The debtors locked up in Newgate?"

Her fingers went to her neck, and Tristan knew instinctively she was grasping for the locket that was no longer there. For reasons he didn't understand, he found it unbearable to watch the panicked movement of her hands. "Don't. Stop it, Sophia." He seized her wrists and dragged them away from her throat.

"You saw Jeremy, Tristan." Her voice broke on his Christian name. "You saw what they'd done to him. Is the law working for him? Do you fool yourself into thinking he'll see justice? A man who doesn't even understand the crime of which he's accused, condemned and sentenced to die. Is that justice?"

It was true. Every word she said about Jeremy was true. Justice wasn't perfect. It never would be, yet it was all they had, and it served more people than it hurt. Tristan leaned over her, and let his forehead touch hers. "I don't fool myself, no, but the answer to an injustice isn't another crime, Sophia. Would you free every prisoner at Newgate?"

"No! Just one. The one I know to be innocent."

"If everyone in London did the same, what then?" He released her wrists to cup her face in his hands. "Flawed justice is preferable to no justice, Sophia."

"For some people, there's little difference between the two." Her green eyes were dark with anger, but her lips were soft, and still parted for him, and there was nothing more to say, nothing he could do but cover her mouth with his own.

This wasn't a soft, tentative exploration. It wasn't gentle. Tristan took her lips hard, his tongue insistent, demanding she take him into the slick warmth of her mouth. She opened to him at once, meeting him stroke for stroke, the kiss angry and desperate, each demanding the other yield and both of them resisting, their lips clinging together in a battle of wills that threatened to drive Tristan to the edge of his sanity.

He wasn't a man who allowed his passions to overrule his logic, but he hadn't counted on Sophia Monmouth, the wild temptation of her. He was on the edge of tumbling into a madness where he dragged her to the settee in the middle of Lady Clifford's drawing room, hiked up her skirts, and covered her body with his...

"No." Tristan tore his mouth from hers with a gasp.

They stood there staring at each other, both of them panting for breath, until he forced himself to turn away from the temptation of her swollen pink lips. He dragged in a few calming breaths until he subdued the demands of his body, then he turned back to her. "Where's Ives, Sophia?"

"He's safe," she whispered. "Safe at last."

Tristan dragged a hand through his hair. "Tell me where he is. For your own good, you need to tell me where you've taken him."

Her face grew as hard as stone, but underneath her coldness she was trembling, her chest heaving as she struggled for breath. "I don't know what you mean, Lord Gray. I haven't taken him anywhere. I told you. Jeremy Ives is dead."

Tristan knew she'd say no more about Ives, but he wasn't yet finished with her. "None of this was really about Sharpe, was it? It wouldn't surprise me to discover I was your target all along."

"My target?" She looked puzzled for an instant, but then her face drained of color. "No! It wasn't...you weren't—"

"You must have realized only I would be able to see you on the roof of Lord Everly's pediment." Tristan had promised himself he wouldn't touch her again, but his hand seemed to move without his consent, reaching for a loose lock of her hair. He rubbed it between his fingers, his gaze holding hers. "Perhaps this was about me from the start."

She opened her mouth, but he dropped her hair and held up his hand before a word could pass her lips. "No. I don't want to hear any more." Because a part of him was afraid she could make him believe anything she said.

"Tristan—"

"No. This ends here."

For her, it *did* end here. Sophia's part in this business was done. Jeremy Ives was innocent of the crime of which he'd been convicted, but he was free now, and all of London believed him to be dead. It had all ended just as she'd hoped it would.

But it hadn't ended for Tristan. It would never end for him until Henry's murderer was swinging from the end of a rope. Henry had been a good man, a just man, and a loyal friend. He and his wife and son deserved justice.

But none of that had anything to do with Sophia Monmouth. "You should be pleased, Sophia. Jeremy is safe. Isn't that what you wanted all along?"

"I don't know," she whispered. "I don't know what I want."

Tristan had no answer for that, other than that it didn't matter what either of them wanted. He didn't say it. Instead, he reached into his coat pocket and drew out her locket. He cradled it in his hand for a moment, warming the silver against his skin, then he held it out to her. "I took this from Hogg yesterday. I thought you'd want it back. Take it."

Her hand trembled as she reached for it. He dropped it into her palm. "There's nothing more that needs to be said between us, and no reason for us ever to meet again."

She said nothing, just closed her fingers tightly around the locket.

"Goodbye, Miss Monmouth." Tristan offered her a formal bow, then went through the door without another word, and without a backward glance.

The housekeeper, Miss Browning, was nowhere to be seen, but the three young ladies were still hanging over the edge of the railing on the landing. Their eyes followed him as he came down the hallway and let himself out the front door.

They might as well look their fill now, because he had no reason to ever return to No. 26 Maddox Street, or see Sophia Monmouth again.

He went directly back to Great Marlborough Street, where he ordered Tribble to say he wasn't at home to any callers, not even Lord Lyndon. After that, there was nothing to do but wait for the long, empty day to pass into dusk.

He spent it at his library window, staring out at the roof of Lord Everly's pediment. He watched the shadows lengthen, and told himself he couldn't still feel the strands of silky dark hair drifting through his fingers, see the glitter of tears on dark lashes, or taste the full lips that had opened so sweetly under his.

Chapter Twelve

Sophia was sitting on the edge of the settee staring down at the locket in her hands when the door of the drawing room opened, and Cecilia peeked around the edge of it. "Sophia?"

She had to take a moment to compose her face before she dared to glance up at her friend. "It's all right, Cecilia. There's no need to look so dejected."

No need to *feel* so dejected, either. It wasn't as if Lord Gray's fury had taken her by surprise. She'd been waiting for him for several hours before he arrived, pacing from one end of the drawing room to the other, rehearsing how she could reconcile him to Jeremy's sudden disappearance from Newgate without revealing the truth.

She hadn't realized how difficult it would be to lie to him.

Every time those gray eyes met hers, she'd been in danger of blurting out the truth. Somehow, she'd managed to cling to the story she and Lady Clifford had agreed on, but even now she wasn't sure how she'd managed it. It was all a bit of a blur.

Looking back on it now, she couldn't understand how she'd expected it to go any other way than it had. Lord Gray might have seen for himself how dire Jeremy's condition was, but Sophia had known he'd never believe the lie, not matter how plausible it was.

He knew her too well for that.

And really, that was the worst of it, wasn't it? Somehow, she'd ended up revealing so much of herself to him, he no longer believed her lies. *That* had certainly never happened before. Then there'd been that kiss. She hadn't expected that, either, but even that wasn't as shocking as what *she'd* done.

That is, she'd...well, dash it, she'd kissed him back, hadn't she?

Sophia pressed her fingers to her lips. They felt tender, bruised, the soft flesh swollen. She shivered, her eyes sliding closed at the memory of his hard mouth on hers, his scarred hands in her hair, the drag of his rough fingertips over her skin.

That kiss had ruined everything.

Before that kiss, she'd done an admirable job of convincing herself she didn't care a whit if she never laid eyes on Lord Gray again. Then he'd gone and kissed her, and moments later he'd severed the connection between them. Those two things together had startled her into an uncomfortable confrontation with the truth.

She was a trifle…preoccupied with Lord Gray.

Tristan.

Fascinated with him, even, against her will and better judgment.

The truth was, she *did* care if she never saw him again. She cared very much, indeed.

"Sophia?" Cecilia took a hesitant step into the room. "You look strange. You're scaring me."

"It's all right, dearest." Sophia beckoned her friend into the room with a weary hand. "Come on, then. Come and cheer me up."

Cecilia hurried across the room to join her on the settee. Sophia waited to be petted and soothed and diverted until her usual sangfroid returned, but Cecilia remained oddly still and silent.

The seconds turned into minutes, and might have turned into hours if Sophia hadn't nudged her. "Well, Cecilia? I thought you were going to cheer me up?"

Cecilia's brow furrowed. "I'm thinking."

"Oh." It was that bad then, was it? "Do take your time." Sophia rested her chin on her hand, lost in her own glum thoughts. What had she been thinking, letting Lord Gray kiss her like that? She'd been holding steady enough until then, but that kiss had scattered her wits like—

"Adeline!" Cecilia cried out suddenly.

Sophia jumped. "My goodness, Cecilia! You scared the life out of me. Adeline? The heroine of *The Romance of the Forest?*"

"Of course, that Adeline. We don't know any other Adelines, do we?"

"No, but I don't see what that Adeline has to do with anything."

Cecilia sighed with exaggerated patience, as if Sophia was being unbearably dim. "Think of it, Sophia. Adeline encounters a ruined abbey and a scheming marquis. She's locked into haunted bedchambers, and tumbles through trap doors. She battles terrible storms and wanders darkened forests, and her story still ends happily."

Sophia blinked. "I don't see what this has to do with me. This isn't a romance, Cecilia, and I'm not one of Mrs. Radcliffe's heroines." Far from it. Seven Dials didn't produce many of those, and as far as Sophia knew, Mrs. Radcliffe had never written a heroine who lounged on rooftops, or ran about the dark streets of London dressed in boy's clothes. Her heroines were pure, sweet maidens, not liars and thieves.

Cecilia gave her a reproachful look. "Every lady is the heroine of her own story, Sophia. My point is, Adeline's prospects look grim indeed, but even when she's in her darkest hour she never gives up, and in the end, she earns her happy ending. Why should you be any different?"

Because happy endings were a thing of books only? Because she wasn't a fictional character, but a real person, and a dreadfully flawed one, at that? There were dozens of reasons, but Cecilia's eager, relentless and utterly impractical optimism was a rare, precious thing, and Sophia wouldn't be the one to smother it.

So, she held her tongue, and instead reached for Cecilia's hand. "Well, when you put it that way, I suppose—"

"Your mother's locket!" Cecilia interrupted with a surprised gasp. "You told me you used it to bribe a prison guard. How did you get it back?"

Sophia closed her fingers around the locket still nestled in her palm. "Lord Gray. He gave it to me this morning. It seems he, ah…he took it back from the guard."

It must have cost him to do it, too. There was no way a man like Hogg would relinquish a silver locket without securing something valuable in its place. Money, and a good deal of it.

I thought you'd want it back.

Sophia *did* want it back, quite desperately, but in her experience wanting a thing rarely resulted in actually getting it, and it wasn't as if Tristan owed her anything—

"Well, how lovely of him!" Cecilia tapped Sophia's fist, which had closed around the locket again. "I confess I didn't care much for Lord Gray when we met him the other day. I thought him a bit stiff, really, and too severe, but I must say this improves my opinion of him."

Sophia's lips quirked. Yes, it was just the sort of extravagantly romantic gesture Cecilia adored. Sophia thought it more likely he wished to tie up any loose ends between them so he could thoroughly wash his hands of her, but once again, she wouldn't be the one to shatter Cecilia's romantic illusions. "I don't deny it was a gentlemanly thing to do."

"Indeed, the act of a true gentleman—"

"Who's a true gentleman?" a voice demanded.

Sophia and Cecilia looked up to find Georgiana peering around the door, with Emma right behind her, peeking over her shoulder.

"Lord Gray." Cecilia patted the empty space beside her on the settee, and Georgiana and Emma hurried in and crowded onto it.

"Lord Gray? More troublesome than gentlemanly, I'd say." Georgiana tapped a finger against her chin, thinking. "He doesn't look much like a Bow Street Runner, does he?"

"No," Emma agreed. "Very much like an earl, though."

"It's his cheekbones, I think," Cecilia said. "Have you ever noticed all aristocrats have the same cheekbones? High, and rather sharp."

They waited, but Sophia, who recalled in vivid detail how those cheekbones felt under her fingertips, said nothing.

"Well, it's just as well he's gone. The last thing we need is a Bow Street Runner hanging about, poking his nose into our affairs. Or an earl either, come to that." Georgiana gave an airy wave of her hand.

Emma nudged Sophia's shoulder. "Georgiana's right. Earls and Bow Street Runners are disruptive creatures, and Lord Gray more so than most, given he's both at once."

"His nose!" Cecilia cried, then flushed when they all turned to gape at her. "He has a noble nose, I mean."

"He's not a biddable sort either." Georgiana frowned. "One need only look at his face to see that, but he's not rash, is he? No, he's altogether too clever. It would only be a matter of time before a man like that uncovered all our secrets."

"Yes, and goodness knows we have plenty of those," Emma said with a sigh.

Sophia fell back against the settee and threw an arm over her face. "You're right, of course. It's just…"

It's just that I'm a great fool.

"You're fatigued, dearest." Cecilia patted her knee. "Everything seems worse when one is fatigued, doesn't it?"

"Yes, indeed. Come now, Sophia," Emma said, pulling Sophia's arm gently away from her face. "Once you've rested, you'll see for yourself we're well rid of him—"

"I'm afraid it's not that simple, my dears."

All four girls looked up in surprise. Lady Clifford was standing in the doorway. None of them had heard her come in, and now Sophia thought of it, she realized Lady Clifford had been conspicuously absent all morning.

"No, because nothing ever *is* simple, it is?" Georgiana grumbled.

Lady Clifford closed the drawing room door and seated herself in the chair beside the settee. "I won't deny Lord Gray's a bit troublesome, but we need him still."

"What do you mean, my lady?" Sophia asked, then cringed, heat flooding her face at the hopeful note in her voice. "That is, who needs him? Not *me*, certainly."

Lady Clifford's brow rose, and a faint smile touched her lips. "Oh no, of course not, Sophia. But I didn't mean just you, my love. No, what I mean to say is, if we want to find out what's at the bottom of this business at St. Clement Dane's Church, we need Lord Gray."

Emma, who didn't care for the idea of needing anyone, particularly a man, frowned. "I don't see why. Jeremy's safe. Isn't that an end to it?"

"Certainly, if one doesn't mind a murderer running amok in London. After all, *someone* killed Henry Gerrard." Lady Clifford gave Emma a mildly chastising look. "Then there's the matter of Peter Sharpe, who's no doubt being paid well to accuse innocent men of theft. Not quite the thing, is it?"

"But Lord Gray's the sort to cause trouble," Georgiana warned, her tone dark.

"Yes, I'm afraid so," Lady Clifford acknowledged with a sigh. "It's a trifle tedious, but think of it in terms of access, girls. As a former Bow Street Runner and an earl, he has a great deal more of it than we do. He got Sophia into Newgate, didn't he? Then there's the matter of his living next door to Mr. Everly, who, I think we all agree, is somehow entangled in this affair."

"He won't help us. Just before he left, he said…" Sophia's voice hitched. *There's no reason for us to ever meet again.*

Lady Clifford studied Sophia, her gaze thoughtful, then turned to the other three girls. "Leave us alone for a bit, won't you, dears? Sophia will join you soon, and then you may fuss over her as much as you like."

Lady Clifford never ordered anyone to do anything. Every wish was phrased as a polite question, but her students knew a command when they heard one. Cecilia, Georgiana, and Emma rose from the settee at once.

"We'll wait for you upstairs, Sophia." Georgiana and Emma paused at the door while Cecilia dropped an affectionate kiss on the top of Sophia's head.

"Now, Sophia," Lady Clifford said when the girls were gone. "You look a bit downcast, my dear. Why don't you tell me what Lord Gray said to you?"

To Sophia's horror, tears stung her eyes. She leapt up from the settee and retreated to the fireplace to hide them. "He thinks I used him. He said he wouldn't be surprised to find *he* was my target all along, and not Peter Sharpe."

"Did he, indeed? Well, we both know that's not the case. What else did he say?"

Sophia bit her lip, but it didn't stop the torrent of words. "He knows Jeremy isn't dead, and that we're behind his escape. He said because he was the one who brought me to Newgate, I'd implicated him in the crime."

"Hmmm. I hadn't thought of it quite that way, but I suppose there's some truth to it." Lady Clifford shrugged. "Anything else?"

Sophia hesitated. "Ought we to have done that? Implicated him, I mean?"

Lady Clifford gave her a serene smile. "Oh, I shouldn't worry about Lord Gray if I were you, dear. Mr. Hogg is the only one who witnessed his involvement, and he isn't likely to reappear in London, is he? In any case, Lord Gray is more than capable of taking care of himself. Now, did he say anything else?"

Sophia wandered back to the settee and settled in next to Lady Clifford. "He said this was an end to it, or something of that nature, and then he said there was no reason for us to ever meet again. He meant it, too, my lady."

His eyes had looked like two chips of cold, hard gray stone. When she'd looked into them, she could hardly believe he'd been kissing her with mad passion just a moment before.

Once again, Lady Clifford looked more thoughtful than concerned. "Yes, I'm certain he thought he did, but I'm not quite ready to dispense with Lord Gray's services yet."

Sophia gave her a blank look. "I don't understand."

"Peter Sharpe is a dangerous man, Sophia, and he's had a good look at your face. Aside from the question of access, there's the issue of your safety. Daniel is off tending to Jeremy, so we no longer have his protection. Lord Gray may not be pleased with you, but he's far too honorable to allow anything to happen to you."

Sophia jumped to her feet again, more agitated than she cared to admit by this observation. "Certainly, he will. I daresay he'd be pleased at it. You didn't see his face this morning, my lady."

"He's angry, Sophia, and I daresay he feels betrayed. One can't blame him, really, but he's wrong, of course. You and Lord Gray still need each other, despite what he may think. I suggest you return to Great Marlborough Street tonight, my dear."

"Tonight!" Sophia cried. "How will I manage that? It's not as if I can simply stroll into his townhouse as I did yesterday. He'll have me turned away at the door."

Lady Clifford smiled. "My dear child, who said anything about the door?"

* * * *

"Well, Gray, here you are," Lord Lyndon announced, pausing in the doorway to Tristan's library. "I'll have you know Tribble lied to me. Told me you weren't home, the scoundrel."

"That's because I ordered him to lie to you."

"That wasn't very gentlemanly of you, but perhaps I should have gone away while I had the chance. What's the trouble *now*, Gray? For a man with a glass of port in his hand and a roaring fire at his feet, you look grim enough."

"What are you doing here, Lyndon? It's late." Foolish question, really. Lyndon was like a bloodhound when it came to sniffing out mischief. Whenever something was afoot, he always appeared sooner or later.

"Call it curiosity, if you like." Lyndon strolled into the library, pausing at the sideboard to help himself to a glass of port. "So, I repeat, Gray. What's the trouble *now*?"

"No trouble. I'm perfectly content." So content, he'd been sitting alone in his library for hours, sipping port and sulking like a spoiled child.

"Content, eh? Well, I'm glad to hear it." Lyndon dropped into the chair beside Tristan's, rested his feet on the grate, and raised his glass to his lips.

Tristan knew Lyndon far too well to believe he'd leave it there. He waited for the next round of volleys, and Lyndon, who could never stay quiet for long, didn't disappoint him. "This contentment of yours, Gray. May I ask if it's the result of your visit to the Clifford School today?"

"More or less." Rather less than more, however.

"Good, good. Then you discovered Jeremy Ives is, in fact, as dead as the *Times* claims he is, and that he was, in fact, guilty of Henry's murder?"

Tristan blew out a breath. Lyndon had a charming way of getting straight to the heart of a matter. "Not exactly, no."

Lyndon's eyes widened in mock surprise. "*No*? Why, you can't mean to say Miss Monmouth *lied* to you, can you? That she and that coven of witches at No. 26 Maddox Street *didn't* stuff a convicted murderer into a coffin and smuggle him out of Newgate before dawn this morning?"

"Ives is no murderer. It would be a great deal easier if he were." This business with Sharpe and Ives and Sophia Monmouth had more heads than a Gorgon, each of them writhing with dozens of hissing snakes, but Tristan knew beyond any doubt Jeremy Ives was innocent.

"Not a murderer, you say? Well, is he dead, or isn't he?"

"He's not that, either."

Lyndon frowned. "Well, where the devil is he, then?"

"I haven't the vaguest idea. Miss Monmouth was less than forthcoming this morning." At least, she'd been tight-lipped about Jeremy Ives. Otherwise, she'd had plenty to say, and none of it pleasant to hear.

Do you truly believe you know anything about guilt and innocence?

He *had* thought so, yes. God knows he'd seen enough of both to have an opinion on the matter, but Miss Monmouth had a talent for throwing his every thought into disarray. It was...disconcerting.

Laws were imperfect, and the execution of them even more so. Tristan had always thought so. Now he was taking his brother's place in the House of Lords, he was in a position to do something about it. But questions of guilt and innocence, goodness and evil—they were concepts he'd always accepted without question as absolute. Thanks to Miss Monmouth, they'd now become a great deal trickier than they'd ever been before.

You saw Jeremy. Is the law working for him?

The trouble with Sophia Monmouth was, she wasn't entirely wrong. He understood her frustration, yet he shuddered to think how dangerous London would be if everyone thought as she did.

"You know what I think, Gray?"

Tristan swallowed the rest of his port and abandoned his glass on the table. "No, but I suspect you're going to tell me."

"I think your little pixie has you turned inside out."

Tristan wished with everything inside him his friend was mistaken, but there was no use in denying it. In a few short weeks, Sophia Monmouth had upended the carefully arranged pieces of his life as easily as if she'd tipped over a chessboard.

Now all was chaos, with the king, queen, and pawns scattered everywhere.

"You *are* aware she's the only one who can turn you right way 'round again, aren't you? Or not, as the mood strikes her. Make no mistake about it, Gray. We're but slaves to the whims of those ladies who slither under our skins."

Tristan rolled his eyes. "You're quite a philosopher tonight, Lyndon, but Sophia Monmouth isn't under my skin, or any other part of me. I'm as good as betrothed to another lady."

"Ah, that's the spirit, Gray. Curious thing, though. It's been ages since I heard you say a word about this other lady. Tell me, what was her name again?"

"You think to catch me out? I'm sorry to disappoint you Lyndon, but I know very well her name is…is…"

Damn it, what the devil was her name again? Lady Emilia? Lady Emily, wasn't it, or…Lady Emma?

Lyndon snorted. "That's what I thought. You can't marry Lady Esther—"

"Esther? Is that it?" How odd. The name didn't sound even vaguely familiar.

"You can't marry Lady Esther if you're besotted with Miss Mon—"

"*Besotted!*" Tristan jerked upright in his seat. "Are you mad? I'm not besotted with her, Lyndon."

Lyndon raised an eyebrow. "I beg your pardon. I was under the impression you were."

"No. I *want* her. Desire her. Can you blame me? You saw her. It's a purely physical urge, for God's sake, not an emotional one. I've never come across a more stubborn, quarrelsome lady in my life. How could I possibly be besotted with her?"

The very notion was ridiculous. He'd never permit himself to become enamored with a willful, unpredictable, reckless termagant like Sophia Monmouth. No, when he decided it was time for him to become enamored with someone, he'd choose much more wisely than that. He preferred quiet, proper sorts of ladies, not unruly ones like Miss Monmouth.

Ladies very much like Lady Emilia, in fact.

Esther, that is. Lady Esther.

Lyndon might know a great deal more about romantic entanglements than Tristan did—he'd had enough mistresses he should have learned *something* by now—but he was wrong about this.

"Very well, Gray. If you say you're not besotted with Miss Monmouth, then I have no choice but to believe you. I beg your pardon. It seems I misunderstood the depths of your feelings."

Tristan eyed his friend suspiciously. Lyndon had the most peculiar look on his face, as if he were doing his best to hold back a smirk.

"It's just as well you're not besotted with her. She's more trouble than she's worth, I daresay. Indeed, I don't see why you don't simply leave London for Oxfordshire at once. I imagine your mother is in fits by now, and anyone can see you're expiring with impatience to see Lady Esther again."

"I won't leave London, Lyndon. Not until I've seen Henry's murderer dangling at the end of a rope. I've got Abigail and Samuel's welfare to consider, as well."

"Of course," Lyndon murmured, his face softening at mention of Henry and his family. "But that hasn't anything to do with Miss Monmouth. It's no concern of yours if she's in danger. She's not your responsibility."

Tristan was well aware Lyndon was manipulating him, but it didn't stop a thread of unease from winding through him. He'd been in a bit of a daze since he'd left the Clifford School this morning. His hard, sharp focus had been blunted with frustration and one too many glasses of port, but at Lyndon's words it returned with a vengeance.

"Pity she should have been so foolish as to get involved in this mess with Peter Sharpe, but it's her own fault." Lyndon shrugged. "She only has herself to blame for it if Sharpe comes after her. I assume he got a look at her when she planted her locket on him?"

"He did." Peter Sharpe had gotten a lengthy look at a face most men would find it difficult to forget. Even if Sharpe didn't realize she'd been following him for weeks, he still had reason enough to resent her, given the scoundrels in front of Ye Old Mitre Pub had nearly kicked his head in at her bidding.

Sharpe was a liar, and a man without scruples or conscience. He'd been perfectly happy to see Jeremy Ives hang for a crime Sharpe knew damn well the boy hadn't committed. But Sharpe was a fool, and also a coward. He was utterly incapable of devising a complex scheme like the one that had trapped Ives, and just as incapable of carrying it out.

For all his viciousness, Sharpe was a pawn, not a king.

Sophia could manage a man like Sharpe easily enough, but the fourth man Jeremy Ives had spoken of, the one who'd murdered Henry...

He was another sort of man entirely.

A villain such as that, one who'd slit an innocent man's throat and stand by while his life's blood seeped into the dirt—that sort of man was capable of anything, and Tristan didn't doubt he knew all about Sophia.

He shot to his feet, unable to sit still a moment longer.

"I see you understand me, Gray." Lyndon finished off the rest of his port.

Tristan recalled what he'd told Sophia this morning, and a dry laugh rose to his lips. "I told Miss Monmouth her part in this thing was over, and warned her to stay away from me."

"A bit hasty, that, but I shouldn't worry too much, Gray. I doubt she'll listen. Miss Monmouth isn't the sort to take orders from you. Well then, this has been a tidy night's work, if I do say so myself." Lyndon rose to his feet. "I'll take my leave now. You will send word if you find yourself in need of assistance?"

"Yes, yes." Tristan stopped his pacing and lifted his head. "Lyndon?"

"Yes?" Lyndon paused by the door.

"Thank you."

Lyndon grinned. "We'll see if you're still thanking me tomorrow. Good night, Gray."

He strolled from the library into the hallway. A few minutes later Tristan heard him scold Tribble for being a lying sot, before he cheerfully bid the butler a good evening.

The front door opened, then closed again.

Tristan remained in front of the fire for a bit after Lyndon left, staring down at the flames, but it wasn't long before he found himself drawn to his library window.

He couldn't have said what drew him there. Had he gone to make certain Lyndon made it safely to his carriage? Or had there been something else, some whisper from deep inside him that told him what he'd find? Whatever the reason, what he saw when he glanced outside his window froze him where he stood.

His first thought was he'd imagined her.

But no. He wasn't foxed, and he wasn't seeing things. That small, black-clad figure was no ghost, and no delusion. Not figment, but flesh. Not shadow, but substance.

There was a woman, lying on the roof of Lord Everly's pediment.

Chapter Thirteen

Perhaps this wasn't such a good idea.

Sophia lay on her back, still as a corpse, and gazed up at Tristan's library window above her, blinking against the dampness that clung to her eyelashes. The mist was so heavy it felt suffocating, like fistfuls of damp soil were pressing her into the cold slate roof beneath her.

Her own little grave.

The only thing darker than the sky was Tristan's townhouse. It was as silent as a tomb, every window shrouded in heavy silk draperies. It didn't look as if he were home, but it didn't matter much whether he was or not. Even if he was looking out his window at her at this very moment, she doubted it would make any difference.

Sophia wasn't one to doubt Lady Clifford—she'd never known her ladyship to be wrong before—but in this particular instance, she wondered if her mentor had missed the mark. Lady Clifford hadn't seen Tristan's face this morning, or heard his tone of cold dismissal when he'd told Sophia there was no need for them ever to meet again.

This ends here...

Sophia didn't imagine another sojourn on Lord Everly's roof would change his mind.

It had been a simple enough thing to climb his lordship's columns again, but it wasn't nearly as much fun as it had been the first time. Tonight, the patter of raindrops on the slate roof didn't sound like a symphony, or like bells chiming. It sounded, and felt, like a depressing drizzle, and chillier than it should be for August in London.

Worse, it was all to no purpose. She was dallying on a roof, wasting her precious time. There were only two reasons for her to linger on Great

Marlborough Street. One was a man she'd sworn not to follow, and the other a man who'd never come.

She given her word to Lord Gray she wouldn't follow Peter Sharpe again, and she intended to keep it, but just in case that wasn't reason enough to curb her reckless tendencies, Lady Clifford had also made her promise she'd come directly back to No. 26 Maddox Street if Lord Gray didn't appear.

He *hadn't* appeared, for all that Sophia been lying here for what felt like an eternity. If she *had* been in her grave, the worms would have devoured her by now. Her spine ached from lying for so long on the hard slate, and she even caught herself wishing for a few layers of petticoats. She detested them, but even they'd be preferable to a chilled backside.

Peter Sharpe hadn't turned up, either, but Sophia guessed he'd be back on the prowl soon enough. No doubt he had dozens of nefarious deeds to see to tonight, and because of her promise, he'd be free to indulge in his choice of petty crimes without any witnesses.

Bitter frustration flooded Sophia at the thought of him creeping about St. Clement Dane's Church, the scene of the worst of his crimes, lying in wait for some unsuspecting victim to stumble upon him. It was too maddening to contemplate, but this was what came of making promises, wasn't it? She'd know better than to give her word next time.

Still, she'd given it *this* time, and she wouldn't go back on it now.

Sophia cast one last despairing look at Tristan's dark windows before sliding to the edge of the pediment, shimmying down the columns to the top railing of the wrought iron fence, and dropping silently onto the pavement.

Just as she had the first night, she kept to the shadows as she crept through the streets toward No. 26 Maddox Street. The night was a black one, the moon shrouded by a layer of clouds. It was easy enough to sneak along without anyone taking notice of her.

She headed down Great Marlborough Street, weaving between the townhouses where she could lose herself in the gloom. She stole toward Mill Street, but she hadn't gotten further than half a block when she caught a faint whiff of smoke. Sophia wrinkled her nose with distaste as the acrid stench drifted toward her. Sharpe would do well to give up those pipes if he wanted to skulk about the streets unnoticed. It was the easiest thing in the world to track him with that stream of smoke trailing behind him—

Sophia froze, pressing her back against the wall.

But she *wasn't* tracking him, was she? Yet there was no mistaking that hint of smoke. Either Great Marlborough Street was crowded with pipe-loving criminals, or...

Or Peter Sharpe was tracking *her*.

Sophia melted into the thickest of the shadows and waited. A moment later she heard the steady tread of footsteps coming up Great Marlborough Street behind her. The hair on her neck and arms rose, just as it always did when she felt an unfriendly presence nearby.

He wasn't particularly skilled at stalking his prey. He shuffled clumsily along behind her, almost as if he wanted her to *know* he was there. She couldn't imagine what he had to gain by revealing himself, but one thing was clear enough. He'd known she was waiting outside Lord Everly's townhouse tonight, but instead of informing Lord Everly, who would certainly have sent for the night watchman, Sharpe had come after her himself.

Peter Sharpe wasn't clever, but after that ill-advised scene in front of Ye Old Mitre Pub, it wouldn't take amazing powers of deduction for him to conclude *someone* had been following him, and to guess she was the most likely culprit. Now it seemed he'd decided to return the favor.

Blast it. Ill-advised was putting it far too kindly. The foolishness of that stunt was now being impressed on her with a vengeance. Her throat tightened as Lady Clifford's last warning before she'd left this evening echoed inside her head.

He's dangerous, and he's seen your face.

Still, how difficult could it be to evade him? He might *try* to come after her, but he'd never catch her. No one ever did, with the notable exception of Lord Gray. *He'd* caught her, and given how disappointed she'd been when he hadn't come for her tonight, it seemed he had a hold on her still.

Now wasn't the time to dwell on it, however.

Sophia focused her attention on the thump of heavy boots hitting the pavement, her ears pricking as she neared Pollen Street on their right. They were getting too close to No. 26 Maddox Street for her comfort. Sharpe had seen her face, yes, but he might not yet have realized she was connected with the Clifford School, and she'd just as soon he didn't have that information.

She paused at the corner of Pollen Street, debating whether to continue on toward No. 26 Maddox, where Lady Clifford was likely watching for her, or to lead Sharpe away from the Clifford School.

That single, brief moment of hesitation was her undoing.

When the attack came, she wasn't ready for it. Not because she hadn't anticipated it, but because it didn't come from behind her.

It came from *in front* of her.

Later, Sophia would recall there'd been a sound first—a faint, rhythmic tapping echoing in the empty street. She jerked her head toward it, but by then, it was too late.

By then, it was already happening.

There was no time for her to flee, or even to a draw a breath before the dark figure that emerged from the shadows crashed into her, throwing her to the ground. She tried to catch herself with her hands, but the blow knocked the breath from her lungs, and her face hit the pavement.

She was vaguely aware of the thump of pounding footsteps behind her, but even as she opened her lips to cry out for help a blinding pain exploded at the side of her head, stealing the words from her lips.

Unnecessary risk, Sophia...

She should have listened to Lady Clifford. She'd warned Sophia her recklessness would catch up to her someday.

Now, that day had come.

* * * *

Tristan's every muscle was tensed to spring into action, but he forced himself to wait until he heard the thud of retreating footsteps fade into the foggy London night before he peeled himself off Sophia's prone body. "Sophia?"

No answer, and she'd gone frighteningly still, her small body crumpled against the damp pavement, the blow forceful enough to have knocked her senseless.

Tristan turned her as gently as he could onto her back. As soon as he saw her face, his heart rushed into his throat. Her cheek was scraped raw from the dirt and grit on the street, her lower lip and forehead were gushing blood, and her temple was swelling with a knot the size of a fist.

And those were just the injuries he could see.

There'd be others, likely worse than these. Tristan hadn't gotten a good look at the man who'd attacked her, but he'd seen enough to guess the villain had outweighed her by at least three stone. He'd fallen upon her like a fury, slamming her face-first into the street, then Tristan had made things worse by leaping onto the man's back.

He hadn't had any other choice, but as Tristan slid his arms underneath Sophia and gathered her against his chest, that didn't make him feel any better. He'd knocked a tiny young woman to the ground. He was a monster, a beast, a hulking, clumsy brute of a man—

"Don't take me...Lady Clifford."

Tristan gazed down into her face, his heart pounding. Dear God, the wits had been knocked clean out of her head. "I'm not Lady Clifford. It's Tristan—that is, Lord Gray."

She cracked open one eye and peered up at him through the slit. A furrow appeared on her forehead as she stared at him, but then her brow cleared. "Yes, you are Lord Gray, aren't you? What I mean is, please don't take me to the Clifford School. Take me home with you."

Tristan hesitated. There was no denying the idea of taking her to Great Marlborough Street filled him with a rush of possessive satisfaction, but it wasn't proper, and No. 26 Maddox was closer—

"Please, Lord Gray. My friends will fall into a panic if I return in this state." She raised a hand to her temple, wincing as her fingers found the knot there. "Oh, dear. There will be no hiding *that*, will there?"

"I'm afraid not." Tristan took her wrist in gentle fingers and eased her hand away from the wound. "It's a pity you discarded the enormous hat you wore to Jeremy's trial. It might have done the job."

Incredibly, a weak smile crossed her lips. "I promised Lady Clifford I'd be careful tonight. If she suspects I've been reckless, she'll have my head for it."

A short, incredulous laugh fell from Tristan's lips. "I would think, Miss Monmouth, she'd be so pleased to find your head still attached to your neck, she'd let the incident go."

A small hand curled into the edge of his coat, silencing him at once. "Please, Tristan?"

He blinked down at her, found a pair of wide, pleading green eyes gazing up at him, and that was the end of the argument. Tristan turned toward Great Marlborough Street without another word.

Tribble was hovering in the entryway. The butler had been standing at the door when Tristan rushed out earlier after Sophia, and like the meticulously trained servant he was, Tribble had wisely deduced his master might require his assistance when he returned.

If he was shocked to see Tristan return with a bleeding lady in his arms, one would never know it by the perfectly impassive expression on his face. "Have you brought a guest, my lord?"

Under any other circumstances Tristan might have laughed, but he couldn't quite find the humor in the situation while Sophia was slumped against his chest, the blood from her cut lip now trickling down her chin. "You could say that. Bring a basin of water, some bandages, and whatever else you deem necessary to tend to the lady's injuries to the library, Tribble."

A generous measure of brandy was certainly necessary, but he had a vague idea he'd need other supplies.

Tristan had never doctored anyone before, but he was strangely reluctant to turn Sophia over to anyone else. So he carried her down the hallway to his library and approached an overstuffed leather sofa near the fireplace.

Sophia winced when he put her down. "Was it you, Lord Gray, who knocked me to the ground?"

Tristan winced. "I didn't knock you down, no, but I…ah, well, once you were there, I fell on top of you. I beg your pardon, Miss Monmouth."

I beg your pardon?

Tristan grimaced at this absurdly inadequate reply. He hadn't stepped on her foot during the quadrille or spilled tea on her gown, for God's sake.

Sophia was once again prodding gingerly at the lump on her head. "You're a rather large man, Lord Gray. Really, I can't think why it's necessary for you to be so large. I feel as if I've been trampled by a horse."

Tristan stood awkwardly beside the sofa, not sure what to say. He'd never fallen on top of a lady before—at least, not under these circumstances. He cast about for something sophisticated and gallant to say, but what came out instead was, "Seventeen stone."

She blinked up at him. "Seventeen stone? What, you mean you weigh seventeen stone?"

Heat rushed up Tristan's neck. Why the devil had he blurted that out? "I, um…well, yes."

"That's all?" Sophia studied her palms, which were scraped raw. "It felt like more than that."

Tristan didn't answer. He was staring down at her, appalled. Her hands were bleeding, her lip was swelling, and the knees of her breeches were ripped to shreds. He might have gone breathless at the glimpse he got of those smooth, bare legs if her flesh hadn't been torn to pieces.

"Tribble!" Tristan rushed to the library door and stuck his head into the hallway, ready to shout the entire house down. "For God's sakes, man, what's taking so…oh, here you are."

Tristan stepped back from the doorway and Tribble, who was bearing a large silver tray loaded with doctoring supplies, entered the library and laid his burden down on a table near the sofa where Sophia was stretched out. "May I help you, my lord?" he asked, taking in Sophia's injuries with a shake of his head. "Perhaps one of the maids could be of service?"

"No, thank you, Tribble. That won't be necessary." Tristan, who hadn't any intention of letting anyone other than himself touch Sophia, had to resist the urge to shove poor Tribble out the door. "I'll tend to Miss Monmouth."

"Very well, my lord." Once again, if Tribble was shocked, he did an admirable job of hiding it. "I wish you a pleasant evening, my lord." He offered each of them a solemn bow, then made his way out the door.

"A pleasant evening," Tristan muttered as he sat down on the large table in front of the sofa. "Not much chance of that." He pulled the tray closer and held out his hand to her. "Give me your hand, Miss Monmouth."

She held out her hand, palm up. She was quiet for some minutes, watching as he gently cleaned the blood and loose rocks away before reaching silently for her other hand. She gave it to him, but this time as he worked, Tristan could feel her curious gaze on his face.

"I don't wish to be presumptuous, Lord Gray." She winced a little as he swabbed at her palm with the wet cloth. "But why did you leap on me?"

Tristan froze, his hand still wrapped around hers. "You don't remember the attack?" He'd have to have a careful look at the injury to her head. That villain had dealt her a vicious blow.

"Who attacked me? Sharpe? I knew he was following me, of course. He's as subtle as a herd of cattle."

Tristan didn't answer right away. He finished tending to her hand, then laid it carefully on her lap. "Not Sharpe. The other man."

Sophia frowned. "There was another man?"

Tristan braced his hands on his knees and met her gaze. "Yes. Did you think I simply leapt on you and nearly knocked the brains from your head on a whim?"

"Well, no." She kept her gaze on her hands, avoiding his eyes. "Though after that business with Jeremy, perhaps you had reason to."

Tristan stared at her. It was the closest she'd come to confessing her part in the business with Jeremy Ives. Strangely enough, as determined as he'd been this morning to have the truth out of her, it no longer seemed to matter now. He gripped his knees to keep himself from touching her. "I won't pretend I was pleased by it, but I wouldn't hurt you, Sophia. Not ever."

They looked at each other, and Tristan had to force himself not to touch her, to take her soft hand in his again.

Sophia cleared her throat. "There was another man, then? Aside from Sharpe?"

"Yes. I saw him slip from the shadows after Sharpe disappeared. Sharpe knew you were on the pediment roof, Sophia. As soon as you dropped to the ground, he went after you."

She blew out a breath. "I was afraid of that. I nearly took him straight to No. 26 Maddox. I know he saw my face at Ye Old Mitre Pub, but I was hoping he didn't know who I was, or where I came from."

"He knows." Tristan's tone was grim. "So does the man who attacked you. Sharpe was there to distract you from his partner, who was hiding in the shadows, waiting for you. They knew you'd likely head toward Maddox Street. If you'd veered off, one of them certainly would have grabbed you."

"The fourth man," Sophia whispered. "The man Jeremy said was at St. Clement Dane's the night of Henry Gerrard's murder. It has to be him."

Tristan set the cloth aside. "Yes. I didn't see the man's face. He was wearing a cap, but he was dressed all in black, and he was carrying a weapon. A stick, perhaps, or a club of some sort."

Sophia swallowed. "A club?"

"Yes, and he didn't hesitate to use it." Tristan caught her chin in his fingers and turned her head to get a look at the injury on her temple, brushing a fingertip over the knot. "He leapt on you, and then I leapt on him. I still don't know how he managed to squirm free of me."

Or more to the point, *why*. Sophia's attacker and Sharpe together might have had a chance at subduing him. Tristan hadn't the faintest doubt the mysterious man who'd leapt from the shadows had intended to kill Sophia, but instead of persisting, they'd both fled into the night.

"You, ah…you saw me on Lord Everly's roof tonight, then? You followed me?" The look she gave him from under cover of her thick, dark lashes was almost shy.

Tristan glanced down at her small hands, which were resting palm up in her lap. Her tender, olive-tinted skin was shredded to ribbons and oozing blood, despite his efforts. Her knees were even worse, and her forehead was smeared with blood from the nasty cut there.

How many bruises, as yet invisible, would appear on that smooth skin before the night was over? Yet it could have been worse—so much worse. He thought of the club in that scoundrel's black-gloved hand, and a shudder of fear wracked him.

What if he hadn't happened to see her on Everly's roof tonight? What would have happened to her then? Even now she could be lying in a bloody heap in the middle of Pollen Street, alone and breathing her last breath.

Just like Henry.

He'd failed Henry, and tonight he'd nearly failed Sophia.

Tristan slid from the table onto the settee, dragged the silver tray with the supplies toward him, then reached for her legs and draped them over his thighs. He didn't ask her permission, but she didn't object—just watched him with huge green eyes.

He plucked up the damp cloth again, wetted it in the basin and began to dab at her knees, but he hardly knew what he was doing.

A cracked skull, a slit throat, a broken neck...

When he thought of all the possible ways she might have been hurt tonight, he was overwhelmed by a staggering array of conflicting emotions, each more confusing than the last.

Anger, panic, fear, regret...

The first good look he got at her knees didn't help. Her skin was as ragged as the cloth that had covered them. Tristan's mouth went dry as he stared down at the bloody mess, his throat working helplessly. He should have taken it as a sign to be silent, because when he did find the words, they only made things worse.

"Why were you on Lord Everly's roof again, Sophia?" Tristan's voice was much harsher than he'd intended. "You had no business being up there. What did you think you were doing?"

"I thought—that is, I'd h-hoped..."

Tristan had never heard her stumble over her words before. Her little stammer went straight to his heart, but when he'd seen Sharpe go after her tonight, he'd been so damn afraid for her, and that fear made him lash out. "You hoped I'd see you there, and come after you? Why would you think that, when just this morning I told you I didn't want to see you ever again?"

"I didn't think you'd—"

"You didn't think I'd be able to help myself? Well, you were right." He laughed, but it was hard and bitter. "I saw you from my window and told myself it was best to just leave you alone, and let you return to No. 26 Maddox where you belong. What if I'd decided to do that, after all? What if I'd waited another ten minutes before going after you? You'd be dead by now!"

She said nothing, but her face drained of color.

"Look at you." He jerked his chin toward her bloody knees, then snatched her hand up and dragged it toward him, his breath coming faster as he stared down at her ravaged palms. "You're hurt, and this is nothing—*nothing*—to what it might have been."

Sophia snatched her hand away. "It's a few scrapes and bruises, Tristan. I've had worse. I'm a bit battered, yes, but I'm hardly at death's door."

"Damn you, don't make light of it." The words felt as if they'd been ripped from Tristan's throat. "You might have ended this night at death's door. It's mere chance only you didn't. Why did you come here tonight, Sophia? You've gotten what you wanted. Jeremy Ives is free. Your part in this business is finished."

"Nothing is finished until Peter Sharpe and Henry Gerrard's killer are made to pay for their crimes. What did you think, Tristan? That I'd skip blithely away once Jeremy was safe? Patrick Dunn, and Mr. Gerrard's wife and son—do you think it doesn't matter to me if they ever see justice?"

He...*had* thought so. Not just Sophia, but Lady Clifford, and Daniel Brixton. All of them. How could he have been so blind? She'd spoken to him of justice many times, told him over and over again she believed it should belong to everyone equally, but he hadn't truly listened to her, and now he'd made a terrible mistake.

Sophia read the truth on his face, and her own face fell. "Oh. You *did* think so."

"Sophia—"

She jumped to her feet so quickly she sent the tray crashing to the ground. "I-I think it's best if I return home, after all. I won't trouble you again, Lord Gray."

"*No*. Wait." Tristan shot to his feet and went after her, his heart in his throat. "I'm sorry. Can you...will you forgive me?"

She kept her face turned away from him, but Tristan could feel her trembling. God, he couldn't let her leave, not like this. "Please, Sophia. I should never have said it, or even thought it. I know it's not true. I want... will you let me take care of you?"

She hesitated for what felt like a lifetime to Tristan, but then finally, a silent nod.

He took her hand in his, careful not to touch her wounded palm, and led her back to the sofa. "Your hands and knees, and your head." He brushed her hair back from her forehead, frowning as he traced the knot there. "Your mouth." He brushed a fingertip over her lower lip, his chest squeezing at the drop of blood at the corner. "I'm sorry I hurt you."

He wasn't just referring to having knocked her down, and Sophia seemed to understand this. Her green eyes darkened as they flickered over his face. "You followed me tonight. I needed you, and you were there."

Needed him...

Tristan stared down at her, stunned, but he didn't press her on how she meant those words. Perhaps he would, later, but now he needed to touch her. He took her face between his palms and stroked his thumbs over her cheekbones. "Sophia?"

She knew what he was asking, and parted her lips in invitation. He brushed his mouth over her lower lip to soothe her hurt, and tasted her blood on his tongue.

Chapter Fourteen

If their kiss earlier that day had been darkness, this one was pure, sweet light.

Tristan didn't let himself think about whether he should be kissing her. He didn't think about anything but the heady taste of her lips under his, her warm sighs in his mouth, the silky curls of her hair tickling his fingers.

He caught a loose lock of it and caressed the thick strands. "I've never felt anything so soft."

Sophia twined her arms around his neck, sifting her fingers through the hair at the back of his head. "Softer than my lips?" she asked, a teasing glint in her eyes.

"There's nothing in the world softer than your lips." Tristan's cheeks heated at the extravagant compliment. He wasn't the sort of man who indulged in poetic ramblings about his lady's lips, but then not every lady had lips like *hers*. He couldn't stop his gaze from dropping once again to that sultry pout.

He ducked his head to take her mouth again, more insistently this time. He slid the tip of his tongue over the seam of her lips, then dragged his finger down her cheek to the corner of her mouth. "Open for me, Sophia," he murmured, stroking the tender skin

She opened her mouth with a soft gasp and a low, hungry growl vibrated in Tristan's chest. He sank into her damp, pink mouth, knowing as he did, he could only savor her for the briefest moment. It was like offering a starving man a single grape from a feast spread out before him.

I can't make love to her...

She was in a vulnerable state, her body scraped and bruised. Only the worst sort of rake would take advantage of a lady who'd just been attacked.

Tristan was no rake, but even so the warning drifted through his head, there and then gone again.

He couldn't make himself release her. Not when she was so close, her sweetly parted lips a mere breath from his. He sank his hands into her hair and eased her head back so he could feast on her neck. He nibbled at her silky skin, chasing her flush of arousal to the hollow of her throat. Her pulse fluttered against his tongue, the skin there warm and faintly scented with honeysuckle, and he couldn't stop himself from scoring it lightly with his teeth before skimming lower to drop kisses between her breasts.

She was so beautiful, her curves slight but perfect. As if in a daze, Tristan cupped one of her breasts in his hand and teased at her nipple with his thumb.

Sophia let out a breathless cry and he groaned at the needy sound, his mouth going dry. His gaze darted between her flushed face and the straining peak under his thumb, a desire unlike any he'd ever known curling hotly in his belly as she went boneless beneath his hands.

Tristan eased her onto her back on the sofa and lowered himself gently on top of her, nudging her legs wider to make a place for his hips. His cock twitched against his falls as he moved closer to her tantalizing heat, but he didn't try and take it further than that—didn't move his hips against hers or try and unfasten her breeches—but he did continue to stroke and tease her, brushing his thumb around her nipple again and again, his lips parting with his panting breaths.

She arched her back, offering herself to his roaming hands. "Tristan, please."

God, it drove him mad to hear her breathless whimpers, to see her writhing for him. "I want to suckle you here." He pinched her nipple gently, a groan tearing from his throat when her body shuddered against his. "Will you let me?"

Her only answer was to clutch at him. She twisted his shirt between her fingers, urging him closer until he was leaning over her, then she buried her hands in his hair and tugged his head down to her breasts.

Tristan groaned at the slight sting in his scalp, then groaned again as he closed his lips over the stiff peak. "So hard for me." He dragged his tongue over the swollen tip until the fabric of her tunic was damp, and her nipple was straining for his mouth.

"Tristan." She dropped her head back, baring her neck for him.

Tristan pressed a half-dozen open-mouthed kisses over her tender skin before pulling slightly away. "Not here. Come to my bedchamber with me, Sophia."

She didn't answer at once, only looked at him, her pupils huge and dark, crowding out the green he'd grown to love so well. He could see the struggle on her face, the uncertainty in her trembling lips. He wanted to go to his knees, to clasp her around the waist and beg and plead with her, but he kept quiet, a bead of sweat sliding down his back as he waited for her to make her decision.

He saw the answer in her eyes before she spoke a word. The green depths softened as she gazed at him before she hid them behind her thick black lashes. She took his hand in hers, neither of them speaking as they rose from the sofa. Tristan led her to the stairs and together they climbed to the second floor, where Tristan's apartments lay at the end of the hallway.

He took her into his bedchamber, closed the door behind him, then turned to her and held out his arms. "Come here."

She went to him without hesitation, wrapping her arms around his waist and pressing her body flush against his. He captured her hand and raised it to his lips, kissed each of her fingertips one by one, then swung her up into his arms, carried her to his bed and lay her down on top of the coverlet. Her cheeks flushed as he looked down at her spread across his bed, his gaze touching her everywhere. "You're beautiful."

That word felt wrong, too weak to capture what he truly felt when he looked at her. A rueful smile quirked his lips. No, he was no poet. He *did* think Sophia beautiful—breathtakingly so—but her beauty was so much deeper than green eyes, silky hair, and pouting lips.

He couldn't put it into words, but he could show her how he felt, how much he wanted her. Slowly he reached for the hem of his shirt and tugged it over his head, his breath catching at the expressions flickering across her face.

Desire, hesitation, anticipation…

"Oh." Her chest rose and fell rapidly as his naked skin was revealed. She cast him a shy look from under her eyelashes, then she reached for him and dragged her fingers across his bare stomach, letting her fingertips slide just beneath the waistband of his breeches.

Tristan sucked in a breath, his head falling back at the sweet caress. "*Yes*. Touch me, Sophia."

She did as he asked, watching his face as she learned his body, pausing to linger on the secret skin behind his ear, the base of his neck—wherever her tentative strokes made his breath catch, or his eyes drift closed.

When he couldn't take another moment of her sensual exploration without going mad, he took control, turning her gently in his arms so her back was pressed against his bare chest, and slid his arms around her waist. He brushed a kiss over the nape of her neck, then moved lower, following the path of her spine with his lips, testing each of her vertebrae with his tongue. Her skin was hot, but she shivered under his touch. By the time he pressed a final kiss to the base of her spine and drew away, she was quivering.

He traced his fingertips down the graceful line of her back, following the path his mouth had taken before pausing to brush his lips over her hair. "Your hair, Sophia. Take it down."

Her hands were shaking as she pulled her hairpins out one by one. Tristan waited until every pin was gone before he gathered the thick locks of her hair into his hands then let it fall loose, watching the dark waves spill over her back. "I love it loose like this. Like a waterfall."

Sophia let her head fall back onto his shoulder with a sigh, and Tristan buried his face in her wild curls, inhaling the sweet scent of honeysuckle. "I want to see your hair against your bare skin," he murmured into her ear. He fingered the edge of her black tunic. "Take this off for me, pixie."

She caught her breath at the nickname, but any hesitation she might have felt earlier, any misgivings she had seemed to have faded away, and she turned to face him. His breath grew harsh as she slowly drew the black tunic up her body, revealing a flash of the tempting skin of her belly, but he only caught a teasing glimpse of the lower curves of her bare breasts before she stopped, hiding herself from his avid gaze.

"Let it drop, Sophia. Let me see you." Tristan hardly recognized his own voice it was so raw and hoarse.

She did as she was bid, but she wouldn't have been Sophia if she hadn't shown just a hint of teasing defiance. Slowly, so slowly Tristan was certain his knees would give way before she was finished, she raised the tunic, revealing inch after inch of smooth, olive-tinted skin.

A small smile curved her lips as she watched his gaze follow her progress, swallowing as each bare inch of her was revealed. Her trim waist, the delectable curves of her breasts, and higher still, her...

Tristan drew in a sharp breath.

The plump, dark pink buds of her nipples, swollen from the caress of his fingers and lips. Tristan's tongue touched his bottom lip as a powerful tremor of desire shook him. God, he wanted to taste her there, without the barrier of her tunic between them.

He squeezed his eyes closed and prayed for control.

That was something that couldn't happen. Not tonight, not after what Sophia had been through, and not when the promises he'd made to his mother about his future still hung over his head.

A future that didn't include Sophia Monmouth. It wasn't a future Tristan wanted.

He wasn't a man who broke promises, but with each passing day Oxfordshire, his mother, and Lady Esther felt further away from him than they ever had before.

But with every breath he took, every stroke of his fingers over Sophia's warm skin, she grew more real to him. Not a shadow, and not a ghost, but a living, breathing woman, one he desired more than any woman he'd ever known. But a gentleman of honor didn't take a lady to his bed when he had nothing but his desire to offer her. He'd never make love to Sophia only to abandon her.

"Tristan?" Sophia's uncertain voice pierced his daze. He opened his eyes to find her staring at him, her tunic once again shielding her nakedness. "Is something wrong?"

"No, I—forgive me." He tore himself away from her with an effort, then reached behind her, plucked up a blanket from the bed, and wrapped it tenderly around her shoulders. "I want you so much, Sophia, but you're injured, and I didn't think you…I didn't think we'd…"

She pressed her fingers to his mouth to hush him, a playful smile quirking her lips. "A gentleman, Lord Gray, turns a lady away from his bed *before* she takes her tunic off. But when I left home this evening, I didn't intend to spend the night in your bed. Neither of us expected this to happen, and really, perhaps it's just as well if it doesn't."

Tristan tipped her chin up so he could see her eyes and murmured, "It's a few hours until morning. Stay with me here, Sophia."

It wasn't safe for her to venture out in the dark. Sophia's attacker could be watching Tristan's townhouse, waiting for her to emerge so he could finish what he'd started tonight. That alone was enough reason for Tristan to keep her with him, but it wasn't the only reason he wanted her to stay.

He just wanted *her*.

She considered him for a long moment, her eyes unreadable, but then she smiled and reached out to brush a finger over his upper lip, tracing the tiny white scar near the corner of his mouth. "If I stay, will you tell me how you got this scar?"

He caught her hand in his and pressed a sweet kiss to her fingertip. "No."

* * * *

Every lady is the heroine of her own story, Sophia.

Sophia gazed out into the darkness, one elbow resting on the windowsill. Such a lovely sentiment, and perhaps there was even some truth to it, but what Cecilia hadn't said was every lady, heroine or not, wasn't destined for a happy ending. Sophia's own story, well…it might be a drama or an adventure, a comedy or a fairy tale, but it hadn't ever been a romance.

That hadn't changed tonight, for all that her lips were still swollen from Tristan's kisses, and her skin still tender from his caresses.

She glanced over at his sleeping form. He'd dropped off soon after he'd gathered her against his chest and urged her head onto his shoulder. He'd felt warm and solid against her, and she thought she'd drift to sleep at once with the steady beat of his heart under her cheek, but that hadn't happened. Her eyes remained open as one hour after the next passed, until at last she slid out from under the coverlet and padded over to the window.

She didn't belong here.

He was the Earl of Gray. An aristocrat, a gentleman, and a Bow Street Runner, and she was an illegitimate street urchin born in Seven Dials to an unknown father and a prostitute mother. A girl who'd grown up to be, if not quite a criminal, not an innocent, either, and certainly not a heroine.

Perhaps even more telling, she'd never aspired to be either. A woman like her had no business being in Tristan's bedchamber or in his bed, but she'd persuaded herself to forget that truth for a few stolen moments in his arms.

But the truth would out. It always did. That had been the lesson of some other heroine's story, hadn't it? She couldn't recall the heroine's name now, or if she'd had a happy ending.

Sophia dropped her chin onto her hand and waited for the first shy streaks of light to illuminate the sky. She'd promised Tristan she wouldn't leave while it was still dark. A bit absurd, given she'd spent endless hours creeping about in the night. She knew how to manage the darkness. What she *didn't* know how to manage was a stubborn, overbearing, irresistible earl whose touch left her breathless.

It was a lucky thing, then, that she hadn't promised him she'd stay past the first hint of sunrise. Really, she should have left hours ago. She'd spent the night away from No. 26 Maddox before, but Lady Clifford and Sophia's friends would be wondering where she was.

She rose to her feet, set aside the blanket she'd wrapped herself in and hurried into her tunic, which she found in a crumpled heap on the floor.

She paused by the bed before creeping from the room, unable to leave without taking one last look at Tristan.

He was asleep on his back, his eyes closed and his breathing deep and even. Sophia drew in a long, slow breath as she gazed down at him. A lock of his dark hair had fallen over his forehead. It made him look younger, even boyish. Her fingers itched to brush it back, but she was afraid to touch him. If he wakened, he'd try and coax her to stay, and all it would take was one kiss, one touch for her resistance to crumble.

So, she left Tristan sleeping and stole into the hallway. She crept down the stairs, but paused once she reached the entryway. Her attacker would be long gone by now—criminals tended to scatter like rats as soon as the sun rose—but after last night's near miss, Sophia had vowed to herself she'd take to heart Lady Clifford's warnings against unnecessary risk.

The front entrance to the townhouse was riskier than the servants' entrance, so she ducked down a set of stairs leading to the kitchens, and made her way toward the door that let out into the mews.

Sophia opened the door, ready to dart out and hurry back to Maddox Street, but she stopped short on the threshold, her eyes widening. She'd assumed the mews would be deserted at this hour, but a smart, bottle green carriage with yellow wheels was there, standing in front of Lord Everly's stables.

She paused just behind the kitchen door, foot tapping as she waited for the carriage to leave before she ventured outside. The servants would be stirring soon—any moment now she could be caught out by Tristan's scullery maid—but she was reluctant to leave the safety of the kitchens while the carriage still lingered in the mews.

With her dastardly luck, Peter Sharpe was probably in it.

If the kitchen hadn't been so quiet, she might have missed the low murmur of voices.

She lifted her head, eyes narrowing. The voices were coming from what was presumably Lord Everly's carriage, with Lord Everly presumably inside it. How peculiar that his lordship should find it convenient to conduct his business from his carriage, at dawn, hidden from sight in the mews. Of course, he could be just returning from an evening of debauchery, and the voices nothing more than a squabble with his mistress, but it sounded as if…

Yes, it was.

Two male voices, one slightly raised. Lord Everly's, if she wasn't mistaken. She'd heard that nasal whine before, droning orders at his servants.

She hesitated, biting her lip.

Approaching the carriage might be considered by *some* to be an unnecessary risk, but given the strangeness of its appearance in this place, at this time, Sophia deemed it a calculated one. Fortunately, the respective locations of Tristan's and Lord Everly's stables meant the carriage was facing away from her, so she kept low, out of sight of anyone who happened to glance out the back window.

Step by step, slowly, closer, and closer still…

"…don't like it, this shifty business with Ives."

Sophia froze at Jeremy's name, a chill rushing over her skin.

"I don't know why you're in such a fuss over Ives. He'd dead, and we're better off for it. Good riddance to him, I say."

It was Lord Everly's voice, sounding bored. Sophia clenched her hands into fists. *Bored,* as if the question of Jeremy's life or death wasn't of the least consequence.

Because to him, it wasn't.

"So ye say, but Ives was taken out afore a single soul at Newgate could see 'is corpse, my lord. Only way to make sure 'e's dead is to see 'im swing at the end of a noose," another voice growled, this one harder and colder. "And we've that other matter to take care of."

What other matter would that be? Sophia inched closer. She was almost certain she hadn't heard the second voice before, but she didn't dare peek through the back window of the carriage to check.

"I told you, it will be dealt with soon enough." Lord Everly again, this time with an irritated huff.

"When will that be, my lord? If this thing goes wrong, it'll be my neck on the noose. If I swing, I'll see to it yer right beside me, Everly."

There was a brief silence. When Lord Everly spoke again the languid note in his voice had disappeared. "Tomorrow night, then. I'll give Sharpe his orders. Make sure you're at the church in good time, and in the meantime, don't come back here again. I told you once before I can't be seen talking to you."

The other man's only reply was a muttered curse. Next came the unmistakable click of a latch, then the carriage door was thrown open. Sophia paused long enough to see a booted foot and the tip of a cane emerge, then she scurried back to the safety of Tristan's kitchen as quietly as possible, taking care to keep low. She ducked through the door and pressed herself against the wall, her heart pounding.

When no one came after her, she peeked around the edge of the door, hoping to get a look at Lord Everly's partner—the man, she was certain—who'd executed Henry Gerrard.

Unfortunately, Lord Everly's blasted carriage was still there, blocking her view of the mews. By the time it rolled into the stables, she only had time to catch a glimpse of a tall, wiry dark-haired man, dressed all in black, disappearing around the corner.

He were biggish, and thinner...tall, with black hair.

The fourth man.

Between Jeremy's description of him and the snatches of conversation she'd just overheard, Sophia knew it must be him.

The fourth man had been talking with Lord Everly—scheming with him.

Lady Clifford had suspected all along there was someone else involved in this business, pulling the strings from behind the scenes. Someone with much more power than Peter Sharpe.

Someone like an earl.

Lord Everly, a member of the House of Lords, a devoted supporter of William Pitt's government, and a respected peer of the realm, was involved in a murder.

Chapter Fifteen

Something had woken him, but this time, it wasn't a nightmare.

Tristan cracked one eye open but remained still, half-afraid if he moved, the nightly terrors that had haunted him these past weeks—ghosts and white marble crypts, blood-stained corpses and an innocent boy clad in prison irons—would reappear, and drag him down once again into his nightmares.

But the terrors didn't come. For the first time in weeks, all remained peaceful and quiet.

What had woken him, then? A sound, so soft he felt it more than heard it, a slight weight settling on the edge of the bed, the subtle shift of the coverlet sliding over his bare skin, and then…stillness, and silence.

His eyes snapped open, but he didn't have to look to know what he'd find.

An empty bedchamber.

Sophia was gone.

Fool that he was, he'd expected to wake with her beside him, wrapped in his arms, her warm curves pressed against him, the scent of honeysuckle teasing his senses.

He gave a hopeful sniff, but not a trace of honeysuckle remained.

She'd taken *that* with her, too.

He struggled upright and reached for the coverlet she'd been wrapped in when she fell asleep beside him last night. It was cold, much as his bedchamber was. The servant hadn't yet been in to build up the fire. A thin slice of moon was still visible in the sky, but the sun's first rays were driving it back as they crept over the edge of the horizon.

She'd left when it was still dark, then. Given he'd been wrapped around her when she fell asleep, she must have been stealthy indeed to slip from his bed without waking him. But then he already knew she was stealthy.

If she could climb to the roof of Lord Everly's pediment, then she could certainly leave Tristan's bed without his knowing it.

Perhaps it was just as well she'd left. He was...well, not *quite* betrothed yet, but only because he'd remained in London. If he'd gone to Oxfordshire as his mother demanded, Lady Emilia—that is, Lady *Esther*—would be well on her way to becoming the Countess of Gray.

If he'd been another kind of man, he might have tried to coax Sophia into a passionate affair regardless of a betrothal, but Tristan didn't trifle with young ladies, or indulge in scandalous liaisons. He was no rake, and he wouldn't become one now, no matter how much he desired Sophia Monmouth.

She'd done the right thing, leaving him alone in his bed this morning. It was better for them both this way. He lay back down and dragged the coverlet up his chest. The only reasonable thing to do was go back to sleep. The sun hadn't even fully risen, and he'd gotten precious little rest the night before.

He squeezed his eyes closed and waited, but sleep had fled his bed, much as Sophia had. He rolled over onto his back, then shifted onto his side, then his other side, squirming and kicking at the coverlet until it was tangled so tightly around him his legs began to tingle from lack of blood flow.

Only his legs, though. His cock seemed lively enough. It was wide awake and throbbing maddeningly. He slid his hand under the coverlet and gave it a comforting squeeze, but it refused to be pacified.

It wanted Sophia. *He* wanted Sophia, a lady he had no right to want, and no claim on. It occurred to him with a jolt of panic he might never want anyone else, ever again. Certainly not Lady Emil—Lady Esther. Perhaps if Lady Esther did become the Countess of Gray, he'd be able to remember her name.

As for Sophia...

Tristan couldn't understand how things had come to such a pass so quickly. He wasn't the sort of man who lost his head over a woman. He'd had liaisons before, but they'd always been discreet, tidy affairs with discreet, tidy widows. He'd never lost control with any of them—it had been rather like scratching an itch. Satisfying in the moment, but forgettable.

Nothing like the wild, messy, desperate passion of last night.

A few short weeks ago he'd been on his way back to Oxfordshire, reconciled to his fate, but now here he was flopping about uselessly in his bed with a throbbing cock, worrying over a wild, dark-haired pixie of a woman who bent the law to suit her whims.

And he didn't *care*. He, the Ghost of Bow Street, a man who'd spent years of his life dedicated to eradicating crime in London, didn't *care* if the lady he'd taken to his bed climbed columns, dressed in breeches, and bribed a prison guard to free a convicted murderer from the dungeons at Newgate. An *innocent* convicted murderer, to be fair, but a bribe was a bribe, and breeches were breeches.

How could he have become so besotted with a headstrong, willful chit like Sophia Monmouth? Worst of all, she was reckless. Not five hours after she'd been threatened by a club-wielding villain, she'd gone wandering off into the dark again, as if it were inconceivable the blackguard who'd attacked her once already might decide to have another go at her.

Sophia Monmouth was going to be the death of him. Of him, or herself.

Tristan tossed the covers back and threw his legs over the side of the bed. What had he done with his breeches? He rose and stumbled about in the dark until he found them tangled in the bed hangings. He pulled them over his hips and yanked the bell to summon a servant, then strode over to his desk. He snatched up paper and a quill, scrawled a quick note, then paced from one end of the bedchamber to the other as he waited for a servant to appear.

A few moments later, Tribble himself came in. "Good morning, Lord—"

"Never mind the pleasantries, Tribble." Tristan handed the paper to him and waved a hand toward the door. "Have one of the footmen take that to Lyndon, and hurry, man. Tell him it's urgent, and to come at once." Lyndon wasn't going to be pleased to be rousted from his bed in the wee hours of the morning, but it couldn't be helped.

As it happened, Lyndon *wasn't* pleased, particularly when he discovered the reason he'd been summoned. He stood in the middle of Tristan's bedchamber, his clothing askew and his hair standing on end, frowning as he listened to Tristan explain his dilemma.

At last, he held up a hand for silence. "A moment, if you would, Gray. Do you mean to tell me you spent the night with Miss Monmouth, then woke to find she'd left you alone in your bed? *That's* why you dragged me out here in the middle of the night?"

Tristan blinked. "Well, not *just* that."

"Good Lord, Gray. You said it was *urgent*. I thought your bloody townhouse was on fire!" Lyndon threw himself into a chair and thumped a booted foot down on the ottoman. "I left Lady Cerise in such a pout I feared a bird would fly through the window and land on her lower lip. Nothing less than sapphires and diamonds will sooth her hurt feelings. I'll make certain Rundell & Bridge send the bill to you."

Tristan had resumed pacing, but now he turned to Lyndon with a frown. "Lady Cerise? When did that start? I'm not sure she's a wise choice as mistresses go, Lyndon."

Lyndon dragged a weary hand down his face. "It's…we were…oh, for God's sake, Gray! What difference does it make when it started? Let's concentrate on the matter at hand, shall we? The way I see it, you've taken a thief into your bed, yet you're quibbling with me over whether Lady Cerise is a suitable mistress."

"She isn't a thief!" Tristan burst out, then snapped his mouth closed, surprised at his own vehemence.

"Ah. Changed your mind about that, have you? Well, I won't say I didn't see that coming." Lyndon studied him with narrowed eyes. "Very well, then. She's not a thief, but she's not an innocent, either."

Tristan pressed his lips together to stop himself from leaping to Sophia's defense again. The truth was, she wasn't innocent. She'd already confessed to helping Jeremy Ives escape from Newgate. Then again, questions of guilt, innocence, and justice had become considerably murkier since he'd met Sophia. "In any case, Miss Monmouth's not my mistress."

Lyndon snorted. "Not if you have your way about it. Anyone can see you're besotted with her."

"I'm not besotted, just…" Tristan trailed off. Once again, Lyndon was right. If wanting Sophia more than any other woman he'd ever known— if finding her fascinating and worrying about her safety meant he was besotted—then he was certainly besotted with her. Since he'd met her, he'd hardly spared a thought for anything else.

That was rather a problem, wasn't it? Tristan dropped into the chair across from Lyndon with a sigh. He'd spent one night with Sophia. They hadn't made love, yet he already found it intolerable to wake without her in his bed.

"Let me ask you this, Gray. Do you trust Miss Monmouth?"

Ah, that was the crux of the issue. Given the business with Ives and Sophia's association with Lady Clifford, he *shouldn't* trust her, yet…

"I do. I've never known anyone like her before, Lyndon. She doesn't think as we do, but I don't question her honor. My every instinct tells me she's a lady of conscience."

"I see." Lyndon studied the tip of his boot. "Do these instincts originate in your brain, Gray, or between your legs?"

Tristan's eyebrows shot up. Well, that was plain enough, but then Lyndon had never been one to mince words. He glanced at the bed, a pang of longing piercing his chest as he took in the rumpled sheets. Only mere hours ago, Sophia had been tucked into a blanket beside him, her legs pressed against his, her hair scattered in a wild tumble across his chest.

He met Lyndon's gaze. "I don't know, Lyndon. I can't deny I want her. That's the problem. I haven't the faintest bloody idea about anything anymore."

Lyndon let out a long sigh. "Christ, Gray. I liked you better when you were dull and responsible. When did you start making such a bloody mess of everything?"

"Yes, well, I *did* say it was urgent." A small smile crossed Tristan's lips. "My apologies to Lady Cerise."

Lyndon didn't reply right away, but rose to his feet and wandered over to the window. The moon had disappeared while they'd been talking. The sun was feeble yet, still struggling through the fog of dirt and grime, but the city had begun to stir. Lyndon rested his palms on the sill, his head down. "You might be better off turning this business with Miss Monmouth back over to Sampson Willis." Lyndon turned back to face Tristan. "You're an earl now, Gray, not a Bow Street Runner."

Tristan thought of the menacing figure who'd leapt out of the darkness last night, the sickening crack as Sophia's head met the pavement, and shook his head. "No. I can't simply walk away now. Someone attacked Sophia last night, Lyndon. I came upon them just in time, but I have no doubt he would have left her dead if he'd had the chance."

Lyndon paled. "Jesus. This business is foul to the very core, isn't it? I'm worried this won't end well for you, or for Miss Monmouth. Your feelings for her are complicated, and it only becomes more so when you throw Lady Clifford into the mix. She plays fast and loose with the law, and those in London who are aware of the Clifford School know it."

"I'm no longer so certain about Lady Clifford's character, either. I don't deny her code of ethics differs from mine, but she *does* have one." That had surprised Tristan, given what he knew about Lady Clifford, but it shouldn't have. Gossips, after all, rarely troubled themselves much with the truth.

Lyndon sighed. "I met Miss Monmouth, talked to her. I don't believe she's a thief or a criminal, but I'm not sure it makes sense for you to trust her either, Gray. You hardly know her, for one, and you already know her hands aren't entirely clean."

Tristan knew it to be true, but it was difficult to hear it from Lyndon. Lyndon saw his struggle, and turned back to the window to give Tristan privacy, but the more Tristan tried to sort out his thoughts, the more they slipped from his hands. So, he sat quietly, utterly still, and let every encounter he'd had with Sophia since he first saw her on Lord Everly's roof drift through his mind.

The boy's tunic, and that black cap—he shook his head, a half-smile on his lips. Now he'd seen her curves laid bare, he couldn't imagine how he'd ever mistaken her for a boy.

The nimble grace with which she'd slipped through that wrought iron gate, the look on her face when he'd climbed it. She'd led him on quite a chase through London that night, and in truth, she hadn't stopped since. He was still chasing her, not knowing which corner she'd dart around, which direction she'd lead him next.

She was reckless, stubborn and willful, yes, but more than anything else, she was *alive*. Her vibrancy, her determination, the way she was a little too much to handle. It was like galloping through a forest on a magnificent horse that wasn't quite broken—risky, even dangerous, but breathtaking. That wildness in her called to something inside him, the same thing that had turned him into a Bow Street Runner. They weren't so very different, really. In some ways, Sophia was more like him than anyone else he'd ever known.

In the ways that mattered.

Tristan lifted his gaze to Lyndon. "Sophia isn't a thief, and she isn't a criminal. She's as ethical as you or me. She simply sees things differently than we do."

Lyndon didn't appear to hear him. "Gray? You may want to see this." He was looking at something outside the window, his shoulders tense.

"I can't walk away from this now, Lyndon," Tristan murmured. His feelings for Sophia *were* complicated, but they were too powerful to deny. He'd always been wary of intense emotions because he hadn't wanted to become like his mother or his elder brother, Thomas, who were both victims of their passions. He'd never wanted that for himself, but perhaps he was more like them than he'd ever realized. He'd been swept up into the whirlwind of Sophia Monmouth before he was even aware his feet had left the ground.

Lyndon leaned further over the sill to get a better look out the window, and a soft exclamation fell from his lips. "What the *devil*? I tell you, Gray, you'll want to come and take a look out the window."

Tristan stayed where he was, his gaze hardening as he fixed it on Lyndon's back. "Did you hear me, Lyndon? I'm not turning this business over to Sampson Willis. I can't."

Lyndon made an impatient noise in his throat, then beckoned to Tristan with one hand, keeping his gaze on whatever was taking place outside. "For God's sake, Gray, cease your blathering and come here, will you?"

Still, Tristan didn't move. "You're wrong about her, Lyndon. She's unconventional, but—"

"Unconventional? Er...yes. You could say that." Lyndon flapped a hand toward the window. "See for yourself."

Tristan crossed his arms over his chest. "I grant you she's unpredictable, and not the sort of lady we've ever known before, but for all her unpredictability, I don't believe she's up to anything truly unscrupulous."

"No?" Lyndon turned and leaned back against the windowsill with his eyebrow raised. "Well, then. I suppose there's a perfectly reasonable explanation why I've just seen her darting about in the mews, dressed as a milkmaid, with a yoke over her shoulders and a bucket of milk in each hand."

Tristan stared at him for one frozen moment, then leapt from his chair and rushed to the window. He glanced from one end of the mews to the other, then peered directly below before turning to Lyndon with an incredulous expression. "Have you gone mad, Lyndon? She's not down there!"

"The devil she isn't." Lyndon crowded into the window beside Tristan, and pointed at the mews below. "She right there, Gray, at Lord Everly's kitchen door."

Tristan nudged Lyndon aside. He could make out Everly's servants' entrance at the edge of the window, and he caught a glimpse of dark hair and drab skirts before the kitchen door opened, and the small figure disappeared into the depths of Lord Everly's townhouse.

Chapter Sixteen

"Yer not Polly." A slovenly-looking creature in a soiled apron stood in the doorway to Lord Everly's kitchen, glaring at Sophia. "What's 'appened to Polly?"

Not a thing had happened to Polly. On the contrary, she'd come upon Sophia at precisely the right time, and met with an extraordinary stroke of good luck. Polly had taken one look at the shiny gold sovereign in Sophia's palm, snatched it up, and turned over her garb, yoke, and pails without a single question or a word of argument.

"Polly's ill. I'm her, er...her sister."

Just before Sophia had knocked on the door, she'd uttered a quick prayer Lord Everly didn't employ one of those despotic French cooks—they were a fussy lot, always asking questions—but it seemed his lordship had gone in quite the opposite direction.

The woman swept a critical look over Sophia, then let out a derisive snort. "Sister, eh? Polly's got two stone on ye, girl. Ye look like yer about to topple over with them pails." She shifted half a step away from the door. "Aw right, then. The master must 'ave 'is milk, one way or t'other."

Sophia stepped over the threshold of Lord Everly's townhouse and into his kitchen, grinning to herself over the success of her plan. Yes, she was trussed up with a wooden yoke over her shoulders like a pair of oxen, but aside from the heavy milk pails she was staggering under, it had worked brilliantly.

Even better than the pediment roof.

Thinking of Lord Everly's roof instantly conjured up thoughts of Tristan, but Sophia pushed them resolutely away. If she could judge by the scowl on Lord Everly's cook's face, she wasn't the chatty, friendly sort, which meant Sophia had only a little time to work out how to get her business done before she was tossed out the door.

She glanced around, noting the layout of the kitchen, particularly the doors and windows. There was a tiny sliver of space underneath the door behind her. Sophia fingered the small metal buckle she'd pried off her shoe and shoved into her pocket. The gap was awfully narrow, but a good shove with her toe might see the thing done.

There was another doorway at the opposite end of the kitchen, but it was impossible to tell where it led. Then there was the one window behind her that looked out onto the mews. Sophia narrowed her eyes, considering it. It was small, but she might be able to slip through it if she were careful—

"Don't stand about gaping like a half-wit, girl. Do yer work, and git." The cook shoved a heaping spoonful of what appeared to be porridge into her mouth with one hand, and waved a meaty hand at the door with the other.

"Er…yes, ma'am."

A timid scullery maid approached and offered her a milk jug. Sophia took it and upended the contents of her pail into it, one eye on her work, the other darting around the kitchens. The doorway on the opposite side of the room might lead into a stillroom with access to the small back garden, but it was difficult to tell from her position in front of the long wooden table. She craned her neck to the side, but all she could make out was a row of cabinets lining one wall, and—

"Ye've spilled the milk, ye clumsy chit! I told ye those pails were too heavy for ye! Ye got no meat on yer bones, girl."

The scullery maid let out a terrified squeak, and Sophia looked down to see a single drop of milk had spilled from the pail onto the table. "I beg your—"

"Give it here." The cook snatched the pail from Sophia's hand, dumped the rest of the milk into the jug, then shoved the pail back into her arms. "Ye tell yer master to send Polly next time, or don't bother coming to 'is lordship's door. Now git!"

The cook turned a menacing look on the poor scullery maid, who darted across the kitchen as if the devil himself were after her and opened the door leading into the mews. "This way, miss."

Sophia trudged across the room after her, muttering a prayer the gap beneath the door was wider than it looked. She didn't necessarily expect her prayers to be answered—heaven didn't look kindly on sinners like herself—but as she was being thrust out the door, she slid the buckle free from her pocket, hiding it in her palm.

"Beg pardon, miss." The scullery maid gave her an apologetic look and stepped back from the door. She pushed it closed behind her, but before it could latch Sophia pressed her fingertips against the wood, stopping it.

She sucked in a breath, half-expecting the cook to descend on her with a rolling pin, but the woman didn't come.

No one did.

Sophia crouched down, slid the yoke carefully from her shoulders, set it down as quietly as she could on the cobbles, and tried to slide the buckle under the door.

It didn't fit.

She gave it a little shove, but it didn't budge.

"Dash it." She sat back on her heels, biting her lip with vexation. It was maddening to come so close only to give it up now, but the blasted buckle was too thick—

Sophia went still as she studied the space, then she got down on her knees to get a closer look, one hand still on the door. It sat crookedly in its frame, as if it hadn't been hung properly. She pressed her fingertips against the bottom edge of the door and slid them from one side to the other. The slit was just a touch wider at the end closest to the hinge, just wide enough to…

Yes!

She jammed the end of the buckle into the space beneath the door, then gave it a shove with the heel of her hand. The buckle slid forward a tiny bit more, just enough so it was securely wedged beneath the door.

Sophia scrambled to her feet, a wide grin on her lips. She took up her yoke, balanced it on her shoulders, and made her way to the other end of the mews, where she handed it back over to Polly, who'd been waiting in a shadowy corner of the stables, out of sight of Lord Everly's door. The girl swung the yoke onto her own shoulders as if it were no heavier than a silk shawl, and disappeared down the street.

Well, that had been a tidy bit of work, hadn't it? Sophia dusted off her hands, flushed and still grinning at her success, but her smile faded a little as her gaze landed on an upper window of Tristan's townhouse, and the memories she'd been holding at bay since she sneaked out of his bed this morning swept over her.

As much as she might wish otherwise, it wasn't the sort of night a lady could forget, any more than *he* was the sort of man she could easily set aside without a second thought.

She shivered, remembering the hot press of his mouth on hers, his wicked tongue slipping between her lips, the rasp of his emerging beard scraping against the tender skin of her face and neck, her throat...

No. Nothing good would come of daydreaming about Tristan—that is, *Lord Gray.* She must remember to think of him as Lord Gray from now on, or better yet, not to think of him at all. It was the reason she'd left him this morning, even as everything inside her had longed to stay, to brush his dark hair back from his forehead and wait for those remarkable gray eyes to open.

Dash it. Sophia squeezed her eyes closed, clenching her hands into fists. She had to find a way to exorcize him, just as the Catholics priests had done centuries ago to rid themselves of their demons. Tristan might be a handsome, tempting demon, but that didn't mean he couldn't be banished. That was why she'd left his bed this morning, never to return again—

"No rooftops today, Miss Monmouth?" A hard arm snaked around Sophia's waist, and she was pulled roughly against a warm, muscular chest. "I can't say I think the mews your most inspired hiding place."

Sophia let out a squeak of surprise, and might have followed it with an elbow to her captor's ribs and a foot to his shin if she hadn't known at once who he was.

"What are you doing, sneaking about Lord Everly's mews, hmmm?" Tristan's low chuckle stirred the hair at her temple. "Shame on you, pixie. But then you make a habit of sneaking about, don't you? Sneaking from my bed, sneaking into my kitchen, sneaking about the mews in the dark." He made a tsking noise, and his hot breath drifted over her ear. "You try my patience, Miss Monmouth."

Sophia opened her mouth to answer, but she never got the chance. His arms tightened around her waist, and the next thing she knew the ground vanished beneath her feet, and a hard shoulder appeared out of nowhere under her belly.

It took her a moment to realize what had happened, but once she did, she began to kick and squirm to free herself. "Tristan! Have you gone mad? This isn't necessary—"

"You wouldn't think so, would you? Yet here we are." He tightened his arm around the backs of her thighs to still her. "Stop kicking."

"You're going to drop me!" Sophia clutched handfuls of the back of his shirt in her fists to steady herself.

"I won't if you stop wriggling. It's not as if you're heavy. I've carried walking sticks that weigh more than you do."

Despite herself, Sophia laughed. "What nonsense. I'm much heavier than a walking stick, especially the hollow ones without the figured gold or silver nobs—"

"The hollow sticks are more properly called canes, but I'm not interested in discussing either canes or walking sticks at the moment, Miss Monmouth."

It occurred to Sophia this might be one of those times when it was wiser to keep her mouth closed, but by then it was too late. "Well, what are you interested in, Lord Gray?"

Tristan hitched her higher on his shoulder. "Milkmaids."

Sophia huffed out a breath. "Oh, for pity's sake. This is absurd. I must insist you put me down this instant, my lord."

"No. I don't think I will." He was striding across the mews toward his townhouse. "Last time I let go of you I didn't care for the result. I wasn't pleased to find myself alone in my bed this morning."

His tone was grim. He was certainly angry with her, but there was an underlying thread of something else in his voice that made her hesitate.

A hint of confusion and...dejection?

Sophia stopped kicking, and her grip loosened on his shirt. Given she was upside down, the blood had already rushed to her head, but there was no denying the way her cheeks heated at his words. Not with guilt, exactly—she'd long since decided guilt was a waste of time—but perhaps she *did* feel a touch of regret.

But under the circumstances, regret was unacceptable, and she wouldn't indulge it. She opened her mouth to remind him she was under no obligation to please him, but what came out instead was, "I didn't mean to..."

What? Hurt his feelings? Well, it was the truth, wasn't it? When she'd fled his bedchamber this morning, she'd assumed she was only hurting herself.

"Didn't mean to *what*, Miss Monmouth? Sneak off like a thief?"

She swallowed. "I thought it best for both of us if I went."

"Why?" He bit out, his shoulder tensing underneath her.

Without realizing she did it, she was running her hands soothingly over his back. He was wearing only the shirt and breeches he'd tossed aside last night, and she could feel his warm skin through the thin linen. "You can't be saying you don't agree it was for the best. Wasn't there a part of you that was relieved to find me gone?"

"*No.*" His growl was so low she almost didn't hear it, but she felt the vibration of it against her palms. "What did I do to make you think I wanted you to go? For God's sake, I begged you to stay last night, and I don't beg for anything, Sophia."

Sophia stilled, her head spinning. In truth, he hadn't said or done a single thing. Just the opposite, in fact. He'd given her more pleasure than she'd ever thought a man could offer, then he'd gathered her against him, wrapped his arms around her, and fallen asleep with his face buried in her hair.

"It wasn't what you said. I just thought…can we have this discussion with me on my feet, please? This is ridiculous, Tristan. Put me down."

"No. Not until I'm sure you can't run away from me again." He paused in front of a door on the other end of the mews and banged his fist on the wood.

There was a shuffling on the other side of the door, and the next moment it flew open, and Sophia heard a scolding voice say, "Why, who do you think you are, pounding on Lord Gray's door like some kind of savage—"

The voice broke off in a shocked gasp, and Sophia felt Tristan chuckle. "I think I'm Lord Gray. I beg your pardon for the intrusion, Mrs. Beeson. I would have opened the door myself, but as you can see, I have my hands full."

Whoever Mrs. Beeson was, she recovered quickly. "Indeed, I can, my lord. Perhaps your…friend would care for a cup of tea, or chocolate?"

The door creaked, and Tristan strode forward into a warm, bright kitchen. He tipped Sophia forward into his arms, then lowered her into a chair at a scrubbed kitchen table.

Sophia took one look around, and her cheeks burst into flames. Half a dozen servants were seated around it, all of them staring at her with identical shocked expressions.

"We were just finishing our breakfast, my lord." Mrs. Beeson scurried around the table, snatching up dishes and teacups and nudging people out of their chairs.

Tristan eyed his startled servants. "There's no need to—"

"Nonsense, my lord." Mrs. Beeson clucked her tongue. "This lot has plenty to keep them busy today. David, you're meant to be helping Tribble in the wine cellar this morning, and Anne and Matilda, you'd best get on with polishing the grand chandelier in the entrance hall. Go on then, get on with all of you." Mrs. Beeson flapped the tea towel at the loiterers until she'd driven the last servant out of the kitchen.

"Er…thank you, Mrs. Beeson." Tristan watched the last straggler scurry out the door. "Miss Monmouth here has had a trying morning, and might like some refreshment to calm her nerves. Miss Monmouth, this is my cook, Mrs. Beeson."

Sophia, who thought Tristan's cook had every right to throw the tea towel in her face, raised a wary gaze to Mrs. Beeson, half-afraid of what she'd find.

Mrs. Beeson was not, thankfully, anything like Lord Everly's cook. She was a plump, ruddy-cheeked lady of middle age, with brown hair pulled back in a tidy bun, and kind blue eyes with deep laugh lines in the crease. "How do you do, Miss Monmouth? Dear me, you do look as if you could use a restorative."

Sophia wouldn't have thought it possible, but those kind blue eyes made her flush deepen. Mrs. Beeson put her in mind of Winnie Browning, the Clifford School's housekeeper, and Sophia knew very well what Winnie would think of a young lady who arrived in her kitchen in the arms of an uppity lord. "Oh, no, please don't go to any trouble on my account."

"No trouble at all, Miss Monmouth." Mrs. Beeson bustled toward a tray resting on one end of the table. She poured Sophia a cup from a pretty white and blue china teapot, put it on the table in front of her, then set the tray with sugar, milk, and a half-dozen warm biscuits at Sophia's elbow. "There we are. Now, if you'll excuse me, Lord Gray, I'm off to the fish market."

Tristan waited until Mrs. Beeson had caught up her basket and left the kitchen before sitting down at the table across from Sophia. "Let's start at the beginning, shall we? What the devil are you up to, wandering about the mews dressed as a milkmaid?"

Sophia pressed her lips together. "What makes you think I'm up to anything? Did it occur to you I might simply be delivering the milk?" It was, after all, the most logical explanation.

He leaned over the table, his gaze holding hers. "Not for one single, blessed second."

* * * *

Tristan had never found it fascinating to watch a woman eat a biscuit before. He couldn't have said whether watching Sophia Monmouth eat one was a truly fascinating event, or if he'd become so foolish over her, he was entranced with everything she did.

Lyndon would say it was the latter.

You're besotted with her.

Tristan shrugged the thought aside. Besotted was a strong word. He was intrigued by her, yes, and he admired her spirit and bravery, but that wasn't the same as—

"Mrs. Beeson's quince preserves are delicious." Sophia caught an errant drop of the sticky sweet on the tip of her thumb, then licked it off. "I've never tasted better, but if you repeat that to Mrs. Browning, I'll deny I said it."

Tristan swallowed, his stomach tightening with want. But then he'd never denied he wanted her. It would be rather difficult to deny it when a bit of jam on her thumb made his cock press eagerly against his falls, but desiring a lady and being besotted with her were two different—

"This cream is lovely, too. I daresay Mrs. Beeson doesn't rely on Polly for her dairy. The milk sloshing about in that pail was filthy." Sophia scooped up a spoonful of the cream, plopped it daintily on top of her biscuit, then bit into it. Her tongue darted out to lick a stray dollop of the cream from the corner of her lip.

Tristan suppressed a groan. Damn it, it would be far better for both of them if she kept her tongue in her mouth. He breathed a sigh of relief when she raised her cup to her lips for a sip of tea. Ah, that was much better. There was nothing seductive about a lady drinking a cup of tea—

"May I take another lump of sugar, Lord Gray? I have a shameful sweet tooth." She grinned at him, her pink lips curving mischievously. "Cecilia scolds me for it, but as I'm sure you can imagine, it doesn't do the least bit of good."

Tristan stared at her lips, mesmerized. Good Lord, he could feel her smile all the way down to his toes.

"Is it wicked of me to be so stubborn in pursuit of my pleasures?" She sank her teeth into her plump bottom lip to stifle a laugh.

Tristan's gaze lingered on her mouth.

"But then we're all sad creatures when it comes to satisfying our cravings, and I daresay a bit of sugar is harmless enough." Her eyes widened as she caught a glimpse of his face. "Tristan? Whatever is the matter? You look flushed."

Tristan had never launched himself over a table before. Earls didn't scramble over tabletops, spilling the cream and sending teacups crashing to the floor. They didn't lose control of themselves and behave like savages. It might be the only thing they had in common with Bow Street Runners. He wasn't even fully aware he'd done it until he'd snatched Sophia into his arms, dragged her over his lap and taken her mouth with his.

His head spun as he teased his tongue between her lips, a helpless groan rising from his chest. Good Lord, but she was the sweetest thing he'd ever tasted. Sugar and tea, quince preserves and her own unique honey flavor, sweet on his tongue. God, he wanted to dive into her and stay there forever, to drown in her.

I *am* besotted with her.

Lyndon was right. Lyndon was always right, it seemed.

Tristan's feelings for Sophia were tangled and confused still, but at the moment, he didn't care. He cared only that he wanted her, and by the way she was sighing and trembling against him, he knew she wanted him, too.

"Why did you leave me this morning?" Tristan groaned, his mouth moving desperately down her neck, tasting her and dropping passionate kisses over her soft skin. "I woke wrapped up in sheets that still carried your scent, but you were gone."

He couldn't stop himself from taking her mouth again, stroking her cheekbones as he drew her toward him. He teased at the seam of her lips until she opened for him, and they both moaned at the first stoke of his tongue against hers. Tristan felt her hands sink into his hair, her fingers tugging at the strands to drag him closer.

He told himself it was enough to kiss her—enough to hold her in his arms—but his control slipped further and further into the abyss the longer their lips clung together, until he stumbled to his feet with Sophia still in his arms and set her down on top of the table.

She let out a breathless laugh. "Take care with the teacups."

He chuckled against her lips, but soon enough he was lost in the sensual glide of her tongue against his, her fingers in his hair, the soft sighs of pleasure on her lips. The next thing he knew her tunic was clenched in his fist, his knuckles grazing the smooth skin of her belly as he dragged it up, higher, then higher...

Mrs. Beeson might have gotten the shock of her life when she returned from the market if, in Sophia's frantic scrambling to help him remove the tunic, her hip hadn't bumped against a saucer and toppled it over the edge of the table. Tristan tore his mouth from hers, and they both cast dazed looks at the smashed china on the floor before turning to each other.

Her cheeks were pink, her lips swollen and damp from his kisses. Locks of her hair had fallen from her neat bun and were curling against her shoulders. Tristan took one look at her, and it was all he could do not to tumble her onto her back on Mrs. Beeson's spotless kitchen table.

Sophia buried her face against his shoulder, smothering a laugh. "Oh, dear. We've spoiled that lovely china set! I did warn you to take care, Tristan."

"Of the teacups, yes. You didn't say a word about the saucers." He tugged gently on a loose lock of her hair. "You haven't told me what were you doing in the mews. Don't think I've forgotten about that, Miss Monmouth."

She patted his chest. "No. I've never known you to forget anything, Lord Gray. Come, I have a story for you. I'll tell you on the way."

He raised an eyebrow. "Where are we going?"

Sophia took his hand and hopped down from the kitchen table. "To the Turk's Head Coffeehouse."

Chapter Seventeen

This conversation wasn't going at all as Sophia had planned.

She'd launched into her explanation of the events of the morning as soon as they were in Tristan's carriage and on their way to the Strand. It began amicably enough, but she'd hardly said a dozen words before Tristan was staring incredulously at her, his face becoming grimmer by the second.

"Let me see if I understand you, Sophia. You sneaked out of my bedchamber before dawn this morning, strolled through my kitchen and out the back door to make a clean escape into the mews, and—"

"Well, when you put it like that, it sounds far worse than it—"

"To make a clean escape into the mews," Tristan repeated, as if she hadn't spoken. "You found Lord Everly's carriage there, with Lord Everly and an unidentified man inside, but instead of remaining safely in the kitchens, or better yet, returning to my bedchamber as a sane person would have done, you—"

"Oh, come now, Tristan. You can't truly think I'd squander such an extraordinary opportunity to find out what—"

"The other man in the carriage was the fourth man. You do realize that, don't you? Did it occur to you if he'd seen you lurking behind the carriage, he would have finished the job he'd begun the night before?" Underneath the flush of anger on his cheeks, Tristan's face had gone white. "For God's sake, Sophia! How can you be so careless with your own safety?"

Sophia cringed at the look in those narrowed gray eyes. His lips, usually so full and sensual, were now pressed into a tight, forbidding line. Oh, dear. He *did* look angry. This wasn't going well at all. "I was extremely careful, I promise you."

"Not careful enough," Tristan snapped.

"Tristan." Sophia's soft voice caught Tristan's attention. "Jeremy was nearly hung for another man's crimes. Henry Gerrard was *murdered*, leaving his wife a widow and his son without a father. You want the men who committed the crimes punished, don't you?"

"Yes, of course, but not at your expense!" Tristan dragged a hand down his face. "You nearly got your skull cracked open last night, Sophia. Do you think I want to see you suffer the same fate as Henry?"

Sophia winced at this description of last night's attack, but she refused to give way on this. If she allowed Tristan's overprotective instincts to run amok now, the next thing she knew he'd have her locked in his bedchamber. "Chasing after criminals involves risk, Tristan. Last night was unfortunate, but despite that near miss, you have to trust I do know how to handle myself."

"It's not that I don't...I *do* trust you, Sophia, but I can't..." Tristan shook his head. "I don't want to lose you."

Sophia touched her fingers to her throat to smooth away the sudden lump there. The worry on his face, the note of fear in his voice—oh, he'd just broken her heart in two. Spontaneously, she caught his hand, raised it to her lips and pressed a fervent kiss to his knuckles. "I swear to you I will take the utmost care."

"See that you do." Tristan's voice was still tight, but his eyes darkened as her lips brushed against his fingers.

They were quiet as the carriage made its way toward the Turk's Head, until Tristan broke the silence with a sigh. "I'm almost afraid to ask, but how did you end up dressed as a milkmaid?"

Sophia turned to him with a tentative grin. "Ah, now that was a stroke of genius, if I do say so myself. I'd retreated to your kitchen and was peeking out a crack in the door, waiting for Lord Everly to leave before venturing out again. So, you see, I *was* being careful."

Tristan rolled his eyes, but a reluctant smile twitched at the corner of his lips. "I'm relieved to hear it, but the milkmaid outfit, Sophia? Unless Lord Everly tossed it out his carriage window, I fail to see how you ended up dressed in it."

"Yes, well, that's the genius part. As soon as Lord Everly's carriage was out of the way, who do you suppose I saw coming down the mews?"

"Let me see if I can guess. A milkmaid?"

Sophia beamed. "Yes, just so. I offered Polly—that was her name—a guinea to loan me her garb and let me take her milk buckets to Lord Everly's kitchen. She was quite amenable to the idea, and agreed to duck into the stables and wait for me to come back out. The thing was done in a trice, as easily as snapping my fingers."

Tristan nodded slowly. "Yes, that's very good, but what did you hope to gain from a visit to Lord Everly's kitchen?"

"I wanted to have a look around to see if I could determine the easiest way to get from the kitchens to the ground floor. That way when we go back tonight, we won't waste time fumbling about in the dark."

Tristan raised an eyebrow. "You want to break into Everly's house."

It wasn't a question.

Sophia gave him a shocked look. "Certainly not, Lord Gray. Why, that would be a *crime*. We won't need to break in. We'll walk right through the kitchen door."

His gray eyes narrowed. "What did you do to Lord Everly's kitchen door, Sophia?"

She shrugged. "Nothing much. Just wedged my shoe buckle into the crack at the bottom. The door wasn't hung properly, which is rather shoddy of Lord Everly, if you ask me. As long as none of his kitchen servants notice it—and I daresay they won't, as they're not the most observant lot—we can get into his townhouse through the kitchen door and make our way up to Lord Everly's study."

"Everly's study isn't anywhere near the kitchens, Sophia. It's up a flight of stairs and on the other side of the entrance hall. His servants might not be the sharpest in London, but even they are bound to notice the two of us strolling about. So, how do you intend to get from the kitchens to the study?"

Sophia cast a look up at him from under her eyelashes. "Er...carefully?"

Tristan blinked. "Carefully? That's the extent of your plan? To sneak about Everly's house *carefully*, and hope for the best?"

Sophia bit her lip. "Well, yes. It worked with the roof, didn't it?"

"No, it bloody didn't. If you recall, I saw you up there and chased you halfway across London!"

Sophia crossed her arms over her chest, nettled at this disparaging account of her rooftop scheme. "*You* saw me, yes. Lord Everly never did."

Tristan dragged a hand through his hair. "That may be true, but Everly's far more likely to see you wandering his hallways than lying on his pediment roof, and that's to say nothing of Sharpe. It's too dangerous."

Dangerous. Sophia blew out a breath at the word. They were back here, again?

"It isn't even just Everly and Sharpe, either. What of all the other servants? Housemaids, footmen—"

"Tristan." Sophia lay a hand on his arm to quiet him. "I don't deny it's risky, but we're running out of time. We've known since our visit to Jeremy whatever's happening at St. Clement Dane's Church didn't originate with Sharpe. Now we know Lord Everly has a hand in it." She met and held his gaze. "An important piece of the puzzle has just fallen into place, but we'll never find out how it fits into the whole without taking some risks."

"I'll go see Everly myself, then. I'll invent some business or other I need to discuss with him. I'll call on him, he'll take me to his study, and I'll—"

"You'll what?" Sophia interrupted, beginning to lose patience with him. "Interrogate him? Demand to see his private papers? No, Tristan. We know Jeremy didn't murder Henry Gerrard. Lady Clifford asked me to find out who did it, and why, and that's what I intend to do."

Silence.

Sophia turned her face to the window, her throat closing. She'd suspected it would come to this sooner or later, but with Tristan, she'd hoped it would be later. "This is who I am, Tristan," she murmured, still not looking at him. "It's…I know it's too much for most people."

She was too much for most people. Even Lady Clifford, who'd seen the worst London had to offer, occasionally despaired over Sophia.

"No." Tristan's warm fingers touched her chin, and he turned her face back to his. "Not for me, pixie."

Sophia's gaze met his, and she swallowed at the tenderness in those gray eyes.

Tristan cupped her face in his hands. "You're not too much for me."

Sophia let her forehead fall against his sturdy chest, her fingers curling into the edges of his coat. Even when the carriage turned onto the Strand, she didn't move away from him. His soft, warm breath stirred the wisps of hair at her temples, his words echoing in her head, stilling her.

You're not too much for me.

She'd never before wanted to believe a man's words quite so badly as she did now.

Tristan rested his big palm against the back of her head until the carriage drew to a stop in front of the Turk's Head. Then he stirred, and pressed a kiss to Sophia's forehead. "Come. Let's see what we can find out, shall we?"

* * * *

"Dunn, ye say?" Will Pryor, the proprietor of the Turk's Head rubbed a hand over his bristly jaw.

"Patrick Dunn, yes." Sophia leaned eagerly toward him. "Have you heard the name before?"

Pryor thought for a moment longer, then shook his head. "Afraid not, miss. It sounds familiar, but I can't recall why. Beg pardon, but I doubt I'll be much help to ye."

Tristan glanced at Sophia, then turned to Pryor. "Dunn was taken up for theft a few months ago, for stealing a man's pocket watch. The crime took place just down the street from here, at St. Clement Dane's Church."

The story seemed to jog Pryor's memory. "Oh, aye," he said with a slow nod. "I remember him now. I recall thinking it was odd when he was taken up. Seemed a good bloke, did Dunn."

"Not the thieving sort, then?" Tristan asked.

"Not a bit of it, no. Quiet bloke, studious like, and respectable. Didn't overindulge in the drink either, not like some of 'em who come here. He's a silversmith, or some such, I think."

"A weaver. Or he was, before he was convicted of theft." Sophia's face darkened. "Now he's confined to a prison hulk on the Thames, awaiting transport to Australia, and his wife and two children are left alone with no protection."

Pryor's mouth twisted. "That's not right, that isn't. Not if he didn't do it, leastways."

"We have good reason to think he didn't. That's why we're trying to help him. So, you can see, Mr. Pryor, why it's so important you tell us anything you can remember about the night he was taken up."

Pryor gave a helpless shrug. "I'd help you if I could, miss, but that was months ago. This is a busy place, and the days tend to all run into each other, ye see."

Sophia's face fell. "I do see, of course."

"Just one more thing, Mr. Pryor, if you would." Tristan braced his elbow on the bar and gave Pryor an affable smile. "Another customer of yours was also taken up for a crime committed at St. Clement Dane's Church, this one a great deal more serious. Do you recognize the name Jeremy Ives?"

Pryor had been running a damp cloth over the bar, but at Jeremy's name his head snapped up. "Ives? 'Course I remember *him*. He was the blackguard what murdered that Bow Street Runner. I told my wife, I says, Ives must have slit that poor man's throat not more'n half an hour after he left here that night. Gives ye the shivers to think about it, don't it?"

"Had you ever seen Ives here before?" Jeremy had told them he'd never been to the Turk's Head before that night. Tristan believed him, but this was a good way to gauge Pryor's honesty and the accuracy of his memory.

"Nay, never laid eyes on him before." Pryor frowned. "Now ye mention him, I don't mind telling ye he was the last lad in the world I ever would have said were a killer."

Sophia opened her mouth, but Tristan shot her a warning look. This wasn't the time to argue Jeremy's innocence. "Indeed, why is that, Mr. Pryor? He's a—that is, he *was* an unusually large man, from what I understand. Certainly, he was large enough to easily overpower his victim."

"He was a big one, aye, but a gentle bloke, for all that. More childlike, ye understand, than ye'd expect for a bloke that size. He didn't seem like the violent sort." Mr. Pryor braced his hands on the bar, his brow furrowing as he thought back to that night. "He was soft-spoken, like, and polite. The place was stuffed to the rafters that night, ye see, it being a meeting night, but he waited patient as a saint while everyone around him was demanding their drink—"

"A meeting night?" Sophia interrupted, a sudden tension in her voice. "What sort of meeting?"

"LCS meeting. They come the first Tuesday of every month, ye see, just like clockwork."

"LCS? You mean the London Corresponding Society? They meet here at the Turk's Head?" Tristan asked, his casual tone utterly at odds with the chill rushing over his skin.

Mr. Pryor gave him an odd look. "Aye. Every first Tuesday of the month, like I said."

The London Corresponding Society had formed in January of the previous year, and had been a thorn in the government's side ever since. And, by default, Lord Everly's side, and the side of every one of William Pitt's supporters in Parliament. Pitt tended to frown upon radical reform groups in general, but he'd singled out the LCS for his particular ire. Not surprisingly, he didn't care for the idea of every citizen in England having a vote.

"You wouldn't happen to recall, Mr. Pryor, if Patrick Dunn was a member of the LCS?" Under the bar, Sophia reached for Tristan's hand. "That is, was he generally here on meeting nights?"

Mr. Pryor's face cleared. "Aye, he was. I didn't recall that at first, but now ye ask I remember he came on Tuesdays with the other LCS blokes."

Sophia's palm had gone damp against Tristan's, and he knew she was thinking the same thing he was. "Thank you, Mr. Pryor. You've been very helpful."

"My God, Tristan," Sophia whispered as he took her arm and led her out to the carriage. "Lord Everly's even more of a villain than I supposed. He's got Peter Sharpe going after members of the London Corresponding Society! Sharpe accuses them of theft, and the fourth man…what of the fourth man? He lurks in the shadows, and if Sharpe's business goes awry, he leaps out, and sets it right again?"

Tristan gave a grim nod. "That's my guess. Today is Monday, and tomorrow is the first Tuesday of the month. Whatever it is Everly's planning next will happen tomorrow night at St. Clement Dane's Church."

Sophia ducked inside the carriage. "Yes, but who's their next target? We have to find out, and make certain he stays away from St. Clement Dane's churchyard tomorrow night."

"No." Tristan closed the carriage door behind him and sat back against the seat, his brow furrowed in thought. "No, whoever it is, he'll have to go to St. Clement Dane's, and let the thing play out. It's the only way to catch Sharpe and his accomplice at the crime. If their victim doesn't come, there's no one for Sharpe to accuse, and no reason for the fourth man to intervene. We may never get a look at him then."

Sophia turned a stricken gaze on Tristan. "The fourth man will be waiting to pounce as soon as Sharpe accosts their next victim. We have to find out who they're targeting next, Tristan, and warn him of the danger. He has to know what to expect when he passes by the church, or this thing could go terribly wrong."

"We'll see what we can discover at Everly's tonight. Whatever else happens, I intend to be at St. Clement Dane's tomorrow night to catch Peter Sharpe, and find out who this fourth man is before he hurts someone else. Brixton and a few of Willis's Bow Street Runners can come with me."

Sophia shook her head. "Daniel's not in London at the moment. Lady Clifford sent him off somewhere with Jeremy."

Tristan blew out a breath. "Damn it. How far have they gone? Can he be brought back to London quickly?"

"I truly don't know where they are, Tristan. I wasn't lying to you about that. Lady Clifford is careful to keep each of us focused only on whatever part of a task we've been assigned. There's fewer chances of errors that way."

"Clever of her," Tristan muttered, then tapped on the roof to signal the driver. "Will you come back to Great Marlborough Street with me?"

"No, not just yet. Drop me at No. 26 Maddox, will you? I need to speak to Lady Clifford. I'll let her know what we've discovered about Lord Everly and the LCS, and see if Daniel can't be made available tomorrow night. I'll return to Great Marlborough Street later for our foray into Lord Everly's study."

Tristan's gray eyes were dark with worry. "Or you could stay at the Clifford School. I promise I'll come and see you as soon as everything is—"

Sophia pressed her fingers to his lips before he could say anything more. "You're wasting your breath, my lord. You know very well I'm going with you."

"Yes, I suppose I do. Very well, then, we'll do this your way. But I'll have my way, as well." He turned her hand to press a kiss to her palm, his gaze meeting hers. "Don't keep me waiting long tonight, Miss Monmouth."

Chapter Eighteen

Darkness had settled over London by the time Sophia returned to Great Marlborough Street. Tribble opened the door to her knock, and offered her a solemn bow. "Good evening, Miss Monmouth."

"Good evening, Tribble." Sophia sank into an equally solemn curtsy and followed Tribble obediently down the hallway, but when they reached the library door, she pressed a finger to her lips before he could announce her. Tribble's eyebrow ticked up a fraction at this untoward request, but he didn't make a practice of arguing with Lord Gray's guests. He offered her a stiff bow and disappeared back toward the entryway.

Tristan was standing in front of the window, his back to her. Sophia didn't announce herself, but paused in the doorway. She couldn't recall ever having had the opportunity to watch him without him noticing, and she took it now, studying his broad shoulders and muscled back. Her gaze lingered on his elegant fingers wrapped around the tumbler he held in his hand, and a shiver tripped down her spine.

He'd touched her with those strong hands, those long, teasing fingers. He'd made her squirm and writhe for him, cry out for him...

Perhaps he felt the intensity of her stare, because Tristan turned from the window, his eyes meeting hers. Surprise flashed in the gray depths, and something else that looked like relief, as if he hadn't truly believed she'd return this evening, despite her promise. That flicker of doubt was so fleeting another person might not have noticed it, but Sophia did. She noticed everything about this man.

"You look surprised to see me, Lord Gray. Did you think I wouldn't come? I did promise you I would." She strode into the library, a smile on her lips.

"Not at all, Miss Monmouth. I simply expected you to come through the window rather than the door."

"The evening's just begun, my lord. We may yet find ourselves climbing through windows and dangling from rooftops. I do hope you're prepared."

He took a leisurely sip of his port, watching her approach over the edge of his glass. His gray eyes heated to molten silver as he swept his gaze over her. "I see *you* are. Dressed for prowling, are we?"

Sophia paused to glance down at her black tunic and breeches. "You may call it prowling, if you like. I prefer to think of it as pursuit of the guilty."

"They're one and the same for you, Miss Monmouth." He linked his fingers with hers and drew her forward, turning her so her backside was against the edge of his desk. "May I offer you a drink? Some sherry, perhaps?"

Sophia cocked her head to the side, eyeing the ruby red liquor in his glass before taking it from his hand and sipping from it. "I prefer port."

He laughed softly, his gaze darting to her mouth. He touched his thumb to her chin to raise her head, and leaned in to taste her lips. "I prefer port as well, particularly from your mouth." He pressed his glass to her lips once more, tipping in another sip of port, his eyes gleaming as he looked down at her.

Sophia licked delicately at the corner of her lip, but when he let out a soft hiss and leaned toward her again, she pressed her hands to his chest. "You do remember why we're here, Tristan? Let's concentrate on the matter at hand." She nodded to the window behind them.

"That would be easier if you weren't wearing breeches." Tristan ran his hand up her thigh and over her hip. "I can see your—"

"I beg your pardon, my lord, but your hand on my backside isn't helping my concentration. Or yours, I'd wager."

"On the contrary. I'm perfectly able to concentrate on your backside."

A grin stole over Sophia's lips. "Pay attention, will you? Has anyone left Lord Everly's house this evening?"

He sighed, but he removed his hand and shoved both of them into his pockets. "Not yet. I only hope he has an engagement tonight. If he leaves, he'll call his carriage and go through the front door. We're not likely to miss him, but it will be far trickier to track Sharpe's movements, as he might go out the servants' entrance."

"He may have already done so." Sophia tapped her lip, thinking. "I'm not as concerned with Mr. Sharpe, however. He isn't likely to be lurking about Lord Everly's study."

Tristan frowned. "It's risky to assume that, Sophia. He could be anywhere on the ground floor, or in the kitchens."

"We should be able to tell if anyone is in the kitchens from outside the door. We'll wait until it's dark and silent, then sneak inside."

Tristan rested his forehead against hers for a quiet moment, then he drew her toward the window. "Watch for Everly." He wrapped his arms around her waist and rested his chin on the top of her head. "As soon as he leaves, we'll go."

Midnight came and went, but there was no discernible activity from Lord Everly's townhouse. Sophia grew more anxious as the moments slipped by, but at last a carriage emerged from the darkness, rattled down the street, and stopped in front of Lord Everly's townhouse.

"About bloody time," Tristan muttered. "I thought he'd never go."

The door opened, and the light illuminated Lord Everly's round figure as he hurried down the front steps. He climbed into the carriage, and it disappeared down Great Marlborough Street.

Tristan dropped a quick kiss on the top of Sophia's head, then took her hand and led her from the library. Tribble had vanished, and none of Tristan's other servants were about. No one saw them as they crossed the hallway toward the staircase leading to the lower floor, and within minutes they were standing in the mews outside of Lord Everly's kitchen door.

They listened for a few moments, but it was silent on the other side, and no lights shone through the narrow crack underneath the door.

Sophia sucked in a breath, rested her fingers against the wood, and pushed. The breath rushed from her lungs when the door opened with a soft squeak. For all her brave talk about the carelessness of Everly's servants, she couldn't quite believe they hadn't discovered the buckle under the door.

"This way." Tristan guided her across the dim kitchen to the doorway Sophia had noticed that morning. It was a small alcove with a series of cupboards on one side and a narrow staircase on the other. They crept up one set of stairs, then peered around another door at the top of the landing.

"We're under the main staircase, at the back of the entrance hall. The layout is similar to my townhouse." Tristan tipped his chin toward a shadowy hallway on the other side of the entryway. "Everly's study will be down there on the left."

Sophia could hear the soft tread of footsteps above their heads. A servant, likely snuffing the candles, but it was impossible to tell whether they were coming down the stairs, or ascending to the upper floors. Tristan and Sophia waited, hardly daring to breathe, but no one appeared, and the footsteps faded.

"Now." Sophia laced her fingers with Tristan's, her heart racing as they darted across the entryway. She didn't dare look anywhere but straight ahead until they reached the relative safety of the dim hallway on the other side. They paused there, but when silence continued to reign over the house she peered around the corner.

No one was there. Aside from her and Tristan, this part of the house was deserted.

"Everly's not the trusting sort," Tristan whispered as they tiptoed toward the study door. "What's more, given his position and connections in the House of Lords, he considers himself very important, indeed. Be prepared for his study door to be locked."

He said no more, but Sophia heard what Tristan didn't say.

If it's locked, we're not breaking in.

But the door wasn't locked. In fact, it stood wide open, as if beckoning them inside. Sophia's heart leapt with hope, but it crashed again seconds later when they crossed the threshold and their eyes adjusted to the dim room.

Aside from an inkstand and quill and a half-empty glass of brandy, Everly's desk was bare. The handsome mahogany credenza against the wall was equally disappointing, the polished surface also bare. The only pieces of furniture in the room that looked as if they'd been touched were the leather chair behind the desk, which was worn in the seat, and the liquor cabinet.

"It looks as if he uses this room primarily for sitting and drinking." Tristan pulled the brass knob on the drawer in the center of the desk. It slid open easily, but there was nothing inside but a letter opener. Another drawer contained a set of uncut quills, sticks of wax and a seal, and third a small stack of blank, loose paper. Otherwise, the desk was empty.

Sophia stared at it in disbelief. "I don't understand. What sort of earl doesn't have a scrap of paper in his desk? Lord Everly's a member of the Lords, for pity's sake."

Tristan was staring at the empty drawer, his eyes narrowed. "No, it doesn't make sense. Everly does more running and fetching for William Pitt than any other lord in the house. His desk should be crammed with documents and papers. Suspicious, wouldn't you say?"

Sophia met Tristan's gaze from the other side of the desk. "Everything about Lord Everly is suspicious, and grows more so by the moment."

"There's only one reason a man like Everly would take such care to make certain not a single shred of paper can be traced back to him."

A shiver darted up Sophia's back at Tristan's foreboding tone. "What reason is that?"

Tristan slid the drawers closed. "To make absolutely certain whatever he's up to, he doesn't get caught at it."

"But there must be something here, Tristan. How else could—"

Sophia broke off, and their heads snapped toward the door. They'd both heard it at once—a soft thud, like the sound of a door closing above. They waited, frozen, and a moment later they heard the sound of footsteps shuffling down the stairs.

"They're coming this way. Quickly." Tristan grasped Sophia's hand and tugged her to the far side of the room, away from Everly's desk and the muted glow of the fire, but there wasn't time to do more than tuck themselves against either side of a massive bookshelf, and hope the shadows would hide them.

A moment later, a man strolled into the study, whistling to himself, as if he hadn't a care in the world. Sophia shrank back against the wall, not daring to draw a breath as he strode toward the desk and slid open one of the bottom drawers. He rummaged about, digging under the neat stacks of blank paper until at last he pulled a tiny scrap out from underneath it.

He closed the drawer with a click, then crossed to the fire. It was late enough the servants had let it die to embers, but there was enough feeble light to reveal Sharpe's rodent-like features. He held the slip of paper between his fingers, moving it closer to the light. He squinted down at it, his lips moving as he read it once, then once again.

Sophia couldn't see much from her place by the bookshelf, but she already knew what was written on the paper.

A name.

Sharpe read it over a few more times, obviously committing it to memory, then with a careless flick of his fingers he tossed the slip of paper into the fire, and strolled back out the way he'd come in. Neither Tristan nor Sophia moved until the muted thud of Sharpe's footsteps faded, then both of them shot up and hurried across the room toward the fireplace.

"Can you still read it?" Sophia hung over Tristan's shoulder as he knelt down and snatched the slip of paper out of the fire.

"Mr. Sharpe's as careless in this as he has been in everything else." Tristan read it, then held it up so Sophia could see it. "Thelwall."

The paper was singed and the edges curled enough to obscure the first name, but it didn't matter. The last name was clearly visible, and it was enough. Sophia gasped softly. "Francis Thelwall?"

"They're either getting bolder, or more desperate." Tristan shoved the paper back into the fire. They both watched as the embers devoured it until it was nothing more than scorched ash in the grate, then Tristan grasped Sophia's hand and led her from the study.

They tiptoed back down the hallway and across the entryway to the kitchens below. Sophia took care to remove the buckle she'd inserted under the door, then she and Tristan hurried into the mews and back to Tristan's kitchen, where he threw himself into one of the chairs at Mrs. Beeson's table. "Not a single paper in the desk, yet a fruitful visit, all the same."

Sophia shook her head. "I don't understand it, Tristan. Do you think they're really foolish enough to target Francis Thelwall? He doesn't enjoy the same obscurity as Patrick Dunn."

Francis Thelwall was one of the founding members of the London Corresponding Society. He was clever, charismatic, and an outspoken critic of William Pitt's Parliament. All of London knew who he was. If he was suddenly arrested for thievery, uncomfortable questions would arise.

"Patrick Dunn may have been an experiment to see if the scheme would work," Tristan said. "Not many people in London would connect Dunn to the LCS. They likely targeted him to see if they could get away with it, and now they have, they're going after Thelwall."

Sophia nodded slowly. "It would be convenient for Mr. Pitt if Francis Thelwall was shipped off to an Australian penal colony, particularly now the LCS has connected with other reform groups."

"Yes. They likely think it's worth the risk."

The LCS had members in Norwich, Manchester, Sheffield—even Scotland, and they were growing more powerful by the day. "A theft charge would be a tidy way to get rid of Thelwall."

"It would be even tidier if he were hung." Tristan's tone was grim. "Six thousand members of the public signed the LCS's latest petition, and it was presented to Parliament in May. When did the rash of thefts begin at St. Clement Dane's?"

Sophia's head was spinning as all the disparate puzzle pieces began to fall together. "Jeremy was accused in June, and Patrick Dunn a month or so before that. What of Jeremy, though? He's not a member of the LCS. What do Sharpe and Everly gain by accusing him?"

"Yes, I thought of that, too. Sharpe must have made a mistake. He likely saw Jeremy approaching St. Clement Dane's, and not being the cleverest criminal, mistook him for someone else, and sprung his trap only to find he'd got the wrong man."

"Yes, of course." Sophia drummed her fingers against the table, thinking. "Sharpe got the wrong man, and if that weren't enough to end the scheme, Henry Gerrard caught them out at it. He knew to go to St. Clement Dane's on the first Tuesday of the month, and he caught Sharpe attempting to frame Jeremy for theft."

Tristan fell back against his chair. "Jeremy told us the fourth man was there that night. He must have leapt from the shadows when he realized Henry had uncovered the scheme, and stabbed him. Who better to blame for his murder than Jeremy? He was already there, and likely too confused to put up much resistance."

"We still don't know who the fourth man is. It can't be Everly." Sophia had seen Everly and the fourth man together herself, in Everly's carriage this morning. "Everly might maneuver it from behind the scenes, but he wouldn't soil his hands with something so gruesome as a murder, which means…" Sophia met Tristan's gaze over the scrubbed tabletop, and her voice trailed off. "Tristan? You look strange. Are you ill?"

* * * *

Tristan gazed across the table at Sophia, into the lovely green eyes he'd fallen into the first time he'd seen them—the eyes he was still drowning in today—and his stomach lurched with fear.

If Everly had had his way, it wouldn't have been a single murder.

It would have been two.

"Tristan? Are you unwell?"

Tristan opened his mouth to answer her, but no words came out. The fourth man had murdered Henry Gerrard, and only two nights ago he'd tried to murder Sophia.

Tried, and nearly succeeded.

If Tristan hadn't spotted Sophia on Everly's pediment roof that night, the villain would have spilled her blood all over Pollen Street. Panic rose in Tristan's throat when he thought of how near a thing it had been.

If he'd come upon them even a few seconds later, he would have lost her. Now, sitting across from her, looking into her eyes, he knew without a shadow of a doubt if the worst had happened, he never would have recovered from the loss of her.

I'm in love with her.

This wild, reckless lady, so small and dainty yet so fierce, this dark-haired pixie, half-angel and half-thief, with her devastating green eyes and her troubling tendency to climb onto roofs and slip through fences. Stubborn, clever, brave—perhaps just a bit broken. She wasn't at all the sort of lady he imagined he'd ever fall in love with, yet she was all he could think about, all he could see.

He stared at her, dumbfounded. Did she love him back? Did she even trust him? If not, would she ever? The questions spun inside his head, but no sooner did they arise than he tossed them aside again, unanswered.

It didn't matter. He was in love with her, and there was no going back from that. She might walk away from him and never look back, and it wouldn't make any difference. He'd go on loving her against reason, sanity, or logic. He'd go on loving her even after he'd lost all hope.

She reached across the table and grasped his hand, her green eyes troubled. "Tristan? Are you all right? You're scaring me."

Tristan forced a smile to his lips. "Just reminding myself you're here with me, and you're safe and well. Well, aside from scraped palms and knees."

Her eyes went soft as they moved over his face. "Only because of you. I had no right to expect you to follow me that night, but you did."

It was on the tip of Tristan's tongue to tell her he'd follow her everywhere, anywhere for the rest of his life if she'd let him, but this wasn't the time to declare himself. He wouldn't speak to her of love with the same breath as he spoke to her of murder.

"Henry's mistake was in thinking Sharpe and Everly were working alone." Tristan's lips twisted with sadness as he thought of his friend. "He hadn't counted on there being a fourth man there that night, lurking in the shadows."

"You realize what this means, Tristan." Sophia's voice was quiet. "At the least we're accusing Everly—a member of the House of Lords—of sending innocent men to prison to put an end to the London Corresponding Society, which is a perfectly lawful reform group. At worst, we're accusing him of being an accessory to murder."

"We are, and that's to say nothing of Pitt himself. There's no denying he's the primary beneficiary of the scheme, and Everly doesn't stir a step without Pitt's approval. I find it difficult to believe he'd go as far as this without Pitt knowing of it."

Tristan had known all along this business went much deeper than a few thefts—a Bow Street Runner doesn't get murdered over a stolen pocket watch—but he'd never imagined it might reach such staggeringly high levels. At the very least, Everly was involved.

As for Pitt, they'd likely never know whether or not he'd set the whole plot in motion. If he had, they'd never be able to prove it. But Sharpe, Everly, and the fourth man—the murderer who'd killed Henry and tried to kill Sophia? Tristan's jaw hardened. They'd be held accountable for their crimes.

He rose, and held his hand out to Sophia. "Come with me."

She took his hand without hesitation, and hope shot through him. Perhaps she did trust him, after all. "The library. I've got copies of the Proceedings there. We may find this business didn't start with Patrick Dunn, after all. Peter Sharpe may have accused a number of men of theft over the past year, all of them members of the London Corresponding Society."

Sophia had only gone back as far as May in the Proceedings, but it turned out Tristan was right. It took hours of pouring over the published accounts, but they found Peter Sharpe had been the unfortunate victim of two additional thefts since the start of the year, both of which had taken place at St. Clement Dane's Church. He'd been careful to leave months between each incident to prevent anyone becoming suspicious, but the dates of the thefts corresponded with LCS meeting dates at the Turk's Head.

"I need to let Lady Clifford know about Francis Thelwall." Sophia set aside the Proceedings from the last session she'd been reading and rubbed her hand over her eyes. "Peter Sharpe will have a great deal more company at St. Clement Dane's Church tomorrow night than he anticipates, but we need to warn Francis Thelwall first."

"Tomorrow, pixie," Tristan murmured. "It's late. Come upstairs, and I'll put you to bed."

He half-expected her to demand to be taken back to No. 26 Maddox Street, but she didn't. Instead she gave him a sweet smile, took the hand he offered, and let him help her to her feet. Tristan led her upstairs to his bedchamber and tucked her into his bed. He unclasped her locket from her neck and set it carefully aside on the table, but he didn't dare strip her of her clothing. He left her safely covered by her tunic and breeches, so he wouldn't be tempted by her soft skin or supple curves.

It didn't make any difference, of course. Sophia didn't even need to be in the same room for him to be hard and aching for her, but it had been a shocking evening, and Tristan had already made up his mind not to trouble her with his amorous attentions.

So, he was still clothed when he slid into bed beside her and gathered her into his arms. "Go to sleep, pixie," he murmured, dropping a chaste kiss on her forehead.

He eased her head down onto his chest and settled back against the pillows, determined not to lay a finger on her. He might have succeeded, too, if Sophia hadn't had other plans.

It started subtly enough—just her fingers stroking lightly over his chest. Even such an innocent caress as that was enough to challenge Tristan's better intentions, but he gritted his teeth, ignored his cock's hopeful twitching against his falls, and remained still.

That is, he did until Sophia's hand moved a tiny bit, sliding lower until she was stroking his ribs, then lower still, her fingertips gliding over his stomach. It was so gradual Tristan could almost persuade himself he was imagining it until her fingers brushed over the straining head of his cock.

"Sophia!" Tristan groaned, his body arching. "What are you doing?"

She shot a teasing glance at him from under those thick, dark eyelashes. "My goodness, Tristan. If you have to ask, I must not be doing it right."

Tristan let out a strained chuckle. "Oh, you're doing it right, pixie, but it's late, and you need to rest." It took every bit of his will to do it, but he captured her wrist and tugged it gently away from his body.

Sophia put it right back on him again. "I'm not tired." She stroked his aching length through his breeches, her warm hand squeezing gently, and Tristan jerked again, letting out a gasp. "You don't appear to be all that sleepy either, my lord."

The gentle pressure of her hand on his hard cock made Tristan's eyes roll back in his head, and he couldn't hold back his hungry groan. "Ah, Sophia."

"See? Wide awake." She leaned over him and dropped a kiss to his chest before wriggling her way down the bed, her warm body sliding against his. "Though if you really insist, I'll stop, and we'll go to sleep."

Tristan tried to insist. A half-hearted protest gathered in his throat, but as he was groping for the words, she tugged his shirt from his breeches and pressed her open mouth to the heated skin of his lower belly, scraping her teeth lightly over his flesh. His hips shot up from the bed and he squeezed his eyes closed, an inarticulate groan on his lips as she loosened his falls, tugged them down his hips and took the head of his cock into her warm, welcoming mouth.

There were no more arguments then, and no more objections. Tristan sank his hands into her hair, tipped his head back against the pillow and let the woman he loved drive him to madness.

Chapter Nineteen

Tristan wasn't Sophia's first lover. She'd been betrothed once, to a kind, quiet man who'd slipped out of her life without a trace when he realized he was too kind and quiet for *her*.

It seemed like a lifetime ago.

This time it was different. Hadn't she known it would be, from the first moment Tristan's lips touched hers? Just as she'd known, one way or another, she'd find herself in his bed.

It wasn't different between them because he was an earl, or because he'd been a Bow Street Runner. It wasn't because the bed was draped with sumptuous blue silk hangings, or his bedchamber was the most luxurious she'd ever seen.

It was because he was *Tristan*.

Sophia lay beside him, trembling as his warm fingers slid under the edge of the boy's tunic she wore. His lips parted, his breath coming faster when he saw she wore nothing underneath. "Soft," he murmured, brushing his fingertips across the bare skin of her belly. "So perfect, every inch of you."

Perfect. No, she was far from perfect. He'd find it out for himself sooner or later, and she'd go back to who she'd been before him—the heroine of an adventure or a fairy tale, but never a romance. The thought made Sophia draw back slightly, away from him, but Tristan didn't give her a chance to go far. He slid his hands up her body, buried them in her hair, and turned her head gently to one side. "I want to see you." He caught her earlobe between his teeth and nibbled at the tender flesh until he'd tugged a soft gasp from her lips. "Show me, Sophia."

Sophia lowered her hands to the bottom edge of her tunic and then hesitated, twisting the fabric nervously between her fingers. Privacy was in short supply at the Clifford School, so she'd never been shy about her body, and it wasn't as if Tristan hadn't seen her before.

But he hadn't seen *all* of her, and he must be accustomed to London's most beautiful ladies, voluptuous courtesans and wealthy widows with smooth, white skin, who wore the finest silks and knew how to seduce a man. She was small, her curves slight, a waif dressed in coarse black linen with scraped palms and scarred knees....

Tristan was nipping at the sensitive skin behind her ear and trailing his firm lips up and down her neck, but when she paused, he raised his head and looked down at her. Whatever he saw in her face made him close his hands over hers, still frozen at the edge of her tunic. "You're exquisite, Sophia."

Sophia gazed up into those burning gray eyes and her hands relaxed, her fingers going slack around the hem of her tunic. Together they drew it up and over her head. Sophia held her breath, half-anticipating and half-dreading the moment his gaze would fall to her bare curves. He'd seen her breasts before, the first time he'd taken her to his bedchamber, but this... this time it was different.

More, somehow.

Tristan's eyes held hers as he lowered his mouth to her lips, the tunic drifting from his fingers to the floor. His lips were tentative at first, softly coaxing, opening her for his tongue, but his control slipped when she let out a little moan and sank her fingers into his hair. His kiss became more demanding then, his mouth growing hotter and more insistent as she pressed closer to him, chasing the delicious slide of his tongue against hers.

"I want to taste you." Tristan's low growl vibrated against her neck, making her shiver. He scraped his teeth gently over her, his tongue darting out to lick her heated skin before moving lower to suck at the hollow of her neck. He let out a low groan as he felt the frantic flutter of her pulse under his tongue. "Do you want that, Sophia? Do you want my mouth on you everywhere?"

"Yes." Sophia gripped his hair, closing her eyes at the slide of those silky dark strands between her fingers, the rough scrape of his emerging beard against the center of her chest as he nuzzled his face between her breasts.

"Here, pixie?" he whispered, rubbing his bristled cheek over one stiff nipple. "Do you want my mouth here?"

Dear God, *yes*. Sophia plunged her fingers deeper into his thick hair and tugged hard, nearly clawing him with her nails in her desperation to feel that friction against her tender nipples again. He growled low in his throat at the sting and dragged his cheek over her other nipple, making her jerk in his arms. "Ask me to suckle you there," he demanded, withholding his mouth until she was moaning incoherently for him, begging between panting breaths for his lips and tongue on her breasts.

A lifetime passed before he obliged her, or so it felt to Sophia as he tormented her with the rasp of his cheek against her nipples. By the time she felt his hot breath against the straining peaks she was clinging to him, her body arching against his in desperation.

Then, in the next breath he was where she'd begged him to be, his wicked tongue circling and teasing her nipples until Sophia wasn't sure if she'd scream or swoon. He was no less frantic, his hands closing around her waist to still her as he devoured her, drawing one nipple and then the other into the heated cavern of his mouth, making her squirm and gasp in his arms. He grew more passionate, more desperate with every tug until one of his hands fell away from her waist and a ragged groan dropped from his lips. "Look at me. This is what you do to me."

Sophia looked down, dazed. Tristan had kicked his breeches off and was stroking himself from his base to his tip, his big hand wrapped tightly around his hard length, the swollen, damp head flushing a deeper red with every pull.

She watched in fascination as his cock twitched and throbbed, her own skin flushing with every broken moan that left his chest until all at once, she couldn't wait another moment for him. She took his face in her hands and pulled his ravenous mouth away from her breasts to tug at the loose neckline of his shirt. "Take this off."

Tristan gazed up at her for a moment, his lips as red and swollen as her nipples, his hand still moving up and down his cock. One stroke, two, then he released himself with a hiss and raised his arms. Sophia gathered handfuls of the fine linen in her fists and tugged the shirt over his head. "Make love to me, Tristan."

"God, yes." He slid lower to press a hot, wet kiss to her belly.

Sophia lay back against the bed to take in the sight of his smooth, golden skin pulled taut over his broad shoulders and powerful arms. His chest and torso were long and lean, the hard muscles twitching under her stroking hands as she explored him, fascinated. "You're so...so..."

She trailed off, flushing. The word that came into her head was "beautiful," but it wasn't a word used to describe a man, so she held it back, uncertain how he'd react, even as she thought no other word did him justice.

He *was* beautiful.

He didn't look like the one other lover she'd had, or like any man she'd ever seen before, and Sophia couldn't stop herself from trailing her hand over his bare chest, reveling in the warm, tight skin under her fingertips.

His body went rigid when she teased a fingertip around his belly-button. She dragged her fingers through the line of soft, dark hair underneath, a smile curving her lips when she made him gasp.

"Sophia." He let out a harsh groan when she traced one finger down his rigid cock, reveling in the heat of that velvety skin and the way it twitched against his stomach, as if inviting her touch. She stared down at the straining length of him for a breathless moment, then cradled him in her hand, her breath coming faster when Tristan's eyes dropped closed. High spots of color painted his cheekbones, and his lips parted as he dragged in one ragged breath after another. "Are you teasing me?"

Was she? Sophia hardly knew. She wanted to touch him, to see him pant and groan for her as she'd done for him. "Perhaps I am," she whispered, her gaze locked on his face as she tightened her fingers and stroked him up and down, as she'd seen him do to himself.

His hips shot up and a sharp hiss fell from his lips. "Harder, pixie. *Yes*, like that. Your touch drives me mad, Sophia."

Sophia loved touching him, loved listening to the helpless moans on his lips as he arched and shuddered under her hands. She tightened her grip around him, stroking him faster now. Desire unfurled inside her lower belly when his head fell back and he thrust into her fist, once and then again before he caught her wrist with a strangled groan. "No…no more, or I'll lose my seed in your wicked little hand."

A light sheen of sweat covered his chest. She ceased stroking him, but his cock was still twitching insistently against her palm. She knew what it meant for a man to lose his seed, and for one mischievous moment she was so tempted to see him spill into her palm her hand began moving again of its own accord.

She didn't get far with her teasing, though. Tristan twisted out of her grip. "No. I want to be inside you." He raised an eyebrow at her boy's breeches, a devilish smile curving his lips as he neatly plucked one button loose, then the other, and dragged the breeches over her hips. "Much easier than skirts, stays, a chemise…"

Sophia let out a breathless laugh. "To say nothing of a corset."

He made quick work of the breeches, his throat moving in a convulsive swallow when she was bare before him. "Sophia," he breathed. He took in every inch of her with his heated gaze before reaching out to run his hand over the smooth skin of her thigh. "I want you so much."

She rose to her knees in the middle of the bed, her gaze still fixed on the slick, flushed head of his cock. Tristan let out a husky groan as it responded to her rapt gaze, throbbing insistently against his stomach. She watched as it twitched and jerked, straining for her, a soft gasp leaving her lips when a drop of fluid beaded the tip.

"Oh." She touched her tongue to her bottom lip.

Tristan stared, his mouth opening, and all at once, playtime was over. He let out a hoarse growl and snatched her into his arms. "I need you, Sophia. Come here."

She hesitated for an instant, as if trying to decide whether it would be more fun to obey or defy him, then she flung herself into his arms and her hands slid around to the back of his neck.

"That's it, pixie," Tristan whispered. He tumbled her onto her back in the bed, the long, hot length of his body pressing against every inch of hers, from her shoulders down to her toes. He dropped a sweet kiss on her lips, and cupped her face in his palms, his gray eyes serious. "Tomorrow, when I wake, I want to find you right here, in my arms. Don't leave me again, Sophia."

Sophia's heart rushed into her throat. "I didn't want to leave you yesterday morning, Tristan. You were asleep, your limbs flung wide and your hair falling over your face. You looked so warm, so peaceful I wanted to curl up next to you and fall asleep with my head on your chest."

He touched his forehead to hers. "Then why didn't you?"

Sophia heard the hurt in his voice, and a soft sob rose in her throat. "Because it's hopeless, Tristan. Surely you see that? You're the Earl of Gray, and I'm no—"

"Brave and passionate. Clever, kind, and beautiful." He tipped her chin up. "You're everything. I don't want only a single stolen night with you, Sophia. I want all of you, always."

She sucked in a shocked breath, but his lips took hers in a devastating kiss, and her thoughts scattered. When he drew away again, he was breathless. He gazed down at her, lingering on her bare breasts, her lips, the spill of her dark hair against his pillow. "Have you ever had a lover before, Sophia? I don't want to hurt you."

Whatever lingering nervousness Sophia felt vanished at his words. That he'd thought to ask, that he'd take such care of her made warmth rush through her, curling her toes. She wrapped herself around him, as close as she could get, and pressed her lips to the center of his hard chest before burying her face against his neck. "I've had…I'm not innocent, but it was only a few times, and it was a long time ago," she whispered, letting her fingers drift down the taut plane of his stomach.

Sophia didn't know whether it was her words or her touch that led to it, but something shifted between them then, as if the last thin barrier holding them apart crumbled and fell away. Every last vestige of the proper, elegant earl disappeared, and he was only Tristan, the strong, determined man who'd chased her across London the first night they'd met.

Not the detached lord, not the distant earl, and not the Ghost of Bow Street. Tristan Stratford, the *man*.

He was gentle with her, so careful, yet at the same time he was demanding, relentless in pursuit of her pleasure and his own. Sophia wasn't a submissive sort of woman, but there was something breathtaking about having such an intense, physically powerful man take command of her body.

"Put your arms over your head," he murmured against her throat, shifting them so she was reclined against the pillows. "Don't move unless I give you leave."

"*Give me leave?*" Sophia squeaked, but her objection died in her throat when he pushed a long, muscular leg between hers and began kissing his way down her body. It should be impossible his mouth could find her every curve and hollow, but that was how it felt to Sophia—as if his hot breath and seeking tongue touched every secret part of her. She held her breath, arching into his mouth as he dragged his lips down her neck and between her breasts.

She let out a soft cry of protest and reached for his head to still him when he didn't pause to lavish attention on her nipples, but as soon as her fingers caught in his hair he lifted his head, one eyebrow arched, his sultry gray eyes gleaming as he grinned down at her. "Hands over your head, Sophia."

Sophia squirmed against the sheets as she battled with herself. She wasn't one to back away from a challenge, and certainly not one to let a man order her about, but he was wreaking havoc on her body with his sinful mouth, and all she could think about was how badly she wanted him to keep going, to move lower....

So, she did as he bid her, lifting her arms and resting them on the pillow over her head, just as he'd placed them originally. He made an approving noise deep in his throat. "Hold onto the headboard...*yes*. Now wrap your fingers around the posts."

He waited for her to obey his command before he resumed his sensual assault, dragging his lips down the center of her ribcage, pausing to nibble at the skin there, leaving a damp streak from his tongue as he drifted lower, dropping tiny wet kisses across her belly.

She was half-lost in the pleasure when she felt his large palms against her inner thighs, the scratch of his emerging beard against the secret skin there, and then he—

"Tristan!" Sophia twisted away from him, more from shock than anything else. "Did you just…"

He'd…it felt as if he'd just *licked* her. *There.*

Now that, *that* she'd never done before.

She jerked upright and stared down at him. He was lying on his belly between her spread legs, his hands still holding her thighs apart, his lips glistening and a curious mixture of amusement, desire, and impatience on his face. "I did, and I'd be pleased to do it again if you'd do as I bid you." He nodded at her hands, which were braced on the bed on either side of her hips.

"But that's…you can't…I've never heard of such a thing!"

A low chuckle met this protest. "Are you asking me to stop?"

Sophia squirmed at the sensation of his hot breath drifting over her damp flesh. "I didn't say that, exactly."

She felt the vibration of another chuckle against her core, but then he was devouring her again, his mouth hot against the tender pink skin between her legs, his lips and tongue stroking into her throbbing center, ruthlessly wringing shudders from her writhing body and incoherent whimpers and pleas from her lips. Sophia clutched at the posts above her head, her knuckles white as Tristan teased and circled, sucked and licked.

"Tristan, please. I need…I need you." Sophia arched against him to urge him to move on top of her. He swirled his tongue over her tender bud once, and then again before he slid up her body with one quick move and settled his hips between her open thighs.

Sophia gazed up into that handsome, harshly elegant face and braced herself for the first thrust of his body into hers, but instead of taking her at once, Tristan paused to brush the tangled hair from her face. "You look nervous, pixie." He leaned over her to press a soft kiss to her lips. "I'd never hurt you, Sophia."

She cupped his cheek in her hand. "I know you won't."

Sophia opened her legs wider, offering herself to him, and he pressed the head of his cock against her slick entrance. He gasped when he felt her heat, then gave one restrained thrust, just enough so the broad head slipped inside her.

She let out a soft gasp, but it wasn't a gasp of pain. She wrapped her legs around his hips and tilted her pelvis up to draw him in deeper. "I want all of you, Tristan."

Tristan groaned. His eyes were squeezed shut, and beads of sweat clung to his skin. "You're so tight, sweetheart. I'm afraid I'll hurt you." He strummed his thumb over the sensitive nub hidden in her damp folds as he eased inside her, driving them both mad with every careful inch until at last he was seated deep. "Sophia, you feel so good."

"You feel so *big*." Sophia gave an experimental nudge with her hips that made Tristan moan. "You feel huge inside me."

Panic flashed across his face. "Is it too much? Am I hurting you?"

He began to draw back, but Sophia wrapped her legs around his hips to hold him in place. "No! Don't move. I mean, *do* move, just not...out."

Tristan let out a quiet laugh, but he did move inside her then, each thrust so slow and careful Sophia felt her throat close with emotion at how gentle he was with her. He murmured into her ear as he coaxed her with his body, telling her how good she felt, how much he wanted her, how beautiful she was, and before long Sophia's hips were moving in tandem with his. "Tristan, I...*Tristan*." She opened her mouth against his shoulder and scraped her teeth over his damp skin.

Tristan's breath left his lungs in a hiss when he felt her tiny bite. He tangled his fist in her hair and drew her head back, staring down at her as his hips jerked against hers, all restraint at an end. "Come for me, pixie. *Yes*. Take your pleasure, Sophia."

His fingers moved feverishly between her legs, coaxing and teasing. Sophia's head thrashed against the pillow, her fingernails scoring his back as her center drew tighter with his every wicked stroke until at last, she shattered beneath him with a cry.

"Yes, Sophia. So *good...*" Tristan drove into her once, then again before he stilled, holding himself deep inside her as a low, guttural moan fell from his lips, his powerful body shaking with his release.

Afterward, he collapsed onto the bed beside her and buried his face in her neck. As their ragged breathing began to calm, he lifted his head and looked down at her. His eyes were soft and sleepy as he traced his finger over her lips. "I already want you again."

He gave her a crooked grin that made Sophia's heart lurch in her chest. She smiled and reached up to stroke his dark, damp hair back from his face. "Well, I'm not going anywhere."

"That's right, you're not. Because if you leave my bed, I'll come after you, throw you over my shoulder, and bring you back here." The arrogance of this statement was somewhat offset when he leaned down and dropped a kiss on the end of her nose.

Sophia slid closer and draped herself over his chest, resting her chin on her folded arms. She stared at him, her nose wrinkled in thought, then reached out to tease a fingertip over his scar. "A highwayman shot at you, and the ball grazed your lip?"

He toyed with a loose lock of her hair. "No."

"A criminal knocked you down, and your face hit the edge of a cobblestone, bloodying your lip and leaving the scar?"

He rolled his eyes, but his grin was back, twitching at the corners of his mouth. "No. Do I look like the sort of man who'd let a criminal, or anyone else, knock me down?"

"No," Sophia admitted, still studying the scar. "A kick to the face, and the boot heel caught your lip? A thief attacked you with a broken bottle?"

Tristan tugged gently at the lock of her hair between his fingers. "No."

"Did someone bite you? Someone with very sharp teeth?"

He drew the coverlet over them, then cupped the back of her head and eased it onto his bare chest. "Go to sleep, Sophia."

"Don't be ridiculous. I can't possibly sleep until I know how you got that scar."

His low laugh rumbled against her cheek. "Yes, you can."

Sophia made a doubtful noise, but then Tristan wrapped her in his arms, and his big hand moved in slow, rhythmic strokes over her hair, and he was so warm and solid, and her eyes so heavy...

Within seconds she'd fallen into a sleep too deep for doubts, and too peaceful even for dreams.

Chapter Twenty

Sophia peeked over the edge of the coverlet and frowned at the pale sun struggling against the thick silk drapes of Tristan's bedchamber. The coverlet on top of her was soft and warm, the bed like a fluffy cloud cradling her pleasantly sore body.

This must be why aristocrats tended toward laziness—they hardly ever rose before noon because their beds were too enticing. Sleeping in such plush magnificence was certainly making her indolent.

Or was it just sleeping in an earl's bed, with an earl?

That is, not *any* earl, but *this* earl.

Then again, they hadn't done much sleeping the night before—

"You've only just opened your eyes, but you've already made me cross, Sophia."

Sophia rolled over and found Tristan wide awake. His head was propped in his hand and he wore such a delightfully teasing smile on his lips, she couldn't stop her own lips from curving in response. Goodness, the morning suited him, didn't it? He looked warm and tousled, his eyes still sleepy and his dark hair standing on end. "How in the world can I have made you cross? I haven't said a single word yet."

"No, but you woke with a frown." He brushed a lock of hair back from her face and smoothed the furrow from her brow with his thumb. "A lady who is satisfied the night before doesn't wake with a frown on her lips."

Sophia blinked up at him, entranced by the mischievous sparkle in his gray eyes. She hadn't often seen this playful side of him, and dear God, it was irresistible. *He* was irresistible. That cheeky little grin made her want to leap upon him and kiss him until her breath came short and her toes curled.

But surely there wasn't time for any toe-curling antics this morning. They had a church to guard, a man to protect, criminals to apprehend, and…and…

"Of course, I wasn't satisfied." Sophia slid her foot up the long, lean line of his calf. "How can I be, when you won't divulge a single detail about the origin of that intriguing scar on your lip? I could hardly sleep for wondering about it."

"Perhaps I can offer you something else in place of my secrets." He nudged her legs apart and wedged a hard thigh between them. "My fragile male vanity demands you be smiling when you wake in my bed."

It was on the tip of Sophia's tongue to deliver a lecture about lounging in bed when there were villains roaming the streets of London, but as soon as she opened her mouth to deliver the scold his lips were there, and her thoughts scattered, lost in the delicious slide of his tongue against hers.

It was some time before they emerged from the tangled sheets. By then the morning and part of the afternoon had slipped away. Sophia was a trifle amazed at her wanton behavior, but even so, she might not have noticed the time if she hadn't heard Tristan's stomach growl, and realized how hungry she was. She wriggled free of his arms and sat up in the bed, clutching the coverlet to her breasts. "What time is it?" She glanced at the window and groaned. "Dear God, it must be past one!"

Tristan indulged in a long, lazy stretch, then dropped a hand on her bare hip. "It's no wonder I'm famished. I'll ring for a tray. That way we can remain in bed all—"

"We most certainly will not remain in bed." Sophia gave him a little shove toward the edge of the bed, then while he was distracted, she scrambled out the other side. If he kissed her again there was no telling when they'd rise—long after poor Francis Thelwall was dragged off to Newgate, most likely.

"First a frown, and now a shove?" Tristan flopped back against his pillows, but his lips were twitching. "I'll begin to think you don't like me, pixie."

Sophia snatched up a dressing gown draped over the back of a chair— Tristan's dressing gown, judging by the way it swallowed her—and paused while tying the belt to glance at him.

He was sprawled on the bed, his long limbs thrown across every available inch of space. He was idly scratching his bare chest, and Sophia's gaze caught on those long, sensitive fingers stroking his golden skin. His thick hair was curling in a wild tangle around his face, and his cheeks were shadowed with dark stubble.

Sophia stared, her heart thundering as her gaze moved from his chest to his hands to the lazy grin quirking his lips. He was wrong. She *did* like

him, and far more than she should. Far more than was wise for her peace
of mind, or her future happiness.

How had this happened? For a woman who was most resoundingly *not*
the heroine of a romance, she was ridiculously besotted with a gentleman
who would never be hers.

If all went as planned, tonight would mark the end to Peter Sharpe and
Lord Everly's machinations. They'd identify the fourth man, this business
would be done, and there'd be no reason for her ever to see Tristan again.
She'd go back to her friends and Lady Clifford, and Tristan would leave
London to go off and do...well, whatever it was earls did at their country
seats, just as he'd planned before he got tangled up with her.

He'd likely be relieved to be free of her, whereas she...

Whereas she, *what*? It wasn't as if she were in love with Tristan. It
wasn't as if he'd be leaving her behind with a broken heart. Her heart was
made of sterner stuff than that.

Of course, it was, and yet...

Sophia hurried across the bedchamber, nearly tripping over the hem
of the dressing gown in her haste to find her clothes. Ah, there they were,
in a crumpled ball at the bottom of the bed. "I should have returned home
hours ago. Lady Clifford will be wondering where I am."

"Running away, Sophia?"

She hadn't heard him move, but in an instant, he was there, his big
hands on her shoulders, his body so warm and strong at her back it took
everything she had not to lean into him, close her eyes, and let him wrap
himself around her.

When had this happened? When had she begun to need his arms around
her to feel safe? The thought made her panic, and she tried to squirm away.
"It's not...I'm not running away."

"Yes, you are." His hands and his voice were gentle—so gentle
tears stung her eyes—but he didn't release her. "You don't need to run,
Sophia. Not from me."

Yes, I do. Especially from you.

But even as the words drifted through her consciousness, she was
already sinking into him, absorbing his heat into her skin.

Dear God. It's already too late.

It was too late to run. She might scale every column in London, flee
from one rooftop to the next as if the devil were chasing her, and it wouldn't
do the least bit of good. She didn't know when or how it had happened,
but somehow, Tristan had become as much a part of her as her own flesh.

Unnecessary risk, Sophia.

As many times as Lady Clifford had uttered those words, Sophia had never really taken them to heart until now. Perhaps because this time it wasn't Lady Clifford's voice in her head, but her own.

Yet her heart was already destined to shatter, wasn't it? A few more hours, a few more kisses, a few more stolen moments with him...surely, it wouldn't make any difference? Sophia swallowed the lump in her throat, and against her better judgment, she turned to face him and twined her arms around his neck. "I suppose I can send her a note."

Some powerful emotion flared in his gray eyes, but before she could decipher it, it was gone. "Yes, I suppose you can," was all he said. Then he gathered his dressing gown more securely around her, and went to ring the bell for a servant.

They dined in his bedchamber—another novelty for Sophia. Afterwards she wrote out a quick note to Lady Clifford, asking her ladyship to meet them at St. Clement Dane's that night, and to bring Daniel, who was meant to return to London this afternoon.

Peter Sharpe was a coward, but he was cunning, and then there was a fourth man to consider. There was no telling what such a brutal fiend would do once he was cornered. Sophia didn't choose to leave anything up to chance. She scrawled a line at the bottom of the note for her friends, telling them she'd see them soon, then folded and sealed it and laid it on the table, ready for a servant to deliver it.

Tristan was writing his own note to Sampson Willis, the magistrate at Bow Street, directing him to come to St. Clement Dane's that night as well, promising it would all make sense once they apprehended Peter Sharpe and got him to confess his part in the crime.

Afterwards they sat together in front of the fire, neither of them speaking, but each stealing glances at the other. The silence between them grew heavier the longer they sat, heavy with all the unsaid words between them.

Sophia didn't speak them, but instead sat quietly, her gaze moving over his face, memorizing every curve and angle. Tristan stared back at her, his own gaze tracing the bare skin of her neck, visible under the gaping neckline of his dressing gown.

"You're beautiful, Sophia," he murmured at last, his gray eyes meeting hers. "Inside and out, from your face to the depths of your heart. All of you, so beautiful."

It was at once the last thing Sophia expected him to say, and the one thing she wanted to hear more than any other. She tried not to melt for him, tried to keep her heart from softening, but it was no use. She rose to her feet and went to him, her heart leaping in her chest when he opened his arms for her. She would have crawled into them, and they would inevitably have spent the rest of the afternoon in bed, if a knock on the door hadn't interrupted them.

"What is it?" Tristan barked, impatience in every syllable.

Sophia bit her lip to smother a laugh, even as she pitied the servant who'd earned that irritable reply.

"I beg your pardon, my lord." Tribble peered cautiously around the edge of the door. "Mr. Willis is here. I told him you weren't at home to visitors, but he says he has urgent business with you." Tribble paused. "I'm afraid he was quite insistent."

"Sampson Willis has abominably bad timing," Tristan snapped, his eyes never leaving Sophia's face.

"Yes, my lord."

Tristan sighed. "Very well. I'll be down in a moment, Tribble."

"Yes, my lord." Tribble bowed himself out, closing the door behind him.

Tristan rose to his feet, took Sophia's hand, and pressed a lingering kiss on her palm. "It seems Willis doesn't care to wait until tonight for his explanation."

"It seems not." Sophia shrugged, but a smile tipped her lips as she looked up at Tristan. "Perhaps it's just as well if you speak with him now."

"Yes, I suppose I'd better." Despite his words, Tristan didn't move. He stood staring down at her, letting moment after moment slip away until at last, he reached out to trace the heavy silk neckline of the dressing gown, his finger brushing her skin. "I'll be quick."

"See that you are, my lord. I'll be waiting."

Muttered curses fell from Tristan's lips as he made his way out the door, leaving Sophia alone in the quiet bedchamber.

But despite his promise, Tristan *wasn't* quick. He was gone so long Sophia—who'd stretched out on the bed to wait for him—fell asleep. When she woke, it was near dusk. She crawled from the bed, still drowsy, and wandered to the window. Deepening purple shadows fell over Great Marlborough Street. Another half hour passed, dusk fading into evening, and still Tristan didn't come.

Finally, unable to stand the silence any longer, she threw off Tristan's dressing gown, donned her breeches and tunic, and made her way downstairs. She turned toward the hallway that led to the library, intending to go into the music room beyond, which also had a clear view of Lord Everly's front door, but as she passed the library, she stopped short, her brow furrowing.

"…should know better than to trust Lady Clifford, Gray."

The library door was open a crack, and Sampson Willis's voice carried clearly into the hallway. Instinctively Sophia drew closer to the wall, her heart lurching unpleasantly in her chest at the mention of Lady Clifford.

It wasn't at all unusual for powerful gentlemen in law enforcement to speak of Lady Clifford and the Clifford School in that contemptuous tone, but Sophia's back still stiffened at Willis's dismissive manner. She pressed closer to the door, curious to hear what Tristan would say in reply.

He hadn't, after all, made any secret of his feelings about Lady Clifford.

"I was suspicious of Lady Clifford at first, but in this instance, she hasn't done anything wrong." Tristan paused, then added, "That is, nothing that would land her in prison."

Sophia thought of Jeremy's escape from Newgate, and sucked in a quick, stunned breath. She'd as good as admitted to Tristan Jeremy was still alive, and they were behind his miraculous escape. Tristan was well aware spiriting away an accused murderer before a noose could find his neck would most certainly land them in prison.

He was *lying* for them.

Her pounding heart calmed a bit as warmth filled her chest, but it started thrashing again at Sampson Willis's derisive snort. "I see. I suppose that little dark-haired chit you've been gallivanting about with is equally as innocent, isn't she? What's her name again? Sophia something?"

"Sophia Monmouth." Tristan's voice was even. "Yes, I was wrong about her, too. She's innocent in this business."

Wrong about her? A sharp arrow of hurt pierced Sophia's chest. That meant he'd thought her guilty at some point, but then she already knew that. He hadn't made a secret of it, and she could hardly blame him. She wasn't, in fact, innocent at all, and hadn't been since the age of seven, when she'd begun to see the law as a thing to be bent and shaped according to her needs.

As suggestions, not imperatives.

To a man like Tristan, a former Bow Street Runner, she was closer to being a criminal than she was a proper, law-abiding citizen, yet he was defending—

"Tell me, Gray. Does your belief in the girl's innocence arise from her spotless behavior, or might there be something else influencing your opinion?"

"I don't know what you mean." Tristan's voice was tight with warning.

"Oh, I think you do." There was a brief pause, then the sound of footsteps. When Willis spoke again, he was closer to the door. "She's a pretty thing, Miss Monmouth. Perhaps I should have taken that into account when I assigned you to investigate her."

"Miss Monmouth's appearance has nothing to do with—"

"But it's been days since you brought me a report of her activities," Willis went on, as if Tristan hadn't spoken. "I should have realized then the girl had turned your head. Ah, well, perhaps it was inevitable, what with the way you've been scrutinizing her every move. We all have our weaknesses, don't we, Gray?"

Tristan said something in reply, but Sophia didn't hear it. A dull roar filled her ears, and she sagged back against the wall. It was one thing to suspect her, but quite another to investigate her. Another still to—how had Willis put it?

Scrutinize her every move.

The meaning of Willis's words sank in, and everything that had happened since that first night Tristan had chased her suddenly took on a more sinister cast. Of course, he'd been investigating her. Why, she couldn't imagine how she hadn't suspected it from the start.

A pair of gray eyes and tempting lips, that's how.

But if he'd intended to turn her over to Willis, mightn't he have done it when he found out about Jeremy's escape? A tiny thread of hope rose in Sophia's breast. Perhaps he *had* come to care for her, just as he claimed, but hadn't known how to tell her the truth.

Except he'd had plenty of opportunity to confess it, and he hadn't said a single word.

Still, that didn't necessarily mean he—

"Perhaps it would be best if you returned to Oxfordshire, Gray." It was Sampson Willis again, his voice heavy with derision, and something else, a hint of something that was more difficult to identify. It sounded like…a warning.

"I'm not going anywhere until this matter is brought to a satisfactory end." Tristan's voice was edged with ice.

Willis let out an impatient huff. "Come now, Gray. Isn't your mother expecting you at your country estate? Aren't you meant to be marrying soon, as well? Surely, your betrothed is anxious for your return."

The tiny spark of hope still flickering in Sophia's breast stuttered, then died.
Tristan was betrothed.

A laugh tore loose from her throat, silent and bitter. Had she really thought he *cared* about her? Dear God, how could she have been such a fool? He was an *earl*, a Bow Street Runner, and she was a grubby little orphan from Seven Dials with a shadowy past, and very likely a shadowy future.

Gentlemen like the Earl of Gray didn't fall in love with common criminals.

"Lady Esther Whitstone, isn't it?" Willis asked. "Lovely girl, Lady Esther. She'll make an admirable Countess of Gray. Substantial portion on her too, eh?"

Sophia's hands came up instinctively to cover her ears, but it was too late for that. She'd heard it, and she couldn't unhear it. Couldn't undo it.

Her throat closed. She'd taken Tristan to No. 26 Maddox Street, given him access to Lady Clifford, and shared everything she knew about Peter Sharpe with him. She'd fallen right into line, and right into his bed. He'd been damn clever, the way he'd gone about it, but then he was the Ghost of Bow Street. He knew how to manage a suspect, and his efforts had paid off.

Lady Clifford, Cecilia and her other friends, Daniel and Jeremy—she'd put them all at risk when she'd brought Tristan to them. They trusted her judgment, and in return she'd exposed them to a man who'd lock the lot of them up in Newgate if given the chance.

There was a brief silence, then Tristan said stiffly, "My personal affairs have nothing to do with this business, Willis."

It wasn't a denial.

Willis said something in reply, but Sophia had heard enough. She backed away from the library door and hurried down the hallway.

The entryway was deserted.

She paused at the bottom of the stairs, but there was no reason for her to return to Tristan's bedchamber. No reason for her to have been there in the first place.

As quickly and quietly as she could, she stole toward the door. No one saw her open it and slip out into the dusk.

* * * *

Sampson Willis was trying Tristan's patience.

He'd always admired Willis—had thought him a decent man, an honest one—but at the moment Tristan would have been happy to toss the magistrate out his front door.

He'd never known Willis to be so obstinate before, but no matter what Tristan said, Willis seemed to be determined to argue with him.

Tristan drew a breath, and tried again. "Listen to me, Willis. Jeremy Ives wasn't the first man Sharpe accused of theft. A few months before the incident with Ives, Sharpe claimed a weaver from Clare Court—a man named Patrick Dunn—had tried to steal his pocket watch."

Willis was pacing from one end of the library to the other, but now he paused in front of the fireplace. "Sharpe was the victim of two thefts? That's hardly unheard of in London, Gray."

"Not two, Willis. *Four*, two of them earlier this year. All four thefts took place at St. Clement Dane's Church. If you doubt me, then check the Proceedings yourself. It's right there for anyone who cares to look."

"That's…I grant you that's a rather startling coincidence." Willis fumbled in his coat, withdrew a handkerchief, and used it to mop his brow.

"Not startling, Willis. Suspicious. Sharpe is a liar. He's been falsely accusing innocent men of theft for the better part of a year, and he's not simply choosing any man who happens to be unlucky enough to cross his path. His victims aren't random."

Willis stilled, his back to Tristan. "What do you mean?"

Tristan paused, knowing Willis wasn't going to care for what he had to say next. "Lord Everly's been feeding him the names. All of the men Sharpe has accused are members of the London Corresponding Society. Odd coincidence, wouldn't you say?"

Willis whirled around, and his face had drained of color. "My God, Gray. You're accusing a *peer* of committing a crime?"

Tristan's eyes narrowed. "You aren't suggesting an aristocrat is above the law, are you, Willis? Or are you arguing an earl is too noble to have committed a crime?"

"No, I…n-no, of course not. It's just all rather shocking. I…well then, Gray, I'll do as you ask and dispatch a Runner to St. Clement Dane's Church tonight." Willis pressed a hand to his forehead. He looked shaken, as if he were trying to regain his wits. "After that cockup of Sharpe's, Poole knows his way around St. Clement Dane's."

Tristan froze.

Cockup of Sharpe's…

Willis didn't seem to realize what he'd revealed, but it was as if lightning had struck Tristan with a deafening crack, illuminating the truth in one cold, harsh flash of light.

Willis could only be referring to one thing.

Henry Gerrard's murder.

Poole had somehow been involved in Henry Gerrard's murder.

Had he been at St. Clement Dane's Church that night? According to both Willis and Sharpe's accounts, there'd been only three people there that night—Sharpe himself, Jeremy Ives, and Henry Gerrard. Willis had come later, after Sharpe ran to No. 4 Bow Street to fetch help.

No one had said a single word about Poole being there.

Until now.

Tristan slowly raised his gaze to Willis's face, an icy chill racing over his skin.

Willis, who was now in a tearing hurry to leave, didn't notice Tristan's stare, nor did he realize he'd let slip a small detail he'd much better have kept hidden. "Right then, Gray. I'd best be off—great deal to do, you understand."

He didn't give Tristan a chance to respond, but hurried from the library with the haste of a criminal fleeing the scene of a crime.

Because that's *precisely what he was.*

For silent, endless moments after the front door slammed behind Willis, Tristan stood utterly still, images from the night Sophia was attacked drifting through his mind. He could recall with perfect clarity the man emerging from the shadows, a club gripped in his black-gloved hands.

As for the man himself...

He was tall but slight, lean and wiry. His face had been covered with a cap, but Tristan had a vague impression of pale skin, and sparse, dark hair.

The last time he'd seen Poole was the day Tristan had gone to Bow Street, the morning after he'd caught Sophia chasing after Peter Sharpe. Poole had been slouched on a bench outside Willis's office, a black cap on his head, his fingers wrapped around—

A walking stick.

A heavy wooden one, with a brass knob. The rhythmic tap of it against the heel of Poole's boot echoed in Tristan's head.

Hadn't Sophia said something about a cane, or a walking stick, on the day of Jeremy's trial? Something about Sharpe claiming to have used a cane as a weapon again Jeremy—a cane that had since gone missing.

There was only one explanation, only one way to fit all the pieces together, and the picture that emerged made Tristan's blood run cold.

Richard Poole is the fourth man.

Tristan flew into the hallway and up the stairs two at a time—to the second floor, where he burst through his bedchamber door. "Sophia?"

No answer. He ran from the sitting room toward his bedchamber, ducking his head into his dressing-room on the way. She wasn't there.

When he reached his bedchamber, he turned around in a circle, hoping with everything inside him she'd come to him, his dressing gown trailing behind her, the smile that had somehow become everything to him lighting up her face.

She wasn't there. His apartments were empty.

Where *was* she? He strode toward the bed, his heart pounding with sudden fear. The room was dim, but the muted light caught on something on the table beside his bed—a dull gleam of silver.

Tristan strode across the room and snatched it up.

Sophia's locket. He closed it in his fist.

Her locket was here, but Sophia was gone.

Chapter Twenty-one

The last faint streaks of light faded in the sky as Sophia made her way down Great Marlborough Street, leaving Tristan's townhouse behind, her steps taking her toward St. Clement Dane's Church.

Lady Clifford and Daniel would be leaving No. 26 Maddox Street by now. She could have gone to meet them at the Turk's Head, but somehow, Sophia couldn't bring herself to turn toward the Strand.

There was an uncomfortable tightness pinching at her chest, like a stone wedged under her breastbone. It wasn't guilt, precisely...regret, perhaps, but there was something else there that was worse than regret.

Shame.

She was ashamed of having allowed herself to believe, even for such a short time, that a man like Tristan Stratford could ever have any tender feelings for a woman like her. As soon as Lady Clifford saw her face, she'd read the truth there, and Sophia didn't want her to see what a fool she'd been.

It was difficult enough to bear her disappointment in herself. She couldn't bear to disappoint her friends, especially Cecilia, who truly believed every lady was the heroine of her own story, and that love could be their saving grace. Perhaps it was even true, for the good little girls Sophia's mother had so often spoken of.

She'd never told Sophia what happened to wicked little girls.

There was no sign yet of Peter Sharpe at St. Clement Dane's, so Sophia ducked into the deserted graveyard beside the church, taking care to keep to the deepest shadows at the back, where cracked stone angels and broken crosses kept vigil over the moldering crypt with the iron gate hanging by a single, broken hinge.

Sophia slipped through the gap, shivering at the breath of cold air inside the crypt that whispered over her skin. She didn't venture deep inside, but lingered close to the gate, peering between the iron bars into the churchyard beyond.

The sky turned a dark midnight blue above her and the shadows grew longer and thicker around her as she waited. London had been rainy this summer, but tonight there was no rain—just the thin, icy air inside the crypt, so steeped in decay and death it was a struggle to draw a deep breath.

An hour passed. The moon tucked herself behind a bank of heavy clouds, plunging the graveyard into a murky darkness. Sophia's limbs began to ache from standing too long in the same position, and still, no one came. Unease rose in her chest. Despite Tristan's lies to her, she couldn't believe he'd leave her to face Peter Sharpe and the fourth man alone.

And what of Daniel and Lady Clifford? Surely, they should be here by now. They were meant to follow Francis Thelwall from the Turk's Head to St. Clement Dane's, but there was no sign of any of them. Lady Clifford would have sent her a message if plans had changed, but it might have arrived at Tristan's townhouse after Sophia left.

She wrapped her fingers around the iron bars, leaned her forehead against her hands, and did her best not to think about Tristan. Was he still arguing with Sampson Willis, or had he returned to his bedchamber and discovered she'd gone? He'd come after her once he did, if not for her sake, then for Henry Gerrard's—

Sophia's head snapped up, her body tensing as she peered into the darkness. She'd seen something, a flash of movement, like...

Yes, there it was again. A figure clothed in black, hardly discernible from the shadows surrounding the entrance to St. Clement Dane's Church. Sophia strained to see into the gloom before her, waiting, until at last the shape broke free from the shadows, the dark silhouette of a man, creeping toward the churchyard.

But which man? Peter Sharpe, Francis Thelwall, or the fourth man? It was too dark and the man still too far away for her to tell, but she knew it wasn't Tristan. She'd recognize him instantly from the shape of his frame and the fluid, arrogant grace with which he walked, as if he assumed everyone in his path knew him to be Lord Gray and the Ghost of Bow Street, and would scurry out of his way accordingly.

Which, of course, they always did.

Sophia edged around the side of the iron gate, keeping her gaze fixed on the lone figure as she crept to the west side of the graveyard, closer to the church itself. The man was moving steadily away from the entrance to the church, his head down and his hands shoved into his coat pockets. Closer, just a bit closer and she'd be able to see his face...

It wasn't Francis Thelwall. The man approaching was rather tall, but he was slender and wiry, much too slight to be Thelwall. Sharpe, then. It had to be Sharpe, here on Lord Everly's orders to accuse Francis Thelwall of theft.

Sophia paused, searching the front of the church, the churchyard behind her, and the rows of gravestones on either side of her. Where was Tristan, and Daniel and Lady Clifford? She bit her lip. It was possible they were hiding nearby—that they'd seen Peter Sharpe and were waiting for him to accost Francis Thelwall before revealing themselves, but if they were hidden in the graveyard or the churchyard, Sophia couldn't see them.

She skirted the edge of the graveyard, careful to keep low to the ground, where she was hidden by the thick gloom surrounding the headstones. She peered down the Strand in the direction of the Turk's Head, her breath catching when she saw it was still deserted. She could handle Peter Sharpe, but there was no telling where the fourth man was lurking—

"Oof!" Sophia let out a shocked gasp as her foot came up against something hard, half-hidden in the shadows. She stumbled and fell, but dragged herself up again on her hands and knees and scrabbled about, patting the ground around her, searching for whatever had tripped her.

It was as dark here as it had been inside the crypt, the moon not having reemerged from the clouds. She couldn't see a thing, but she crawled blindly forward until her hand landed on what felt like...the sleeve of a woolen cloak? She reached out cautiously, patting at the object, until her forward movement brought her knee up against...

Sophia sucked in a breath.

A man's legs.

She leaned closer, and her hand landed in something wet, a warm, thick puddle that clung to her fingertips before dripping off in slow, heavy drops, like...

Blood.

It was a man's body, covered in blood. Unmoving, but still warm.

Sophia's own blood froze in her veins. A cry rose in her throat but she bit it back and crawled closer, her hands moving over the still figure in front of her.

A man, yes. She felt her way down to his feet, running her palm over the rough heel of a pair of heavy boots, then upward, over a torso and arms clad in a thick, woolen coat, and then upward again until her fingers brushed over flesh. She felt a faint trace of warmth under her fingertips, but the man's skin was rapidly cooling, and soon enough she found out why.

His life's blood was gushing from a long, jagged slit in his throat. Sophia gagged as a heavy, metallic smell filled her nostrils and more of the thick, sticky warmth flowed over her fingers. For one endless, dreadful moment she froze, her mind reeling, but then she jerked her fingers to the pulse point behind his ear. The blood was flowing so quickly from the gash in his throat she despaired of finding any flutter there, but she pressed her fingers hard against his flesh.

No, not a twitch. She hovered her damp fingers over his nose and mouth, but he was no longer breathing.

Dead.

Another man murdered in St. Clement Dane's churchyard. Sophia fell back against her heels, her heart squeezing with shock in her chest. Another man, nameless and faceless, lying lifeless in his own blood, his throat glutted with it, breathing his last alone in a deserted graveyard.

Who was he? Not Thelwall.

Who, then?

Tristan.

Dread rolled over her, but she'd spent hours touching Tristan's body, his face—had spent the night wrapped in his arms. She'd never forget the warmth of his skin under her fingertips, the long, smooth muscles of his body moving over hers.

Sophia's brain recognized at once it wasn't him, but her heart wasn't so easily convinced. It was thrashing about inside her chest like a frantic bird, demanding certainty. She reached for the man with shaking hands, trying to avoid touching his blood again as she searched his face with desperate fingers. His chin, the bones of his cheeks, his lips, gasping all the while with hope and terror.

She might have stayed there all night, her hands moving over the dead's man's face, rocking and muttering incoherent pleas and prayers if a sudden dull gleam of light hadn't fallen over her. Sophia stared down at the features under her fingertips, and her heart rushed into her throat.

It wasn't Tristan.

It was Peter Sharpe, blood still oozing from his ravaged throat, his eyes open and staring blankly up at her.

"Shame about Sharpe, innit it, Miss Monmouth?"

Sophia froze. The light that had fallen across Peter Sharpe's ghastly face had come from a lamp. Again, her first thought was it must be Tristan, but it wasn't Tristan's voice. No, there was someone else looming over her, a lamp in his fist. She turned slowly, holding up her hand to protect her eyes from the light.

"I been after ye for days, but yer a cunning one, aren't you? Sneaky, like."

Sophia couldn't see his face. The light blinded her, rendering the man before her nothing but a dark, hulking silhouette, his features hidden in shadows, but she recognized his voice at once as the same voice she'd overheard arguing with Lord Everly yesterday morning.

The fourth man.

The man who'd killed Henry Gerrard all those weeks ago. The man who'd let Jeremy stand trial for his crime, and who'd gladly have seen him hang for it.

The man who'd killed Peter Sharpe tonight.

Sophia's mind was sluggish with shock, and she had to grope for the connection between the man standing over her now and the villain who'd made an attempt on her life on Pollen Street two nights ago. Tristan had said he'd had a club, or a stick…

Her gaze darted to the heavy walking stick in his hand. He let it dangle loosely between his fingers, tapping it repeatedly against the heel of his boot with a careless flick of his wrist.

"Knew I'd get ye alone sooner or later, an' now here ye are."

He grabbed the brass knob at the top of the stick, and Sophia heard the unmistakable clash of steel being drawn from its sheath. She gasped as a long, wicked blade emerged from the hilt.

He run the sword across the man's throat…

It had to be the same walking stick that had disappeared from the scene of Henry Gerrard's murder, and inside it was the murder weapon. Jeremy had called it a sword, but the lamplight revealed the deadly edge and the ornately carved hilt of a dagger.

"Looks like yer luck's run out, girl."

There was no time to speak, to move, or even to think before he grabbed her by her hair. Sophia cried out in pain when he wrenched her to her feet, but it died to a whimper when he pressed the cold blade of his dagger to her throat.

Sophia reacted instantly, without thought or reason, her defense born of an instinct honed by years spent wandering the most dangerous streets in the grimmest neighborhoods of London.

"No!" It was a deafening scream, pitched high enough to carry to every corner of St. Clement Dane's churchyard and into the Strand beyond. If anyone was near—Lady Clifford or Daniel, Thelwall, or Tristan—they'd hear it.

The scream had been building in her chest since she'd stumbled over Peter Sharpe's mangled body, and she gave voice to it now as close to her attacker's ear as she could manage. With any luck, it might shatter his eardrum.

"Shut yer mouth!"

The man kept his arm pressed tightly to her neck, but the shock of her scream threw his balance off, and Sophia took immediate advantage of it. She slammed the heel of her foot back, connecting with his knee. He let out a pained grunt as his leg buckled, and the arm around her neck loosened.

Sophia tore loose from his grip and fled, her harsh breath drumming in her head as she flew over the uneven ground of the graveyard towards the entrance to the church.

She didn't get far.

Her attacker was a hardened criminal who'd survived much more powerful blows than hers. He came after her, caught her by the hem of her tunic and yanked her backwards, sending her sprawling into the dirt. Another cry left her lips as her head slammed into the ground with a loud, dizzying thump.

"Bloody little bitch," he spat, and then he was on her, wrenching her to her feet with a vicious tug on her arm. This time he didn't give her a chance to scream, but slapped a hand over her mouth with such violence she tasted blood as her teeth cut into the inside of her lip. There was no chance for her to bite him, or even to draw a breath before his forearm jabbed into her throat.

She raked her fingernails over his flesh, clawing him as hard as she could, but he'd snatched hold of her hair again, and now he yanked her head backwards, exposing her vulnerable neck. Sophia kicked and flailed in his grip, but this time her feet didn't find his knee, only empty air.

"Quit yer fussing, girl. It'll be over quicker that way."

His hot breath drifted over her ear, and she just had time to think, *this is what happens to wicked little girls* before she felt the tip of his blade prick her neck, and she didn't think at all.

* * * *

Tristan raced across London, his horse's hooves pounding the streets between Great Marlborough Street and St. Clement Dane's Church into powder.

But no matter how quickly he flew, it wasn't quickly enough.

How long had it been since Sophia left his house? An hour? Longer than that? How much time had he wasted, listening to Sampson's Willis's lies?

If only he'd told Tribble to send Sampson Willis on his way. If only he hadn't left Sophia alone in his bedchamber, or returned to her sooner, or caught her before she slipped out the door...

If only, if only...

He leaned over his horse's head, a mumbled prayer on his lips. He didn't know what he prayed for, only that his words grew more desperate when St. Clement Dane's spire appeared in the distance.

Nearly there. Past Arundel and Aldwych, another block further along the Strand...

His heart eased a fraction in its frantic pounding as the entrance to the church and the churchyard came into view. It appeared deserted. He knew Sophia was here, but she would have taken care to hide herself well.

There was no sign of Sharpe, either, but that was little consolation to Tristan, who knew there were far more dangerous men hiding in the darkness than Lord Everly's cowardly servant.

Men like Richard Poole.

Wily, quick, and a ruthless murderer. He'd ended Henry's life with a swipe of a blade, and if given a second chance, he'd do the same to Sophia.

Tristan didn't intend to give him a second chance.

As soon as he made it to the church he leapt from the saddle, drawing in deep, calming breaths as he stole cautiously toward the entrance. A battle would certainly unfold in St. Clement Dane's churchyard tonight, but by some miraculous bit of luck he seemed to have arrived before it—

"*No!*"

The high-pitched scream rent the air, shattering the silence. Tristan's head whipped toward it, his blood freezing to ice.

Sophia. He'd know her voice anywhere.

The scream had come from the graveyard beyond the church. Tristan tore off in that direction, his long legs eating up the ground at his feet. As he drew closer, he noticed a dim light at the base of a white marble crypt.

A lantern, lying on its side, and beside it, just at the edge of the pool of light was the lifeless body of Peter Sharpe. Tristan didn't gasp or flinch at the sight. He didn't blink, and he didn't pause in his flight. One glance, and he could see by the spreading pool of blood seeping into the ground around the body that Peter Sharpe was beyond help.

But Sophia wasn't. She was here, and she was alive.

He ran for her, the graveyard unfolding at his pounding feet, and suddenly he was trapped in his nightmare of the past few weeks, the white marble crypt at his back as he ran for her, faster, then faster still, drawing closer with each step, his hand reaching for the long strands of her dark hair, catching it between his fingers just as she dissolved into mist.

But he ran on, his heart shuddering in his chest, each breath tearing from his lungs until there, at last, just ahead, at the edge of the graveyard...

He couldn't see them, but he sensed movement, some sort of struggle, and an instant later he heard it. A muttered curse, and a woman's choking cough, as if someone was squeezing her by the throat. Tristan's heart clenched with fear, but as terrifying as it sounded, he wasn't prepared for the sight that met his eyes when he found them at last.

It was the scene out of his worst nightmare.

Poole had a handful of her hair in his fist, her head back to expose her neck, and a dagger, the edge of the blade gleaming, was pressed hard against her throat. Sophia was fighting him, but Tristan could see she was weakening as she struggled to draw breath into her lungs.

Poole was either going to slash her throat, or strangle her.

Tristan bit back the agonized shout that tried to escape his own throat. The only advantage he had was Poole hadn't yet seen him. His body tensed to attack, to leap on Poole and tear Sophia loose from his arms, but once again a tiny shred of reason prevented him.

Poole had a blade pressed to Sophia's neck. All it would take was an unexpected noise or movement for Poole to startle and for the dagger to slip...

No. He couldn't risk it. Before he had a chance to stir a step, Poole would spill Sophia's blood all over the ground at their feet. There was only one way, and it wasn't a battle of blows.

It was a battle of wits.

He crept as close as he dared, his footfalls silent against the soft ground. "You've saved me a good deal of trouble this evening, Poole. I owe you my thanks."

Poole's head jerked up, and his entire body went rigid when he saw Tristan emerge from the shadows. His arm tightened around Sophia's neck, and his fingers curled on the hilt of his dagger. "Stay where you are, Gray. Not one bloody step, or I'll carve a slit in her throat before you've drawn a single breath."

Sophia was retching and choking against the pressure on her throat, and it took every ounce of Tristan's control not to look at her, to wipe all expression from his face. "Go ahead. I don't give a damn what you do to her, though it occurs to me she'd be far more useful to us alive than dead."

"Us?" Poole gave a scornful laugh. "Who's 'us,' Gray?"

"You, me, Everly, and Willis, of course. Sharpe's part is finished, by the look of him. Willis told me you'd manage it, but Everly wanted me to come after you, just to be certain."

"*You!*" Poole's grip on Sophia loosened as he stared at Tristan in disbelief.

Tristan stared steadily back at him. As far as Poole knew, the only way Tristan could know Willis and Everly were involved in this business was if Tristan was involved in it, too. "Yes, Poole. *Me.*"

Poole was staring at Tristan with his mouth open. "What do you know about Everly's business, Gray?"

"A great deal more than you do, I suspect. For God's sakes, man, why else would I be wandering around St. Clement Dane's churchyard in the middle of the bloody night? Sharpe's a loose end Lord Everly wants tied up. You know his lordship too well to think he'd leave something as important as this to chance."

Indeed, Everly was much cleverer than Tristan and Sophia had given him credit for being. As soon as Tristan saw Sharpe's dead body lying in the dirt, he knew they'd made a miscalculation.

Lord Everly hadn't sent Sharpe to St. Clement Dane's tonight to target Thelwall. After that mess with Henry and Jeremy Ives, Everly must have realized his scheme was falling apart, and he'd decided to eliminate the players, starting with Peter Sharpe.

Francis Thelwall wasn't the intended victim of tonight's crime.

Peter Sharpe was.

"Just as well Sharpe's dead," Tristan said with a shrug. "He's made a great many blunders, starting with Jeremy Ives. Bloody inconvenient, the way Sharpe called Lady Clifford's attention to our affairs. One doesn't need her poking about."

"Everly never said a word about you to me."

Poole didn't release Sophia, but Tristan saw the uncertainty on the man's face, and his heart leapt with hope. "Why should he? My business with Lord Everly is none of your concern. It's an agreement between *gentlemen*, Poole."

It was the right thing to say. Poole's utter ruthlessness made him useful to Everly, but Poole wasn't an aristocrat, and Everly would have taken care to make him painfully aware of that fact.

Tristan gave a lofty lift of his eyebrow, ready to press his advantage. "Everly came to me once Lady Clifford became involved. *Someone* had to keep Miss Monmouth occupied, after all. You didn't suppose it would be *you*, did you? Miss Monmouth here may be as common as dirt, but I doubt even she would have fallen victim to your, er...*questionable* charms. Why would Lord Everly send *you* when he has an earl at his disposal?"

Poole's face flushed angrily, but he knew how preoccupied with rank Lord Everly was, how grand he thought himself. He had to be wondering if Tristan was telling him the truth.

"I don't recall Lord Everly saying anything about killing her tonight, though," Tristan added, his voice cool.

He let his gaze wander to Sophia, who was staring at him with huge green eyes, her face a ghostly white. A trickle of blood was running down her neck from where Poole's dagger had pierced her skin, and Tristan could see a livid red mark over her windpipe where Poole had grabbed her. His stomach lurched.

Poole gave him a sullen look. "He didn't know she'd be here, did he?"

"Don't be ridiculous. Of course, he knew. Miss Monmouth has been skulking around St. Clement Dane's Church since Jeremy Ives was taken up for murder here. You had your chance to dispatch her the other night, Poole, and you squandered it. The last thing Everly wants is another dead body to explain tonight."

"What are we meant to do with her, then?" Poole whined. "We can't just let her go. Best way to keep her quiet is to slit her throat."

Tristan suppressed a shudder at the nonchalance with which Poole spoke of murdering Sophia. The man was an utter villain, without scruples or conscience. He wouldn't have thought twice about slitting Sophia's throat tonight. Panic swept through Tristan at the thought, and he had to fight to control his breath. "Why, see her sent to Newgate Prison for murdering Peter Sharpe, of course."

Poole's mouth thinned. He yanked on Sophia's hair, jerking her closer as if he was afraid Tristan was about to march her off to Newgate right there and then. "Thelwall's taking the blame for that. Lord Everly said so."

Tristan gave Poole a bored look. "Did he? Well, let me ask you something, Poole. Do you see Thelwall here? Curious, isn't it, that he hasn't yet arrived, given the LCS's meeting at the Turk's Head broke up more than an hour ago."

Ah. That hadn't occurred to Poole. "But Lord Everly said he'd be here! Where's he gone?"

"Christ, you're dim, Poole. Miss Monmouth here must have sent a note to Lady Clifford, and her ladyship sent someone to the Turk's Head to see to it Thelwall avoids St. Clement Dane's Church tonight." Tristan waved a desultory hand. "Bad luck, eh, Poole? A dead body, and no one to blame for his murder? No one, that is, but you and Miss Monmouth."

"*Her!* Who's going to believe she finished off Sharpe? She's no bigger than a bedbug. How's a little bit of a thing like 'er going to fell a grown man?"

Tristan smirked. "Think about it, Poole. I'm sure the answer will come to you."

But it *didn't* come to him. For all Poole's viciousness, he wasn't a deep thinker. He looked from Tristan to Sophia with a puzzled expression.

"For God's sake, Poole. Do I have to explain everything to you? Very well, then. Let me be more specific. If Miss Monmouth were to invite you to join her for a quick tumble amongst the tombstones, would you refuse her?"

From the corner of his eye Tristan noticed Sophia flinch, but he could see the dawning understanding on Poole's face, and he forced himself to go on. "I don't think there are many men alive who *would* refuse her. I doubt Mr. Sharpe proved to be an exception."

Poole licked his lips and leered down at Sophia. "She's a tempting bit, isn't she?"

Tristan's hand ached to strike the leer right off Poole's face. It closed into a fist of its own accord, but he forced himself to keep his arm by his side. "Very. Once she had him down, it would be the easiest thing in the world for her to slit his throat. It doesn't take strength so much as cunning. One swipe when Sharpe least expects it, and the thing is done."

Tristan waited, his muscles tensed to pounce the moment Poole made a move, but the villain still hadn't released Sophia.

"We'll both claim to have witnessed Sharpe's murder, of course. I doubt anyone will question the word of two Bow Street Runners, one of them an earl, particularly since Miss Monmouth has been seen following Sharpe all over London. But do as you will, Poole." Tristan shrugged, as if he didn't care one way or the other what Poole decided. "Though if you think you have trouble with Lady Clifford now, imagine what she'll do when she finds one of her precious girls has been murdered in St. Clement Dane's churchyard. Ah, well. I'm sure you'll come up with some explanation that will satisfy Daniel Brixton."

Poole went pale at the veiled threat, and while he retained his hold on Sophia's arm, he dropped the one he'd wrapped around her neck. "All right, Gray. What do we do now?"

"Take her up for murder. What else?" Tristan was ready to snatch the dagger from Poole's hand, but he held back, playing for an even greater advantage. "Wipe off your dagger in the dirt first. I'd rather not drag Miss Monmouth off to the magistrate for murdering Peter Sharpe while the man's blood is still dripping from your blade."

He'd hoped Poole would crouch down to clean the dagger in the dirt so he could pounce on him and smash his face into the ground, but Poole only shrugged, and wiped the blade across his pant leg.

"Come here, Miss Monmouth." Tristan beckoned Sophia forward, his gaze holding hers. He didn't dare do more than that until she was out of Poole's reach, but he prayed she'd read his intent in his eyes. "I do apologize our time together had to come to such an unpleasant end. Speaking as a man who's sampled your charms, I daresay I'm more upset about it than you are. You see, I wasn't nearly done with you."

Poole snorted.

Sophia took a shaky step forward, toward Tristan. His fingers twitched subtly, urging her another step closer to him, away from Poole. "Come along, Miss Monmouth. No sense in delaying the inevitable."

She took another step toward him, her green eyes dazed. Another step, another…

"We haven't got all night, Miss Monmouth." Tristan stretched his hand out to her, his gaze steady on hers, but just as she stepped out of Poole's reach, sudden doubt filled the man's face. His eyes narrowed on Tristan, and whatever he saw there made him snatch at Sophia.

But Tristan was quicker. He grabbed her hand and jerked her forward with a wrench so powerful her feet left the ground, and he caught her in his arms and shoved her behind him. He heard her stumble, but there was no time for him to help her, or even to look back and reassure himself she was all right.

Poole was already on him, fury in his face and his dagger raised to strike. It came toward Tristan in a blur, the blade turned outward, aimed right at his throat.

Chapter Twenty-two

A burning pain shot up Sophia's leg as she crashed onto her side on the ground behind Tristan. She lay there stunned, gagging and coughing, her hand flying up to clutch at her throat. It felt as if Poole's punishing grip had crushed her windpipe, and a thin trickle of blood from his blade wetted her fingertips. She dragged in a desperate breath, then another, struggling to fight back the sharp edge of panic.

"Yer a bloody fool. I thought ye were smarter than to think with yer cock, Gray." Poole's menacing voice jerked her back to awareness, and she looked up to find Tristan had managed to throw Poole off, and they were now circling each other. "You've made a mistake tonight, my lord. The last one you'll ever make."

"You'll hang for certain if you murder an earl, Poole, but then you're going to hang anyway, aren't you?" Tristan appeared calm, his tone faintly mocking, but his body was tensed as he waited for an opportunity to strike.

He was the bigger of the two men, but that advantage was more than offset by his lack of a weapon, and Poole knew it. He grinned at Tristan as he toyed with the dagger, tossing it lightly into the air, then catching it by the hilt again. "Not if I kill you. I've never heard of a dead man testifying in court, Gray."

"Another murder won't help you this time, Poole. Lady Clifford knows all about you and Peter Sharpe and Lord Everly, and you can be certain she's told Kit Benjamin. Your neck is destined for a noose whether you kill me or not. Or perhaps she'll simply turn you over to Daniel Brixton." Tristan's lips stretched in a bloodthirsty smile. "I'd rather face the noose, myself."

Poole's face paled with fear. "Then I may as well kill you. I don't have anything to lose, and I've never liked you much, Gray. Always so grand, thinking you're better than the rest of us."

Tristan laughed. "Better than *you*, certainly."

This taunt had the intended effect. Poole let out a snarl of fury and lunged at Tristan. Sophia's heart rushed into her throat as the dagger arced through the air. Anger made Poole clumsy, and Tristan dodged him easily, but it was only a matter of time before Poole struck again, and the next time, Tristan might not be so lucky. All it would take was one well-aimed blow, one slice with the blade, and it would be over.

She staggered to her hands and knees, her first thought to crawl behind Poole and grab him around the legs, but Tristan kept his body in front of her, shielding her as he shifted in a wide arc around Poole. He was doing everything he could to protect her, which put him at a further disadvantage. How could he fend off Poole if part of his attention was focused on her?

A weapon. Tristan needed a weapon, but what? Sophia scrabbled blindly at the ground, praying she'd come across a loose rock or even a branch, but she found only dirt and a few loose pebbles. It wasn't much, but if she could get close enough to Poole and catch him unawares, she might be able to blind him.

Sophia snatched up a handful of the dirt in a tight fist and scrambled into a crouch, ready to scurry around Tristan to get to Poole, but a grunt of pain stopped her. She stumbled to her feet just in time to see Poole drag the edge of his blade across Tristan's forearm.

"That one'll bleed nicely." Poole sprung back with a bloodthirsty smirk and flicked his gaze over the blade of his dagger, his mouth curling with satisfaction at the blood dripping from the tip. "Not feeling dizzy, are you, Gray? It'll be your chest next time."

Sophia watched in horror as blood spurted from Tristan's wound, turning the sleeve of his white shirt a dark red. Nausea swamped her, nearly sending her to her knees again.

Tristan pressed his other hand against the wound to staunch the flow, but he didn't waste his energy replying to the taunt. His gaze darted from Poole's face to the dagger in his hand as he and Poole continued to circle each other.

Poole lunged again, missed, then lunged a second time, aiming his blade at Tristan's chest. Tristan dodged at the last minute and the strike flew wide. Before Poole could regain his balance, Tristan charged at him, grabbing him around the waist and knocking him onto his back on the ground. The breath left Poole's lungs in a stunned whoosh. Tristan fell on top of him and closed his hands around Poole's throat, but Sophia could see his wounded arm was stiff. He was weakened by blood loss, as well, and Poole managed to throw him off.

Sophia rushed forward then, ready to blind Poole with the dirt in her hand while he was down, but for all that Poole lacked cleverness, he was a skilled fighter, as deadly with a dagger as he was vicious. He was up again in a flash, rolling onto his feet in one smooth move.

He saw Sophia approach from the corner of his eye and sent her sprawling with one blow from the back of his hand. She vaguely registered a howl of rage, and the sounds of a furious scuffle as she crumpled to the ground.

Don't swoon. Not now, not now...

The clouds had receded, and a dark sky sprinkled with stars swam above her. Their bright edges blurred together, then began to fade to black as her vision tunneled, but just as consciousness threatened to desert her, the spire of St. Clement Dane's Church came into focus, the light gray stone pale against the midnight sky.

Henry's spire...

That spire was the last thing Henry Gerrard had seen before his eyes closed forever. He would have found serenity in the sight of that spire reaching into the heavens—a final moment of peace before his heart beat its last. Sophia could understand that peace as she lay on her back, her gaze fixed on the spire soaring into the sky.

She'd have to remember to tell Tristan how it felt...

Because she wouldn't die here tonight. She wouldn't die, and she'd do whatever she must to see to it Tristan didn't either. The spire of St. Clement Dane's Church wouldn't be the last thing she ever saw.

It had begun here, but it wouldn't end here.

Sophia dragged in deep breaths as she stared up at the spire, focusing on it until the dizziness receded. One breath, another...slowly, her heart ceased its panicked thrashing, and the darkness receded from the edges of her vision. A calm descended over her, almost as if someone were whispering soothingly into her ear.

Such a good girl, Sophia...

Not a good girl, no. She'd never been that, had never even understood what it meant to be that. But maybe once, just this one time, she could be the heroine.

Sophia staggered to her feet, blood spurting out of her nose from the blow to her face. Tristan and Poole were scrambling in the dirt, each of them trying to pin the other to the ground and gain the upper hand. Hope surged in Sophia's chest as Tristan rolled on top of Poole, but she didn't wait to see who'd emerge the victor.

There was no time.

Instead she flew towards the church, stopping halfway there and falling to her knees in front of the dilapidated crypt she'd hidden inside earlier tonight. There was a heavy marble cross half-buried in the dirt in front of the arched doorway. She'd noticed there was a long, deep crack in it, close to the bottom. One kick was all it would take to break it, but she'd have to land the blow carefully, or she risked the entire thing crumbling to pieces.

The cross tilted crazily in the loose dirt at its base. She clawed at the ground, shoving the dirt to one side, then staggered to her feet and muttered a quick prayer just as she brought her heel down hard right over the crack near bottom of the cross.

The marble fractured with a cold, hollow snap. Bits of chipped stone flew everywhere, but the cross remained mostly intact, and heavy enough to use as a weapon. Sophia heaved it up in both hands and ran with it back to where Tristan and Poole were struggling in the dirt.

What she saw when she drew near made her freeze, and her heart stop in her chest.

Tristan was on his back, with Poole on top of him. Poole's hands were raised over his head, and between them he held the dagger, the point aimed for Tristan's heart. The faint hint of moonlight peeking through the clouds gleamed dully on the blade as it arced downwards. Tristan caught Poole's wrists before Poole could plunge the dagger into his chest, but gravity and momentum worked against him.

He was able to slow the dagger, but not to stop it. Poole's wrists slipped through Tristan's fingers and the dagger plunged downward into Tristan's chest.

A scream echoed around them in the clear, dark night then—a scream filled with an inhuman anguish. At first Sophia thought it must be Tristan screaming with pain, but as her feet pounded across the graveyard towards him, she realized it wasn't.

It was *her*.

She was flying across the ground, running faster than she'd ever run in her life, yet her feet felt sluggish and her legs heavy as she watched Poole raise his hands over his head a second time, and dear God, they seemed miles away still, the expanse of ground between her and Tristan vast, an ocean. She wasn't fast enough—she wasn't going to make it to them in time to stop Poole from stabbing Tristan a second time.

He was going die, to bleed to death right in front of her eyes—

But then suddenly in the next breath she was there, behind Poole, her own arms raised in the air, the stone cross clutched between her hands. He turned just as she swung it at his head, and she saw the knowledge of what was about to happen flash in his eyes before she brought it down in a vicious strike against his temple. She struck him as hard as she could, with every bit of her strength behind the blow.

When Poole fell, he was never going to get back up again.

She winced at the dull crack of stone against flesh and bone. Poole made a faint sound, a gurgle of surprise more than pain before he listed over, blood pouring from an enormous gash in his head.

Sophia didn't spare him another glance. She shoved him hard to the side and he slumped into the dirt. "Tristan? Tristan, look at me." She bent over him, her shaking hands hovering helplessly over his chest. There was so much blood...dear God, he was soaked with it, and she couldn't think, didn't know what to do to stop it, where to even begin. She couldn't see the wound, just great clouts of blood spurting from Tristan's chest, but she pressed both hands against him where the blood seemed to be flowing the heaviest.

It wasn't enough. All she could do wasn't enough to save him. She stared down at his blood spurting between her fingers. She could feel his heart beating weakly under her palms, but she knew it was no use, that there was no way he could survive such a wound, but broken pleas continued to tear loose from her throat, as if she thought she could save him with her words alone. "Tristan, please. *Please—*"

"Sophia!"

She heard her name echo across the graveyard, but Sophia didn't look up. She kept her gaze locked on Tristan's still, pale face, hope struggling inside her even as she was tumbling over the edge of despair. She pushed Tristan's hair away from his eyes, leaving a smear of blood on his forehead. "Tristan, can you hear me?"

This time, her voice seemed to get through to him. He didn't open his eyes, but she was certain she saw them flutter under his eyelids. "Tristan?" She leaned closer, but before she could reassure herself there was some part of him still alert enough to respond to her voice, a pair of large, masculine hands closed over her shoulders.

"No! Don't touch me!" Sophia thrashed against the man's hold, panic making her strong. She heard a muttered curse when her fingernails raked down a muscular forearm. That voice, low and deep and with a pronounced Celtic lilt, it sounded familiar...

"Sophia, look at me." This second voice was firm, calm, and the hands that came up to hold her face were gentle. "Let Daniel move you away from Lord Gray so we can tend to him."

It was Lady Clifford. Sophia stared into that comforting face, a face as dear to her as her own mother's had been, and all at once all the fight went out of her. She sagged as her limbs went liquid, and would have collapsed in the dirt if Daniel hadn't lifted her gently away from Tristan and placed her securely in Lady Clifford's waiting arms.

Sophia buried her face in Lady Clifford's shoulder, her entire body now shaking with the sobs she'd been fighting to hold off since she'd tripped over Peter Sharpe's body.

But the sobs weren't for her. "Tristan. His chest. He's…he's dying."

They were for Tristan.

Lady Clifford, who had yet to meet a crisis that could crack the steel in her spine, soothed Sophia with pats and murmurs. "We don't know that, Sophia. We don't know anything yet. Lord Gray is a strong, hearty gentleman. You won't give up on him quite yet, will you?"

Sophia shook her head, and Lady Clifford patted her cheek with a smile. "That's a good girl. Daniel?" She met Daniel's gaze over Sophia's shoulder and her expression shifted subtly, a slight tightening in her lips that hadn't been there before.

Daniel had been kneeling beside Tristan, assessing his injuries with swift, sure hands, but now he rose to his feet and met Lady Clifford's gaze. "Bad, but not as bad as I thought." Daniel glanced at Sophia, an odd look on his face. "The blade didn't touch his heart."

Sophia stared dumbly at him. She'd seen Poole plunge the dagger directly into Tristan's chest. How could it not have pierced his heart?

She didn't have time to ask, because Lady Clifford was talking quickly, issuing instructions. "Do what you can to stop the bleeding, if you'd be so good, Daniel—just enough so we can get him into the carriage and back to Maddox Street."

Daniel unwound his cravat, folded it neatly, and pressed it to Tristan's chest. "Hold that there, Miss Sophia, and don't be afraid to press down hard. That's it, lass."

Sophia did as she was told, stifling her gasp as Daniel lifted Tristan into his arms as if he weighed no more than a child, and carried him to Lady Clifford's carriage. Sophia scrambled in, and Daniel laid Tristan across the seat, his head in Sophia's lap.

"Thank you, Daniel." Lady Clifford dropped into her own seat on the opposite side. "I believe I saw Lord Gray's horse wandering nearby. Take it, and call on Giles Wakeford. Tell him we need him at No. 26 Maddox at once, and that it's urgent."

Daniel's lips thinned.

Giles Wakeford was the doctor, surgeon, and all things medical for the Clifford School. Wakeford was handsome, amusing, and discreet. All of them loved him—everyone, that is, but Daniel Brixton. No one knew what Wakeford had done to offend Daniel, but over the years Daniel's distaste for the man had remained implacable.

"Once you've fetched Wakeford, call on Kit Benjamin. Explain the circumstances, and ask him to see to it that unpleasant gentleman with the cracked skull is dealt with."

"Peter Sharpe, too." Sophia met Lady Clifford's eyes. "He's in the graveyard. Mr. Poole slit his throat."

Daniel nodded and closed the carriage door, and then Sophia and Lady Clifford were on their way to No. 26 Maddox Street with Tristan. Sophia said nothing as they rattled through the dark streets of London toward the Clifford School, but sat silently on her side of the carriage, pressing the cravat firmly against the wound in Tristan's chest.

Lady Clifford watched her for a moment, then retrieved her reticule, rummaged around inside it, and leaned across the seat to dab at Sophia's nose with a dainty linen handkerchief. "Your nose is bleeding, dearest."

Sophia looked down at herself. Her hands and gown were covered with Tristan's blood. "I think it's too late for that, my lady."

Lady Clifford gave her a cryptic smile. "My dear child, it's never too late for anything."

Chapter Twenty-three

It was a short drive from St. Clement Dane's Church to No. 26 Maddox Street, but tonight London felt as vast as an ocean to Sophia as they made their way through an infinity of dark, endless streets.

She cradled Tristan's head in her lap and murmured soothingly to him, but his eyes never flickered. He hadn't regained consciousness by the time they arrived, and a dark red pool of his blood was spreading across the pale gray velvet carriage seats.

Sophia was able to draw a few calming breaths into her lungs when they arrived at the school at last, but then another lifetime seemed to pass as they waited in the carriage for Daniel and Giles Wakeford to arrive. It wasn't more than ten minutes before a hackney coach skidded up behind Lady Clifford's carriage and disgorged the two men at the curb outside the Clifford School, but by then Sophia was shaking with stark panic.

Lady Clifford ordered Tristan be taken to a downstairs bedchamber, and she, Daniel, and Giles Wakeford remained closeted inside it with him for the better part of the night. Sophia had been left to hover outside the door, her eyes burning with unshed tears and her every breath choked with dread. One hour dragged after the next until finally Lady Clifford emerged to tell Sophia Tristan's condition remained uncertain, and ordered her to her bedchamber to rest.

Rest. Sophia did as she was told, but there would be no rest for her today. She thought of Tristan's wan face, his pale lips, the dark red blood soaking his shirt, and wondered if she'd ever sleep again. She didn't even attempt to lie down in her bed, but stood by her bedchamber window, the drapes fisted in her white-knuckled grip. "Why doesn't someone *come?*"

"Someone would have, if the worst had happened." Cecilia had joined Sophia in their bedchamber, her usually rosy cheeks as pale as Tristan's had been. "Until then, we won't give in to despair, will we? Indeed, I won't allow it, Sophia. Now, come here, dearest."

She held out a hand to Sophia, who abandoned her post by the window to join Cecilia on the bed. "There, that's better," Cecilia murmured, patting Sophia's hand.

Cecilia was making a great effort to remain optimistic, and a less discerning friend might have believed she was. She sat stoically on the edge of the bed, every hair in place, with Sophia's hand securely between her own.

But Sophia wasn't fooled.

Cecilia was more unnerved than Sophia had ever seen her. Of all the bad omens and waking nightmares that had made up this night, Cecilia's disquiet bothered Sophia most of all. If Cecilia was anything less than unrelentingly positive, then things were very bad, indeed.

Sophia spent the next few hours pacing from the bed to the window to the bedchamber door, listening for Lady Clifford's footsteps in the hallway. She and Cecilia didn't speak much, but her friend never abandoned her. The sun had just sent its first tentative rays into the sky when Sophia turned from the window to face Cecilia, and broke her silence at last. "I love him, Cecilia. I'm in love with him."

Cecilia raised her head, and her gaze met Sophia's. "I know."

Sophia managed a half-smile and a shrug, but the tears she'd kept at bay all night glittered at the corners of her eyes. "I'm in love with an earl. It's the most foolish, absurd thing ever, yet I've gone and fallen in love with an earl."

An earl who's betrothed to a lady in Oxfordshire.

It was on the tip of Sophia's tongue to say it aloud, to confide everything to Cecilia, but something held her back.

"I know, dearest," Cecilia repeated with a sigh, then patted the empty space beside her on the bed. "Come here."

Sophia shuffled over to the bed, dropped down beside Cecilia, and wrapped her arms around herself, shivering. When had it grown so cold? "How did you know?"

Cecilia tucked an arm around Sophia's shoulders, squeezing her closer when Sophia lay her head against her shoulder. "Because it's who you are, Sophia. You hang about deserted graveyards at night. You scale earls' townhouses, hide on their roofs, and break into their kitchens. You've never been one to shy away from danger, even at the expense of your own safety. So, why should you behave any differently with your heart?"

"Oh, dear. You do insist on making me into a heroine, don't you?" Sophia asked, with a forlorn little laugh.

"Of course, you're a heroine, a wonderfully brave sort of heroine. You always have been."

Sophia sniffled. "I wish I was a coward. I'd be much better off."

"No, you wouldn't." Cecilia stroked a hand over Sophia's hair. "Falling in love is a great risk, certainly, but it offers the greatest reward. Why, just look at Adeline and Theodore."

Sophia closed her eyes and tried to empty her mind of everything but Adeline and Theodore's happy ending, but the image of Richard Poole on top of Tristan with the knife raised over his head seemed to be painted on the inside of her eyelids. Time and again she saw the knife arc through the air, the blade gleaming in the faint light before it plunged into Tristan's chest, and the blood, thick and dark, spurting everywhere...

She shuddered, and turned her face into Cecilia's shoulder. "What reward? He's going to die, Cecilia. Tristan's going to die, and I'll be left alone."

She'd been alone before. The thought of being so again shouldn't cause her such despair, yet somehow losing Tristan made her feel more alone than she ever had before.

"Hush. You know better than that. You'll never be alone, no matter what becomes of Lord Gray." Cecilia kept stroking Sophia's hair and muttering words of comfort, but she didn't try and convince Sophia Tristan would be all right. She didn't make any empty promises, and she didn't say he wouldn't die.

Cecilia was a true romantic, but she never lied. For all her starry-eyed dreams and fancies, she'd seen too much of life to believe every story had a happy ending.

So, Sophia wept, and Cecilia rocked her gently as the hours crawled by. The summer sun, which had chosen this day of all days to shine with unrelenting cheerfulness, was high in the sky before Sophia gave up her struggle to stay awake, and succumbed to an exhausted sleep.

She startled awake sometime later to a soft knock on the door.

When she opened her eyes, Cecilia was hurrying to open it, and a moment later Lady Clifford entered the bedchamber. She glanced at Sophia huddled under the covers Cecilia had draped over her, and her face softened. "Ah, that's good, dear. You've managed to get some sleep."

"Just for little while, yes." Cecilia wrung her hands, tutting as she gazed anxiously at Lady Clifford. "My goodness, my lady. You look in dire need of some sleep yourself."

Lady Clifford was sagging with fatigue, and her smooth face was creased with worry. Her fair hair had fallen from its elegant chignon and was plastered to her damp forehead. She pushed a lock of it back and gave Cecilia a wan smile. "I don't look nearly as bad as poor Mr. Wakeford does. Another hour, and the dear man would have collapsed."

Cecilia glanced at Sophia, who'd sprung bolt upright when Lady Clifford entered the room, but hadn't yet managed to say a word. "And Lord Gray? How does he do?"

Lady Clifford sat down on the edge of the bed and took Sophia's hand. "I know you've been anxious, dearest. I beg your pardon for not coming sooner, but I wanted to wait until I had something definitive to tell you."

Definitive. Sophia's throat moved in a swallow. Was Lady Clifford trying to tell her Tristan was dead? "Is he…is Tristan…"

"Lord Gray is doing as well as can be expected, given the severity of his injuries. He's resting comfortably at the moment." Lady Clifford frowned. "That is, resting as comfortably as any gentleman who's taken a dagger to his chest can be, which is to say, not so comfortably at all. But one takes what one can get, doesn't one? He's alive and breathing, which is remarkable enough, considering the circumstances."

Sophia was very still for a long moment, staring at Lady Clifford, then all of her strength drained from her at once and she collapsed back against the pillow. "He's…he's alive? He's going to be all right?" Her voice was faint, as if she didn't dare believe Lady Clifford could be telling her the truth.

Lady Clifford squeezed Sophia's hand. "For the moment, he is. Mr. Wakeford can't make any promises regarding Lord Gray's future condition, of course, but he seems inclined to be optimistic."

"But…how? I saw Poole stab him, a vicious blow, right in Tristan's chest. How could he have survived it?" Sophia gripped Lady Clifford's hand, her eyes pleading. "Are you q-quite sure he's all right, my lady?"

"I'm quite sure he's still alive, yes. It's a bit of a strange tale, really. Giles Wakeford was astonished when we removed Lord Gray's shirt, and realized what had happened."

Cecilia looked at Sophia, then at Lady Clifford. "What do you mean? What happened?"

Lady Clifford didn't answer right away. She studied Sophia, her head cocked to the side, but then she reached into the pocket of her skirts and drew something out. Cecilia had drawn the curtains closed to darken the room while Sophia slept, but muted light from a low lamp on the table revealed a glint of silver and a long, heavy chain.

Sophia gasped. "My locket! How do you happen to have it? I left it at…"

Tristan's. He'd taken it off her last night, and laid it on the table beside his bed. She'd left in such a rush yesterday, she'd forgotten it.

Sophia's gaze met Lady Clifford's. The only way Lady Clifford could have the locket now was if she'd gotten it from Tristan. He must have found it on the table, taken it up, and brought it with him to St. Clement Dane's Church last night. "Lady Clifford?"

"I took it off Lord Gray." Lady Clifford was watching Sophia closely. "He was wearing it around his neck."

Tristan had been wearing her locket? Sophia stared at Lady Clifford, her mouth falling open in shock. "H-he was wearing it?"

Lady Clifford fingered the locket in her palm, then took it up by the chain and let it dangle between her fingers. "Look at it, dearest. Here, right in middle."

She held the locket out to Sophia, who took it, laying it face up in her palm. There was something there, right in the center of the plain silver oval. A mark, or...

Sophia's eyes went wide, and a soft cry left her lips. "No. It can't be."

But it was. There, right in the center where the locket rested over the wearer's heart was a small hole, the same size as...

As the tip of a dagger.

Sophia fumbled at the catch on the locket, her hands trembling. She thought she already knew what she'd find when she opened it, yet when she saw it with her own eyes her heart rushed into her throat, and her hand flew up to cover her mouth. "I-I can't believe it."

No one who hadn't seen it with their own eyes could have believed it, but the proof was right there in the palm of her hand.

"Poole's dagger went through the lid of the locket, and left a deep puncture in the bottom half." Lady Clifford traced a fingertip over the gouge there. "It was a near thing, but the blade didn't go all the way through."

The dagger hadn't touched Tristan's heart. The locket had stopped it.

"What is it? Let me see." Cecilia leaned closer to peer over Sophia's shoulder. She let out a soft exclamation and reached out to touch the hole in the center of the locket. "My goodness, that's astonishing! I've never seen anything like that in my entire life."

Sophia ran her thumb over the hole wonderingly, then looked up at Lady Clifford. "But how? Tristan was bleeding. I saw the blood myself—"

"Lord Gray didn't escape unscathed, unfortunately. Giles Wakeford thinks the dagger glanced off the locket when Poole brought it down in the center of Lord Gray's chest. The blade likely skidded sideways.

It left his lordship with a nasty wound, but it prevented the knife from reaching his heart."

Sophia stared at Lady Clifford, too stunned to speak.

Her locket…it was precious to her, special, yet she'd given it up to Mr. Hogg the day she and Tristan had gone to Newgate to see Jeremy. It had pained her to lose it, especially to someone so loathsome as Hogg, but she'd given it up for Jeremy's sake.

Then Tristan had got it back again, for *hers*.

That it should be the locket that saved Tristan's life, when it had been Tristan who'd rescued it for her, that the kindness he'd shown her had been the means by which his life had been saved…dear God, even *she* couldn't deny there was something mystical there, a sort of otherworldly balance.

Fate, or perhaps a perfect iteration of justice.

Lady Clifford's dark blue eyes met Sophia's. "If Lord Gray hadn't been wearing the locket—if the blade had touched his heart—he'd be dead now. Your locket saved his heart, and then *you* saved his life, my dear, when you hit Poole with the cross before he could stab Lord Gray a second time."

"My goodness, Sophia." Cecilia squeezed Sophia's arm, nearly breathless with the romance of it. "A dagger-wielding villain in a dark graveyard, and a magical locket that saves the hero's life? Why, it's a Gothic romance come alive! Mrs. Radcliffe herself couldn't have written a more perfect ending!"

Sophia gave a shaky laugh. It *did* sound like something out of one of Mrs. Radcliffe's romances. She was an unlikely enough heroine—so much so she could hardly credit such an ending could belong to *her*—but despite her many imperfections, she loved Tristan with all her heart.

Perhaps that was all it took for a happy ending?

Lady Clifford wrapped Sophia's slack fingers around the locket. "Lord Gray had fallen into an uneasy sleep when I left his bedchamber just now, but he asked for you over and over again tonight—each time he regained consciousness. Indeed, when he was at his most agitated Daniel was obliged to hold him down. He'll likely sleep for some time, but I think he'll be quite pleased to see you when he wakes again."

"Yes, you must be waiting by his bedside when his eyelids flutter open, Sophia." Cecilia took Sophia's hand and tugged her from the bed. "That's what a proper heroine would do."

Sophia closed the locket tightly in her fist and rose from the bed, leaving her dread behind her in the tangled sheets. She was more than ready to see her hero.

* * * *

Sophia's courage nearly deserted her when she crept into Tristan's bedchamber. She paused at the door, her heart swelling into her throat at how pale and still he was.

He was lying on his back in the center of the bed, his arms laid carefully at his sides. The coverlet was pulled down just enough so she could see his bare chest and torso were wrapped heavily in bandages. A bit of blood was already pooling over his breastbone, despite the fresh dressing.

Sophia edged closer and took his hand in hers. His skin was cool and dry, his fingers slack. He didn't react when she touched him, not even a twitch of his eyes under his eyelids. Tears stung Sophia's eyes as she thought of how close he'd come to never opening those gray eyes again. A few tears escaped down her cheeks, but she brushed them aside and settled herself into the chair beside his bed.

Tristan was alive. She could see his chest moving up and down with each of his shallow breaths. This wasn't a time for tears, but a time for gratitude.

She stayed by his bed for the rest of the day and into the evening, leaving his side only when Giles Wakeford chased her from the room so he could assess his patient's condition and change his dressing. Tristan slept through it all, oblivious to everything around him. Sophia had hoped he would wake, if only for a moment so he'd see her, and know she was there with him, but hour after hour passed and his eyes remained closed. Finally, worn out with watching and waiting, Sophia folded her arms on the edge of the bed, rested her head on them, and fell into a fitful sleep.

When she woke, the bedchamber was dark, the fire having burned down to embers. She blinked groggily, uncertain why she'd woken until she felt the softest touch on her head, like fingers moving slowly through her hair.

She lifted her head and looked up. Tristan's face was turned toward her, and he was gazing down at her with gray eyes so soft her heart melted like warm honey in her chest.

"I knew you were here, pixie. Even before I woke, I knew you were here." His voice was thick and raspy, and though he tried to hide it, Sophia could see by the white lines around his lips that he was in a great deal of pain.

Sophia smiled and slid her hand into his. "How did you know?"

"Your scent. Honeysuckle. You smell like honeysuckle." A faint smile drifted over his lips, but it faded as he searched her face. "You won't leave me?"

"No. I won't leave you." She held his gaze as she raised his hand to her lips. "Never, Tristan."

Chapter Twenty-four

It was five days before Tristan was alert enough to make sense of his surroundings. The time before that was hazy, just a series of images drifting through his head—drape-shrouded windows, soft voices, white-hot, burning pain in his chest, and a tall, dark-haired man with kind brown eyes and silver frosting his temples leaning over the bed.

There'd only been one constant, only one thing that made sense.

Sophia.

Each time he forced an eye open she was there beside his bed, her anxious gaze fixed on his face, her fingers tucked into his hand. He tried to talk to her, to swim to the surface, but the dizziness kept sucking him back down again. At one point he thought he'd spoken to her, had watched her lips moving in reply, but when he struggled to consciousness much later, he wondered if he'd dreamt it.

He couldn't make any sense of time as he floated in this nebulous state. Once or twice he woke and couldn't remember the last time he'd heard Sophia's voice. He'd fallen into a panic each time, and flailed and thrashed in the bed to get to her, but he was too exhausted to struggle for long, and inevitably unconsciousness would wrap him in silken threads and draw him down into darkness again.

Then, late one afternoon his surroundings came into focus at last.

Sophia's was the first face he searched for.

"Well, good afternoon, Lord Gray. How pleased I am you've woken at last. We were growing rather concerned."

That voice…cultured, but with a faint hint of amusement underlying every syllable. He recognized it at once.

Lady Clifford.

Tristan blinked up at her in confusion. Where was he, and why wasn't Sophia—

"You're in a bedchamber at the Clifford School, my lord. I daresay you would have been more comfortable in your own home, but given a good deal of your blood had already vacated your body before we got you into the carriage, time was of the essence." Lady Clifford leaned over him, her brow furrowing as she studied his face. "Not quite yourself still, I see. Do you remember what happened?"

Tristan squeezed his eyes closed. The light from the fire made his head ache, but he tried to think. He'd been at St. Clement Dane's Church, hadn't he? Yes, he remembered riding there, but everything after that was fuzzy, as if it had happened long ago, or to someone else.

But…something awful had happened, hadn't it? Uneasiness stole through him as a memory began to unfold in his head. He recalled hearing someone cry out, and a lantern tipped over onto the ground. It had been dark, but the lantern had given off just enough light for him to see…

Tristan gasped, and his eyes flew open.

Peter Sharpe lying in a puddle of blood. Richard Poole, knife in hand, and Sophia—

"Sophia!"

Tristan shot upright, ignoring the searing pain in his chest, but before he could throw off the coverlet and scramble to his feet Lady Clifford caught hold of his shoulders and eased him back down against the bed. "No, no. That won't do. Listen to me, Lord Gray, and cease that thrashing about at once, or I'll be forced to summon Daniel Brixton."

He continued to struggle, hardly able to hear her beyond the panicked roaring inside his head, but either Lady Clifford was surprisingly strong for such a slender, elegant lady, or else he was as weak as a kitten. She held him fast until he subsided against the bed at last, exhausted by his efforts, his entire body clammy with sweat.

"My goodness, my lord. Sophia warned me you're stubborn, but I confess I didn't expect quite so much resistance from a gentleman who's been stabbed in the chest." Lady Clifford was panting to regain her breath.

"Tell me where Sophia is," Tristan begged, his voice breaking. The last time he could remember seeing her, Poole's knife was at her throat—

"Calm down, if you please, Lord Gray. Now, Sophia is perfectly well, though I couldn't say precisely where she is at the moment. I ordered her to her bedchamber to rest, but I've just been to check on her, and she isn't there. Ah, well. She'll turn up when she's ready. Until then…" Lady

Clifford shrugged. "You know for yourself our Sophia's rather good at keeping herself hidden."

"You're certain she's well? She's all right?" Lady Clifford had said so, but Tristan needed to hear it again.

"Yes, my lord. I promise it. She has a few scratches and scrapes and some bruising on her neck, but otherwise she's quite well." Lady Clifford cocked her head, studying him. "I believe I've misjudged you, Lord Gray. I've always thought you a stern, cold sort of man, but you're truly fond of Sophia, aren't you?"

Fond of her? No. What he felt for Sophia went far beyond fondness.

He was deeply, madly in love with her, but Sophia would be the first to hear those words from his lips, not Lady Clifford. So, he simply nodded. "I—yes, of course I'm...*fond* of her."

A slight smile drifted across Lady Clifford's lips. "You may well be stern and cold, but I'm inclined to overlook these flaws, given your extraordinary discernment in regards to Sophia. Now, my lord, if you're willing to lie quietly and listen to me, I'll tell you what happened."

Tristan didn't want to lie quietly. He wanted to tear through the house and peek behind every curtain and under every bed until he found Sophia, but that was out of the question. He'd collapse before he made it to his bedchamber door. So, he rested his head obediently against his pillows, but kept his eyes stubbornly open.

"Peter Sharpe is dead. Richard Poole slit his throat in St. Clement Dane's churchyard five nights ago, on Lord Everly's orders. May I assume, my lord, that you know all this already?"

Tristan nodded grimly. "I saw Sharpe's body myself." If he'd been a better man, Tristan would have felt some compassion for Sharpe having come to such a grisly end, but he'd felt nothing but satisfaction when he'd looked on Sharpe's bloody, mangled body. "What about Poole?"

"Ah, Mr. Poole. Such a distasteful gentleman, Poole. He did his best to send you the way of poor Peter Sharpe. He succeeded in plunging a blade in your chest, and he might have finished the job if Sophia hadn't crushed his skull with a single blow."

Tristan stared at Lady Clifford, his body going cold. "How? Sophia is half Poole's size."

"Yes, she's always been a tiny little thing, but presence of mind is far more valuable in these matters than size, and I don't think I need to tell *you*, Lord Gray, how wily Sophia is."

"*How?*" Tristan croaked again, pushing the word through numb lips. Had Poole gotten hold of her a second time, while Tristan was unable to defend her? "Did he hurt her?"

He must have looked desperate indeed, because Lady Clifford took pity on him. "He never had a chance to lay a finger on her, my lord. She struck him with a stone cross she liberated from a crypt in St. Clement Dane's graveyard. Richard Poole was dead before he even knew what hit him. Sophia killed him before he could kill you."

Lady Clifford's tone was neutral, and her face carefully blank, but she hadn't made any attempt to soften the facts. Tristan was certain her bluntness was intentional. She was watching him closely, as if searching his face for some hint he'd change his mind about Sophia once he discovered she'd killed a man.

He wouldn't.

Tristan thought of the courage it must have taken her to overcome Poole, the incredible strength of character, the fierceness and resolve hidden inside that dainty body, and his throat closed. Sophia didn't do anything in half measures, and though she hadn't told him so, Tristan believed she loved him with her whole heart. He couldn't imagine his life without her, and nothing—*nothing*—would ever change that.

His gaze met Lady Clifford's. "Sophia saved my life."

"She did, indeed. Not long after you saved hers." Lady Clifford gave him a considering look. "It's almost enough to make one believe in fate, isn't it?"

Tristan didn't answer, because once again, his stomach was roiling with panic. "What's going to happen to Sophia?"

She hadn't done anything she hadn't been forced to do to save his and her own life, but Tristan had come to understand justice wasn't as blind as he'd always imagined it to be. What if Everly saw to it Sophia was taken up for murder, or—

"There's no need to worry, my lord. I've explained the situation to Kit Benjamin, and he's promised to take care of any…oh, shall we call them inconvenient details? You may have heard, Lord Gray, that Mr. Benjamin and I have an understanding."

What Tristan had heard was that Kit Benjamin and Lady Amanda Clifford were involved in a torrid affair, and Benjamin was so blinded by his passion for her, he often overlooked her more…legally questionable activities.

Like most of London, he'd believed the rumor to be true, and perhaps they *were* having an affair, but he'd been wrong about Lady Clifford in one respect, and it was the only respect that mattered. "I misjudged you as well, my lady, and I beg your pardon for it. I assumed you were working on the wrong side of the law, and Kit Benjamin was covering your tracks for you."

She laughed. "Oh, dear. That would be rather dreadful, wouldn't it? But what makes you so sure that's not the case?"

He *wasn't* sure, but whatever Lady Clifford got up to, whether she happened to be working on the side of the law or against it, Tristan believed she was as anxious to see justice done as he was himself.

Lady Clifford gave Tristan's hand a little pat. "Shall we say the law sometimes needs a little nudge in the right direction, and simply leave it at that, Lord Gray?"

"Perhaps that would be for the best."

They exchanged tentative smiles, but then Tristan sobered. Peter Sharpe and Richard Poole might have met their just ends, but this business hadn't begun with either of them. Three men were dead, and Jeremy Ives had been sent to rot away in Newgate for a crime he didn't commit. "What of Lord Everly? He's at the center of this, pulling the strings, and Sampson Willis has been helping him."

Christ, even though he knew it to be true, Tristan could hardly credit Willis could have turned out to be such a villain. All the information he'd given Willis about Jeremy Ives and Sophia and Lady Clifford, Willis had been using against them.

Tristan had always admired Willis—had thought him a good, decent man. It never once occurred to him Willis could be behind Henry's death, and *why?* Because he'd assumed Willis, a magistrate, must be on the right side of the law.

Tristan's blindness had nearly cost Sophia her life.

"Yes, we're well aware of Lord Everly's and Mr. Willis's roles in this business, and don't think for a moment we haven't considered who might be pulling *their* strings."

Neither Tristan nor Lady Clifford said the name, but they were both thinking it.

William Pitt.

"There's no evidence against Lord Everly, unfortunately. The two men who might have implicated him in this, Sharpe and Poole, are both dead. That said, we now know Lord Everly's not *quite* the upstanding peer everyone assumed him to be, and the same is true of Sampson Willis. There's a great deal of power in knowledge, Lord Gray. As for the other…" A troubled look crossed Lady Clifford's face. "I'm afraid there's only so much one can do, and there's a limit to Kit Benjamin's influence, as well. Even he can't reach that high."

"No. No one can." Indeed, that was rather the problem.

Lady Clifford gave his hand another pat, then rose to her feet. "Now, Lord Gray. I advise you to get some rest."

"No, my lady. Not until I see Sophia." Tristan pulled the coverlet aside, determined to go find her, even if he had to climb onto the roof to do it.

"Ah, yes. Sophia. No, there's no need to leave your bed, Lord Gray." Lady Clifford made her way to the bedchamber door, but before she disappeared into the hallway she paused and said, "You can come out of the cupboard now, Sophia, dear."

"The cupboard!" Tristan's mouth fell open. His gaze shot to the tall cupboard on the other side of the bedchamber. The door creaked open, one inch at a time. When Sophia's dark head appeared, his lips curved in a grin. "Well, I'll be damned."

Sophia gave Tristan a sheepish look, then turned to Lady Clifford. "How in the world did you know I was in the cupboard?"

"I know everything that happens at the Clifford School. You should know that by now, dear." Lady Clifford lifted her chin, but there was a gleam of mischief in her blue eyes. "Well, that, and a fold of your skirt was caught in the cupboard door."

Sophia looked down at her skirts. "Blast it," she muttered, her face flushing.

Lady Clifford's soft laugh drifted across the bedchamber, and then she was gone, closing the door with a quiet click behind her.

Tristan's gaze met Sophia's. "Sophia. Come here, pixie."

Sophia gave him an uncharacteristically shy look, but she crossed the room and stopped by the side of his bed. He reached and took her hand in a weak grip. "You look fatigued, sweetheart."

"You developed an infection a few days ago, and I thought…I was worried." Her lower lip began to tremble, and she sank her teeth into it to still it. "You're much better now. Giles Wakeford took good care of you."

Giles Wakeford. The man with the dark hair and brown eyes. Tristan would thank him later. Much later.

For now, all he wanted, all he could see, was Sophia.

"Come closer, sweetheart." After an exhaustive effort and more than one curse and hiss of pain, Tristan managed to shift a little to his left. "Lie down with me."

"No." Sophia hung back. "I don't want to jostle you."

"You won't. There's plenty of room."

Sophia glanced at the door. "Lady Clifford will scold dreadfully if she finds out." But when she turned to Tristan again, her face was filled with longing.

"Lady Clifford is gone. Please, Sophia. I need to hold you and reassure myself you're here, and in one piece."

Sophia's resolve disintegrated in the face of that soft plea. "Oh, well, perhaps for just a moment." She rested a knee on the bed and climbed up beside him, taking care not to hurt him. Once she was settled, she lay her hand gently against his neck and pressed her face into his shoulder.

More than anything Tristan wanted to wrap his arm around her and ease her head down to his chest, but that would have to wait until he'd healed, so he settled for turning his head and burying his face in her hair. "There's something I need to know, Sophia. You overheard me talking to Sampson Willis, didn't you?"

Sophia stiffened. "It doesn't matter now—"

"Yes, it does. It matters to me."

She let out a long, deep sigh, her warm breath ghosting over his neck. "Yes. I…he said you were investigating me."

Tristan heard the tremor in her voice, and pressed a kiss into her dark hair. "I won't lie to you, or pretend it isn't true. Willis did ask me to investigate you, but I agreed to do it the morning after our first meeting at St. Clement Dane's Church, the night I followed you there. I didn't know you then, Sophia."

She sighed. "No, you didn't. I don't blame you for agreeing to investigate me, Tristan. Henry Gerrard was your friend, and anyone would have been suspicious of me, but once you did know me, you should have told me the truth."

"I made a mistake, and I'm sorry for it. You were so skittish at first, I thought you'd never trust me again if I told you, and then later, I…this won't make much sense to you, but I became so preoccupied with you, I didn't think about the investigation at all."

She raised her head to stare at him. "How could you *forget* you were investigating me? You're a Bow Street Runner, Tristan."

He chuckled. "I didn't forget, precisely. It was more that the investigation ceased to matter to me. The mistake I made was in thinking it wouldn't matter to *you*."

She lay her head back on his shoulder. "It doesn't now."

Tristan waited, knowing there was more. Sophia didn't speak for a long time, but then she sniffled, and he felt the trickle of tears against his shoulder. "Are you betrothed, Tristan?"

He pressed his cheek into her hair, regret sweeping over him. "No. I'm not betrothed."

"I heard Sampson Willis say—"

"Shhh." Tristan pressed a kiss to her temple. "I know what he said, but it isn't true. I won't deny there's a lady in Oxfordshire my mother wishes to see become the Countess of Gray, but I'm not betrothed to her. I haven't seen the lady in years. I can't even remember her face." More often than not he couldn't even remember her name, but it didn't seem gentlemanly to say so.

"You don't…you don't love her, then?" Sophia asked with another sniffle.

Tristan's injuries prevented him from taking her into his arms, but he nestled her as close against him as he could, and then the words began to spill from his lips in an awkward rush. "*No*. I've only ever loved one lady. I haven't stopped thinking about you since the first time I saw you, Sophia. Well, perhaps not the *first* time, because I thought you were a boy, but—"

"Yes, I've been meaning to mention that. It's not very flattering, Lord Gray."

Tristan blinked. "In my defense it was dark and rainy that night, and you were dressed in breeches with your hair hidden under a cap."

"Of course, I was. I can't be expected to climb or run in skirts and petticoats, can I?"

Her tone was teasing, and he couldn't help but drop another kiss onto her temple. "No, indeed, and I realized my mistake soon enough." Pain arced across his chest as he reached for a lock of her hair, but he sighed with satisfaction as the silky strands slid between his fingers. "I'll never forget that moment when I took your cap off." His voice dropped lower. "All that thick, dark hair tumbling over your shoulders, and the greenest pair of eyes I've ever seen. So beautiful, I thought I'd imagined you."

Sophia raised her head again. Her gaze met his, and whatever she saw in his eyes made her breath catch.

"I should have known right then what would happen," Tristan murmured, still toying with her hair. "I should have known I'd fall in love with you. Perhaps I did know, even then, because I've been chasing you ever since."

Sophia let out a shaky laugh. "Perhaps I should have known as well, since you're the only one who's ever caught me. But Tristan, I…you're an earl, and I'm just—"

"You're just the only woman I've ever loved, and the only woman I ever *will* love. The only woman I want to spend the rest of my life with." He let the lock of her hair fall onto his shoulder and turned her face to his. "Do you love me at all, Sophia? Because nothing else matters."

She gazed up at him, the firelight catching the tears shimmering in the green eyes he loved so well. "I *do* love you, Tristan. You're good and kind, and the best man I've ever known, for all that you *are* an aristocrat, and terribly proper."

He chuckled. "Perhaps I am, but I see a great many improprieties in our future, my lady."

She raised her hand, and her fingertips drifted over his lips. "Oh, dear. I've ruined a perfectly good earl, haven't I?"

"You didn't ruin me, pixie." He pressed a kiss to her fingertips, then buried his face in her hair with a sigh. "You're the one who saved me."

Epilogue

Three months later.

Tristan woke to the sensation of something soft tickling his lips.

It felt like…a butterfly? With every flutter of the butterfly's wings the delicate scent of honeysuckle drifted like a cloud around him, and he inhaled deeply, losing himself in the sweetness.

Ah, a dream, then. Tristan had left his nightmares behind weeks ago, but it was a bit jarring to leap from blood and gravestones to butterflies in fields of honeysuckle.

He burrowed into his pillow, a smile curving his lips. Not that he was complaining. Who didn't like butterflies? And the scent of honeysuckle always reminded him of…

Sophia.

Tristan opened his eyes to find her leaning over him, brushing soft, teasing kisses over his lips. Ah. Not butterflies or fields of honeysuckle, then, but his lovely wife. Tristan closed his eyes again as he reached for her, wrapping his arms around her waist. "Are you waking me with kisses, Lady Gray?"

Sophia laughed softly. "Certainly not, my lord. Go back to sleep. I'm conducting an investigation, and it doesn't concern you."

"No? How curious. It feels as if it *does* concern me, and rather intimately." Tristan's smile widened as the tip of her tongue grazed the scar on his upper lip.

"The tip of a riding crop might have made such a scar," she murmured, drawing back to study his lips. "Did you accidentally strike yourself in the face with your crop?"

Tristan did his best to look outraged. "How dare you, madam? I'll have you know I'm an accomplished horseman."

Sophia's brow furrowed. "An encounter with a sharp tree branch, perhaps?"

"No. This may surprise you, Lady Gray, but I'm perfectly able to manage London's trees."

"Hmmm." Sophia brushed her fingertip over the scar. "I know! You were drinking tea from a cracked teacup. It fell to pieces in your hand, and one of the shards sliced your lip."

"That's a shocking allegation, Lady Gray." Tristan regarded her with mock horror, then added in virtuous tones, "I will do you the favor of not disclosing to Mrs. Beeson the viciousness with which you've maligned her teacups."

"Very well. Keep your secrets, then." Sophia lifted her chin and glared down her nose at him. "But I don't wish to hear another word from you, Lord Gray, unless it's a confession."

With one final quelling glance she wriggled away from him and tried to scramble over to her side of the bed, but she didn't get far before Tristan caught her by her waist and rolled her underneath him.

"That's a fetching pout, Lady Gray." He brushed his thumb over her lower lip, his blood heating at the hint of damp warmth he found there. "How can I resist teasing you when you pout so prettily?"

Sophia snorted. "You won't find the edge of my teeth quite so pretty, I assure you. Your confession, my lord, or I may be tempted to give you a matching scar on your bottom lip."

"I warned you before it's a dull story, but since you insist on knowing it…" Tristan paused to press a kiss to that pouting mouth. "I fell up a flight of stairs."

"*Up* a flight of stairs?" Sophia blinked at him. "Don't you mean *down* a flight of stairs?"

"No, I mean *up*. There's nothing ridiculous about falling down the stairs. If I'd fallen *down* them, I would have confessed it at once."

"But how does one fall *up* a flight of stairs?" Sophia was trying to smother the grin tugging at the corners of her lips.

Tristan's own lips twitched. "When one is six years old, one stumbles while chasing their brother up a flight of stairs and smacks their face into the edge of a stair above them. It's easier than you'd think."

"Oh, dear." Sophia had lost the battle with her grin, which had chased the pout from her lips. "You're right, my lord, that *is* a dull story. Did it bleed much?"

Tristan fingered the scar. "Gushed everywhere, from my nose and mouth. I even lost a tooth. My mother was in fits over all that blood on her polished staircase."

"The staircase, and not your precious face?" Sophia reached up and stroked her finger tenderly over the scar, her smile fading. "I'm afraid that doesn't surprise me."

After a hasty marriage ceremony in London, Tristan had dutifully brought his new bride to Oxfordshire to present her to his mother. The Dowager Countess of Gray, upon finding her one remaining son had married a commoner, had fallen into hysterics and taken immediately to her bed. She'd remained there in fits until it became clear Tristan was unmoved by her dramatics, whereupon she'd swept back down the stairs in great state, and announced her intention to retire to the dower house.

Neither Sophia nor Tristan offered any objection to this plan, though in the end, it might have been just as well for the Dowager Countess to have remained where she was. Tristan and Sophia left Oxfordshire after only two weeks, and between themselves decided not to spend much time there in the future.

Sophia couldn't bear to be separated from her friends for long, and Tristan couldn't bear for Sophia to be made unhappy, and so they'd returned to Great Marlborough Street, much to the delight of Lady Clifford and the young ladies at the Clifford School, particularly Cecilia, who haunted their townhouse like a cheerful, starry-eyed ghost.

"Have I mentioned how fond I am of this scar?" Sophia asked, gently caressing his lip. "I imagined tasting it long before it was proper to do so."

"You did?" The thought of her gazing at his lips and wondering how they'd taste made his stomach tighten with desire. "How long before?"

"Since the day we went to see Jeremy at Newgate." The dreamy smile on Sophia's lips faded a little, and a shadow crossed her face at mention of Jeremy, who remained tucked away in some obscure part of England. Lady Clifford assured them he was recovering nicely, but Sophia missed him, and it would be some time yet before it would be safe for her to see him.

Tristan stroked his fingertips over her cheek, anxious to distract her. "What else do you imagine? What do you dream of, Sophia?"

"Oh, so many things. Sometimes I dream of Lord Everly and Sampson Willis being brought to justice." She smiled, but there was a hint of sadness to it.

There'd been no sign of Everly in recent weeks. He'd retired to his country estate, and hadn't returned when Parliament resumed. No one in London seemed to know what precipitated this sudden change in Everly's circumstances. As for Willis, he'd abruptly retired as Bow Street Magistrate, and disappeared from London without a trace. Tristan suspected Kit Benjamin had a hand in that, but that was pure speculation on his part. In the end, neither Everly nor Willis had gotten what he deserved, but neither had they gone unscathed.

But Tristan didn't want to talk of Everly, or Willis, or anything that brought shadows to Sophia's eyes. He touched a finger to her lips. "No. Tell me only your sweetest dreams, pixie."

Sophia turned her face to kiss his fingertips. "Jeremy, safe and happy and frolicking in the ocean somewhere. Lady Clifford with Gussie on her lap, and Emma, Georgiana, and Cecilia giggling over Mrs. Radcliffe's novels. But mostly..." A pink flush rose in her cheeks as she gazed up at him. "Mostly, I dream of you, Tristan."

Tristan's heart swelled in his chest, and he had to kiss her then, his mouth taking hers in a gentle, lingering kiss before he drew away to gaze down at her. "And what do you dream of, Lady Gray?"

"Your eyes, soft on my face, and your beautiful, stern lips curved in a smile," she whispered. "I dream of your arms wrapped around me, my head resting on your chest, your heartbeat echoing like music in my ear."

"Ah, pixie." Tristan brushed soft kisses over her brow, her eyelids, and the tip of her chin before gathering her against him and burying his face in her hair. "Those aren't dreams."

Author's Notes

James Scott, the first Duke of Monmouth, was the illegitimate son of Charles II. He was beheaded in 1685 for treason after leading the Monmouth Rebellion against his uncle, James II and VII (England and Scotland, respectively).

St. Clement Dane's Church is located on the Strand in the City of Westminster, London. The graveyard adjacent to the church is a product of the author's imagination.

Ann Radcliffe, *The Romance of the Forest* (London: T. Hookham & Carpenter, 1791).

A gentleman by the name of Sampson Wright succeeded John Fielding as Chief Magistrate of Bow Street. Mr. Wright would have been Chief Magistrate during the year in which the novel is set. The author changed the character's last name from Wright to Willis so as not to impugn Mr. Wright's reputation as a man of honor.

Jack Sheppard, an early eighteenth-century thief and petty criminal, was known for his numerous miraculous escapes from London's prisons. The incident Georgiana is referring to is Sheppard's infamous second escape from Newgate, which he achieved by climbing up a chimney, removing an iron bar that had been set into the brickwork, and using it to break through the ceiling. He made it onto the roof of Newgate Prison, and used a blanket to gain access to the roof of the house next door. He broke into the house, and walked through the front door to freedom.

The Proceedings were published accounts of trials that took place at the Old Bailey, made available to the public after each session. The Proceedings grew from the seventeenth-century ballad, chapbook, and broadside accounts of the lives and exploits of London's famous criminals, which were popular with London's citizens. The Proceedings were generally between four to nine pages long, and though they did not contain comprehensive accounts of every case tried at the Old Bailey, by 1680 most trials appear to be contained in the Proceedings. Sophia may well have found an account of Patrick Dunn's trial there, as well as accounts of previous thefts in which Peter Sharpe was a witness.

Tim Hitchcock, Robert Shoemaker, Clive Emsley, Sharon Howard, and Jamie McLaughlin, *et al., The Old Bailey Proceedings Online, 1674–1913* (www.oldbaileyonline.org, version 7.0, 24 March 2012).

Arthur Griffiths makes references in his book *The Chronicles of Newgate* to an incident that took place in 1593, in which a prisoner was conveyed from the prison inside a coffin. The details regarding this curious incident are scarce, but it appears the scheme involved a corrupt guard swapping the rightful occupant of the coffin with a gentleman who was still very much alive, and who was thus conveyed from the prison. Arthur Griffiths, *The Chronicles of Newgate* (London: Chapman & Hall, 1884).

The London Corresponding Society was formed in 1792, a year prior to the opening date of the novel. Society members believed in the principle of universal suffrage, in which every adult citizen was guaranteed the right to vote, regardless of gender, race or ethnicity, or income. William Pitt's government strenuously opposed the Society's calls for radical governmental change. In May of 1792 the Society submitted a petition signed by 6,000 citizens demanding political reform. Between the petition and the political upheaval caused by the French Revolution, Pitt became so fearful of the Society's influence he risked putting its three principal leaders—Thomas Hardy, John Thelwall, and John Horne Tooke—on trial for the attempted assassination of King George III. The government charges were transparently false, and all three men were acquitted. Pitt's effort to frame prominent members of the LCS for an attempted assassination of the king (a crime for which they certainly would have been executed) inspired the plot between Lord Everly, Peter Sharp, Sampson Willis, and Richard Poole to frame innocent members of the LCS for theft.

William Pitt did eventually succeed in silencing the Society by suspending the Habeas Corpus Act, thereby making it legal for the government to detain without trial persons suspected of radical activities. Under pressure from the suspension of habeas corpus and the Unlawful Societies Act of 1799, which outlawed radical secret societies, the London Corresponding Society ultimately disbanded.

For an enlightening discussion of Ellen Moers concept of "The Female Gothic," please see "Female Gothic: The Monster's Mother" (*New York Review of Books,* 1974).

Printed in the United States
by Baker & Taylor Publisher Services